The Innocent Project

David A. Wiyrick

The Innocent Project

David A. Wiyrick
The Innocent Project

All rights reserved
Copyright © 2022 by David A. Wiyrick

No part of this publication may be reproduced, distributed, or transmitted in any form or by any means, including photocopying, recording, or other electronic or mechanical methods, without the prior written permission of the publisher, except in the case of brief quotations embodied in critical reviews and certain other noncommercial uses permitted by copyright law.

This is a work of fiction. Names, characters, places and incidents either are products of the author's imagination or are used fictitiously. Any resemblance to actual events or locales or persons, living or dead, is entirely coincidental.

Published by BooxAi

ISBN: 978-965-578-043-7

BooX AI

Contents

Prologue	1
Chapter 1	3
Chapter 2	7
Chapter 3	17
Chapter 4	27
Chapter 5	29
Chapter 6	63
Chapter 7	71
Chapter 8	73
Chapter 9	79
Chapter 10	85
Chapter 11	93
Chapter 12	95
Chapter 13	101
Chapter 14	103
Chapter 15	109
Chapter 16	117
Chapter 17	129
Chapter 18	133
Chapter 19	157
Chapter 20	161
Chapter 21	169
Chapter 22	171
Chapter 23	183
Chapter 24	203
Chapter 25	219
Chapter 26	221
Chapter 27	223
Chapter 28	225
Chapter 29	231
Chapter 30	239
Chapter 31	241
Chapter 32	247
Chapter 33	249
Chapter 34	257
Chapter 35	279

Chapter 36	293
Chapter 37	295
Chapter 38	303
Chapter 39	309
Chapter 40	313
Chapter 41	323
Chapter 42	325
Chapter 43	327
Chapter 44	335
Chapter 45	337
Chapter 46	343
Chapter 47	349
Chapter 48	357
Chapter 49	361
Chapter 50	365
Chapter 51	369
Chapter 52	375
Chapter 53	379
Chapter 54	381
Chapter 55	387
Chapter 56	391
Chapter 57	393
Conclusion	395

Prologue

Wheatland is the county seat for Canyon County and had initially been created as a small railroad stop at the turn of the century where the trains traveling through would stop to take on water for their thirsty steam engines.

It is mostly desert area with vast scablands and deep canyons created from the ancient Missoula Ice Dam bursts that flooded and carved the region thousands of years ago.

The soil washed from the land scoured by the floods settled in great deposits that provided rich soil nutrients for a variety of crops.

A defunct World War Two Air Force Base sits in the center of this vast region near Moses Lake, WA where the aircraft industry has assumed control over the Base and is valued as a pilot training center for world airlines.

Local residents have been offered a steady job with good pay and benefits, to support the aviation training industry.

Today Wheatland, Washington is the County seat of Canyon County, and has a fair and healthy population of 1,100 citizens from all ethnicities and income levels.

A slow but steady influx of Methamphetamine, Heroin, Fentanyl,

Cocaine and illicit Marijuana grow sites brought organized gangs and increased violence and a means for enterprising young men to get rich.

Chapter 1

The night was still young when 26 year Ryan Bates laid on his girlfriend's couch in her home on the northeast part of Wheatland and was bored watching the local news story on TV.

Carlene was his girlfriend that he described as his flavor of the month, and her house was clean and comfortable.

He was living there, freeloading off Carlene's income from her job at a local fast food joint.

It was about 9:00 P.M. mid week and Ryan thought, "God, I am starting to get sick," and had the urge to start heaving his guts out and having the shakes from drug withdrawal.

"I'm going out for a while to get something for this fucking withdrawal shit," and headed for the door.

Carlene didn't ask where he was going, she was just glad she had a man in her life.

Ryan would strike her with his fists when he was high on meth and she always thought it was her fault because she hadn't taken care of his wants and needs.

"OK, I will be right here at home and call me if you need a ride home," she told him.

She knew that he was not headed to a friend's house, but was going out to get meth from his dealer at a trap house several blocks away as he had done many times before.

She suspected that when he went out late at night he would be breaking into cars and closed businesses and would sell the stolen property he had acquired to supply his drug needs.

At times she had shamefully asked her parents for money to help with her rent and utility bills and survived on groceries from the once weekly open food bank in nearby Soap Lake.

Ryan knew it was the effects of two days of using high amounts of meth and attending a party at a friend's cabin at nearby Soap Lake in neighboring Grant County.

He was weak and becoming agitated, and his arms were dotted with small red scabs with some sores infected from meth injections.

Tonight, he had no cash to buy meth to quench his fierce addiction and downslide of his body.

Ryan walked to his dealer's trap house and knocked on the door.

"Who's there?" came a voice from the other side of the door and the lights were turned off inside the house except for the front porch light.

A face peered out from a small curtained window at the upper part of the door.

"It's Ryan, man, let me in, it's cold outside," he said softly.

Light snow was falling as it had been most of the day and the night temperature was falling to a few degrees below freezing.

The sound of a sliding lock was heard and Ryan stepped in from the cold to a house that was too warm and smelled like cat urine from the meth that was being cut, weighed and packaged on the small kitchen table.

The man at the door commented, "What the hell do you want man?" Jacob Hunt said as he spun Ryan around and checked him for firearms, and for wires that would reveal Ryan was a snitch for the cops.

Ryan had worn wires for the cops before but not tonight, because this deal was for personal use.

A black revolver laid on the kitchen table within easy reach of a second person named Josh that was processing meth on the table.

Ryan was sweating from his drug withdrawal and felt like he was going to throw-up in the dealer's living room.

He stared hungrily at the bindles of meth and tried to suppress his urge to grab the revolver on the table.

Josh looked up at Ryan and saw the wild look in his eyes.

Josh picked up the revolver and pointed it at Ryan.

"Get the fuck back from this table man, go sit on the couch," he said.

"I know you are starting to get crazy and you better not try to grab our meth, or I will put a round in the middle of your forehead," he said menacingly.

Ryan looked into Josh's unblinking eyes and knew he would die if he tried to take any meth by force or approach Josh.

"Look man, I'm really getting sick and I need a fix to get me by so I can collect some money later tonight."

"If you'll front me a bindle of meth tonight, I will have the money tomorrow," he pleaded.

Ryan pleaded, "Look man, I've been a steady longtime customer of you guys and you have fronted me before, and I've always paid you back."

"I'm one of your best customers," he continued.

Jacob looked at Josh and said, "Give the man a bindle, but Ryan, if you are not back by tomorrow night with the $200.00 for the bindle, I'll hunt you down and get it from your skin."

Ryan looked astonished, "Fuck man, this shit is selling for $100.00 a tenth elsewhere, why are you jacking the price up on me?"

"Supply and demand," said Jacob with a slight smile as he reached over and patted Ryan on the cheek.

You come back tomorrow with the money to buy a full quarter pound and I'll give you a special deal since you have been a steady customer.

"Now get up and take your bindle and get the fuck out of here, you know I don't like the neighbors to see steady traffic in and out of this place."

Ryan got up from the couch and greedily put his hand out as Josh placed the bindle in the palm of his hand.

Jacob looked out onto the street through the door window and not seeing anyone he unlocked the bolt of the door and Ryan stepped outside, hearing the bolt slide back into place.

Ryan walked about half a block down the street and stopped on the sidewalk between street lights.

He placed a small pinch of the powdery substance in a small pipe and lit it up.

"Ahh," he said as he took a deep drag from the pipe and the hot acrid smoke filled the deepest part of his lungs.

Ryan's urge to throw-up started to diminish and he started to feel like he could run for miles without tiring.

He was invincible again.

"Now how am I going to get money to pay my drug debt and buy more," he thought to himself.

"I know a way," he thought as he reached into his coat pocket for his cheap burner phone.

Chapter 2
Juan Garcia

Juan Garcia was 23 years old and a lifelong resident of Canyon County and was born at the local hospital in nearby Moses Lake.

His mother had raised Juan, an older brother and two younger sisters, and worked long and hard hours at a potato warehouse, leaving Juan to take care of his younger siblings during the day at the low income apartment complex where they lived.

His father was just a faded memory and had died in an industrial accident when the tractor his father was driving had rolled over on him.

Juan was bitter towards his older brother Chris who had let his anger get away and he had beat a neighbor with a golf club.

The attack was particularly vicious and the victim was robbed by Chris to support his drug addiction.

When medical response from the local fire department arrived, it was just a few minutes before there was a pounding on the apartment door and Chris was taken away in cuffs by the cops and later sentenced to 6 years in prison.

Chris's girlfriend Susan Mattern was loyal to him while he was in prison and would often come to his mother's apartment and spend the night on the living room couch.

She would make frequent trips to Coyote Ridge Prison in Connell, Washington to visit him.

Juan would often hook up with Ryan Bates from the time they were teenagers.

They would scope out homes for burglaries when there was opportunity and were also prolific car prowlers, often hitting as many as 20 cars in one night.

Whenever Ryan and Juan were observed walking through a neighborhood by the police, the officers would be on high alert, knowing there was a good chance that either burglary or car prowling reports would be reported the next day.

The officers assigned to Crime Analysis would monitor and record property type crime locations and actually kept a connected map of known burglars that had been contacted or observed in the area of the related crimes.

Ryan and Juan usually were at the top of the list as suspects.

On a late evening in December Juan had settled into bed with Tiffanie Weeks after smoking marijuana and putting away a couple of longneck beers.

His brother's girlfriend Susan Mattern was sleeping on the couch in the living room that evening.

Juan was lying on his back and had Tiffanie snuggled onto his left side with her warm breath gently blowing on his neck.

Juan gave a start as he felt the silenced buzz of his cell phone lying beneath his pillow.

Tiffanie stirred and turned away from him with her backside pressing into his side.

"Who is this?" whispered Juan into the phone and was irritated from being disturbed from a comfortable dream like feeling.

"Hey man, it's me Ryan, let's go out and boost some cars, I'm tapped out and have to get some money to pay my dealer for the debt I owe. I know of some places in town where the owners leave their cars parked on the street at night and there are not many streetlights. There has been good stuff in their cars in the past," Ryan spoke quietly over the phone.

"A neighbor that lives on 3rd down the street from my mom's leaves guns in his pick-up truck," said Ryan.

"Should be pretty easy to get in his truck and grab any guns he has in there. We can sell the guns or use them to boost the norteno gang pukes from their meth," he said.

"I know their trap house in Othello gets a large shipment every Thursday from Yakima, Washington. Their source is supposed to be the main man for the area so if we hit them during an early evening there should be a stash of cash and meth. We will have to leave no trace of who we are because the norteno's source is the Sinaloa Mexican Drug Cartel," he continued.

"A gun pointed at the norteno's will open the doors for us," said Juan, relishing the excitement of a takedown robbery.

"I'm with you, let me slip out of here and not disturb Tiffanie and I'll meet you at the church on Division on the hill in about 10 minutes," Juan said before hanging up.

Juan quietly got dressed and placed a pair of gloves into his coat pocket.

He had forgotten Susan Mattern was sleeping on the couch in the living room and was startled when he saw her still form lying on the couch with her back to him.

"Oh hell, I hope she doesn't hear me," he thought to himself.

He slowly and quietly made his way across the living room to a slider door that was always unlocked.

The door made a low scraping sound as it slid open and he watched Susan's form and listened to her breathing.

There was no indication the sound of the door slider had disturbed her.

He carefully slid the slider door closed and then walked across the back lawn of the apartment complex and headed towards the park behind the church parking lot to meet Ryan.

The night was just below freezing and a light snow was falling.

The ambient light of the snow on the ground lit up even the shadows of the houses and cars parked on the street.

The sounds of the night were muffled from the snowfall which would lull people to sleep soundly.

As Juan approached the church Ryan stepped out from the porch entrance to the church.

"This is a damn cold night Bro," quipped Ryan as they met.

"Did you bring the Slim Jim and gloves?" asked Juan.

"I've got them right here," Ryan said as he opened up the small backpack he was carrying.

They had used the slim Jim tool numerous times to insert down beside a car window to the interior door mechanism and unlock the vehicle.

Cars and trucks were starting to be produced more frequently with installed security systems or aftermarket systems, which was a problem they had to consider.

The aftermarket alarm systems would often have a small blue light or red light mounted at the bottom of the interior dashboard which was designed to warn and deter car prowlers that an anti-theft device was installed and active in the vehicle.

"Let's do our prowls on the S/E side of town, the streetlights are far between and we haven't hit that section for a long time," said Ryan.

"Last time we got some good stuff out of the cars, including purses, mostly in plain sight," Ryan said.

"We can pick up enough stuff and cash to go to Jacob's trap house and score some meth and get high while we continue to do our thing tonight."

"Great idea, let's get to it, I got a woman waiting back at my apartment in a warm bed," murmured Juan as he shivered from the damp cold.

They started walking along the east rim of town where more affluent homes were located.

There were great views overlooking the town and the brown treeless mountains in the distance.

The night was quiet and they would have ample warning should a cop leave his warm police station and coffee and drive aimlessly around town with the Police cruiser's studded tires making a loud scratchy sound on the pavement.

As they quietly walked down the street, the first vehicle they spotted was a newer Chevy pick-up that had recently been parked, and the light snow was melting as it struck the metal surface of the warm hood.

"This guy probably came home from a bar since it's later than 2:00 A.M., so he should be in a dead sleep," Ryan whispered to Juan.

They approached on the driver's side and, using a small penlight, looked into the interior of the pick-up truck.

"Don't see anything other than an open 1/2 case of beer with only a couple cans remaining," said Ryan.

Juan excitedly whispered, "No, look under the edge of the center console cover, it looks like part of a wallet sticking out."

Ryan bent down and peered into the interior and when using his small penlight he could also see the object that looked like a man's wallet.

Pulling the Slim Jim out of the backpack Ryan went around to the side of the pick-up door farthest from the residence.

His practiced hands expertly guided the tool to hook on the bar that controlled the door handle lock.

He pulled on the bar which released the latch of the driver's door with the sound of a low click of the door release.

He gently pulled the driver's door open.

The ceiling interior light came on, lighting a small area which afforded a better view of the contents.

He quickly reached up and turned off the interior roof light by pushing the small switch on the side.

Ryan quickly pocketed the wallet in his coat pocket and quickly checked the glove box and interior of the center console.

A small glass jar was located inside the console containing loose change and jewelry.

As quickly as they had entered the pick-up truck, the door of the truck was carefully closed until there was a click of the latch.

They withdrew a short distance from the pick-up and Ryan opened the wallet to examine the contents.

"It's not very thick so probably not much money," said Ryan as he pulled the bills out of the wallet and shined the flashlight on the bills.

Juan almost shouted, "Holy shit, those are Benjamins you got there."

Ryan quickly counted 24 one hundred dollar bills and passed $1,200.00 to Juan as his share.

Ryan threw the wallet down onto the street as they continued quietly walking.

"Let's stop over by this alley and see what's in the jar," said Juan as he looked around at the nearby houses for any activity or lights that were on.

The area was devoid of any activity except for a cat quickly crossing further down the street.

Ryan unscrewed the jar and dumped the contents into Juan's stocking cap that he had carried in his coat pocket and tossed the empty glass jar onto a lawn.

They both examined the contents from the glass jar which contained what appeared to be loose change, and inexpensive jewelry at first glance.

A small white plastic type ring box from the jar was picked up from Juan's stocking cap and Ryan opened the box which contained two diamond mounted gold rings.

Juan picked up the rings and turned them around at different angles. "Hmm, that looks like a wedding and engagement ring set so there might be some value there."

The rest of the contents of the jar contained loose change and Ryan placed the coins into a side pocket of his backpack.

"Doing good so far but let's go along this street a little further," said Juan and they quietly started back down the street.

They checked various vehicles further down the street until they came upon a tricked out late model bright red Jeep wrangler 4 door.

Significant expense had been spent on a lift kit with oversized tires and Black Diamond brand wheels.

Ryan started to insert the Slim Jim into the rear passenger window when Juan hissed at him and pointed to the interior where a small blue light was glowing dim on the lower section of the dashboard below the stereo controls.

Juan hissed, "That Jeep is alarmed, let's get the hell away from it."

They traveled further down the street and about a block away an older 90's Buick sedan was parked on the street in front of a house with numerous kid toys partially covered with snow in the front yard.

"Geez, this car looks like a poor baby mama would drive this car," quipped Ryan as he looked in the window of the unlocked car.

"There's a cell phone on the passenger seat that might be worth some money," Ryan said.

They quietly opened the unlocked side doors of the car and shined pen lights under the seats and never found anything except a couple of empty drug bindles and used syringes.

"Careful man," said Juan, "those syringes could really fuck you up if you get stuck from one of them."

"Don't be reaching around in the seat cracks where you can't see," said Juan.

"Let's go, we got enough shit for the night," said Ryan as he reached over and grabbed the cell phone, then decided to leave it.

Juan responded, "We have money to score some serious meth from Jacob and maybe sell or trade him for a little extra smack."

They closed the car doors until there was a click and started down the street, keeping away from the streetlights, talking in low tones.

Ryan said to Juan, "Let's get our meth at Jacob's now."

"Then we can go down the street to the dude's where he keeps his guns in his pick-up truck parked out on the street," he finished.

John Adams was 26 years old and rented a small one bedroom house in the Northeast blue collar section of Wheatland.

He owned a cabinet and tile business and did installations of his product.

The business was starting to take off.

There were new business buildings and residential structures under construction in Wheatland and surrounding communities.

The larger construction and contractor companies were a distance away in Yakima, Wenatchee or Spokane, so John captured most of the local tile and counter top contracts on construction or remodel projects.

He made a good financial living.

John had hired a full time assistant worker named Greg Walker and his wife Cheyenne to manage his books and finances for his business.

John had suffered through a recent divorce and his ex had married Cam Gentry, a deputy from Canyon County Sheriff's Office.

John knew there were rumors around that his wife had started an affair with the cop a year before their divorce.

The sudden overnight business trips by his wife confirmed in John's mind, there was no way their marriage could be repaired.

John read texts on his wife's I-phone when she would carelessly leave it lying around when she was in the bathroom.

The steamy texts and photos between the Canyon County Deputy and John's wife convinced him there was no way he wanted to be married to such a cheater.

It wasn't but a few months after the final divorce decree that John realized there were women interested in him.

He had a relationship with a married woman named Carmin Martinez that wanted nothing more from him than frequent trysts.

They would meet at hotels in Ellensburg or Wenatchee where she picked up the tab and all expenses.

Her husband Ted was tied up managing his trucking transport contracts in the Bakken Oil fields, hauling crude oil or fracking water from the well sites in far away Williston, North Dakota and the nearby Little Shell Indian Reservation.

John had an on again off again relationship with his girlfriend Nancy, who outwardly seemed ok with the knowledge that John was seeing a young woman named Marianne Shutt.

Marianne had recently moved from Oregon with her mother who worked at local hospitals as a traveling nurse.

On several occasions Marianne had left her cell phone on John's kitchen table while she was distracted outside the house with her son Zachary.

John was always a little suspicious because of his ex-wife's propensity of sending steamy messages and photos on her cell phone to her lover.

John would read Marianne's text messages and found Marianne was still in a relationship with her alleged ex boyfriend Dustin Silver.

He had read her romantic text messages she had been sending to Dustin, some with attached nude photos.

"Here we go again," John said to himself.

John suspected when Marianne would travel to The Dalles, Oregon to visit relatives, she would spend most of her nights with Dustin.

Marianne would sometimes borrow John's Jeep telling John she was going to visit friends in Yakima but would instead meet with Dustin.

When she really got the urge for an intimate meeting, she would meet with Dustin at motels in the Ellensburg, Washington area.

When John first became suspicious of the extra mileage on his Jeep, he placed a small GPS unit behind the third center tail light of his jeep and would download the device on his laptop to map the location and number of stops the Jeep had made when Marianne returned from her carnal trips.

John actually drove the GPS routes displayed in the GPS unit and on three different occasions was able to follow the trail right to motel parking lots, where the GPS would be stationary for 3-4 hours before starting back to Wheatland.

John had thought about his relationship with her and knew he could not trust Marianne enough to ever consider marriage.

In late December, Marianne had spent a couple of nights at John's place and left early in the morning.

John's close friend Nancy came by that evening and shared some wine and talked to John about his relationship with Marianne.

"She's a lying Bitch and there's no way I'd marry her," he growled.

"Fact is, as far as I'm concerned I'm going to break up with Marianne and give her a call tomorrow morning."

'Not even going to respect her enough to do it face to face?" asked Nancy.

"Hell no, I'll do it over the phone," he replied.

"At least I won't have to worry about loaning my vehicle to her so she can go and be with her lover," he sighed.

John lay in bed naked next to Nancy with a beer in his hand while Nancy sipped on a glass of wine while John Lamented over the situation.

"Nancy, let's spend more fun time together," he said.

She replied, "You know this is why I like to hang out with you."

She sat her glass of wine down and rolled over towards him on the bed.

"You are such a great friend with benefits," she murmured and placed her head on John's bare chest.

About 11:00 P.M. Nancy reluctantly got out of John's bed, got dressed and left after one last sensual kiss.

John jumped in the shower and languished from the force of the stream of hot water on his back.

When he got settled back in bed, he phoned Nancy who picked up the phone on the second ring, "Hey babe, I've got an early morning workout at The Club and some construction bids to deliver, but can we meet for lunch. Then we can go out target shooting after lunch tomorrow if the weather clears?"

"Sounds like a plan, we'll have a great time," Nancy said with an excited tone to her voice.

"Good night, I'll call you first thing in the morning," John said.

Chapter 3

Ryan and Juan walked the short distance to Jacob's trap house and tapped on the front door.

The inside lights of the house were extinguished except for the front door porch light.

Josh looked out the small window in the door and recognized Ryan and Juan and slid the lock, then opened the door, looking around for any possible surveillance.

"You guys need to text when you are coming over, I've told you the neighbors watch for traffic coming in and out of this house," growled Josh.

"Come in you guys," Jacob said and directed his attention to Ryan.

"Are you here to pay off your $200 debt?" Jacob asked.

"Let's talk about that $200 drug debt I owe from earlier tonight," Ryan replied, "I want to buy more meth but you have to cut the $200 bill debt back to a hundred."

"We have a stack of Benjamins and I want to score some decent crap that you haven't cut," Ryan said.

"What are you talking?" asked Jacob.

"I want a quarter pound of the uncut stuff and will pay $2,000 and that includes the $200.00 drug debt I owe."

"Man are you fucking crazy? I can cut that meth down and put it into bindles and make $5 grand," said Jacob.

"Yeah, but there is a big risk with all the traffic coming to your house to score your stuff," Ryan continued.

"Just a matter of time till the cops start focusing on you," said Ryan.

"Tell you what, I'll throw in a nice gold wedding and engagement ring set with half Carat diamonds in each ring."

"I even have the receipt from the jewelry store that the rings were wrapped in, where some chump paid $8300 dollars for the set."

"I'll let you have the rings for $2,000 and that will be $4,000 I'll be paying you for the 1/4 lb. of uncut meth," he offered.

Jacob fingered the rings and scratched the sharp point of the diamond engagement ring against a clear water glass he had retrieved from the kitchen.

A clear scratch was observed on the water glass.

Jacob then pulled a compact microscope out of a nearby dresser drawer and set it up on his table.

"Hold the light from the end table lamp closer," he said to Josh as he placed the wedding and engagement rings separately under the microscope examination plate.

After peering into the microscope and looking at both rings, he turned them at several different angles before he raised his head.

"The larger diamonds in each ring settings both have micro etched serial numbers on them which means they are of high quality, but the bad news is that they will be harder for me to sell," he said.

Jacob stepped aside and let Ryan look into the microscope and view the etched serial numbers from both rings.

"You're right," he said to Jacob and glanced over to Juan who had a clear frown on his face.

This wasn't Jacob's first rodeo so next he placed the rings back on the table and returned the microscope back onto the dresser table.

Jacob got a small gold tester kit containing chemical drops from a kitchen drawer and placed the testing kit on the kitchen table.

Jacob tested the gold content with the chemical process which revealed a high percentage of gold, confirming the gold rings were valuable.

Gold price was high per ounce and the gold in the rings was at least worth $3,000, so Jacob and Josh would make a good profit when they melted the gold jewelry down.

"Ok, you have a deal," Jacob said.

"Josh, give the man a 1/4 lb. of meth," said Jacob.

"I would like the 1/4 lb. split into two baggies in equal amounts, one for me and one for Juan," said Ryan.

Ryan looked across the room where Josh was now standing at the table used to cut and process meth.

Josh had been holding his revolver along his side during the transaction and Ryan hadn't noticed.

"No need to come any closer to the meth, I'll give you guys your full amount."

It took Josh a few minutes to measure the meth and he placed the equal amounts into small plastic baggies and placed them at the corner of his work table.

Ryan quickly counted out ten one hundred dollar bills and Juan did the same and handed the money to Jacob.

Jacob walked across the living room into the kitchen where he picked up the two baggies and walked back to Ryan.

Ryan placed one baggy in his coat pocket and handed the other baggy to Juan.

"Thanks, man," he smiled at Jacob while patting his coat pocket.

"I might be coming into some more Benjamins next week and maybe I can get another quarter pound from you," he said.

He thought to himself of how much cash he and Juan could get from a takedown robbery at the norteno's trap house.

"We'll talk a deal when you have the cash," said Jacob.

Jacob glanced out the small window in the front door and looked at the video screen console hardwired to both of the surveillance cameras mounted facing the street and towards the back alley.

It was only then that Jacob slid the bolt lock back and opened the door.

As soon as Ryan and Juan were out the door, it was immediately shut and the clear sound of the locking bolt was heard.

Ryan and Juan gave a hand slap as they walked down the sidewalk.

"What a great night, we got meth to last us for a spell and can double our money," said Juan.

"On top of that, we have two hundred bucks apiece in our pockets."

"Let's head over to the guy's place where he keeps guns in his pick-up," said Ryan.

"The fool's name is John and he drives the blue Chevy Silverado with the black wheels."

"I got into his truck last summer to score some change and the truck was unlocked, but I never got anything because the guy came out of his house and yelled at me so I walked away."

They walked across Division Street on 3rd Avenue, past a Mexican market store on the corner that was closed.

It was nearing 6:00 A.M., but the streets were dark and very few lights were on in the neighborhood houses.

The light snow on the ground made it easy to see their surroundings.

Their target house was about three houses past Ryan's Mother's house on the same side of the street and the blue Chevy Pick-up was parked directly in front of John Adams' house.

There was no outside porch light on at the house but the light snow on the ground created an early dawn light.

They walked on the sidewalk past the pick-up and house and noted the curtains were partially open in front.

A male was observed sitting at a small computer desk with his back to the front window and was intently typing on the computer key board.

"Slip across the lawn around the tree in the front yard and go to the Southwest corner of the house," Ryan directed Juan.

"Watch the guy through the window and give me a whistle if it looks like he is getting ready to leave," Ryan told Juan.

Ryan watched as Juan crossed over to his position by the window after crossing a corner of the neighbor's yard located to the South.

Ryan approached the pick-up truck cautiously and stopped directly in front of the driver's side door.

He could see a partial section of John's torso and right arm as he sat at the computer table with his back to the street.

Ryan turned and looked at the house directly across from John's house.

The living room window curtains at that house were open and he saw a dark haired woman sitting at a table facing the street with an overhead kitchen light on that was very bright.

The woman seemed engrossed in reading a book or newspaper and was not looking up.

He thought the woman would likely not be able to observe many details of the surroundings outside her front window because of the bright kitchen lights reflecting back on the interior glass.

To limit his chances of being seen by the woman, Ryan stayed on the driver's side of the pick-up.

He crouched down by the door and tried the handle.

He pulled on the handle and there was a low audible click as the latch freed from the locking mechanism, and the door opened.

As he opened the pick-up door, the interior ceiling light came on.

Ryan quickly reached up with his gloved hand and pushed the off switch next to the plastic covered interior light.

Ryan swept his hand under the driver's seat searching for a gun.

He found nothing there and opened the upper center console cover.

Other than fast food napkins, a measuring tape and numerous pens and pencils, there was a cup of loose change in the console and Ryan placed the change into his coat pocket.

He knew there was another storage compartment below the center console.

He closed the upper console lid and tilted the console backward, which allowed access to the compartment beneath.

Ryan was nervous because it was about 6:30 A.M. and people would be stirring and getting ready or leaving for work.

As Ryan lifted up the lid of the lower storage container, he saw what he was looking for.

A metal colored semi-auto handgun with a laser attachment was lying inside with several spare ammunition magazines.

A box of ammunition was lying next to the handgun.

Ryan picked up the two spare magazines and box of ammunition and placed them in his large coat pocket.

He grabbed the 45 caliber semi-auto pistol in his right hand and was holding it when he was backing out of the pick-up instead of placing it in his other coat pocket.

He heard a short whistle from Juan and snapped his head around toward John's front door.

The front door of the house was standing wide open and Ryan saw the truck owner standing on the porch with a surprised look on his face.

John immediately recognized Ryan and with a scowl yelled, "You again! What the fuck are you doing in my truck." He stepped off the porch heading towards Ryan while holding his truck key ring in his right hand.

Ryan was in a blind panic and started to run away from the pick-up.

He didn't look when he raised the stolen pistol over his left shoulder and fired blindly one time in John's direction.

Ryan heard a loud gasp and saw John standing but slumped over, holding his stomach coughing and stumbling toward his front porch.

He watched as John disappeared inside the house through the front door.

There was a dark color on the back of John's light colored jacket.

Feeling like a trapped deer caught in the headlights, Ryan turned and ran in a north direction across the front yard and then turned at the corner of the house and ran through the backyard out to the alley.

Ryan ran south down the alley and kept his feet inside the tire tracks of a vehicle that had travelled down the alley.

Ryan heard a whistle and looked behind to see Juan running behind him.

As they exited from the alley, they noticed a man crossing the street from the neighborhood market, holding a paper coffee cup container in each hand. They turned left and ran towards Carlene's house.

"Hey Juan, I'll catch you later, head home and change your clothes."

"What a damn mess you've got me in by your screw-up," Juan said with a dangerous tone of voice.

Juan hoped the guy wasn't dead or he would spend a long time in prison for just being with Ryan if they were identified.

Ryan had a panic event when he noticed he had dropped his handcuffs from his backpack and wasn't sure when they had fallen out.

"Damn good thing I was wearing gloves," he thought.

"I can walk around later and look, but now the neighborhood will be swarming with cops," he thought.

Juan reached the apartment complex and saw no one walking on the street or any moving cars, but he could hear a cacophony of sirens in the area.

He went to the slider-door of the apartment and found it unlocked as he had left it.

He entered quietly but was breathing heavily and was out of breath.

As he started to cross the living room towards his bedroom, he heard a noise and Susan rolled over on the couch and glanced at him, then shut her eyes and went back to sleep.

He went into the darkened bedroom and his girlfriend Tiffanie Weeks was sleeping on the other side of the mattress with her back to him.

Juan carefully undressed and quietly and smoothly got into bed with her.

She gave a small sigh and nudged her backside into Juan's groin and belly, gave another contented sigh and continued peacefully sleeping.

Juan's heart was still racing from the adrenaline surge caused by Ryan's murder of the guy that morning.

He laid quietly, wondering what the day would bring.

Ryan carefully and quietly opened the front door of Carlene's house and made his way to the bathroom.

He was startled when Carlene came to the open bathroom door with an angry look on her face.

"Gone all night again," she said with venom in her voice.

"Which skank were you with tonight?" she said.

"You are scrubbing your face and hands pretty hard, afraid you caught an STD from your Skank?" she challenged.

"Hey, it's not like that at all, I was doing some gambling till dawn and drinking skunk beer. The goddamn cigar smoke had my lungs all fucked up and my clothes stink," said Ryan, defensively.

"Who the hell do you think you're telling your tale?" she rasped back at Ryan.

"I know what another woman smells like," she told him.

"Look Bitch, I don't have time to argue, I'm jumping in the shower and changing my clothes," he said.

"I got lots of crap to take care of today," Ryan blasted back at her.

He stripped off his clothes and threw them on the floor and stepped into a steaming shower.

Carlene picked up his clothes to throw in the laundry and there was an unmistakable odor of another woman on his clothes.

That lying son of a bitch Carlene thought as she started seething again.

Ryan stepped out of the shower and toweled off, then put on a set of fresh clothing, put on his size 12 boots he had been wearing, put on his coat and walked out the front door without saying a word.

Carlene saw that Ryan was holding a piece of dark clothing in his hand and thought it might be his dark t-shirt.

She watched him bend down and reach behind a shrub beside the front door and place an object inside the dark cloth and wrap it up and place the object in his backpack.

"Wonder why he didn't bring his stash inside the house with him," she thought.

"It looked like it was more like a metallic object, maybe the shape of a handgun gun," she mused

"I hate you, Ryan," she said aloud as she reached for the cigarette roller and placed some quality pot in the roller, and rolled a professional looking joint.

I need to chill out, she thought as she lit the joint up and took a big hit, sucking the smoke deep into her lungs and feeling the expansion of her lungs until she started to cough in spasms.

When the spasms passed she took another deep inhale and the coughing spasms were not as severe.

Another couple of hits and a few minutes later she could care less about Ryan and his whore from the last night.

Chapter 4
John Adams

John Adams had gotten up early, about 6:00 A.M., and dressed for the Fitness Gym Center in town where he would do hard workouts with the business owner Rufus Jennings, who had become a close friend.

They were both single and would share their stories of conquest they had with the local women and had no secrets from each other.

John turned on his computer and sat in front of the screen to print out bids to drop off at the local mortgage company later that morning.

"I'm going out to the truck and warm it up, it's damn cold," he thought as he grabbed the keys and headed for the door.

While waiting for his pick-up to warm up, he would go back inside to his warm kitchen and have a glass of protein drink and a protein bar to fuel his body as part of his hard core exercise regime.

As John stepped onto the front porch he saw movement by his truck and easily spotted Ryan crouched by his truck door.

He yelled at Ryan and stepped off his front porch.

He heard a loud blast and immediately felt a hard impact and numbing in his left chest area and felt like the breath had been knocked from him.

He turned and stumbled into his house and bumped into the

computer table trying to reach his cell phone that was lying on the computer table, knocking it off onto the floor where it slid from sight.

He was gasping and fell face forward on the kitchen floor and knew he was going to die on the floor.

He lowered his head and the last of his lifeblood pumped from his body.

Chapter 5
Bonnie Crawfoot

Bonnie Crawfoot was a woman in her late 60's and was hard as leather from her hard life working on her fruit and vegetable 10 acre farm located just outside of the town of Wilson Creek, Washington

She sold her farm products to the local schools for the student lunch programs.

She used the fruits and berries from her farm to make delicious scones and pastries that she sold to the local coffee shops.

At 4:00 A.M. each morning she would do her baking and read the local daily newspaper at her kitchen table while her goods baked, before heading out to deliver her baked goods.

The large window in her living room gave her a great view of the street in front of her house and she felt secure enough in her neighborhood that she never closed the drapes.

Bonnie's home was across the street from John Adams house.

About 6:30 A.M. she was sitting in her usual spot at the kitchen table reading her newspaper, when she heard a loud gunshot or fireworks.

She saw a male subject in the front yard of the house across the street and there was a flurry of activity near him.

She recognized John Adams in his workout clothing and light

jacket shuffling on the sidewalk towards his front porch and observed him stumble inside the house, with the door shutting behind him.

She noted how light it was outside, almost like the turning of dawn, but it was actually a combination of light from the snow covering the ground and the approaching dawn.

Bonnie was on the alert, knowing something bad may have happened to John so she picked up her phone and telephoned his phone number.

There was no response and the phone ring changed to voicemail.

Bonnie put on her coat and boots and walked quickly across the road to John's front porch and stood on the front steps.

She knocked on the wooden front door with no response from inside.

"Oh Lord," she thought as she walked back across the street into her home and dialed 911.

"911, what's your emergency?" said the Communications Officer on the end of the phone.

"I live at 173 N 3rd and I think I saw my neighbor directly across the street possibly get shot and stumble into his house, his name is John Adams." she gasped out.

The Dispatcher asked, "Did you see anyone else or a car in the area?"

"When I heard a gunshot I saw a flurry of activity in the front yard and I think it could have been John's son Devin and someone else but can't give much of a description. I thought at first it was John and Devin shooting off fireworks in the front yard. I tried phoning John but there was no answer so I walked over to his house and knocked on the door and no one came to the door. I didn't hear any voices from inside and I'm also worried about Devin, his son." she finished

"Ma'am, we have units coming and the officers will be there in just a few minutes. Keep an eye out and if you see anything else suspicious, call back," said the 911 Operator.

Bonnie kept her heavy winter coat on and stepped out of her house and stood on the sidewalk across the street from John's house.

As she made her way to the sidewalk in front of her house, a car approached and turned into her neighbor's driveway.

"Oh, no," she thought, "that's John's younger sister Olive who lives next door."

She knew Olive had just arrived home after spending the night with her boyfriend.

It was a regular pattern.

"What's going on?" Olive asked as Bonnie walked up to Olive as she was getting out of her car.

"I think something happened to your brother," she said to Olive.

"I heard a gunshot and saw John stumble into the house," she explained breathlessly.

"I called 911 a couple of minutes ago and the 911 Operator said the cops are on their way."

They both turned to the sound of studded snow tires on the street approaching them.

They saw three clearly marked Wheatland Police cars with their lights off creeping down the street and they came to a stop on the east side of the street about two houses south of John's residence.

Bonnie and Olive crossed the street and walked towards the three dark clad uniformed officers approaching down the sidewalk.

"That's the house there," Bonnie explained to the officers and pointed to John's house.

She told the officers the details of what she had earlier heard and observed.

Sgt. Joe Harmon travelled close to the front of the neighboring houses as he approached John's house.

He set up his position on the S/W corner of John's house.

Cpl. Quinn Baker and Officer Jack Bellows approached at an angle across the lawn.

Cpl. Baker knocked on the front door and stepped to the left as an officer safety procedure while Officer Bellows peered in the window on the south side of the front door.

Officer Bellows whispered excitedly, "Quinn, we got a male subject lying face down on the floor in the kitchen."

Both Officers had drawn their handguns.

"Let's go in," Bellows whispered and turned the front door knob and discovered the door was unlocked, making a forced entry unnecessary.

Baker was first to enter the residence and turned to the right making a sweep of the kitchen and living room area for a possible suspect still on scene.

He reached down and felt for a pulse on John's neck as he continued keeping his handgun in his other hand.

Officer Bellows brushed past Corporal Baker and began a search of the interior of the residence.

Satisfied there was no one in the residence, Officer Bellows returned to the living room where Cpl. Baker was contacting the 911 Center calling for fire and medical response and provided the limited information that the male victim had a gunshot wound and was possibly DOA.

Bonnie and Olive had followed the officers and had stood outside on the front porch until they saw through the open doorway the man lying on the kitchen floor was Olive's brother, John.

They stepped into the living room and Olive Adams began moaning softly and started to sink to the floor with her eyes rolling back. Officer Bellows stepped over and grasped Olive under the arm to keep her from falling as her eyes opened up.

"Devin," screamed Bonnie because she thought it was Devin that she had observed outside the house with John at the time of the fatal shot.

Officer Bellows said, "There is no one else in the house, Devin is not here."

"Both of you have to leave, this is a crime scene," he said.

"Bonnie, can you take Olive to your house and we'll come over and speak to both of you after we have the scene secure and the medical crew can examine Olive's brother," he continued.

"He is deceased, possibly from a gunshot wound," Cpl. Baker said in a soft tone.

Bonnie held her arm around Olive's waist to support her as they walked back across the street to Bonnie's house.

"Oh Gawd, I have to tell my Family," Olive sobbed as she sat at Bonnies kitchen table.

Bonnie handed Olive her phone and went into the living room to allow privacy so Olive could tell her family the horrible news.

Olive notified her shocked parents and after sobbing at both ends of the telephone line a plan was made to notify other friends and family members.

Olive knew John's girlfriend Marianne Shutt should be notified as soon as possible before she heard of John's murder on the news.

She telephoned Marianne Shutt's phone number and after 6 or 7 rings a female answered the phone.

Olive was sobbing and Marianne's mother Terri had answered and identified herself when she answered the phone.

Olive proceeded to tell her the horrific news and asked if she would tell Marianne of the death of John.

Marianne was sleeping heavily in the upstairs bedroom, but when she heard steps coming up the stairs, she rolled over on the bed and was facing the door when her mother stepped in.

Terri sat at the edge of the bed and gently rubbed Marianne's shoulder.

"Honey," she said in a soft voice, "I've got some bad news that's going to hurt."

Marianne was fully alert now and sat up in the bed.

Terri told her, "Something bad happened at John's house this morning and he was shot and killed. The Police don't know what happened or who killed John but they know it wasn't suicide."

"OMG," said Marianne, breaking into deep, uncontrollable sobs and having difficulty catching her breath.

She sat on the bed sobbing and holding her face in her hands.

After about a half hour she stood up and looked at her mother, who had been sitting by her side comforting her.

"I've got to go there and find out what happened, I will go to Olive's house where the rest of John's family are gathered," she said.

In the back of her mind she wondered if Dustin Silver might have something to do with the murder.

Driving from her home on the way to Wheatland, Marianne picked up her cellphone and dialed up Dustin.

"Hello," Dustin cheerfully answered the phone.

"Where are you?" shouted Marianne.

"That's a weird question, where are you?" he replied.

"Somebody just shot John and I want to know where you are this morning."

"I'm in Oregon and headed up to pick up some car engines," he replied.

"Are you accusing me of shooting John? Is he alive?" quipped Dustin.

"I've never ever threatened the guy and it was you that was always trying to make me jealous of John and you know it," Dustin angrily told Marianne.

"I don't know what I'm thinking, but if you are responsible, I will come to The Dalles and kill you, and yes, John is dead," she spat out.

"I know that you have never threatened John, but I had to ask you so I would have peace of mind," she said.

"You are crazy, Marianne," Dustin shouted into the phone and hung up.

Nancy Williams had also received a call from Olive at her home and was in far worse emotional condition than Marianne.

Nancy was alone and she slid down the kitchen wall, dropping her phone without hanging up, and stumbled to her living room sofa where she lay on her side, sobbing uncontrollably.

She thought she was having a horrible nightmare and didn't know when the nightmare would end.

There was a knock on her front door which stirred her.

As she made her way to the door the knocks became incessant.

She opened the door to find her neighbor Allison Brooks telling her there had been a murder on the street where her friend John lived.

Nancy told Allison that Olive had already phoned her and John Adams was dead.

Nancy broke into tears as Allison came into the house and they sat together and hugged as Nancy sobbed onto Allison's shoulder.

Wheatland Officer Jack Bellows, Sgt. Joe Harmon and Cpl. Quinn Baker were the three officers present when the local fire department EMT's rolled up, followed shortly by the local ambulance service vehicle.

Baker opened the front door and waved to the fire EMTs and the local ambulance crew.

Oh shit, he said to himself as the fire EMT team cut across the front lawn, contaminating the potential crime area where evidence might be located.

He yelled at the ambulance crew to stay on the sidewalk and come directly to the front door and enter.

The EMT fire team walked across the living room to the kitchen.

EMT Scott Zanger reached down and felt for a pulse of John, who was lying facedown.

"Come on, Burel," Scott Zanger said to his partner, "we have to place the patient on his back to attach an EKG for signs of life."

At this time, the ambulance crew had arrived and entered the kitchen.

They had brought their portable defibrillator into the room and almost immediately began placing EKG pads on John's chest and sides after he had been placed on his back.

The ambulance EMT attendant Tom Ford had attached the electrodes and made sure all the connections were secure.

The machine gave a low hum and began scrolling out data on the portable EKG Machine that was wirelessly transmitted to the Wheatland Basin Hospital Emergency Room where an E.R. Doctor could view the screen in real time.

His partner Jonas Patron slowly shook his head side by side and replied, "No sign of life."

They noted the bullet hole and expansion of the entry wound where the body had swelled up directly around the entrance.

Basin Hospital ER doctor James Riggs watched the EKG printout on the hospital monitor.

Dr. Riggs directed the ER nurse to notify Jonas Patron on the portable radio that the EKG reading did confirm the victim was deceased.

"Thanks for responding," Cpl. Baker told the EMT fire crew and ambulance attendants.

"I think there's not much you guys can do further, so when you leave the scene, be sure and leave down the front sidewalk and into the street where you can get to your vehicles," continued Cpl. Baker.

Tom Ford and Jonas Patron detached the EKG electrodes from John's lifeless chest and packed up their equipment and left through the front door.

"Please complete your incident reports and send over to the Wheatland Police Investigative Division," Cpl. Baker instructed.

Sgt. Joe Harmon was the Wheatland Police Department senior officer on scene and he had knowledge of the Incident Command System (ICS) which is the national procedure for fire and crime scene management and disasters.

He would be the Incident Commander until a senior Officer responded and took command.

"I'm going out to the car and get my camera," he told Officer Jack Bellows.

Maintain control of our crime scene inside the house and I will go out and take some exterior photos.

As Sgt. Harmon stepped out onto the front porch he noticed several Canyon County Sheriff vehicles that were parked on opposite ends of 3rd Street and had erected yellow tape barriers to block traffic about a block on either end from the crime scene.

Cpl. Baker contacted Sgt. Harmon at his police cruiser where he was obtaining his camera from the trunk of his vehicle.

"Hey Sarge, what do you think of the scene?" Cpl. Baker asked.

"The deceased male on the kitchen floor looks like he was killed with a larger caliber handgun. It looks like the guy was actually shot outside near the front porch and he made it back inside his house to the kitchen where he died," Sgt. Harmon opined.

"There are at least 7 or 8 rifles or shotguns in the living room in a gun cabinet and a couple of handguns are visible in the bottom drawer of the cabinet, and there was no sign of a struggle inside," he continued.

"Cpl. Baker, would you direct a couple of police officers to do a canvas of the neighbors in a three block area to see if anyone saw anything or anyone in the area around 6:30 A.M.?" Sgt. Harmon directed.

"We have been hit pretty hard with car prowls in this neighborhood so there could be a connection," said Sgt. Harmon.

Sgt. Harmon received a message to contact the Communications Center by telephone. The Dispatcher told Sgt. Harmon the center already received a call this morning from a man reporting a vehicle prowling of his pick-up that he had noticed when he was leaving for work at his regular time.

"Someone had got into the guy's pick-up truck and stole his wallet and a set of gold wedding and engagement rings with expensive diamond insets from inside the center console. He had paid over $8K for the wedding ring set and he found his wallet laying on the street near his pick-up truck minus $2,400 in 100 hundred dollar bills. He said he had locked his vehicle but had not turned on the security alarm system. The victim said he never heard anything during the night and his dog had been sleeping inside because the temperature was so cold," said the 911 Operator.

Sgt. Harmon notified the Communication Center to have all involved law enforcement units respond to the staging area on the South end of the closed off street so there would be some semblance of accounting for officers and support staff and Cpl. Baker could assign officers to canvas the immediate neighborhood.

The staging area would be located next to the Mobile Command Vehicle.

Sgt. Harmon directed crime scene tape to be stretched completely across 3rd street on both sides of the house property lines.

About 30 minutes had elapsed and no senior staff had arrived to take control of the crime scene.

Two additional Wheatland patrol officers in their cruisers arrived on scene and parked on the street beyond the outer crime scene tape.

Sgt. Harmon met the two officers on the sidewalk, who identified themselves as Doug Harrison and Matt Winslow.

"I want you guys to start a methodical search of the front yard, but be careful of any footprints you may see in the snow and throw a placard down when you see one," he said.

"If you find any evidence or possible evidence, put down a marker and let me know."

Sgt. Harmon drew a rough draft of the front quadrant of the yard and showed Officer Winslow and Officer Harrison where they were assigned to search.

Officer Winslow started a methodical search of his assigned area and almost immediately observed a pair of metal handcuffs splayed open on the lawn.

He looked carefully around and saw no footprints near the handcuffs.

He thought it looked as though someone had thrown or dropped the handcuffs.

Officer Winslow peered closely at the handcuffs and could not see a serial number on the dark metal handcuffs.

He took a photo of the leaves partially covering the handcuffs with his personal cell phone.

There were several leaves partially covering the handcuff where the serial number would be located.

He carefully removed three larger maple leaves that had been lying partially on top of the handcuffs, covering the serial number.

He picked up the handcuffs by several inches and turned the handcuffs at an angle so he could check the other wrist portion of the cuffs and noticed the serial number had also been defaced or filed off and was unreadable.

He placed the handcuffs backdown in the position he thought he had first found them.

He unknowingly had placed the handcuffs down on the grass and bent the grass beneath the handcuffs in the opposite direction the grass had been pointing when he had lifted the handcuffs.

Officer Winslow thought about putting the leaves back on the handcuffs.

He surmised, "These cuffs are not connected to this incident so I'll just leave the leaves off, it won't make any difference."

Winslow marked the location of the handcuffs with an evidence numbered placard, took a photo of the tampered evidence on his cell phone, and continued on the search of his assigned area.

Meanwhile Officer Harrison was searching his assigned part of the lawn when he spotted what looked like a spent shell casing lying on top of the grass.

He marked the location with a numbered placard.

He gently reached down and carefully picked up the shell casing with his bare hand and noted that it was a 45 caliber shell casing.

"Oh hell," he said, when he realized he had not put on protective evidence gloves and N-95 face mask to prevent contamination of evidence.

He looked around to see if anyone had observed him pick up the shell casing and he put it back down at the location where he thought he had first picked the shell casing up.

He took photos of the spent shell casing with his cell phone.

He looked around, put on an N-95 face mask and surgical gloves and picked up the shell casing and carefully placed the shell casing in a small paper bag, folded the top and put it inside his uniform jacket pocket.

"Hope my DNA didn't contaminate the spent shell casing," he worried.

Officers Harrison and Winslow continued to another quadrant of the front yard and split into smaller quadrants again.

Officer Harrison started checking along the front of the house on the lawn and noted a set of larger footprints that ran across the lawn and appeared to run around the side of the house.

He marked the area with crime scene cones placed next to the footprints.

Officers Harrison and Winslow contacted Sgt. Harmon and pointed out the handcuffs and spent shell casing location they had found, as possible evidence.

Neither reported to Sgt. Harmon the crime scene evidence had been contaminated by both of them.

Police Chief Sam Fife rolled up on scene with the Medical Examiners vehicle closely behind at about 7:30 A.M.

The Crime scene tape had been lifted by Ryan Bates who had been standing at the end of the street, watching the activity with acute interest.

Wheatland Officer Sam Hufmunster would later comment in his report that Ryan Bates had been standing at the end of the street and was actually raising the crime scene tape to allow responding police cars entry.

Both the Chief and Medical Examiner's cars were parked on the East side of the street a short distance from the crime scene.

They were met on the sidewalk by Sgt. Harmon who had assumed command of the crime scene until relieved from that duty.

Sgt. Harmon briefed the two newcomers on the preliminary findings and tasks performed at the early stage of the investigation.

They walked down the sidewalk and stepped onto the porch without observing the large spot of blood on the outdoor carpet covering the porch floor.

Coroner Teagan tracked blood from the bottom of his shoes when he walked onto the vinyl floor in the kitchen.

He bent down wearing a pair of vinyl gloves and opened the victims eyelid and closely looked for Subjective Petechial Hemorrhage in the eyes.

Not finding Subjective Petechial Hemorrhage in John's eyes, he moved to the chest area and examined the entry wound located at the left upper chest.

He noted the ENT's had left an EKG monitoring sticker below the entrance wound on the upper left side of John's chest.

He withdrew a medical thermometer with a sharp tube attached to the device from his medical bag.

He pierced the victim's skin above the liver in the back and slid the device 3-4 inches into the victim.

This method of checking the deceased person's liver temperature was commonly used to assist the county Medical Examiner and Law Enforcement investigators to determine the time of death.

"Time of death was about 2 hours ago, internal temperature is 96.3 which coincides with the reported time a gunshot was reported to 911 about 6:30 A.M. this morning," Teagan said to no one in particular.

"We'll know more at autopsy to see how much damage there was to the internal organs and how rapid the blood loss occurred," he continued.

"Judging from the entrance wound in the upper left chest area, it was a high powered bullet that killed this man," he noted.

"The exit wound was near the lower right back area that left a nasty exit wound and has the bullet been located?" he asked.

"Not yet, we will be bringing in searchers with metal detectors and explosive detection trained K-9 dogs trained to locate bullets, shell casings and related firearms," said Sgt. Harmon.

"Have you made an identification on this victim yet?" asked the Coroner to Officer Bellows.

"The sister of the victim was standing on the street when we rolled up about 6:30 A.M. this morning," he replied.

"Olive Adams and the neighbor Bonnie Crawfoot stepped inside the living room while we were checking and they told us the victim was Olive's brother John Adams."

"Why the hell did you let them come into the active crime scene?" asked Chief Fife.

"Chief, Corporal Baker, Officer Bellows and myself were busy trying to determine if Adams was still alive and I had just cleared the rest of the house to see if anyone else was present inside the house," Sgt. Harmon replied.

"We didn't notice them until they had already entered," he continued.

"I did check the back door and it was unlocked," Officer Bellows said.

"Were you wearing evidence protective gloves when you touched the door knob?"

Officer Bellows' face turned a slight red and he sheepishly replied that he hadn't thought about putting on gloves.

"Jesus," Coroner Teagan said as he looked up at Chief Fife with a disgusted look on his face.

Officer Bellow's said, "The neighbor, Bonnie Crawfoot began screaming the name Devin over and over again and yelling that he must be there inside the house."

"I told her the only person in the house was the victim and no one else."

Officer Bellows advised Bonnie was adamant that she had observed a flurry of activity in the front yard when John had been shot, but said she would have to think on it for a while.

"Stay with the victim," he directed Officer Bellows, "until we get investigators on scene and he can be examined and processed."

"From what I've observed, this incident is going to take more resources than the Wheatland Police Department can effectively investigate."

The Chief and Coroner walked out the front door directly down the sidewalk to public sidewalk where Sgt. Harmon was standing, awaiting their approach.

"Chief, I called for the Mobile Command Post and it just arrived."

It's parked at the outer perimeter of the crime scene and communication equipment is being spooled up as we speak.

"Sgt. Harmon, I have started the Incident Command System protocol and you are currently the Incident Commander until you relinquish that position to someone else," said Chief Fife.

"Make sure a log book is kept by an assigned officer of the changes in command and every officer or civilian that enters," he said.

"Sgt. Harmon, I believe this investigation will entail the use of substantial manpower, so the CBIT Unit will be in charge of the investigation and their supervisor will be selected from the CBIT (Columbia Basin Investigation Team)," he continued.

"Until then, follow ICS, Incident Command System guidelines. If I were you, I would assign a person for Logistics to supply the material and equipment needed for this event," he told Sgt. Harmon.

"Assign someone for Operations and work with you to develop your action plan and post it somewhere so all of the responders will know what's going on. Assign Detectives, Tom Zollars and Jesse Massee, to assist in interviewing potential witnesses. Massee has ten years in the agency and is a recently promoted Detective," Chief Fife said.

"Call out reserve police officers and assign them to man the security posts on both ends at the crime scene tape so we can free up the regular assigned police officers and we're pretty short handed right now and need our officers out there to handle calls.

Any related information the officers obtain from their door knocks needs to be forwarded when they obtain it, and pass the information to our investigators right away.

Contact Amy Bently, our investigative assistant, and have her set up in the Mobile Command Post to assist the incident commander and keep track of the information coming in and place the information by time and location as part of the incident action plan. Use the white board and place information and status in order to check that we're covering all the on scene intricacies of this investigation," he directed the Sergeant.

The Joint City County forensic team will be in charge of evidence collection, photographs and scene identification, and they will be working hand in hand with our two detectives and CBIT," Chief Fife said, then left the scene accompanied by Coroner Teagan.

Sgt. Harmon contacted Detective Zollars, Massee, and Forensic Officer Beth Johnson.

He motioned to Cpl. Quinn Baker to come over to his location.

Quinn said, "I'm headed to the office to write up a search warrant and have the judge sign it so we can enter the crime scene and process the scene and get the body moved out of there."

"The victim's family and one or two of his girlfriends are across the street at Bonnie Crawfoot's house, watching out from her big front room window."

"Remember, when the Medical Examiner's assistants take the body out, make sure they are told the family is watching closely how the body is being handled."

"Let's show as much compassion as we can under the circumstances," he continued.

After an hour and a half Cpl. Baker came back with the search warrant in hand.

As he handed the search warrant to Det. Zollars he commented, "I was damn lucky I caught Judge Cooper during recess, because the rest of the District Judges are at a law convention in Seattle until tomorrow gaining their CEU credits."

"Judge Cooper just briefly looked over the warrant request and never asked any questions, he just scribbled his name and requested the search warrant return be sent to him in 3 days." Cpl. Baker said.

Detectives Zollars and Massee walked up the sidewalk to the front door and stepped into the living room accompanied by Forensic Officer Beth Johnson.

Massee placed the signed search warrant on the kitchen table.

Officer Bellows gave up control of the crime scene and returned to the Incident Command Vehicle parked on the street.

Detectives Zollars and Massee stood to the side while Johnson began taking a series of photos of the interior of the residence and the position of the body.

Detective Zollars directed Johnson to take photos of a pair of jeans laying on the table less than five feet from the victim's body.

Det. Massee carefully picked up the jeans and went through the pockets examining several coins, a house key for an unknown residence and removed the brown leather wallet from the left rear pocket.

He opened up the wallet and a woman's Washington State Driver's license was in the first clear wallet holder with the name Janice Azevedo with an Ephrata address.

The rest of the wallet contained fourteen dollars, a social security card and a local bank debit card.

Massee thoughtfully held the wallet in his hand while thinking about how the pants and wallet could be involved and decided there was no connection.

He slid the wallet back into the back pocket, then placed the jeans back on the seat of the chair.

Zollars noted a partially full bottle of local late harvest wine, a wine glass with a small amount at the bottom of the glass and a Rocky Mountain Blue beer can.

"Looks like our boy John here had a female visitor over here last night," he said.

"She might have left her pants here, so I wonder what she wore when she left," Detective Zollars winked at Detective Massee and smiled.

After checking out the kitchen area for other potential evidence, a decision was made to roll the victim over to check for evidence that may have been located on the floor beneath the body.

When John's body was rolled over onto the floor, a set of car keys was found beneath his body.

Johnson photographed the set of car keys and Det. Massee picked up the set of keys while wearing his evidence collection gloves.

"Looks like a couple of car keys, one like an ignition key, a door lock key and a house type key," said Massee as he examined the set.

"We'll have to check and see if the keys fit the ignition and door lock of the blue pick-up parked out front," he said.

Massee placed the keys in a small plastic evidence bag and placed them on the kitchen table.

John Adams was wearing sweat pants, a wife beater type shirt, Jogging type shoes and a light jacket when he died.

Detective Massee searched through the light jacket pockets and discovered three 45 caliber cartridges and six spent shell casings.

Detective Massee peered closely at the three cartridges and six spent shell casings and made a note they were 45 caliber cartridges and held one of the six spent shell casings up to show Detective Zollars the caliber.

Beth Johnson took photos of the cartridges and empty shell casings as they were being held in Detective Massee's gloved hand.

He placed the cartridges and spent shell casing in a small plastic evidence envelope, carefully marking the location it was found and placing them in his coat pocket.

A wine bottle, wine glass, and beer can were all packaged after Beth Johnson photographed their location.

Detective Zollars stepped to the front door entrance and shouted to Sgt. Harmon to have the two Coroner Assistants come into the house to transport the body to the morgue.

The attendants brought in a gurney and set it near the body, and laid out a black zippered body bag.

One attendant placed his hands beneath the armpits and used his forearms to cradle John's limp neck and head.

The other attendant grasped the ankles and they gently lifted John's body upwards about 6 inches and moved him over the body bag, and gently lay him down with his hands on his chest.

The body bag was zipped up.

There were two handles sewed into each side of the bodybag.

Detectives Zollars and Massee each grasped a handle while the attendants grasped the other handles and lifted John's body unto the gurney where he was strapped in to prevent the body from falling off the gurney.

The attendants rolled the gurney down the sidewalk to their awaiting converted delivery mini-van.

Forensic Officer Beth Johnson walked through the interior of the house and noted a gun cabinet with the door partially open against the east wall on the south side of the living room which was also in view of the kitchen table.

There were 5-6 rifles placed in the soft brackets of the gun cabinet and assorted ammunition sitting atop the cabinet.

The bottom of the cabinet had a drawer that was opened a few inches and several handguns were partially in view.

Detective Zollars opened the drawer and two revolvers, one a 357 Mag and the other a western style 22 cal. revolver were inside the drawer.

A S&W semi auto 40 cal. pistol was also located in the same drawer as the two revolvers.

Misc. rifle and handgun boxed ammunition was neatly stacked on the left side of the drawer.

The firearms were photographed by Beth Johnson.

Hmm, I wonder where the 45 caliber semi auto pistol might be located, Detective Massee thought to himself as he recalled the 45 cal. semi-auto cartridges and spent shell casings he had located in John Adams jacket pocket he was wearing when he was killed.

Detective Zollars looked on the top of the gun cabinet and located a partially full cartridge box with the label, high velocity 45 Caliber Cartridges, imprinted on the box.

"Be on the lookout for a 45 cal. handgun, I found the ammo for a 45 semi-auto pistol located on the top of the gun cabinet," he told Detective Massee.

They completed the search of the interior of the home without locating any obvious evidence or locating other handguns.

As Detective Zollars stood at the doorway he looked down on the outdoor covered carpet concrete porch and spotted a quarter sized splotch of blood on the indoor carpet covered step.

He could see what looked liked a small footprint that had stepped directly on the blood splash and the footstep was pointed away from the front door towards the street,

He thought to himself that whoever stepped on this blood splotch has spread that blood everyplace they had stepped.

Detective Zollars called for Forensic Tech. Beth Johnson to take photos of the blood drop on the carpet on the front porch.

When finished, Beth Johnson took out a scalpel and cut around the margin of the blood spot and placed it in an evidence container.

"Now, how can we figure the location where the victim was shot?" Detective Zollars thought to himself as he looked at the blood prints from the shoe that led out onto the sidewalk and disappeared in the confusion of the many footprints made by persons walking on the sidewalk.

They walked to the Mobile Command Post and met with Officer

Bellows, and deposited the packaged evidence on the front table of the Command vehicle.

Officer Bellows told them, "Officers Harrison and Winslow searched the yard and located a spent 45 caliber shell casing and a set of handcuffs lying in the yard."

"Officer Winslow found a set of boot tracks near the handcuffs and followed them around the Northside of the house and across the yard where they ended at the alley, and there was a set of car tracks there," he continued.

Detective Massee, Detective Zollars and Beth Johnson left the Mobile Command Post and stepped over to the inside crime scene perimeter.

"Hey guys, can you show us where you located the cuffs, shell casing and footprints?" Detective Zollars asked Officers Winslow and Harrison.

"Sure," said Officer Winslow, and led the group single file across the lawn to prevent contamination of other evidence that might still be on the lawn.

As they neared the handcuffs, they saw the handcuffs lying on the lawn were in the open position and not closed.

That is strange that the handcuffs are in that open position thought Detective Massee too himself.

The grass beneath the handcuffs was bent towards the street, indicating the direction the cuffs had been dropped or thrown.

There were no footprints located between the handcuffs and the back fence of the yard.

"Hmm, I wonder how long those handcuffs have been lying there," Detective Zollars commented.

"Looks like the handcuffs have been there before this small skiff of snow, which probably explains the lack of footprints," mused Detective Massee.

"Leave the handcuffs in place and don't disturb, I'm calling for our additional Forensic Recovery Team to process the exterior of the crime scene," said Beth Johnson.

"We must keep the evidence pristine and not disturbed," she said.

"Also, call in the Total Station team, we need to have accurate measurements," she continued.

Officer Winslow never said a word or disclosed that he had indeed tampered with the handcuffs.

A faint boot heel print had been located about 6-7 feet on the lawn in a northern direction.

A small evidence cone was placed near the boot print.

They continued across the yard to the corner of the house where a series of footprints with the same heel print were observed leading around the side of the house, across the backyard, to the alley behind the residence where they disappeared at the alley.

There was a set of highway type car tracks in the alley and it appeared there were faint footprints stepping into tire tracks heading down the alley towards Division street," Officer Winslow informed.

Evidence cones were set down beside each footprint so the forensic team could locate and measure the footprints and take photographs.

They retreated from the backyard and walked on the south side of the neighbor's yard when Detective Zollars looked down and saw a faint footprint in the snow leading towards the alley about 10 feet away.

Other tracks of the same shoe print were more visible, and had a small circular mark in the middle of the heel pattern and they appeared to have been left by a boot heel.

Detective Zollars followed the shoe prints and noted where they turned south along the side of the alley and disappeared in a pine needle buildup under the trees that lined the alley.

There were several scuff marks of the shoe print a short distance with the same circular heel marking in the tire track which indicated that same person had ran down the alley and used the tire tracks to help conceal the direction of his travel.

Detective Zollars looked at the shoe print with the circular mark in the heel and thought to himself that there may have been two people involved in the murder.

"Mark the locations of those unusual heel prints and add it to the check list for the forensic team to photograph," he told Officer Winslow.

Officer Winslow then directed them to the location in the front yard where he had located the spent shell casing.

The placard was posted there but the shell casing was missing.

"Where is the shell casing?" Zollars directed his question to Harrison.

Harrison answered, "I picked up the shell casing and placed it in an evidence envelope as he reached into his jacket pocket and displayed the shell casing for everyone to view."

Zollars words were biting when he addressed Harrison with the proper method of collecting evidence, including the shell casing, which should happen only after the location of the item has been measured and photographed by the forensic team.

"I put it back down in the exact location and photographed it, then picked it back up," he responded lamely.

Harrison mumbled his apologies and asked whom he should give the packaged shell casing to maintain the proper chain of evidence.

"Take it back to the Mobile Command van and have Officer Bellows place it with the other collected evidence," said Detective Zollars.

The forensic team and Total Station Traffic Officers arrived on scene and reported to Forensic Supervisor Beth Johnson.

She pointed out the location of the evidence that had been marked with evidence placards.

"When you are finished with the exterior of the property you need to check for additional evidence such as blood on the steps, fingerprints, DNA and do a video of the interior of the residence and take photos," she ordered.

Minutes later the three member CBIT Team arrived at the Mobile Command Post.

Coulee City P.D. Detective Ben Skates, Canyon County Sheriff's Detective Ralston Hannigan and Wheatland P.D. Detective Joel Fitz made up this particular CBIT Team.

The CBIT team members would rotate through the team after a two year assignment and a new team would be selected from the local and state law enforcement agencies.

All members would be required to have prior experience in the investigation of serious crimes.

Detective Ralston Hannigan had taken the role of leadership of the CBIT Team as he had the most experience.

He spoke briefly to Sgt. Harmon, the Incident Commander and requested the team be escorted through the crime scene to survey the layout of the interior house and surrounding yard.

Sgt Harmon said, "I will walk you through the crime scene."

Sgt. Harmon revealed the progress of the investigation explaining that the victim has been removed at the Medical Examiners direction and is currently located at the County Medical Examiner facility.

"Collected evidence such as a wine bottle, wine glass, beer can and a splotch of blood was removed from the carpet on the front porch, and will be sent to the Washington State Patrol Forensic Crime Lab, to check for fingerprints and DNA," he explained.

"A pair of opened handcuffs was located on the lawn in the front yard and a spent 45 caliber shell casing was found lying on the grass where the sidewalk in the yard connects with the public sidewalk," he said.

"We did locate footprints leading around the Northside of the victim's house but they ended out in the alley and were soon lost where the two suspects ran and stepped in a vehicle tire tracks," he continued.

"There are so many footprints leading to the house on the sidewalks and street that they are an unreadable series of shoe prints, not of much value," Sgt. Harmon explained.

Sgt. Harmon said, "The neighborhood residents are being contacted as far as 3 blocks away and also on neighboring 2nd and 4th Streets."

"Several neighbors reported they thought they heard fireworks or a gunshot but never heard any vehicles start off from the area. Bonnie Crawfoot is the neighbor across the street that called 911 and reported the shooting," he said as he pointed out her residence.

"The victim's sister Olive Adams lives in the house next door on the Southside of Bonnie Crawfoot's house and the victims family and friends seem to be gathering there," he finished.

Detective Hannigan thanked Sgt Harmon and conferred briefly with the rest of the CBIT Team.

"Detective Skates and Detective Fitz, would you start witness interviews while I walk the crime scene more with Sgt. Harmon and we can get moving on this case," he said.

"Interview Bonnie Crawfoot together as she seems to be our only witness identified so far," he directed the two Detectives.

Det. Hannigan and Sgt. Harmon walked on the sidewalk leading to Johns Adam's front door.

"I noticed some small blood marks on the door and the side door jambs," Hannigan said.

The blood spots on the door and jamb were high velocity blood stains and were narrow on one end and expanding out to a shape similar to an exclamation mark which showed the direction the blood was traveling.

Sgt. Harmon replied, "The victim had been shot in the left upper chest with an exit near the right rear kidney area and the caliber was suspected to be large bore gun from the size of the ragged exit hole."

"Probably was a long shot," Detective Hannigan thought to himself.

They stepped over the threshold into the living room, stopped and looked at the bloodstains and pool of blood on the kitchen floor where the victim had been found.

They walked through the other rooms in the house and did not observe anything of evidentiary interest except for the gun cabinet that contained the five rifles, three shotguns and three handguns.

"Make sure those firearms and ammo are collected and identified by make model and serial number," Hannigan told Sgt. Harmon.

"Not sure if they are directly involved in this case but there have been other cases I've worked where the intent of the shooter or shooters was to obtain guns," he said.

"I will get it done," replied Sgt. Harmon.

"Do you recall if the backdoor was unlocked when the first responding officers arrived on scene?" asked Hannigan.

"I'll have to check, I don't recall if anyone mentioned it," he said.

They walked out of the residence and down the sidewalk to the Chevy pick-up that was parked in front of the house.

"What about this truck?" Detective Hannigan asked Sgt. Harmon. "Is it the victim's truck?"

"Yes, it is," said Sgt. Harmon, "we have walked around the truck and can't tell if anything was disturbed or removed from the unlocked pick-up."

"Did anyone take photos of any shoe prints around the vehicle before it was trampled all over?" asked Detective Hannigan.

"No, I don't believe any photos were taken," Set. Harmon answered softly.

"What a cluster," Detective Hannigan said out loud to himself.

"Let's have the vehicle transported to the vehicle processing garage and then have WSP techs go over the truck for prints or DNA and make an inventory of the contents," Detective Hannigan stated.

"The Forensic Crime Technicians have already called for a tow truck" Sgt. Harmon advised.

"I'm particularly interested in any firearms or ammunition in the truck so make sure everything has an inventory number and description," said Detective Hannigan.

"I can see a couple of boxes of ammo lying on the floor in front of the center console and there's a rifle rack in back, so we will need to find out how many guns the victim had and how many are missing," Detective Hannigan said.

The victim could have had some rifles in the rack at the back window, Detective Hannigan thought to himself.

Detective Hannigan asked Sgt. Harmon to send a message to all law enforcement agencies in the state requesting information on any 45 caliber handguns, ACP cartridges or spent shell casing that they had located in their cases.

Hannigan said, "If anyone finds or locates these items, they can notify us and we can send them to the WSP Crime Lab for comparison to the 45 caliber shell casing recovered in this event."

"If the doors were found unlocked, I'm interested if someone used a Slim Jim or other instrument to reach down by the window and unlock the door, and there may be tool marks or scratches on the mechanism which could indicate the pick-up was entered with a slim Jim or similar instrument," Detective Hannigan said to Sgt. Harmon.

They walked over to the Southside of the front yard and followed a path that had been used by other investigators and responders.

They stopped near the placard where the handcuffs had been found and carefully looked for footprints.

Finding no footprints near the handcuffs, Det. Hannigan said, "It looks like those cuffs may have been lying there for a lengthy period of time."

"Have there been any recent residential burglaries where the home owners had reported a set of handcuffs stolen?" he asked.

"None that I am aware," Sgt. Harmon replied.

"The handcuffs lying here are Smith and Wesson but they were modified with bigger connecting rings and the officer that found them told me it looked like the serial number on one cuff had partially been filed off," Sgt. Harmon detailed to Hannigan.

Several steps away towards the front of the house, one lone boot print was observed and appeared to be heading across the lawn in a northern direction.

They continued walking across the lawn and the sidewalk continuing Northeast where the boot tracks disappeared around the corner of the house.

"Looks like the suspect jumped the fence and went down the alley," Hannigan mused.

"Did anybody go south down the alley to see if they could locate any footprints?" asked Hannigan.

Sgt. Harmon's face turned red in embarrassment.

"Two sets of faint footprints were found traveling South down the alley in tire tracks for a short distance and were lost because the news media satellite truck drove down the alley and parked, and the reporters have been stomping around in back and covered up any other tracks that we may have found," Sgt. Harmon said.

"Jesus," Detective Hannigan thought to himself, "were any officers stationed behind the house as security to keep trespassers off the property or to keep evidence from being destroyed?"

They walked back to the Incident Command Vehicle and stepped inside.

"Sgt. Harmon, has your Scribe been taking notes of the names of persons arriving and created timeline log of when the person arrived and left the scene?"

"We never kept a log for the first hour because we never had the manpower to keep track of everyone coming and going or exactly what duties they accomplished," Sgt Harmon said.

"We are relying on the communications dispatch time stamps when the person checks out on scene, and Officer Bellows has been assigned to provide security for collected evidence here at the Command Post and will log in all persons entering the crime scene and the time the person exits the scene."

"Sgt. Harmon, I know this case is important to you as a first line supervisor because I understand you have only recently been promoted, so I would advise you to have an after action meeting with everyone that was here today, including the law enforcement command staff and do a critique of what worked well and the things that could have been done better," Detective Hannigan said.

"It will help you out tremendously next time you are assigned as the Incident Commander at a crime scene or disaster," he advised.

"The news media are standing along the perimeter, so if you haven't done it yet, you should prepare a basic press release here at the Command Post and make copies for the media," he commented.

"Announce that you are providing a written press release to the media and advise the media there will be a more detailed announcement by the Chief Medical Officer and Chief Fife tomorrow morning," he continued.

"Don't name the victim in your release, we want to be sure the appropriate relatives have been notified. I believe they have been, but request the department Chaplain to come to the scene and contact John's parents that are staying with their daughter across the street from the crime scene," he said.

"And one last thing, leave the Mobile Command Post in place overnight so the officers can rotate and come in and take a break, it's damn cold out there."

"If no one has done it yet, have Communications contact the Red Cross and request that they come to the scene and park their van next to the Mobile Command Post. They will supply hot coffee, sandwiches and protein bars for the officers and the officers will appreciate it," he said.

"I don't mean to be stepping on your toes, but I have been through the same thing as an Incident Commander and I know how rough it can be if you have never been assigned as the Incident Commander," Detective Hannigan said to Sgt. Harmon.

"I appreciate your suggestions and no offense taken," Sgt. Harmon said to the Detective.

"We can review the progress of our investigation tomorrow and if we don't need anything else at the crime scene, we can release the house to John Adams' parents."

"If you would tell all officers at the scene to complete their reports in a timely manner, download all the photos that have been taken, and place all evidentiary items in Evidence Property Storage."

"Detective Fitz, Detective Skates and myself will be doing the follow-up interviews with witnesses that are located and Detectives Fitz and Skates are doing an interview with the neighbor Bonnie Crawfoot and Marianne Shutt today," Det. Hannigan finished.

Bonnie Crawfoot sat at her kitchen table at the location where she had been sitting when she heard the gunshot and looked out her living room window. Detective Joel Fitz and Ben Skates both sat at the kitchen table.

The newspapers were still lying on the kitchen table where Bonnie had laid them down earlier that morning.

"I was sitting in this same chair this morning reading the newspaper, having my cup of coffee when I heard a loud bang," she said.

"The only light I had on was the one in the kitchen," she pointed out.

"I looked up and through my living room window and I saw some activity in John's front yard on the other side of his pick-up truck. I thought it was John and his son Devin shooting off fireworks," she said.

"There was just a flurry of motion, kind of a motion of several people and then my eyes focused on John, as he stumbled into the house kind of holding his stomach. That was the only thing I remember, except with a little more time I will probably remember and have more details. I'm so damned shaken up right now that I can hardly remember my own name," she continued.

"Was there only one gun shot that you heard?" Detective Fitz asked.

"There was only one gunshot, but what may have alerted me to look over there," she said, "I swear I heard a loud whistle just before the gunshot, but that doesn't make a lick of sense, so I probably imagined it."

"What did you do next?" enquired Detective Fitz.

"I picked up my phone and called John's phone number and there was no answer. Then I put on my coat and grabbed a flashlight and went up to John's door and knocked real loud several times but there was no answer. Then I went back home and called 911 and waited for the cops to show up. No, actually, after I called 911, I went outside and stood on the sidewalk, and that was when John's sister, Olive, drove into her driveway and I contacted her," Bonnie said.

"When the Police showed up, we followed them over to John's house, and when they all went inside the house, Olive and I stepped inside the living room and were watching the officer check John's pulse to see if he was still alive. That's when I kind of went hysterical and was screaming Devin's name because I thought he was in the house somewhere. I think I startled the officer because he told us to leave the house and John's son Devin was not there. Olive and I left and she went into my house for a few minutes and then went next door to her house," Bonnie said.

"Did you ever actually see anyone on the street or running away?"

Bonnie answered, "When I was walking over to John's there was one man and he was walking north down the street. I see this guy just about every morning walking down the street about 6:30 A.M. or a little later. This morning he was walking down the middle of the street and headed back to his house from the store. He was holding two cups of coffee, one in each hand as he always does. He walks down to Division Street Market every morning and gets his girlfriend her coffee. His girlfriend's name is Lynn Bennet and she lives a couple houses down from me, same side of street in the brick rancher."

"I have talked to the guy in the past and he is a friendly sort, I think he said his name was Steve, maybe Steve Paulson. He mentioned to me that he is a carpenter by trade and I have seen him coming home at Lynn's wearing construction jeans and heavy boots," she said.

"Lynn Bennet had the cops at her house a lot in the last couple of years because her worthless ex-husband Carl was always beating the shit out of her. They finally got a divorce and he still lives in town but I never see him around here anymore. He has a hell of a temper and hates cops because he's resisted arrest a few times after pounding on Lynn, and came out on the losing end with the cops. Served him right, the lazy bastard was a leech on Lynn and she paid all the bills," she continued.

"Did John have girlfriends coming over to his house?" asked Detective Skates.

"He had at least three girlfriends that he was seeing that I know about," she said.

"One was a pretty woman in her thirties that drives a nice blue Mustang. She would usually come by in the afternoon and only stay for a few hours and then leave a little ruffled looking. I knew she was married because she would usually look down the street both ways and would take a few minutes to pretty up her face in the rear view mirror before driving off. Once I saw her driving her car downtown in Wheatland about 2 months ago, and a guy about her age was actually driving the car and she was a passenger. We both stopped at a red-light and the guy had pulled up beside me on the left. She looked over at me and seemed startled when she recognized me," she said.

"Right at the edge of town here in Wheatland is a workout facility called The Club, and I have seen that blue Mustang parked there early in the mornings when I drive by on my way to Wilson Creek where I tend to my small acreage where I grow my organic garden vegetables and berries and have a small orchard," she continued.

"I sell locally to the local school districts and at farmers markets. I also make baked goods like scones and fruit filled tarts and consign my stuff at the three coffee stands here in Wheatland. That's how I make my living," she said proudly.

"That's nice, I bet you're pretty proud of making a living from the soil," said Detective Skates politely.

"Getting back to this Mustang, how do you know that is the same Mustang you would see at John's house?" he asked.

"Well," she paused and thought. "The Mustang is a dark metallic blue, almost the same color as John's pick-up truck. The side of the front fender has a snake emblem with the words 429 Cobra under the emblem. I used to be really into cars and rods so I still take notice of the small markings and makes of cars, and that's why I noticed it was parked at the workout facility," she continued.

"I asked John one time the name of his girlfriend and he told me her name was Carmin Martinez."

"John was also seeing a young woman from here in Wheatland."

"Her name is Nancy Williams and she used to stay at John's 3-4 times a week. They would do a lot of bird hunting and also would shoot at the Wheatland shooting range. They seemed like a real happy couple and John's son Devin would often be with Nancy and John when they were camping," she continued.

"I would see her unloading John's truck and carrying guns into his house when he was parked in front. I really liked Nancy, she seemed like a good fit for John. Nancy and John would both go to Devin's little league baseball games. I was invited over to John's this last summer for a birthday party for Devin's 11th birthday. Even John's ex-wife Tammy came to the party and everyone got along just fine. I would often see Tammy looking at John and sitting close to him like she wanted him back. A woman can always tell when another woman is interested in a man," she quipped.

"Tammy's new husband is a Mattawa City Police Officer named Cameron Gentry and he came by in his patrol car. It was a very relaxing event and John spoke to Cameron and they were friendly to each other and John did tell me one time when I was over visiting, that the best thing that ever happened to him was when he and Tammy got a divorce. He told me it made him realize he had only been staying with her because of the child in common," she revealed.

"There were some hostilities for awhile because Tammy had been having an affair with Gentry and they would meet at a motel over in Coulee City. John told me that he happened to be working on a job site in Coulee Dam and was headed back to Wheatland for more supplies. He said he was driving on the highway past the Sunset Motel and saw Tammy's car parked behind the Motel. John started knocking on doors, it was only a 10 unit motel. It wasn't long before Cam Gentry answered the door of one of the units and there was Tammy in the background frantically trying to get dressed. From what I heard, John never said a word to them and turned around and walked back to his truck and drove away. John never came back to his house until Tammy moved out and the divorce papers had been served and the divorce finalized. The custody of their son Devin was amicable and John always had access to Devin," she advised.

Det. Skates asked, "Do you think Tammy or Cameron Gentry would have had a reason to kill John?"

"I don't think so, like I said, Tammy and Cam were at the birthday party a few weeks ago, and all three of them were friendly and relaxed with each other," she quipped.

"What about Nancy Williams? Did you ever hear John or Nancy quarreling or can you think of a reason why Nancy would want John dead?"

"Not at all, they were always close, and even after John started seeing this other woman named Marianne, Nancy would still go to events with Devin and go out in the country shooting with John. I didn't understand this penchant John had for Marianne," she said.

"I'm not sure what he saw in her other than a physical attraction," Bonnie continued. "Marianne was not real friendly and always wore skin tight pants that made the local boys pant," she said with a chuckle.

"She has a little boy, but I would hardly see him with her when she was across the street. The neighbor boys down on the corner used to come over to John's and play on the trampoline in John's back yard. I would see Devin, Marianne's boy Zachary and Lynn Bennett's two boys playing over at Lynn's house. Lynn Bennet's boyfriend is the guy that I would frequently see, early mornings walking down the street from the Market holding a cup of coffee in each hand," she said to Detective Skates.

"Getting back to Marianne, do you know how to get in touch with the woman?" Detective Skates asked Bonnie.

"If you want to talk to her, I think she's next door at Olive's right now," she answered

"Thanks for talking to us, Bonnie, you have been real helpful and it looks like you're the only witness to this murder," said Det. Skates.

"If you need anything else, I'm up at 4:00 A.M. and in bed by 6:00 P.M., so give me a phone call before you come by," she replied.

Chapter 6
Marianne Shutt

Detectives Fitz and Joel Skates went to Olive's house next door, knocked on the door and identified themselves to the elderly man that had opened the door.

"I'm John Adam's father, my name is John Sr.," he revealed to the Detectives. "I thought you guys would be showing up over here at some time."

"We're sorry to have to meet this way, Mr. Adams, but we are trying to find out exactly what happened and are trying to find the responsible person for your son's death," Det. Fitz said.

"We are in the process of trying to locate anyone that may be helpful and I understand Marianne Shutt is here with your family."

"Yes, she's here at the house, in the kitchen with my daughter Olive, I'll go get her," he said.

It was only a few minutes before a young woman with dark long hair walked across the living room and introduced herself to Detectives Fitz and Skates.

Her eyes were red from crying and her voice was still choked with emotion.

"I'm Detective Joel Skates and this is Detective Fitz," he said.

"Miss, we're sorry to bother you at this time but we are trying to find the circumstances that lead to the death of your friend John Adams."

Marianne wiped her tears and said, "I'll try to help in any way that I can."

"Would you mind coming down to the Sheriff's Office where we can sit down in private?" Det. Skates asked Marianne.

"No, I don't mind going with you, to tell you the truth, the atmosphere here is unbelievably sad, we all loved John, so just give me a minute to grab my coat and tell John's mother I am leaving to talk to you and Detective Fitz," she said.

Detective Skates made a phone call to Detective Hannigan and gave him an update of their interview of Bonnie Crawfoot.

"We are going to do an interview of Marianne Shutt and thought you might like to be here. We are going to be downtown at the Sheriffs Office," he said.

"I will be right there," Det. Hannigan answered.

Det. Skates, Det. Fitz and Marianne travelled to the Canyon County Sheriff's Office where they walked back to one of several designated interview rooms.

Detective Hannigan arrived several minutes later and was introduced to Marianne Shutt.

"Would you like anything to drink, we always have hot coffee brewing in the break room and soda or water?" Det. Skates asked Marianne.

"A bottle of water would be helpful, I have a dry mouth," she said as she propped her elbows on the table and held her head on each side with her hands.

Skates returned in less than a minute and handed the cold bottle of water to Marianne who took it and thanked him.

Det. Fitz sat on the same side of the table as Marianne and Detectives Skates and Hannigan sat on the other side.

Detective Fitz placed an open note book and pen on the table in front of him.

"Marianne, we have some questions for you that may help us with the investigation. If you know the answer, please say yes, but don't guess, just let us know what you know. Do you understand?" he said in a kindly tone and Marianne shook her head in a motion of agreement.

"Alright, if you would just tell us what you know and then we will follow up with questions," he said.

"I think I know who may have killed John," she said.

"My ex-boyfriend's name is Dustin Silver and he lives in The Dalles, Oregon," she started.

"I knew him when I lived in The Dalles, Oregon with my mother. Dustin was a few years older than me and would have parties at his house where there was liquor and plenty of good looking guys," she said.

"My friends and I would go to the parties. He didn't know that I was only 18 at the time, and one time when Dustin asked me how old I was, I lied and told him I was 20 years old. He seemed OK with that since he was about 23 years old. I started seeing more of Dustin and before long I was his girl and everybody knew it," she said. "I fell in love with Dustin and we soon became intimate and I thought, this is the man I want to spend my life with," she said.

"Dustin would be gone for up to a week at a time and he traveled down to Nevada and southern Oregon, picking up hard to find classic car parts. He knew where every wrecking yard was located in the smaller towns and was always on the lookout for farms and ranches where vehicles were located, and not running or wrecked. He would sell the auto parts online in his business called "I Find Parts" and he would ship throughout the United States. He would also haul parts to a classic auto parts dealer in Pocatello, Idaho where he would get good prices," she continued.

"Dustin always had a wad of cash in his pocket. We had a wonderful time when Dustin was back home in The Dalles and he quit having parties at his house. We would spend evenings together or go hiking in the mountains and cliffs along the Columbia River."

"Dustin had left on one of his trips and I missed a period while he was gone. I wasn't worried because my periods were not very well regulated. When Dustin came back from his trip we were laying in bed and Dustin noticed that I was unusually quiet since he had returned. He asked me why I was acting that way. I told Dustin that I was pregnant and I expected him to be angry for not using birth control. Instead, Dustin told me he was elated and would take care of the baby and me," she said.

"My family was quite religious and I knew my family would not accept Dustin because of the reputation he had," she continued.

"After dinner at my house, a few days later I took my mother aside and broke the news to her that I was pregnant. She asked who the father of the child was and I told her it was Dustin. She broke down sobbing and asked if Dustin knew I was only 18 years old. I told her I had lied and told Dustin that I was 20 years old. She became very angry and got in my face and told me that she hadn't raised me that way and that I strayed away from God's teachings. She forbade me to have any further relationship with Dustin. She told me I was going to start going to church with her on Sundays and hope that I would be forgiven," Marianne said as tears welled up in her eyes.

"My mom went to the Police and told them Dustin had raped me by getting me pregnant because I was 18 years old. The Officer told her the age of consent was 16 years of age and I had been 18 years of age, so there had been no criminal law violation and my mom was real disappointed," she said.

"I would meet with Dustin at his house and one day I told Dustin that our relationship was breaking up my family, and I told him that I needed some time apart from him to work things out in my head," she said sadly.

"Dustin was broken hearted and said he would give me time to sort my feelings out. I left and went back to live with my mom, but couldn't sleep and was really stressed out just thinking of Dustin and how much I missed him." She said as Detective Hannigan handed her a Kleenex.

"After about 6 weeks I phoned Dustin and told him how much I missed him and wanted to see him, and after that I would slip away and meet Dustin for a few hours," she said.

"Then my mother took a job as a nurse at a medical office in Waterville, Washington and we packed up and moved there," she continued her story.

"I had the baby boy at the local Good Samaritan Hospital there and made a phone call to Dustin and gave him the good news," she said.

"We named him Zachary, after Dustin's middle name. By then I was 19 years old. I heard infrequently from Dustin after that and he always seemed to be on one of his out of state trips. When Dustin was back home in The Dalles, he would travel to Waterville and give me money to help pay expenses for myself and the baby," she said.

"We would go to other towns and stay at motels and spend time playing with Zachary, and would go out shopping to buy clothes and toys. In spite of our best efforts, we drifted slowly and further apart because Dustin always seemed to be working down in Idaho and rarely spoke on the phone with me," she explained.

"Usually, about once a month, I would receive a Money Order from Dustin that pretty much covered Zachary and my living expenses," she said.

"I started going to church again with my mother and one day I met John Adams and he seemed friendly to me in spite of me being a single woman with a child. Our family had been friends with John's relatives in The Dalles, Oregon, and our families both went to church together there and had pretty conservative values. It wasn't long before I started dating John who was about five years older, and my thoughts of Dustin seemed more distant. Dustin was so exciting and lived like a free soul and John was solid and settled down," she continued.

"I built up the courage to tell Dustin the next time he called me that I was seeing a local man from Wheatland. I told him it was just a casual relationship because I was lonely and missed him and John seemed like a decent man. Dustin was really upset and I could tell from his voice that I had hurt him deeply. Dustin told me that he was going to bow out of my life. He told me that he would like to check with me from time to time to find out how his son Zachary was doing," she said.

"I felt so bad and was depressed and couldn't get over my depression for what I thought was a mistake of pushing Dustin away from me." She said as tears welled up in her eyes. "I tried contacting Dustin at least a dozen times by phone calls and text messages, but he never answered me," she continued.

"My mother took me to a doctor and I started taking medication and started seeing a counselor to help me through my depression," she revealed to the three Detectives.

"A few months later Dustin came into my life again when I got a phone call from him that he was in Waterville visiting the local wrecking yards for hard to find classic car auto parts. We met at the city park and I brought Zachary with me because Dustin had only seen recent photos of Zachary that I had texted to him, prior to our break-up," she continued.

"I realized that Dustin would always be in my life because I never lost my feelings for him," she said.

"Dustin told me he wanted me to stop seeing John, but he never threatened John or anything, and laid the decision on me to quit seeing him," she said.

"John was getting more involved with his construction business and I would only spend the night with him one or two days a week. Periodically Dustin would contact me and I would drive John's Jeep to meet with Dustin and we would stay overnight at hotels in Quincy or Moses Lake. Every time I thought about telling John we were through, I would choke up and not say anything to him," she said.

She said, "A couple of months later John came to me and was holding a small metallic device with a magnet on it. John told me it was a GPS unit that he had placed on his Jeep. He told me he had followed the coordinates on the GPS unit and found where his Jeep had been parked several times for 3-4 hours at the Sun Best Motel in Quincy and the Top Western Hotel near the freeway in Moses Lake. John was really angry when I admitted to my trysts with Dustin."

John said, "Maybe I'll take a trip to The Dalles with my 45 and we'll settle things."

"I begged John not to do anything like that and I lied and told him I was breaking up with Dustin. John looked me in the eye and told me that he really hoped so, but he never mentioned again, of going to The Dalles to settle things with Dustin with his 45 caliber gun. After that conversation I phoned Dustin and warned him and told him what John had told me. After that Dustin and I decided to let things cool down until after I had broken up with John. That was about October or November last year and I only saw Dustin one time when he dropped off some toys and stuff at my Mom's while she was at work. The last time I talked to Dustin was when I phoned him this morning when John was killed and I accused him of shooting John," she said.

"Dustin said he was in Oregon on a road trip and became angry with me when I accused him of killing John and he hung up on me," she said.

"Can we get his phone number from you?" Detective Fitz asked her.

"Yes, it's right here," she said and read the number to Detective Fitz.

"Do you think Dustin was jealous enough of your relationship with John that he would kill him?" Detective Skates asked.

"I don't think so but I'm so confused right now, I need to clear my head."

"Anyone else that you can think of that would have a reason to kill John?" Detective Skates persisted.

"I would never accuse Nancy Williams, but she was one of John's girlfriends before John and I had started seeing each other. When she found out John and I were spending time together she was upset but things settled down the more time John, Nancy and myself spent time together. All three of us would go to his son Devin's baseball games and often be together at John's house and watch movies and hang out," she told the three Detectives.

"I knew they still spent time together and would hunt and fish together and go out to the shooting range and shoot trap. I wasn't really comfortable handling guns and once I went out to target practice at a makeshift shooting range that everyone used along the canyon road. John had a semi-auto pistol with some kind of device on the lower front of the gun that had an on switch on the side of the device. When John turned it on, a red beam of light would come out the end and wherever the beam of light was pointed, when the gun was fired, the bullet would hit right where the red beam ended. John may have told me it was a laser sight. I fired the gun five or six times but it had a heavy recoil and hurt my hand," She said.

"He did take a photo of me holding and shooting the gun with his cell phone when we stopped along Canyon Road outside of Wheatland. John told me the gun was a 45 caliber Smith&Wesson and he had bought it from one of his customers," she continued.

"I'm not accusing Nancy at all, but I thought it was a little weird that she hung out with us."

"Was there a chance they were getting back together? I mean, didn't John find out you were still seeing Dustin on the side," asked Detective Skates.

"We hear John was on the verge of ending his relationship with you," Det. Skates said to Marianne.

Marianne snapped her head up and looked directly at Det. Skates.

Then she held her head down and tears welled up in her eyes.

"No, not a chance," she said, "John told me he would give me some time to break it off for good with Dustin."

"He knew I would also have some contact with Dustin because of our son Zachary," she said.

"That also could make you a suspect since you know how to shoot a firearm and had access to John's guns," Skates said as his eyes probed into Marianne's eyes.

"I know it could look bad for me, but I swear I was not involved, I cared for John. I was home in bed sleeping when Olive phoned my mom at about 7:00 A.M. and said that John had been shot and killed and my mom can confirm my alibi," she replied.

"Stay available for further interviewing," Det. Skates said, "We may have more questions about your other boyfriend, Dustin."

They dropped Marianne off at Olive Adams' residence.

"I'm going to get a couple of search warrants to track Silvers's phone pings and another search warrant to obtain text messages and photos between Silver and Marianne Shutt's phones," Detective Hannigan said to Detectives Fitz and Skates.

Chapter 7
Juan Garcia

Garcia lay quietly in bed with Tiffanie and felt her warmth against his side as he lay on his back.

She lay her arm across his chest and snuggled her face into his neck and shoulder.

He could hear her peaceful breathing as he felt her warm breath.

"God, what did I get myself into with Ryan," he thought to himself.

It was only supposed to be car prowls to get enough stuff to trade for some meth.

He was starting to get restless and feeling like the room was closing in on him.

When he could not stand it any longer, he climbed out of bed and looked around for his best dirty shirt and put on his jeans from the night before.

He put on his thermal boots with the unusual oval marking on the heel and stumbled into the kitchen where he took a long drink of water and splashed his face in the kitchen sink, toweling off with paper kitchen towels and combing his long hair with his fingers.

He noticed a pizza box on the kitchen table and opened it up to see a small slice of dried, curled cheese pizza and outer crust pieces that someone had thrown in the cardboard pizza box.

Juan sat at the kitchen counter and started to eat the pizza slice and crust remnants.

There were several partially full soft drink cans sitting on the counter by the pizza box and Juan lifted them and found there was still liquid in both of the soft drink cans.

The fizz was long gone and the liquid was room temperature when he emptied one can, then drank from the second can to help send the dry pizza remnants down his throat.

Wiping his mouth with the back of his hand he went back to his bedroom where Tiffanie was still sleeping.

She had a habit of normally sleeping until late mornings and was never awake at 10:00 A.M. as Juan looked at the clock on the wall.

He reached down and tapped her on the shoulder and she stirred, looking up at him.

"Babe," he said in a low tone, "I'm going over to see Trampus and hang with him for a while."

"Ok," she murmured and rolled back over and fell asleep.

Juan quietly stepped across the living room to go out the same rear slider door he had come in earlier in the morning.

His brother's girlfriend Susan was lying on the sofa with a pillow propping her head and watching TV with a low volume.

"It must have been a real good party last night, Juan, for you to get home at 6:45 this morning," said Susan.

"You must be mistaken, I was here all night," he said.

Susan smirked, "Look, I know what I saw and what time it was when you came through the slider so don't pull that crap on me."

"I'm pretty good at keeping secrets so don't worry, I'm not going to snitch you off to Tiffanie," she said with a snicker.

Juan looked at Susan and replied, "Sorry, I didn't want Tiffanie to know I was out all night with Ryan."

Chapter 8
Trampus Byrnes

Juan opened the rear slider, closed it and walked the three blocks to his friend's single story house, which was only four blocks from the murder scene.

Juan went to a window located to the right of the front door.

He kept knocking on the glass and would stop and wait for a response.

"Come on, Trampus," he whispered loudly three or four times without a response.

The next time he knocked on the window with more force and noise.

Juan was startled when the front door opened and Trampus' mother Leslie leaned around the door frame and looked towards Juan.

"What do you want and how come you just didn't come up and knock on the door like a normal person?" she asked.

"Sorry, I didn't want to wake up the family and I know Trampus is usually up at this time playing on his video games."

"It's 10:00 A.M., Juan, you weren't going to wake up anybody," she replied.

"What have you been doing, you look like you've been exercising or something, you're all sweaty and shaky," she said.

"I'm all right, I just ran from my house," he answered.

"Kind of took my breath away," he said.

"You need to quit smoking, "she said, "you look pretty pale."

"Come on in and close the door behind you," she said as she walked down the main hallway of the house leaving Juan waiting in the living room.

Leslie tapped on the door several times and opened the door to Trampus' bedroom.

Trampus and a 19 year friend named Martin Nelson were inside, sitting on a couch that was also used as a bed.

They were intently playing a war time video game with lots of action.

Leslie called for Juan to come down the hallway to the bedroom.

"Hey Juan, find a spot, we're almost at the end," said Trampus as he turned his attention back to the video game at hand.

She closed the door to the bedroom, but as all curious mothers would do, she stood outside the cheap hollow core door of the bedroom and listened to conversations coming from inside her son's room.

She had a mistrust of Juan because he always seemed to have money and nice clothes but never seemed to have a job.

She knew Juan's mother was on Public Assistance and there was no real explanation for how Juan obtained the folding money and nice clothing.

She suspected Juan had to be involved in some nefarious business, so she listened from the hallway.

She listened to the exciting sound of Trampus and Martin's voices until the game reached a climax and ended with a laugh from Martin and a cussing comment from her son.

"Man, you look like shit," Martin pointed out to Juan.

"You're all pale and look like you saw a ghost, what's up man?" Martin said loudly.

Juan sat at the end of the sofa and was holding his head in his hands with his eyes closed.

"Man, I think I'm in big trouble and will be going to prison for something that whacked out Ryan did this morning!"

"Tell us what you're talking about?" they both said in unison.

"Ryan and I were out all night boosting cars and we got some cash out of a guy's wallet he left in his car along with some change, and some jewelry. We took the jewelry and the money and went over to a trap house where Ryan scores his dope and we traded for a 1/4 lb. of meth and split it. Ryan had done a couple of bindles of meth and was really flying high and bouncing off the walls. I used a teener bindle myself and it was good grade so I was flying but not as high as Ryan," Juan said.

"We decided to try and steal a gun out of a pick-up that was parked on the same street as Ryan's mom's house about a block away, so we go down the street and there was only one front porch light on at the house where the guy lived, that owned the pick-up truck," he continued.

"The lady living across the street was sitting in her kitchen but she wasn't paying attention. We walked down the sidewalk past the truck and checked the driver's door and it was unlocked. We noticed the guy that owned the truck had his window curtains partially opened in his living room and we could see him using his computer with his back to the street," he said.

"Ryan told me to sneak over to the corner of the house and watch the guy through the window, and if the guy looked like he was putting on a coat and leaving, to do a whistle so we could get away," he said.

"I stood at the corner of the house and watched the guy, and then he looked at the watch on his arm and stood and walked across the room and picked up his jacket and put it on, and I whistled a warning to Ryan and it was just about the same time the guy came out the front door of his house and stepped off his front porch," Juan said.

"He yelled, and Ryan was holding something in his right hand as he turned and started to run and I saw Ryan turn to the left a little and he held up a pistol and fired it blindly in the direction of the guy," Juan said with his voice quavering.

"I heard the shot, a loud whack, like something hit the side of the house," he said.

"The guy turned right after he was shot and was holding his chest when he looked me in the eye with a look of astonishment on his face. The guy kind of stumbled up the porch steps and went into his house. Geez, I was in shock and almost pissed my pants, it scared me so bad," Juan said.

Juan paused and sounded out of breath, then continued with his story.

"I took off running and then ran around the next door neighbor's house out onto the alley, then I ran down some tire tracks that had been made in the snow. I saw Ryan running down the alley in front of me so he must have run across the guy's backyard and into the alley and I yelled at Ryan and caught up with him," he continued.

He said, "We came out of the alley onto Division Street and ran towards Ryan's girlfriend's house. I glanced over my shoulder and saw a man stopped in the middle of Division, holding what looked like a couple of coffee cups. He appeared startled and looked right at Ryan and me as we ran away."

"We continued running on the street in front of Ryan's girlfriend's house where we split up after agreeing to meet up later in the day," Juan continued.

"Before we split up, Ryan removed a 45 caliber semi auto pistol he had stolen that had been stashed in his backpack and showed it to me," he said.

"Ryan told me he was going to hide the gun in the bushes at his girlfriend's house for now. I think it had a laser sight on the gun and it looked like a large caliber semi-auto pistol," he said and finished telling of the horrible incident.

"What are you going to do about this?" Trampus asked.

"Are you going to the cops and tell them you never had anything to do with it?" Martin asked.

"I don't know what to do because I may have a pretty good alibi if the cops come around," Juan answered.

"My girl will say I was with her all night," he said.

"I was in bed with Tiffany last night and she was stoned on CBD Gummies and Rum and went right to sleep and was not awake when I left."

"She was still sleeping when I got back home and got into bed with her after the shooting," Juan said.

"The only hitch in my alibi is my brother's girlfriend Susan saw me leave last night and when I snuck in through the sliding door in the living room this morning she rolled over and looked directly at me. When I left this morning, Susan and I had a short conversation and she knows I wasn't at home last night," he said.

"Let's just chill out and play some games," said Martin as he turned to load a new game in the game console.

Chapter 9

Around noon, Trampus' mother came to the bedroom door and knocked.

"Ryan is at the door and wants to see you," she said.

"Oh shit," Juan said, "I don't want Ryan to know that I'm over here and that I have talked about what we did."

Martin said, "Look, I'll go out front and meet with Ryan and take him over to my house."

Martin stepped out onto the front porch and greeted Ryan.

"Hey man, what are you doing here?" Ryan asked.

"We played video games all night and Trampus is crashing so I'm leaving."

"Hey, you look a little wired, everything OK?" Martin said to Ryan.

"You want to come back to my place and chill out for a while?" he asked.

"That would be cool, I need a place to chill out and talk to a friend," Ryan replied.

"I got some meth with me that I scored at the trap house this morning if you want to smoke a bowl," he told Martin.

"Naw man, that shit lights me up too much and makes me act like the Devil," replied Martin.

"But I got some fresh bud right off the farm," Trampus said.

They sat on the back porch while Martin professionally rolled a joint and lit it up.

He took a deep drag and held it in his lungs until they expanded and he coughed heavily as he passed the joint to Ryan.

Ryan greedily took a long drag from the joint and held the smoke into his lungs before exhaling as Martin had done.

A couple more drags off the joint and they both sat relaxed on the back porch.

"I really did it this time," Ryan said in a shaky voice as he held the last of the joint between his fingers.

"I was out last night and early this morning boosting cars with Juan and we found a truck that had $2,400 in a wallet and some jewelry," he said.

"We took the stuff back to a trap house and traded the jewelry and cash for a 1/4 pound of meth," he continued, "and I used some of the meth and got feeling like I was superman."

"We had talked about checking a truck for guns that might be in the truck," he said, "and the truck was parked just down the street from my mom's."

"If we obtained a gun, we were going to do a robbery takeover at a norteno trap house in Othello," he said.

"A pretty reliable source tells me of prime meth that comes directly from the Sinaloa Cartel up through California to the norteno trap house in Othello. There should be a large quantity to grab and there could be a substantial amount of cash. The local dealers from the area will be bringing cash to pay for their product," he said to Martin.

"Are you interested in doing a takedown?" Ryan asked Martin.

"No man, I've got a wife and two kids and can't take a chance," he replied.

"Tell me what happened to get you so worked up," Martin pushed.

"After we left the trap house we walked down where the guy's truck was parked on the street. It was only about a block from my mom's house. We were walking down the sidewalk and there was only one porch light on at one house," Ryan said to Martin.

"We walked past the truck and looked in the guy's front window and saw the guy was sitting at a desk or something with his back to the street. He was on a computer or something and wasn't paying attention outside," said Ryan.

"I saw a lady across the street sitting at a table and it looked like she was reading the paper," he continued.

"Her light was pretty bright and I doubt if she could have seen anything past her living room window because of the reflection back to where she was sitting," he continued.

"Just to be safe, I had Juan watch the guy from the corner of the house and he was going to whistle and warn me if the guy looked out or anything," Ryan said.

"I stayed on the driver's side of the truck, away from the ladies point of view. The door to the truck wasn't locked so I got in and searched around the back seat, under the seats on the floor and in the center console, and never found any guns. I remembered on that pickup model there is another hidden storage unit beneath the flip up center console of the pickup truck," he told Martin.

"I looked under the console and lifted the lid up and that is where I found a semi auto pistol with several magazines and a box of ammo. I grabbed the pistol and stuck the magazines and ammo in my coat pocket, and was holding the pistol when I backed out of the truck," he continued.

"Just as I clicked the door shut I heard Juan whistle and I turned just as this guy came out the front door and started walking towards me. He yelled something like 'You again!' and I knew he recognized me from the time he had caught me in his truck this past summer and he knew where I lived," said Ryan.

"I just panicked as he approached and I shot blindly in his direction, and I heard a grunt from the guy and saw him clutching his stomach and turn towards his house and stumble through his front door and close it. I ran around the back of his house and down the alley and met up with Juan and as we came out of the alley, a guy saw us running out of the alley," Ryan said.

"After I split with Juan I went to Carlene's, took a shower and changed clothes and left after getting in a fucking screaming match. She accused me of sleeping with another woman. I left her house and walked to my mom's and got there about 7:30 A.M. and we watched all the activity going on down the street," he said.

"My mom and I went outside for awhile and stood looking down the street and I would raise up the tape barricade for the cop cars coming and going," Ryan said.

"It looked like some cops were walking to each house," he continued, "so I walked back inside my mom's house so the cop wouldn't talk to me and might have had an outstanding warrant for my arrest."

"That's when I left my mom's place and went to see Trampus," he said.

"I got some meth on me if you want to really get blasted," Ryan said.

Martin said, "Get that shit away from me man, you know I'm on probation for possession of that crap and it's probably been cut with that killer Fentanyl."

"Nah, it's pure stuff and hasn't been cut at all," he assured Martin.

"I want to show you something," he said as he reached into the backpack he had been carrying.

Ryan pulled out an object wrapped in black cloth and opened the cloth to reveal a semi auto pistol with a laser sight.

He handed the gun to Martin who examined it.

"It's a Smith and Wesson 45 caliber semi-auto pistol with a laser sight attached to it," Ryan told Martin.

"Where did you get this gun, was it the gun you took out of the truck and killed the guy with?" asked Martin in a cautious tone.

"Yes, that's the gun," Ryan replied.

"Are you crazy walking around with the murder weapon with all the cops around here asking questions?" Martin said with an angry tone towards Ryan.

"You need to get rid of it," Martin said to Ryan.

Martin feverishly wiped the gun down with the front of the cotton t-shirt he was wearing.

"Dammit man, if the cops find you with that gun and my fingerprints or DNA are on it along with yours, then I'm fucking going away to prison with you!"

"You know better to hand me a hot gun," he growled at Ryan.

"I don't want you at my house in case the cops show up," he glared at Ryan.

Ryan placed the gun into his backpack, stood up and walked around the side of the house.

Ryan took a circuitous route into the alley that led to his mother's back yard and entered through the back door.

Ryan walked outside to the front yard and looked down the street towards the crime scene.

There were still officers sitting in marked patrol cars on each end of the street and the Mobile Command Post was parked in front of Bonnie Crawfoot's house.

His mother was now at work at the local Eagles Club as a bartender so Ryan removed the murder weapon from his backpack.

"I've got to get rid of this gun or at least hide it so it can't be found, unless I need it," he thought.

Chapter 10
Jenna Edwards

Jenna Edwards just got back into town a couple days ago and she has a car and I need a ride, Ryan thought to himself.

He called her phone number at least five times and Jenna finally picked up her phone.

"When did you get back in town and are you staying for a while?" Ryan asked.

"I got back in town two days ago and will be here for about two years while I attend my classes at Big Bend Community College," she replied.

"I'm staying at my Aunt Laura's place on S. River Road," she divulged.

Ryan and Jenna had been friends with benefits for a couple of years but had a nasty breakup just before Jenna had moved to Seattle.

"I'm hoping we can maybe spend some time together while you're back in town," he said.

"I would like that," Jenna said, but there was some hesitancy in her voice.

"I've got a favor to ask you if you're not too busy for a couple of hours," Ryan said to Jenna.

"What did you need?" Jenna asked with a little suspicion in her voice.

"I need a ride up the Rocky Gulch Road, I need to get rid of something that could get me in big trouble," he replied.

"As long as I don't get in trouble, I guess I can," she replied back.

"Great," he replied, "can you meet me at the church down on 1st street in about 10 minutes? I'll be out back in that little park?" he asked.

"Be right there," she said, then hung up the phone and walked out the front door.

This might be a fun afternoon, Jenna thought as she got behind the wheel of her car and headed towards town with lewd thoughts in her head.

Ryan might get lucky today and get a wild ride in my backseat when he is done with his bullshit, she thought to herself.

Jenna remembered their intense physical acts from the past.

I don't really like the guy anymore but he is good for a romp or two, she thought.

Jenna drove her car behind the church and spotted Ryan walking across the street from the small park.

He looked around the immediate area apprehensively and opened the right front passenger door and slid into the car.

Jenna leaned over and gave Ryan a hard long kiss, then leaned back, looking into his eyes.

"Hello stranger," she gushed, "glad you phoned me," and gave him a wink and a sly smile.

"If you don't mind, we need to get moving," he told Jenna as he looked around for any police cars in the area and placed his backpack on the floor in front of him.

She drove through town on the main street, obeying the speed limit and driving as if she was in a driver education car.

Luckily for her, as she was leaving town in the area where the speed limit changed from 30 mph to 60 mph, she saw the front fender of a patrol car parked on a side street facing the main roadway.

She recognized a Wheatfield Police Car and saw Officer Nick's face through the side window of his cruiser.

He was holding a portable handheld radar which was pointed at her vehicle.

She subconsciously tapped her brake but she was already driving the legal speed limit.

Ryan's heart skipped a beat when he saw the patrol car and anxiously looked over his left shoulder, to see if the patrol car had pulled out and may be following them.

As they left the city limits Ryan leaned back and relaxed.

"There's an old pump house along a road just off Rocky Gulch Road towards the top of the plateau and I need to get rid of something," he said to Jenna.

Rocky Gulch Road was just a few miles out of town that meandered up to the flat plateau that overlooked the town of Wheatland and was about 600 feet higher in elevation.

It was a prime location for the local kids to have their beer parties and have their backseat romances while overlooking the town 6 miles away.

As they gained elevation on Rocky Gulch Road, fog started to form and the higher they travelled the fog continually turned more dense until the fog seemed as thick as pea soup.

Jenna slowed the car to a crawl as Ryan peered through the thick fog, trying to locate the road leading to the small pump house.

"I think the old driveway is on the left side of the road that leads to the old homestead where the only building remaining is the dilapidated wooden pump house," said Ryan.

"I think it's called the old Smith Farm," he told Jenna.

They drove through the deep fog to the top of the plateau without locating the road that led to the pump house.

There is a gravel parking lot scattered with garbage, mostly empty beer cans, hard liquor bottles and condom packages.

Many Wheatland children would be born as a result of their young parents' adventures in this very same parking lot.

"Let's turn around and head back and see if the fog is clearing," said Ryan.

Jenna drove slowly down the road, headed back towards Wheatland far below.

"Stop!" Ryan suddenly said, "I think this might be the road."

Jenna slammed the brakes and if she would have been going at a higher rate of speed, Ryan would have planted his face into the windshield since he was not wearing a seatbelt.

He stepped out of the car carrying his backpack, and was soon lost from sight in the swirling fog when he walked down a faint road.

When he hadn't returned as 10 minutes passed, Jenna was getting anxious sitting alone in her car with the swirling fog around the car.

She was nervous sitting in the car by herself and pushed the door lock button.

She had seen too many low budget horror movies as a high school student and those type of gruesome movies were imbedded in her mind.

Before she realized it, there was a dark form at the driver's window tapping on the glass.

She gave a sharp gasp, then saw it was Ryan and unlocked the doors so Ryan could get into the vehicle.

"I looked all over and could not locate the old pump house so we may as well go back to town," Ryan told Jenna.

Jenna looked over at Ryan and noticed he no longer had the backpack with him.

Hmm, she said to herself, he did hide something down the road, probably some dope or something from his car prowling.

They drove back to Wheatland and on the way Ryan seemed more at ease and was not tense.

She drove him back to the park behind the church and stopped and had a short conversation with him.

Jenna looked into his eyes and gave him a long hug.

"Look," she said, "I'm pretty much free and you look like the only cowboy in town, so if you want a good bucking give me a call."

Ryan looked at her and gave her a wink as he was stepping out of Jenna's car.

Jenna drove to a friend's apartment in Soap Lake who lived in a small apartment unit with an open courtyard in front.

She hadn't seen her friend since she had left Wheatland 6 months earlier.

She knocked on the door and looked around as several neighbors glanced towards her from their chairs near their front doors.

"Does Danielle Strawn still live here?" she queried.

"She should be home," said one elderly lady in a friendly voice.

"She was just outside visiting me not more than 15 minutes ago," she said.

"Thank you, ma'am," Jenna replied.

She turned and knocked louder and longer at the door, which was suddenly jerked open.

"Oh my God, what a wonderful surprise, come on in, Jenna, when did you get back in town?" Danielle said with a large smile and gave Jenna a long hug.

"I got back two days ago and I'm staying at my aunt Carol's until I can get my own place," she answered.

"Sit down girl," Danielle said and smiled and sat next to Jenna, holding hands with her.

"My job in Seattle was great but I was one of about a thousand employees there, with low seniority. I am off work from a back injury and State Labor and Industry Insurance pays me almost as much money as I was earning when I worked. State L&I has retraining programs for up to two years at Community Colleges to learn new skills and I have signed up at Big Bend Community College in Moses Lake. I will continue to receive full benefits while I attend. My heart is in Wheatland and not Seattle with all the people and horrendous traffic. The constant rain and clouds were depressing and all I thought about was getting back to the sunny side of the state," Jenna said with a sigh.

"It's so quiet over here and folks are friendly," she opined.

"I wouldn't say that it's all that quiet around here," said Danielle.

"In Wheatland, someone shot and killed a guy named John Adams and no one knows what happened," she said.

"I think the guy lived a short distance from Ryan Bate's house on the same street. John Adams' family has already offered a $5,000 reward for anyone that can help the police find out who did the murder and if that person gets convicted," Danielle said out loud.

Jenna suddenly sat upright and her face turned pale.

"What is it girl?" asked an alarmed Danielle.

"Well, I got a phone call from Ryan Bates and he asked if I could pick him up by the old church in Wheatland, that he was in big trouble and had to get rid of something right away," she said pensively.

"He had phoned at least five times, so I finally answered and his voice seemed strange when he asked me to pick him up. When I picked him up he was carrying a backpack with him. He had me drive him up the canyon on Rocky Canyon Rd. The higher we drove, the thicker the fog became and I could barely see the road," she continued.

"Ryan said he was looking for an old well house on a little side road but we could not find it in the fog and we drove clear to the top of the plateau. We sat up there for a while," Danielle said.

"He kept mumbling something that it was the biggest mistake he had ever made. I thought he had me drive him up to the top so we could have some privacy and see how things worked out, but Ryan was genuinely scared. I drove back down the canyon going real slow and all of a sudden Ryan snapped at me to stop. He pointed to a faint, hardly used lane on the Northside of road and asked me to back into the lane off the main road. Ryan told me to wait in the car, that he would be right back, then he picked up his backpack and stepped out of the car," Jenna told Danielle.

"Ryan came back to my car after about 10 minutes and his hands were all dirty so I think he buried the backpack. He had me drive him back into town and he was slumped down in the front seat like he didn't want anyone to see him. I dropped him off at the church and he looked all around like he thought someone was after him. I think that's more than a coincidence," Jenna said to Danielle.

"Why was he so serious when he phoned you and said he was in more trouble than he'd ever been and he had to get rid of something?" Danielle asked.

"He had you pick him up after he was hiding behind the church, and he's got something in his backpack and he buries it by the old pump house up in Rocky Canyon, and that is suspicious," said Danielle.

"When he came back to my car he warned me not to tell anyone about our trip to Rocky Canyon," Jenna said.

"Tomorrow is New Year's Day so let's talk about it after New Year's," Danielle said.

After that intense conversation Jenna picked up her mood and soon they were talking and laughing about the life changes they had both endured over the past year.

After having a cold beer, Jenna announced that she had to be going and they promised to meet again the day after New Year at Danielle's place.

Chapter 11

Sgt. Harmon came back to the Incident Command vehicle and located Det Ralston Hannigan, Det. Joel Fitz and Det. Ben Skates in the meeting room.

"Sgt. Harmon, has anything helpful been found since the murder?" Det. Hannigan asked.

"There were only two people that had heard what they thought was a gunshot but had not seen anyone or vehicles leaving the neighborhood, with the exception of Kat Bates who lived about 1/2 block away from John Adams. She told me about 6:30 A.M. she was in her backyard after letting her dogs out to do their duty when she had observed a black car driving through the alley south bound really fast and only one person was in the car," as he paused to breathe.

"She thought it was a woman that was driving," he finished.

"Thanks," Hannigan said with a sigh, "we'll probably have to do a follow-up neighborhood canvas of the immediate area to talk to the folks that were not home or didn't answer their door."

He said, "let's take a break tomorrow and meet on January 2nd in our CBIT War Room."

"We can lay out our plan of attack and look at all the evidence and reports filed by the responding officers. Sgt. Harmon will finish up with the Command Post details," Hannigan said to the group.

"If we need to go back into the house, the parents can sign a search consent document and we won't need another search warrant," he concluded.

"The parents will receive a copy of all the property we have removed as evidence but they need to notify us if they discover other items missing in the house after they have taken possession," he finished.

Chapter 12

Monday Morning at 9:00 A.M., Detectives Hannigan, Fitz and Skates were at the War Room, waiting for Chief Fife to come to the meeting room with other investigators that could help piece the murder mystery together.

Chief Fife walked into the conference room with Medical Examiner Jack Teagan and Detectives Massee and Zollars.

A few steps behind was Beth Johnson from the Joint Forensic Evidence Recovery Unit.

Walter Colvins, the elected Prosecutor of Canyon County, walked into the room accompanied by his Special Victims Deputy Prosecutor Sophrinia Patrick, who was regarded as one of the best "no nonsense let's not make a deal" Deputy Prosecutors in Colvin's office.

The Wheatland Mayor had also been invited to the meeting after an agreement had been made that he would not speak to the public about the incident unless the content of his release was agreed upon by the Police Chief and Det. Hannigan.

Selective information would be provided to the Public Information Officer and he would prepare the printed News Release and disseminate after final approval to the media.

Everyone was warned that conversations with other persons outside of the War Room regarding the case, would be a direct violation of the protocol unless approved.

The entire west wall of the room located on the second floor was a whiteboard.

Numbered names were displayed on the large whiteboard:

1. Marianne Shutt
2. Dustin Silver
3. Nancy Williams
4. Cam Gentry
5. Tammy Gentry
6. Carmin Martinez
7. Ted Martinez

Hannigan stepped to the front of the room as all the participants took chairs across the room in no special order.

"Good morning," he addressed the room.

"Before I get started I would like to thank all of the elected officials and participants of the task force we are developing. I am the Lead Detective assigned with Detectives Fitz and Skates on the CBIT Team to focus on the John Adams Homicide, but as most of you know, we cannot solve this murder without help from the various agencies that we are asking to assist. You will see our phone numbers written on the whiteboard. The telephone number located in this room is also listed right below our numbers. We have installed a combination security lock on the door," he said.

"The combination security lock code numbers should not be shared and no one should be granted access other than members of this team," Hannigan continued.

"Moses Lake Police Department is a distance away but we are going to use their Crime Check Tip-line phone number for citizens that wish to phone in a tip. There has been a $5,000.00 reward offered so hopefully some good tips will come in on that line and we can do a follow-up," he continued.

"If you look at the main whiteboard , you will see 7 names that we have determined will require a follow-up as they are all possible suspects for the murder of John Adams," he said.

#1 "Marianne Shutt is listed as a current girlfriend of Adams but the jungle beat out there is Adams found out she was still in a sexual relationship with her ex-boyfriend Dustin Silver and Adams was going to break up with her the same day that he was murdered."

#2 "Dustin Silver is Marianne Shutt's ex-boyfriend and they have a 3 yr. old child in common. In the initial interview with Marianne on the day of the homicide she was hesitant but voiced some concern that Dustin could have traveled from The Dalles, Oregon to Wheatland and shot Adams but she later said Adams had threatened to shoot Dustin out of jealousy with a 45 gun but Dustin had never threatened John Adams. We will be having some long sessions with that young lady," he continued.

#3 "Nancy Williams was a side chick for Adams but she was also an ex-girlfriend of Adams, and continued to hang out with Adams and Shutt, including going out and shooting, watching Adam's son Devin playing sports, etc. She had shot Adam's 45 caliber Smith and Wesson semi auto Pistol with Laser attachment recently, and that gun has not been located. We know Nancy would have knowledge of where the gun was located and how to manipulate, load and fire the weapon."

#4 "Cam Gentry is a Mattawa Police Officer that is married to John Adams' ex-wife, Tammy Gentry," said Hannigan.

#5 "Tammy Gentry should be questioned but there has been no information that would point to her as being involved. There had been some minor visitation issues between Tammy Gentry and her ex-husband, John Adams, over visitation of their son Devin," he explained.

#6 Det. "Carmin Martinez was one of John's identified married girlfriends he had at the time of his death. She would meet with John at various motels around Canyon and Grant County."

#7 "Ted Martinez is Carmin's husband and is a successful business man that spends a lot of time out of town managing a trucking company that is doing contract work at the Bakken Oil Fields and nearby tribal reservation in North Dakota," he finished.

Hannigan looked across the room and said, "I would like to introduce Beth Johnson, the supervisor of the Forensic Crime Recovery Unit."

She moved to the podium as Hannigan stepped aside.

Beth stepped up to the podium with a small sheaf of papers and placed them on the podium shelf.

"My team and I have conducted an extensive crime scene recovery investigation and are in the process of processing key items that may help resolve this case," she said.

"We have the spent shell casing found at the crime scene and will be sending the shell casing to the Washington State Patrol Crime Lab for DNA analysis in the near future and are hoping the firearm can be located to send to the WSP Lab at the same time," she continued.

"The same for the Peerless brand handcuffs found in the front yard. We have noticed the handcuffs are quite unusual as the original factory rings connecting the handcuffs have been replaced with two larger rings, and there are partial serial numbers on each handcuff, but we did use acid etching to bring out some additional serial numbers, but unfortunately we don't have the complete sequence," she noted.

"A partially full wine bottle, wine glass and beer can were found on a table near the victim and all three were checked for fingerprints and DNA."

"Nancy Williams fingerprints were located near the bottom stem section of the wine glass, and the victim's fingerprints were found on the wine bottle and the beer can," she continued.

"The heel print found near the Southwest side of the house match size 12 footprints made by an unknown person running around the Northside corner of the house. The tracks lead through the backyard and over a short fence into the alley."

Beth paused and pointed out a large photo of a footprint that was on display taped to the whiteboard behind her location.

"We located another set of footprints in the neighbors yard located on the Northside of the victim's house, and the footprints were headed in the same direction as the other set of footprints," she continued.

"A vehicle had driven down the alley and there were faint footprints of two persons running and stepping in the vehicle tire tracks. By the time we started to examine the footprints, the media was already there. The news media parked their vehicle in the alley and obliterated any usable tracks or evidence," she said.

"It's hard telling if anyone may have picked up evidence lying along the road," Beth said to the group.

"One of my forensic team had to keep the media at bay while we did our scene process," she said.

Chief Fife was red faced and said, "I'll get to the bottom of that shit show after this meeting,"

"People, we are not here to start attacking the shortfalls of this investigation. They will be resolved as we find problems," Hannigan addressed the group.

"Meanwhile, we will start the follow-up investigation and contact the potential suspects we have discussed in our meeting. As soon as WSP Lab reports are complete we will need to be immediately notified and all document copies will be placed in files in this War Room. As this case develops, Wheatland Detectives Tom Zollars and Jesse Massee have been cleared by Chief Fife to transfer their cases to other Investigators," he disclosed to the group.

"Chief Fife has assigned Administrative Assistant Carol Whitaker to move a desk and support equipment to keep all of our files in one location in the War Room. Assisting investigators in the Wheatland Investigative Division will work inside the War Room until this crime is solved. All press releases related to this case will be prepared by the Public Information Officer and will be reviewed before dissemination. Remember folks, no leaks in this investigation because we don't know where this case is going to lead us," Hannigan said sternly as he ended the meeting.

"We'll meet at 10:00 A.M. every Monday unless the investigation starts heating up, then you will be notified," he continued.

"Detective Zollars and Detective Massee, please wait and we will discuss our team assignments," Detective Hannigan said as he turned and looked at both of them.

Chapter 13

After the room cleared Hannigan said, "Ok guys, let's look at this list of potential witnesses and we can split them up."

"I will work with Det. Skates to interview Carmin Martinez and her husband. Detective Fitz, pair up with Detective Zollars and contact Cam and Tammy Gentry. Then when you guys complete that assignment go back and do another interview with Bonnie Crawfoot," he continued.

"Detective Massee, would you check the list of all the witnesses in the neighborhood that heard a gunshot and also attempt to locate residents that weren't contacted through the neighborhood canvas the day of the homicide?" he said.

"Make reports on every contact and circumstance and have Carol Whitaker file and make a copy and post on the whiteboard," he said.

"File all your handwritten notes when no longer needed and they have been transcribed," he directed.

"The combination to the door is # 494949 and will not be disclosed to anyone without my permission, folks."

Chapter 14

A week had passed and the CBIT Team met for an update and to let all the supporting members know of their findings.

"Detective Fitz and Zollars, did you contact and interview Officer Cam Gentry and his wife Tammy?" he asked.

"Yes, Zollars and myself finished our interview with Tammy yesterday which required some follow-up but she has been cleared," Fitz told the group.

"Tammy Gentry works for Federal Delivery and we were able to track her movements the day of the incident from 4:30 A.M. when she reported for work at the Federal Delivery warehouse in Moses Lake near the airport until she got off work in the early afternoon. Her electronic activity log timed all her stops and company GPS tracked her location by the delivery addresses she stopped and delivered. On that day she traveled from Wheatland to Elmer City where she dropped off packages at the local Federal Delivery Store at 6:15 A.M. The rest of her delivery route took her out to Nezpelem on the Colville Indian Reservation. She stopped at the Mexican restaurant in Soap Lake and then returned to the warehouse a few minutes after noon and she got off work logging out at 1:00 P.M. Wednesday we stopped by the 911

Joint Communication Center in Moses Lake and got a printout of all the calls for service the day of the homicide that Officer Cam Gentry responded to in Mattawa. Cam Gentry worked 1st Shift Graveyard from 22:30 hrs. until 08:30 hrs. on Patrol. He never had much activity the first part of the shift other than a Domestic Violence Assault and the another officer actually made the arrest and transported the suspect to the Grant County Jail. About 5:00 A.M. Officer Gentry responded to a single car rollover on Road B west of I-90 near George, Washington which turned out to be a fatal, a 17 year old female driver not wearing a seatbelt. WSP was called to investigate the investigation, but Gentry stood by to assist with traffic control until 7:15 A.M. Gentry drove back and checked out at the Mattawa P.D. office and wrote a report on his involvement in the investigation," said Fitz as he finished his verbal presentation.

"Good work," Hannigan remarked as he looked at Detectives Fitz and Zollars.

"OK, we can check both Cam and Tammy off our list of suspects," he said as he marked an X beside each name on the whiteboard.

"Did you have time to do another interview on Bonnie Crawfoot since the shooting last week?" Hannigan directed his question to Detectives Fitz and Zollars.

"Det. Zollars and myself attended the funeral of John Adams at the Holy Cross Cemetery," Det. Fitz said.

"We had Officer Tom Beeman from the Regional Drug Task Force park his undercover surveillance van mounted with surveillance cameras at a vantage point and video or photograph the people that attended the funeral in hopes of identifying a possible suspect in the small crowd," he said.

"Bonnie was interviewed again by Detective Fitz and myself at her home," said Det. Zollars.

"We sat at the kitchen table with Bonnie and she pointed out what she had observed through her living room window. Her story is about the same as the interview that was done on the day of the homicide. Bonnie seems to be stuck on her observation of a flurry of commotion that she saw in John's front yard at the time she heard the gunshot. She thought there were at least two persons in the yard when she looked up after hearing the single gunshot."

"Thanks," Detectives Hannigan said.

"Detective Skates and myself did a follow-up on the Martinez woman and also to determine their whereabouts at the time of the Homicide."

"Yesterday we checked at their residence and neither of the Martinez couple were home but the housekeeper Lupi Garcia answered the door," Detective Skates reported.

"Ms. Garcia advised us the Martinez family was vacationing in Belize, Central America and had left the day after Christmas for an extended 2nd honeymoon," Detective Skates said, barely able to suppress a grin.

"They won't be back until January 30th when they fly to Spokane to pick up their car and come home. I believe we can cross both Carmin and Ted Martinez off as potential suspects since they were out of country."

He walked over to the whiteboard and placed an X to the left of their names.

"Nancy Williams was transported to the Wheatland Police Department and interviewed on the day of the homicide," Detective Hannigan told the group.

"As a background we know that Nancy and John had been in an intimate relationship not long after John's divorce from Tammy Gentry was final," he continued.

"She had been a back-up babysitter for Devin when John was working late on a project and she would also pick up Devin from baseball practice and take him to John's place. She would take care of Devin until John came home. Most of the time she would spend those nights with John at his house. John's parents tried to discourage his relationship with Nancy because she was not of the same faith, and they thought she was rough around the edges because of the rough and tumble hobbies she had," he explained.

"John would often take Nancy and his son Devin to the firing range to trap shoot or just up Rocky Canyon Road to shoot ground squirrels with his 22 caliber rifles. We checked Nancy's alibi and she did admit she had been at John's house the night before where they had cleaned his shotguns then had a quiet dinner and she told us John had a beer and she had a glass of wine," Det. Zollars revealed.

"She left John's place about 11:00 P.M. and when she got home she phoned John to say good night, and he sounded upbeat because he had a big project he was going to bid on the next day," he continued.

"Nancy is enrolled in a online management class at Spokane Falls Community College and was at an early 6:00 A.M.-7:00 A.M. Zoom meeting. We have contacted her instructor Professor Calvin Forbes and he did confirm Nancy did attend his 6:00 A.M. to 7:00 A.M. Zoom class. Nancy did say that while she was on the Zoom Management class she did note a phone call at 7:45 A.M. from John's sister but did not return the call until after her class. Olive told Nancy the terrible news and she drove directly to Olive's house. Nancy told us that she and John had been friends and romantically involved since John's divorce and she had no other men in her life other than John," Detective Skates finished and looked around the room.

"I think we can cross Nancy Williams off the list as a suspect," Detective Hannigan said as he walked across the room and placed an X beside her name on the whiteboard.

"The only two potential suspects are Marianne Shutt and her ex-boyfriend Dustin Silver," he said.

"At this point the only reason we are considering Dustin Silver is because he is an ex-boyfriend and Marianne mentioned his name when she was interviewed the day of the homicide. We reviewed Marianne Shutt's interview from the day of the homicide and we contacted her in Waterville. Her mom confirmed that Marianne was in bed the morning of the homicide and she had to awaken her to give her the bad news. The mother confirmed Marianne was there all night and Marianne did not have a car because it was in the shop getting new snow tires installed. Marianne borrowed her mom's car to drive to Wheatland to Olive's house. However, I think she knows more than she is saying and," Hannigan said as he walked over and put an x beside Marianne's name on the whiteboard.

"The last suspect on our list is Dustin Silver, Marianne's ex-boyfriend but Marianne has not directly said she was suspicious of Dustin," he mused.

Chapter 15

The following Monday morning Detectives Fitz, Skates and Hannigan sat in the War Room planning the week's assignments.

Detective Skates was reviewing the in-basket where all new reports and messages, including messages from the Crime Check Tip Line, would be placed.

"What the hell!" he said as he stared at a Tip Line note.

Detective Hannigan and the others stopped what they were doing and stared at Detective Skates.

"A woman called in on the telephone Tip Line at Moses Lake Police Department and listed a guy named Ryan Bates as a suspect in the murder," Detective Skates blurted out.

"She wanted to know about the $5,000 dollar reward," he said.

"The note said Ryan Bates contacted a young woman on the day of the murder and told her he had to get rid of something and needed a ride."

"The woman that called in the tip left her phone number but not her name," Fitz stated.

"Detective Fitz, would you run down the information from the Tip Line and see if we can locate this woman," said Detective Hannigan.

"Sure thing," Detective Fitz muttered.

"What do we know about this person named Ryan Bates?" asked Hannigan.

"I'll run a background on the guy," Detective Fitz said as he sat down in front of a computer screen and started typing in his password to obtain information.

"Ryan Bates is 21 years old and has a pretty lengthy record. Mostly for petty theft, drug possession and assault," he reported.

"There are some field contact notes on the screen that show Ryan Bates and a guy named Juan Garcia are suspects in numerous car prowls and residential burglaries here in Wheatland," Det. Fitz told them.

"Juan Garcia is listed on a field intelligence card where he has been stopped several times in the early morning hours. The officers making contact with him suspected he was out prowling cars. Ryan and Juan are suspected of using a Slim Jim instrument to gain entry into cars and steal whatever they can find," he said.

"Vehicle Prowling Theft reports were entered into the system by Officer Wes Stewart on the morning of the same date as the Adams Homicide," he reported.

"One significant vehicle prowl occurred in town where cash and jewelry were stolen. The Field Intelligence card says scratch marks near the door post on a late model Chevy pick-up truck was the point of entry which would indicate the instrument used to gain entry was like a Slim Jim tool," said Detective Fitz.

The sound of the door opening interrupted the conversation as Forensic Supervisor Beth Johnson came into the room, with documents that she held close to her chest.

"The Evidence Property Unit has sent the handcuffs, and the shell casing to the Washington State Patrol Crime Lab in Cheney Washington, to be checked for DNA source," she said.

"Hopefully they will collect enough DNA from the handcuffs so a test can be conducted. We were not able to lift any latent prints from the handcuffs or the shell casing," she said as she finished the report to the group.

"Think we better look at this Dustin Silver and see what type of alibi he claims," said Hannigan.

"Detective Skates, would you check Wasco County Sheriff's Office in The Dalles, Oregon to see what information they have on Dustin Silver, and while you're at it, check WASIC and NCIC," Hannigan directed.

"Meanwhile, Detective Fitz and myself will have another visit with Marianne Shutt."

The morning meeting ended and Detective Fitz went to his desk and made a phone call to Marianne Shutt's residence.

"Hello," came a sleepy voice.

'I'm Detective Fitz calling for Marianne Shutt, is she available?" he asked.

"This is Marianne Shutt," she replied.

"Ma'am, are you available at 1:00 P.M. this afternoon for another interview with Detective Hannigan and myself at the Wheatland Police Department?" he asked.

"Yes, it's my mother's day off from work and she can watch my son Zachary," she responded.

Marianne arrived a few minutes before 1:00 P.M. at the Canyon County Sheriff's Office and was directed to a small room with a table and 4 chairs.

A large one way viewing window was framed on one wall and a video camera was mounted in a ceiling corner.

A mounted clock in a metal case was sitting on the table close to the wall

The clock actually contained a sensitive microphone to record conversations or statements between the person interviewed and the interviewer.

Detectives Fitz and Hannigan had been waiting for Marianne and she was directed to sit in the chair opposite from Detective Hannigan.

Detective Fitz sat against the wall directly at the head of the table which hemmed in Marianne as she looked nervously toward the closed door.

"Thank you for meeting with us again, Ms. Shutt, can we offer you some bottled water before we start this interview?" Det. Fitz asked.

"That would be nice," she answered, "I always get dry mouth when I'm nervous."

Fitz left the interview room and returned momentarily with a plastic water bottle.

"Before we start this conversation we would like to audio and video record this interview if you will give us permission," Detective Fitz asked Marianne.

"Of course, you have my permission," she replied.

"Thank you," Detective Fitz said as he motioned to an unseen person behind the one way glass to turn on the electronic equipment.

After going through the permission preliminaries required to make the interview legal, Detective Hannigan went over the interview information Marianne had provided on the day John Adams was killed.

"When was the last time you heard from Dustin Silver?" he asked.

"Well, it was only about 3 days before John was killed," she replied.

"Then I phoned him the morning John was killed," she continued.

"Did Dustin say where he was located?" Hannigan asked.

"He didn't really say other than he was on the road somewhere in Oregon, I think he said Bend, Oregon but not sure, and he was going to be home on the weekend," she replied.

"Did you say you phoned Dustin right after you found out John was killed?"

"Yes, the number I called is Dustin's cell phone which is 376-943-8701," she said.

"Did you accuse him of killing John?" he asked.

"I told him John was dead, and I would kill him if I found out he had killed John," she said softly.

"Did Dustin make any comments after you made that comment to him?" he asked.

"Yes, he was very angry at me and asked me if I was off my depression and anxiety medication and hung up on me," she replied.

"I know you have already been questioned about your past history with Dustin and John but we need to go over it again to clear up some questions we have," Det. Hannigan said.

"I will try to help you," said Marianne

"My mother had taken me to a Mental Health Therapist in hopes I would feel better and get over my feelings for Dustin after she told me I had to break up with Dustin when we had lived in The Dalles, Oregon," she continued, wiping her tears and blowing her nose with a tissue.

"The medication prescribed for me cut the edge of my anxiety and my depression started to lift up," she revealed.

"I started going to church with my mother here in Wheatland and it was the same church the Adams family attended. They were friendly to me and I learned they were related to the Adams family in The Dalles and I had attended church there with my mom. On one church holiday I met John Adams at the church function and he seemed like a nice man. Then, I remembered him when I was a child at his relatives home in The Dalles. He was about 5 years older than me at the time," she continued.

"John had a son a few years older than Zachary, his name was Devin and we started hanging out together and Zachary and I would go to the Little League baseball games and see John there as he also watched his son Devin play in the game. As time went on, John and I spent more time together and would often go out to the range and shoot his guns. We became intimate and I thought it would help me get over Dustin's touch but I still had the yearning. Then last fall Dustin phoned me out of the blue and said he wanted to see me and Zachary," she continued.

"Of course, I said yes, and it seemed almost immediately my depression lifted and I could hardly wait to meet him in Moses Lake the next day. John was working over in Coulee City and I phoned him and told him I was going to The Dalles to visit friends. I borrowed John's Jeep and met Dustin in the park near the Inter-state 90 in Moses Lake. Dustin took Zachary and me shopping and bought clothing for Zachary and gave me $1,000.00 cash to help make ends meet. We spent most of the day in the park and Dustin played for hours with

Zachary. We checked in and spent the night at the Coulee Motel in Moses Lake, and it made me realize I would never get over my feelings for Dustin," she said.

"Dustin promised that he would keep in touch with me and wanted to be part of Zachary and my life. The next evening I went to Devin's baseball game with Zachary and met with John. He seemed a little distant to me and after the game he didn't invite us back to his house as usual. I didn't hear from John until late afternoon the next day and he asked me to come by his house for dinner. I went to his house and we had dinner and everything seemed normal. I continued seeing John but could not stop thinking of Dustin and longed to be with him. I would drive to out of the way nearby towns and meet with Dustin at motels whenever he came through the area, usually on a weekly basis. Most of the time my mom would watch Zachary when she had a day off."

"What type of vehicles did you use when you would meet with Dustin?" Hannigan asked.

"I would usually use John's Jeep to meet with Dustin," she replied.

"Were you aware of other girlfriends of Dustin?" Hannigan asked.

"He had an ex-girlfriend named Samantha Fox that lived in Pendleton, Oregon while she attended Blue Mountain Community College," she replied.

"I'm not sure where she is currently living but she could be back in The Dalles. About a month ago when Dustin and I were in a Smiley's Restaurant in The Dalles, Samantha walked in and was surprised to see me sitting with Dustin. She had seen David's car parked in the parking lot and was coming in to say hello. It was a little uncomfortable because she knew that I had been a past girlfriend of Dustin's. I had to get back to Waterville, so I left them after kissing Dustin on the cheek. I looked over at Samantha and could tell by the look in her eyes, that she was jealous."

"How many phones do you currently have?" Detective Skates asked Marianne.

"I only have my current phone that Dustin had bought for me the last time we spent together," she replied.

"Can you describe Dustin's car that he would use when you were meeting with him," asked Detective Skates.

"Dustin drove a red Nissan pick-up with a canopy on the back that he would use to haul smaller car parts he would obtain on his route. He also had an older white Dodge flatbed truck with side racks that he would use to haul larger auto parts like engines and transmissions. I only saw him driving the flatbed truck one time and that was when we met at a motel in Quincy, about three months ago," she replied.

"Would you please provide your phone number, your mom's old phone number from the phone she gave you and Dustin's cell phone number?" Detective Hannigan requested.

She provided Detective Hannigan with the phone numbers.

"Thank you for meeting with us today, and if it's okay, we may have some further questions and hopefully you won't mind getting contacted," Hannigan commented.

"Not a problem," she replied, "but afternoons until about 3:00 P.M. work best with my schedule."

Detective Fitz walked Marianne to the lobby area of the Sheriff's Office, then returned to the interview room.

"We have enough probable cause for a search warrant to obtain phone records for Marianne's phones and do a review of her text messages she sent to both Dustin and the victim as well to obtain a search warrant to obtain phone pings for Dustin Silver's phone," said Detective Hannigan.

Chapter 16

Jenna Edwards had just arrived home about noon after working the 5:00 A.M. to 11:30 A.M. shift part time at the Keystone Bakery in Wheatland when her cell phone rang.

She looked at the Caller I.D. which read "Unlisted Caller".

"What the hell," she said to herself, another telemarketer wanting to sell me something, so she hung up the phone.

Almost immediately the phone rang again with the same Unlisted Caller showing on her phone screen.

Finally, she picked up her cell phone and answered it, expecting the usual sales pitch, but instead she recognized the soft voice of Ryan Bates.

"Hey baby, do you want to hang out today and maybe go for a hike on the trails by Soap Lake? That sounds like a great way to spend the afternoon and maybe more than a hike would be in store."

"Yes, that would be fun," she replied.

"I can get a couple of bottles of Mimosa and snacks and we can have a private picnic along the trail," he said.

"Is it alright if I pick you up in about 30 minutes?" he said in his low voice.

"Just honk when you are out front, and I'll come out," she replied.

They ended the call and Jenna put on a pair of woolen type pants and pulled her hiking boots out of the closet.

She knew it could be chilly where they were hiking so she dressed in layers by wearing a long sleeve cotton shirt under a light pullover sweater and would top it off with a thin ski type jacket and placed a pair of light driving gloves in the coat pocket.

She reached into a jewelry box on her dresser, removed a couple of packaged condoms and placed them in her front pants pocket.

You never know, I might get lucky, she thought.

She smiled as she looked at her image in the mirror on the back of her bedroom door and heard a horn honk on the street in front of her house.

As she crossed the yard to the driveway Ryan reached over and opened the passenger door of his Chevy Pick-up and it swung open as an invitation for Jenna to enter the pick-up.

"You were always such a gentleman," she remarked to Ryan as she got inside the pick-up and sat on the passenger side because of the middle console in his vehicle.

She had noticed a beat-up cooler behind the front seat of the pickup as she was entering the truck.

"I found a really neat trail up by Soap Lake that leads back into a canyon and it's really isolated, and there is a great view from the crest of the canyon," he said to Jenna.

"Sounds like a great place with lots of privacy," Jenna said while smiling at Ryan.

Ryan laughed and placed his hand on her left leg and gave it a light squeeze.

They drove into a Bureau of Land Management maintained parking lot and stopped near the trailhead.

The parking lot was empty and they both exited Ryan's truck.

Ryan stepped around on the passenger side and got his rucksack and placed the Mimosa bottles and snacks from the cooler into the rucksack.

He slung the pack over his shoulder and held Jenna's hand as they started up the trail.

After about 15 minutes the trail had started to climb and they stopped for a short break before continuing to the rim of the canyon.

Finally, after reaching the top of the ridge, Ryan picked a spot that overlooked the trail coming up the hill and removed a blanket from the rucksack and placed it down on a bed of soft pine needles.

They sat under a gnarly old pine tree on the canyon edge.

They caught up on old times and drank from the bottles of Mimosa and noshed on the salami, French bread and cheese.

They laid beside each other on the blanket and Jenna began exploring the front of Ryans' shirt with her hand while hungrily pressing her lips against his lips.

Ryan responded and unzipped her jacket, unsnapped her pants and began exploring with his hand.

Jenna was breathing heavily as Ryan pressed his body into her.

This is what I came for, thought Jenna as they began lovemaking.

Afterwards they lay on the blanket catching their breath.

"Why did you agree to meet with me today?" Ryan asked as he looked directly into her eyes.

"I was lonely and I needed some man company, and was horny," she said as she ran her foot up and down the inside of his bare leg.

Ryan sat up and reached into his coat pocket that he had been using for a pillow.

"Care to share some weed with me?" he said as he displayed a baggy of Marijuana buds and got out a small pipe.

"Yeah, I'd like a hit or two," Jenna replied and stood up, putting her pants back on before sitting down next to Ryan.

Ryan tamped the high quality marijuana buds into the pipe and held a lighter, puffing slowly until the material in the pipe started to smolder.

He took a long drag off the pipe, and as his lungs expanded, he coughed violently as he passed the pipe to Jenna.

She took a slow drawing breath from the pipe into her lungs and she felt the smoke expand into her lungs.

She took another hit on the pipe and passed it back, knowing her sensitivity to smoking weed.

Ryan tapped the remaining ashes from his pipe and placed the pipe back in the bag of Marijuana and placed it in his coat pocket.

"Gawd, I have a nice buzz," she said to no one in particular.

She could still think clearly, but her mood had brightened from the effects of the THC in the marijuana.

After just chilling out for about an hour they packed up and started down the trail with Ryan holding onto Jenna's arm to steady her.

After about 30 minutes they reached the parking lot and placed the rucksack into the pick-up truck.

While standing beside the pick-up truck, Ryan held Jenna in his arms and looked into her eyes.

"Jenna, I really like you and want to get serious with you," Ryan said as he held her in his arms.

"Ryan, I came with you today because I needed you to scratch my itch," she answered, matter of factly.

"I'm attending school at Big Bend Community College for two years and I can't be distracted by a relationship."

"I just have time to be a friend with benefits with you whenever we can get the time together and nothing more while I am in school, so please let's just leave it there," she said.

Ryan's face turned beet red and he angrily struck Jenna hard across the face several times with his hard fist.

As her head snapped back from the blow, Ryan said, "You fucking bitch, I was just playing you to see what you would say."

Jenna was shocked at the sudden transformation of Ryan's mood.

She spat blood from her split lip in Ryan's face.

"You fucking bitch," he said as he closed his hands around Jenna's neck, "I'll kill you just like I did that Adams guy."

Jenna started to see stars from lack of oxygen when he finally removed his hands from around her throat.

He pulled the shoulder of her blouse down and bit her on the top of her shoulder as she cried out in pain.

"Come on bitch, get in the truck," as he pushed her into the passenger front seat.

They did not speak until Ryan dropped Jenna off at the edge of town in Soap Lake, Washington.

Before he drove off, he yelled, "Find your own way home."

With a squeal of tires, he disappeared down the main street.

Jenna realized she was only a few blocks from her friend Laura Strawn's apartment so she slowly made her way to her apartment.

Jenna knocked on the door and Laura opened the door after half a minute.

When she saw Jenna's bloody face she pulled her inside and sat her down on a chair at the kitchen table. "My Gawd, what happened to you?" she asked as she closely looked at her face.

"Ryan got mad at me when he told me he wanted a relationship with me."

"I told him I wasn't interested because I would be attending Big Bend College for two years," she continued.

"He beat the shit out of me and dropped me off at the edge of town. I was lucky you lived so close," Jenna said.

"Let me get out some extra clothes I have," Laura told her.

"We are about the same size and you can take those bloody clothes off and have a fresh shower," Laura said.

"I think you need to get checked out at the ER first, it looks like you will need a stitch or two on your lip," she said.

"That's not all," Jenna said as she slid the bloody shirt off her left shoulder and exposed a human bite mark on her shoulder that had bled profusely.

"I've never seen such a deep bite before on anyone, let's go to the hospital," Laura commented to Jenna.

"I've got to tell you something because I'm afraid Ryan will come after me and kill me," Jenna continued.

"What are you talking about?" asked Laura after they were both seated in Laura's car.

"When Ryan attacked me, he was choking me and said that he would kill me like he killed the Adams guy," she blurted out.

"I thought he was about to kill me after he confessed to killing that Adams guy," she said with a shudder.

They arrived at the E.R. at Wheatland General Hospital and Jenna was ushered immediately into an examination room.

"What happened?" asked Jana House, the Emergency Room R.N, as she looked at the damaged face.

"Were you involved in a Domestic Violence assault?" she asked as she looked over at Laura who was nodding her head yes.

"Yes, it happened in the hills west of Soap Lake," Jenna replied.

"OK, let's get you into a hospital gown and the Doctor can do an examination," she said and closed the door of the small exam room.

Jana House walked back to the nurses' station, giving Jenna time to change into the gown.

Dr. Glen Pierce was on duty and looked up as Jana approached him as he was sitting in the nurses' station writing patient notes on their charts.

"Doctor, there is a woman in E.R. room two that has been viciously assaulted in a Domestic Violence situation."

"Please contact the Police Department and have an officer respond to take a report," the Doctor directed the nurse.

"Yes, Doctor, I will do it right away," she responded.

Dr. Pierce walked down the hallway to the exam room where he introduced himself to Jenna.

A few minutes later Nurse Jana House entered the room and stood by while the doctor did an exam of Jenna to check for further injury.

"Young lady, you have a pretty good cut on your lip that will require several stitches," he said.

"You have a pretty big impact on the right side of your face by your right eye and we need to have an X-ray to make sure the orbital bone is not fractured," he said.

"The blood in your right eye will diminish and should be gone after a week or two," he explained to Jenna.

"If your vision changes, be sure and contact a vision specialist," he continued.

"The bite mark on your shoulder is pretty nasty looking and a human bite is often prone to infection," he said.

"The nurse will clean it up, and if you haven't had a tetanus shot in the past 5 years I can give you the injection and an antibiotic to put on the wound twice a day," he instructed her.

As the doctor finished, a Nurses Assistant assigned to the X-ray and Nuclear Medicine section came into the room with a wheel chair to transport Jenna for her x-ray.

Canyon County Sheriff's Deputy Jason Bell made contact with Laura Strawn as she stood outside the emergency room entrance talking on her cell phone.

"Deputy, my name is Laura Strawn and I am the person that drove Jenna Edwards to the hospital," she explained.

"A guy named Ryan Bates beat the shit out of her when she turned him down after he asked for a relationship," Laura said.

"Before you talk to Jenna, she told me that when Ryan was trying to strangle her, he told her that he was going to kill her just like he did the Adams guy," Laura said.

"Ryan also bit her real hard on the shoulder," she continued.

"I hope her black eye is not worse, and Jenna could lose sight of her eye," she said.

"When Ryan dropped Jenna off he told her that he would kill her and her family if she told the cops," Laura continued further.

"Thanks, I will interview Jenna when the doctor is through treating her," Deputy Bell replied.

Deputy Bell entered the Emergency Treatment location and walked up to the Nurses Station where he contacted RN Jana House.

"I can honestly say that I have never had a DV victim come into the ER with injuries such as this woman has suffered at the hands of her boyfriend," Jana told the Deputy.

"That human bite on her shoulder looks like the guy tried to actually bite a chunk out of her right shoulder," she said.

"Come along, I'll walk you back to the exam room," she said to Deputy Bell.

As they parted the privacy curtain and stepped in, Jenna had a fearful look on her face.

"It's all right, ma'am, I'm here to make sure you are alright and obtain some information from you for my incident report," he said softly, which had a calming effect on Jenna.

She nodded slowly and then replied that she would like to tell him the circumstances of her assault by Ryan Bates.

Jenna sat at the edge of the bed and asked that her friend Laura be allowed to come into the exam room while she disclosed her information.

Laura was summoned by the ER nurse and sat in the bedside chair while Jenna explained the circumstances of her assault by Ryan Bates.

"Jenna, you left out the part that Ryan had told her that he would kill you just like he did the Adams guy," Laura interrupted.

"Is that true?" asked Deputy Bell.

Jenna looked fearful as she described the comment Ryan had made as he was trying to strangle her.

"Yes, Ryan told me that, and I almost forgot," she paused, "Ryan said Juan Garcia was with him when he killed Adams!"

"Please, I don't want Ryan arrested for beating me up, he said he will kill me and my family if I called the police," she pleaded.

"Ma'am, this is a domestic violence and a mandatory arrest will be made if Ryan is located," he replied.

"Do you have someone that can pick you up and give you a ride home?" he asked.

Laura interrupted and told Deputy Bell that she could give Jenna a ride home.

"No, I don't want to go home, if Ryan finds out the police were called, he will show up at my house and beat me some more," she pleaded.

Laura interrupted and told Jenna that she could stay with her in Soap Lake and Ryan would not know where she was at.

Jenna had a grateful look on her battered face.

"Any idea where Ryan could be found this evening?" asked Deputy Bell.

"He has a side chick named Carlene," she replied.

Jenna checked out of the ER after she had been advised the orbital bone that protected her right eye had not been fractured from Ryan's hard fist.

They drove back to Laura's apartment and Jenna took a prescribed pain pill and laid down on the living room couch where the effects of the pain medication had her soon slumbering away.

Deputy Bell phoned in a locate request for Ryan Bates and the Tri-County Communications operator scanned information of Ryan Bates.

"We have a possible address for Ryan Bates," the Communications operator relayed to Deputy Bell. "Several weeks ago there was a fight call at E 613 6th in Wheatland and Ryan was contacted and was staying with Carlene Holland. White female, Brown and Brown, about 5'6", 125 libs. Several weeks ago."

"Thanks, Cindy," he told the Communications Dispatcher.

"Would you put out a BOLO on Ryan Bates, he should be driving a white 4X4 Chevy Pick-up with a bear paw sticker in the back right rear window of his pick-up truck," Deputy Bell requested.

Less than 10 minutes later Wheatland Police Officer Stan Franks called in that the white Chevy pick-up was parked in front of Carlene Holland's residence.

Deputy Bell headed for the address and requested assistance from the Wheatland Police Department.

When he was about a block away he cut his lights and pulled beside Officer Franks who had been maintaining surveillance on Ryan's white Chevy Pick-up.

"Officer Jackson is parked in the alley behind the residence and covering the back door in case Bates makes a break for it," Franks informed Bell.

Officer Franks and Deputy Bell crept upon the house without turning on their flashlights.

Deputy Bell gave a loud rap on the door and waited for an answer at the door while officer Franks stood at the corner of the house, looking down the side of the house.

After waiting a full minute his incessant loud knock brought a response and the woman identified as Carlene Holland came to the door and opened it halfway.

"What do you want at this time of night?" she enquired.

'We're looking for Ryan Bates, is he here?" he asked.

"No, haven't seen him for a week or so," she replied.

"Look, we have good information that he is here," said Deputy Bell.

"If he is inside I will arrest you for providing false information to a police officer and obstructing if I find out you lied to me," Bell sternly told her.

Just then Ryan Bates appeared behind Carlene and identified himself and invited Deputy Bell and Officer Franks inside.

"What's this about?" Ryan asked innocently.

"It's about that little dust-up you had with Jenna this afternoon out at the Canyon," Deputy Bell revealed.

"Oh, that," Ryan replied, "we were hiking up there and Jenna tripped on the way down and got skinned up pretty good."

"That doesn't explain that nasty bite the lady had on her shoulder," Deputy Bell said to Ryan.

Ryan's gaze met Deputy Bell's eyes and he spun around before Deputy Bell could grab him, and ran into the kitchen area of the small house and jerked the back door open and started to run across the backyard towards the alley.

He only made a few steps before Wheatland Police Officer Bill Jackson tackled Ryan and slammed him face first into the lawn with such force that Ryan was incapacitated, trying to suck enough oxygen into his body.

"You're under arrest for 3rd Degree Assault with Domestic Violence enhancement and now we'll add a Resisting Arrest charge to sweeten the pot," Deputy Bell told Ryan.

"These charges could get you some jail time," Deputy Bell said with a smile on his face as Ryan was handcuffed, and none too gently.

Ryan held his head down and said nothing as he turned and was walked over to the police cruiser.

When they arrived at the jail Deputy Bell told Ryan for the second time that he was being charged with 3rd Degree Assault with the Domestic Violence enhancement because of the extensive facial injuries Jenna had received from Ryan's fists and the bite to her shoulder.

"You will make your first appearance tomorrow in front of Superior Court Judge Edgar Spartan and he will take your plea and set the bail amount," Deputy Bell told him.

Ryan was booked on the described charges.

"Tell that bitch Jenna that this isn't over yet and she knows what I mean," Ryan said as he was walked back to his assigned cell by a corrections officer.

"This asshole is really unpredictable so put him in a single cell," Deputy Bell told the corrections officer.

"Put him on a high threat designation for the Correction Staff if you would," Deputy Bell said as he spoke to the Jail Shift Commander.

"Not a problem," replied the Jail Commander, "as a matter of fact, we will place Ryan on a suicide watch in Q segment of the jail and he will be placed in a single cell and be checked every 30 minutes."

Deputy Bell left the jail and went to the squad room where he completed his report and indicated an Order of Protection should be placed on Ryan to have no contact with Jenna by Ryan Bates or through a third party.

Deputy Bell also requested that Judge Abigale Clayton, who is on the bench for First Appearance inmates, not reduce the bail for the defendant in light of the severe beating he has committed on the victim Jenna Edwards.

From past experience it was a 50/50 chance the Judge would reduce the bail low enough, so that Ryan could get out of jail on bond the next morning and could walk over next door to get a Public Defender to represent him.

When Deputy Bell finished reading his report for accuracy, he hand wrote an F. I. card (Field Intelligence card) and included information that Ryan Bates had implicated himself in the John Adams Homicide.

He placed the F. I. card into a narrow slot at the top of a locked wooden box marked "F.I. cards" that was sitting on a table at the front of the Patrol Division squad room.

Returning officers would often sit and review their reports and drop off their FI cards in the box.

Usually, within the week the information from FI cards would be entered into an intelligence file.

This secure file was accessible and the information was available to patrol officers' portable mobile data terminals in their squad cars.

They could also input data into their mobile data terminals which they could send to all law enforcement agencies utilizing the Wheatland Police Department Communications System.

Chapter 17

The following Monday morning Detectives Hannigan, Fitz and Skates met in the War room with the unit.

"OK, people, any new developments in the Adams Homicide to share with the group?" Hannigan asked.

Detective Fitz stood up and walked to the front of the room and stopped at the adjoining table where he picked up a stack of documents.

"People, we have another possible suspect that has made himself a little higher on the suspect list. I will pass around a police report submitted by Canyon County Deputy Jason Bell. Last Thursday Deputy Bell responded to an injured female named Jenna Edwards who was being treated at Wheatland General Hospital for severe facial injuries and a severe bite mark on her shoulder. The victim reported she had been on a hike with Ryan Bates on a trail where the trailhead starts on the west side of soap Lake and travels through wild horse canyon to a ledge about 500 ft. from the canyon bottom. They hiked back down to the parking lot where Ryan Bate's pick-up was parked. There was some type of verbal disagreement between the victim and Ryan Bates. Ryan is alleged to have slapped and beat the female with his fists and bit her on the left shoulder which required several stitches from the deep bite wound. Her lip was split wide open and required stitches and the doctors thought at first that several facial bones were shattered. Ryan had dumped the victim off at the edge of Soap Lake and drove off after making death threats to her. The victim, Jenna Edwards, walked to a friend's house in Soap Lake and her friend took her to Wheatland General Hospital. Since the crime occurred in the county, Deputy Jacob Bell responded and took a report from Jenna Edwards. She described the assault she received from Ryan but also told Deputy Bell that when Ryan was trying to strangle or choke her, he said he would kill her just like he killed the Adams guy. He also told her that Juan Garcia was with him. When Jenna was at her friend's house she had also told her friend named Laura Strawn that Ryan had made the admission of killing John Adams to her," he added for further emphasis.

"I just checked over at the jail and Ryan Bates is still in jail and won't have his first appearance until late afternoon because of the judge's heavy work load," he continued.

"So there has been no bond set yet for Bates. That also means he has not been assigned a Public Defender Attorney yet."

"Detectives Zollars and Fitz, go over to the jail and do an interview with Ryan Bates and make sure you read Deputy Bell's report and pull any files out of police records," Hannigan said.

"I will write up a search warrant for the three phones we recovered from Marianne Shutt, her mother Terri Shutt's old cell phone that Marianne also used, and John Adams's cell phone we have recovered. After the judge signs the search warrant, I will take the recovered phones to the Identification and Forensic unit and have the text messages and photos downloaded. Also, I will have the Judge sign an additional search warrant to be served on Adobe phone service requesting a record of all ongoing and incoming phone calls on all three phones," Hannigan said.

"The Washington State Patrol Crime Lab in Cheney, Washington has notified me and they should have the results of any DNA found on the handcuffs and shell casing found in the front yard at John Adams's residence. Let's get a signed search warrant to obtain DNA swab's from Ryan Bates and Juan Garcia," he said to Detective Massee.

"We're getting some pressure from the brass to get this case wrapped up. The Mayor is getting phone calls from friends and family of John Adams demanding that we do more on this case. John's dad has been interviewed by the local news media and also did an on camera interview with the local TV news station. People, we have been authorized extra funds for travel and overtime so let's get with the program," he continued.

"Thanks, and let's have a good week and follow up on any leads we come up with," he said to the group as the meeting ended.

Chapter 18

Detective Tom Zollars and Joel Fitz walked over to the County Jail, and after locking their weapons in a lock box, were allowed entry into the confines of the jail.

"We're here to see Ryan Bates, if you could bring him down to the interview room," Tom Zollars said to the control room operator, who was stationed in a booth surrounded by bullet proof glass windows.

The interview room they would use was wired with audio and video equipment and could be used as evidence in court if the defendant had approved the use of the equipment to record his interview.

Zollars and Fitz were sitting in the interview room when the two corrections officers brought Ryan Bates into the room and sat him down facing the one way glass window on the wall.

Ryans' hands were placed in front and his handcuffed wrists were attached to a raised metal pipe that had been placed several inches above the surface of the metal interview table.

"I'm Detective Zollars and this is Detective Fitz, and we would like to talk to you about a recent incident," he said.

Ryan looked up at both detectives and replied, "Let me save you some time, I have the right to remain silent, anything I say can be used against me in a court of law, I have the right to an attorney, and if I cannot afford one, then one will be provided for me. Yes, I understand my rights and I would like to wave my rights and talk to you guys."

"Do you mind if we audio and video record our conversation?" asked Detective Skates.

"Heck no, I want our conversation audio and video recorded," he replied confidently.

"Ryan, I still have to read your Constitutional Rights and also obtain permission to audio video our conversation," said Detective Fitz.

Detective Fitz walked out of the room to turn on the audio video equipment and while he was momentarily gone, no questions were asked of Ryan.

"OK, we are recording," he said and walked back into the interview room.

Detective Zollars then introduced himself and Detective Fitz and provided the time and date for the interview with Ryan Bates.

Ryan Bates was advised of his Constitutional Rights which he waived and also verbally gave permission for the audio and video of the Interview.

"First, we would like to talk to you about the assault of Jenna Edwards that resulted in your arrest over at Carlene Holland's house over on 6th."

"I know I was booked into jail for Assault on that bitch Jenny Edwards and for Domestic Violence," Ryan spat out.

"First of all, she was not my girlfriend and we never lived together so I'm not guilty of a Domestic Violence charge," he explained to the Detectives.

"And I never assaulted Jenna, she was the one that invited me for a walk in the canyon so she could have sex with me. She wanted more from the relationship and when I said no, she attacked me and scratched my face and back. I finally got her to calm down so I drove her back to Soap Lake and dropped her off."

"How did she get the black eye and the split lip that took several stitches to close?" Fitz asked.

"When we were walking back down the trail back to the pick-up truck Jenna tripped and fell and planted her face in the ground," he replied.

"How did Jenna get the nasty bite mark on her shoulder?"

"I have no idea how she got that, but it wasn't me," Ryan replied.

Detective Fitz got out of his chair and walked around behind Ryan and pulled up his shirt.

"Well, I'll be," he said. "There are no scratch marks on your back or on your face," Detective Fitz commented.

"Wanna stick with that story or just set down and work this out?" said Zollars.

"By the way, when Jenna's bite mark was treated at the hospital, it was swabbed for DNA and it's obvious your DNA will be identified," he said.

Ryan's face blanched and he looked down at the table and the handcuffs rattled against the pipe as his hands shook.

"With your past criminal record I think the Prosecutor will get you at least a year in the County jail," Detective Fitz Commented.

"Now, we would like to ask you if you knew John Adams," Fitz said as he stared directly into Ryan's face.

Ryan's eyes widened and for a brief second there was a look of panic on his face.

Ryan's hands were frozen and there was no rattling sound of the handcuffs for a good 30 seconds.

Detective Fitz could clearly see that Ryan was thinking of a response that would not implicate himself.

"Let me think about it and if I can make some type of deal, I'll talk," he replied.

"OK, you have my card, and when you decide, let the corrections officer know and he will get in touch with me," Fitz said as he looked down at Ryan.

Without another word they left the interview room and walked back to the War Room.

Hannigan was waiting for them as they walked through the door.

"Well, what did Ryan say when confronted?" he asked.

Zollars responded, "As we thought he would do, he denied the assault on Jenna and said she fell down on the pathway on the hike and sustained her injuries, but he got pretty rattled when he was told the bite mark on Jenna's shoulder had been swabbed for DNA to compare to his DNA."

"We asked him if he knew John Adams and he looked like he was in shock, so about 30 seconds later he made no admissions but did say he would think about it and maybe he could make a deal with us," Zollars continued.

"We stopped the interview and will give him some time to stew over our question about John Adams," said Det. Zollars.

"That sounds like a plan, but don't drag it out too long, the Sheriff and Police Chief want this wrapped up as soon as possible."

"Find us a person of interest that we can feed to the media and will take the heat off us," Det. Hannigan told Det. Zollars and Det. Fitz.

"I think we need to travel to The Dalles and have a talk with this Dustin Silver. Clear your calendars for Wednesday, the day after tomorrow, and pack your overnight bags, no telling where this is going to lead us," Hannigan told Detective Fitz and Detective Skates.

"When we interviewed Marianne Shutt and she advised Dustin had an ex-girlfriend name Samantha Fox that lived in The Dalles, Oregon and attended the local college. Marianne said that over the past year Dustin hardly ever had a place he could call home, so he would use Samantha's apartment as a home base. Marianne thought Samantha's Dad was a cop someplace in Wyoming. Fitz, would you do an NCIC and WACIC search for Samantha so we can get a current address? If she is not in the system, check social media and TLB, the skip trace company the Sheriff's office uses. Detective Skates, please review the recorded interview we did with Marianne and pick out the inconsistencies of her story."

Wednesday morning Detective Fitz, Skates and Detective Hannigan met in the War Room to pick-up case related notes and background on Samantha and Dustin, before leaving for The Dalles, Oregon.

The trip to The Dalles was about a 3 1/2 hr. drive to cover the 200 mile distance so they had plenty of time to discuss their plan.

"Let's talk to Samantha first if Dustin is not there and see if she knows Dustin's whereabouts on the morning of December 28th," Hannigan commented.

They traveled through the Yakima Valley and started up Satus Pass.

The highway surface was broken with ice and packed snow which forced Hannigan to slow the unmarked Sheriff's Unit.

"Looks like we're over the worst of the icy road," he said as they passed over the summit to the west side of the pass.

All of a sudden Det. Hannigan jammed on the brakes when a jack knifed semi truck loomed ahead.

The cab of the truck was lying on it's side, partially obscured by the snowbank at it's final resting position.

The ABS brake system on the Detective's car prevented a total skid and he was able to stop in time.

Hannigan turned on the emergency flashers on his vehicle as Detectives Fitz and Skates walked down to check on the driver.

Detective Skates peered through the windshield and spotted the driver inside trying to kick out the windshield so he could exit the cab.

The outer edge of the windshield was leaning out so Skates grabbed the edge, pulling the windshield outward.

The driver scrambled out of the cab and stood at the side of the road with Fitz and Skates.

"Are you injured?" Fitz asked the driver.

"No, just my pride," the driver answered. "I came around that bend back there," as he pointed behind him.

"There was a car stopped in the middle of the road and some gal had her camera out the passenger window and was taking pictures of some deer," he said.

"I swerved and jammed the brakes to avoid hitting the car, but you can see the results," the truck driver continued.

"I have already phoned my trucking company to get a heavy tow up here to get me going, it looks like the passenger door and mirror and windshield are damaged but otherwise the rig looks pretty good. I was hauling an empty trailer, on the way back to load up in The Dalles. The damn car that was in the middle of the road just drove off without even stopping to check on me," he growled.

A few minutes later two Washington State Patrol vehicles arrived on scene.

Hannigan spoke to the first trooper and told him they had not witnessed the accident but had helped get the driver out of the truck.

He handed the trooper a Canyon County Sheriff business card and the Detectives got into their county car and continued their trip to The Dalles, Oregon.

They crossed the bridge across the Columbia River and arrived in The Dalles about 1 1/2 hours behind their schedule.

They spent another 20 minutes locating the apartment complex about 1/2 mile downstream from The Dalles Dam.

The apartment was located on the second floor of a small complex with less than 40 apartment units.

Detective Skates knocked softly on the door and stood to one side of the door.

A safety method he had retained in his memory since he had been a rookie patrol officer.

Detectives Fitz and Hannigan stood at the other side of the door along the wall.

The vibration of the landing near the door indicated someone was walking up to the door from the inside.

The door opened about 3 inches and was restrained from opening further by a chain lock.

"Hello, who is it?" came a female voice from the other side.

Fitz stood in front of the door where the female could clearly see his face.

"Ma'am, my name is Detective Fitz and I have Detectives Hannigan and Skates with me. We're here to talk to your friend Dustin Silver and understand he is living at this address," he said.

"Do you have identification?' she asked.

Detective Fitz removed his credentials from his inside coat pocket and displayed his photo identification to her.

The door closed and the sound of the security chain being released was audible.

The door opened again and Samantha Fox stood to the side and invited the officers inside.

She directed them to a tall kitchen table with bar height stools and she invited them to be seated.

"As I said, we are here to talk to Dustin about the incident over in Wheatland, Washington," said Detective Fitz as he sat down at the stool.

Is this about the guy that was shot back on December 28th last year?" she asked.

"Yes, Dustin's name got brought up in an interview with a lady living over in Waterville."

"Must have been Marianne," she said without expecting a reply.

"Do you know where Dustin was at on the 27th of December?" enquired Det. Hannigan.

"Well, yes, I do," Samantha replied.

"I work part time at The Dalles General Hospital and when I left for work about 7:00 A.M. he was still in bed," she replied.

"Did you actually see him in bed when you left?" Hannigan asked.

"I slept in the same bed with him so I guess I should know because I walked right by him and gave him a kiss," she said with a quizzical look towards Hannigan.

"His jeans were still laying on the floor by the bed," she added.

"Before I left, Dustin invited me to go on his route to pick up some car parts in Seaside Oregon. I had taken time off from work in the past and rode with him on his route but I couldn't get the time off so he said he was heading to southern Oregon instead," she continued.

"He did call me about 11:00 A.M. and told me he was in Kennewick, Washington, then he was headed for Pendleton Oregon because he had to look at classic Mopar car parts there," she said.

"He telephoned me about 10:00 A.M. on December 28th, he said that his ex-girlfriend Marianne had telephoned him and told him that her boyfriend had been shot and killed. Dustin said Marianne was suspicious that he was involved and she threatened to kill Dustin if he was responsible," she continued.

"Dustin said Marianne wasn't making sense and babbling and told Dustin her boyfriend was shot with a shotgun."

"Does Dustin own a shotgun?" Hannigan asked her.

"I've known Dustin for over 5 years and never known him to have a firearm. Dustin told me that he was going to continue on his route to buy collector car parts. I've got a couple of handguns that I keep for protection and have them here in my apartment," she revealed.

Detective Skates' eyebrows lifted as he exchanged looks with Detective Fitz.

"Why do you have the firearms?" Detective Skates asked as he leaned forward in an attempt to intimidate Samantha.

"I'm sure you guys have heard of the 2nd Amendment, haven't you?" she stared back at Detective Skates.

"What caliber are the handguns?" Detective Hannigan snapped at her.

"Why do you ask?" Marianne said. "The guy was shot with a shotgun."

"Look, young lady, you can find yourself in big trouble if you refuse to cooperate with us," Hannigan said ominously.

"You could be found guilty of being an accessory to the murder," he threatened.

"Either get those guns out and show us or I am going to apply for a search warrant and will tear your place apart looking for evidence," he said directly to Samantha.

"If you continue that line of questioning, you can all get the hell out of my apartment," she said in a tone that left no ultimatum.

"My dad is a cop out of state and I understand you would need to have credible and reliable information that would establish there is probable cause to believe there is evidence related to the Wheatland murder in my apartment," she commented further.

"I won't be intimidated, Detective Hannigan, you're acting like a street thug," she stated directly to Detective Hannigan.

"Change your line of questioning or you thugs can get out and not come back," she snapped as her nostrils flared.

"I'm sorry, Samantha, I didn't mean to offend you and hope we can continue our conversation," Hannigan said.

If Detective Hannigan had been wearing a hat he would have been holding it in his hands as a sign of defeat from Samantha.

Detectives Fitz and Skates leaned back in their seats as a sign for Detective Hannigan to continue speaking with Samantha.

"You've been put on notice," she spoke defiantly to Detective Hannigan.

"Dustin and I were together about 5 years ago and pretty serious, but as time went on we found that we would be lifelong friends, but neither of us wanted a full blown commitment," Samantha mused.

"Dustin has always been honest with me and has told me he wishes the best for Marianne, but knows he could never trust her and her appetite for different men," she continued.

"You might talk to Marianne and ask her what other men have been with her around Waterville or Wheatland," she said to Detective Skates.

"What do you mean?" Detective Hannigan asked.

"She has a habit of developing a few friends with benefits wherever she lives. You might want to grab her cellphone and check it out," she said.

"What would I find?" he asked.

"In the past Marianne used to pose in the nude and take all types of suggestive positions on her cell phone and post them to the different men in her life."

"How do you know that?" Hannigan asked.

"My friend that used to live here in The Dalles worked for a cab company and Marianne would phone him for a ride," she said.

"Marianne never had money for the cab ride, so how do you think she paid for the cab ride before she got to her destination? My friend showed me some photos on his cell phone of Marianne paying for her ride when they were parked along the roadway. She also sent him nude photos and I actually saw them," she continued.

"Dustin was aware of Marianne's behavior because the cab diver had stayed with Dustin for a while and showed him the photos. At the time Dustin was still having sex with Marianne, but it was strictly for the sex and he knew her body was a well used commodity. Dustin didn't want anything to do with Marianne other than for the sex or to see his son once in a while," Samantha mused.

"What kind of vehicle was Dustin driving when he left on his trip this morning?" Det. Hannigan asked.

"Dustin had his pick-up here and when I left for work and came home after work, his pick-up was gone," she answered.

"Do you know when Dustin will be getting back to your place?" she was asked.

"Dustin actually phoned me today on his cell phone and told me he would be coming from Twin Falls, Idaho where he sold a load of catalytic converters he had picked up on his route," she said.

"Dustin was pretty excited that he had found some Mopar parts outside of Boise, Idaho and had bought a load of valuable classic car parts, including some Slap Stick transmissions and two 426 Hemi engines that were in good condition," she continued.

"He keeps all of his parts in a storage unit at the edge of town, so he will be dropping the parts off before he comes here," she said.

"I expect him back about 10:00 P.M. tonight so if you want to see him, come by tomorrow morning," she said.

"It is my day off so I'll also be here," she finished.

"Thanks, Samantha, you have been a great help and we'll stop by tomorrow morning," Hannigan told her.

"Oh, I almost forgot, can I have your phone number in case I need to ask you more questions?" he asked.

"Of course, here is my cell number. I'm still on my dad's family phone plan in Wyoming," said Samantha.

"Please, give me Dustin's phone number in case we miss him tomorrow morning," he asked.

"Dustin's number is 304-424-8899."

"Does Dustin have a toothbrush that he leaves here when on his trips or does he take it with him?" Skates asked.

"If he does have one here, I'd like to take it for DNA testing which might prove David's innocence in the Adams Homicide," he said to Samantha.

As Samantha walked back into the bedroom area, he turned his head slightly towards Hannigan and Fitz and gave them a wink and a slight smile.

Samantha had looked back as she entered the bedroom and turned when she saw Detective Skates winking with a wolfish grin on his face.

She walked back into the living room and faced Detective Skates.

"I saw that smart ass smirk on your face, so if you want Dustin's toothbrush. you better change your tone. Dustin always keeps his bathroom locked for privacy but I know where the key is located and will unlock the door and get the toothbrush if you are asking me to do that," she said.

"I am asking," he replied.

A moment later she came back into the kitchen area and gave Hannigan Dustin's toothbrush and handed it to Hannigan with her bare hand.

Hannigan instinctively reached out and accepted the toothbrush with his bare hand, depositing his own DNA onto the toothbrush.

"Now, get the hell out of here," she spoke loudly and opened the apartment door as the three detectives filed out.

Detective Skates had produced a small brown paper bag from the inside of his jacket, and Det. Hannigan dropped the toothbrush inside and Skates put it back into his coat pocket.

"Wow, that bitch was really pissed at you," Detective Hannigan told Skates.

"I just kind of smirked as she was walking away and she caught me," he replied, and it was obvious from his red face that he was embarrassed.

Samantha stood in the hallway after they left, musing that Marianne was still angry with her because Dustin had moved in with her.

The detectives stood outside their car and discussed their plans.

Hannigan said, "Let's find a place to stay tonight and first thing in the morning we'll knock on Samantha's door."

"I have to tell the wife I won't be home tonight," mused Hannigan. "She is not going to be happy that I'm missing a visit from my in-laws."

"Good idea," answered Fitz and Skates.

They checked in at the Best West Motel and agreed to meet at Fitz's room in an hour and go find a place to eat.

"In the meantime I am going to start preparing a search warrant for the cell activity on both Samantha and Dustin's cell phones," Hannigan said.

"Come Monday or Tuesday, I'll take the Search Warrant Application to the Judge in Wheatland to sign," said Hannigan, "but I'll need to obtain a search warrant from an Oregon Magistrate to obtain Dustin's cell phone."

After a late dinner the three Detectives retired to their rooms for the evening.

Dustin drove by Pendleton, Oregon on the main interstate and continued to Bigg's Junction where he fueled up his pick-up truck.

Biggs Junction, Oregon consisted of four fueling stations and several drive through restaurants with the same tasteless hamburgers and fries.

There was only one sit-down restaurant at the junction and Dustin chose it because he had been driving hard all day.

He knew the food was good from his frequent trips that brought him by there while on his routes to find classic auto parts.

His cell phone rang and he was pleased to see the caller was Samantha.

"Hey Dustin, there were three cops from Wheatland that came by to talk to you."

"Don't worry about it," Dustin laughed, "I don't have anything to do with John Adams murder."

"I'll see you tonight," he said.

"That cop Hannigan is a real asshole," she said.

"He thinks he is a real smart guy and could intimidate me until I basically told him to back off," she said as the conversation ended.

By the time Dustin got back to The Dalles it was about 8:00 P.M.

He stopped by his storage unit and used his portable engine lift to remove the big block Mopar engines from the bed of his truck.

He thought about the fine profit he was going to make from the sale of the car parts he had collected and brought to the storage unit.

Tomorrow he would do a compression check on the engine cylinders of the Hemi engines and the slap stick auto transmissions that are hard to find and used to restore classic Mopar Muscle Cars.

I paid $10,000 cash for all these parts and have the receipt and I know I can get an easy $25,000 out of them, he thought.

Dustin left the storage unit and drove to Samantha's apartment where he parked his truck in the parking lot and used his key to enter Samantha's apartment.

"Oh good, you're home," Samantha said as Dustin dropped his keys on the table and sat at one of the bar stools.

"The cops were here to see you today and I told them you would be getting home late tonight," she said.

She held out a business card with the name of Detective Joel Fitz.

"There were two other Detectives with him, one had a last name of Hannigan and I forget the name of the other cop," she said.

"What did they want, as if I didn't know," Dustin said disgustedly.

"I'm sure Marianne would try to cause me problems since she knows we are living together," he said.

"I know," said Samantha, "she still thinks we are intimate, she said with a wink and a smile."

"They will be back tomorrow morning to talk to you," she told Dustin.

"They asked for your toothbrush so I gave it to give them," she told him.

"One of the detectives said it could help clear you," she said, "but I don't trust those assholes."

"That Det. Hannigan gave me the creeps the way he looked at me when I told him Marianne would send nude photos," she said.

"I swore I saw Hannigan's tongue hanging out when we talked about Marianne's nude photos. That guy is definitely a Creeper so he must really enjoy asking personal questions to women," she chuckled.

"Did the Detective say he had a search warrant to obtain my toothbrush?" he asked.

"No," she said and bit her lower lip.

"I have nothing to hide," Dustin said.

"When they came into our place, did they tell you they were recording your conversation and then ask permission to record?"

"Well, no, they didn't say anything about recording our conversation," she replied.

"Hard telling, but they probably forgot they were out of their jurisdiction since we live in Oregon and they are Washington Cops." he said.

"Did they ask if I was paying you rent for the bedroom and personal restroom," Dustin asked.

"No, I don't recall any of them asking me," she replied.

"But they know your room was locked and I told them that you didn't allow anyone in your bedroom," she continued.

"Let me take a shower and we'll have a beer and watch a movie if you would like," he said to Samantha.

"That would be great, I'll grab a soft blanket and we can lay back on the couch and relax with a good adventure movie. We have some cold tall bottles in the fridge and I'll pop a bowl of popcorn while you're in the shower," she said.

"It will be good to get to bed after the movie," Dustin told her.

Dustin stood in the shower and felt the hot steamy water wash the grime off him, since the last night he had slept in the cab of his pick-up truck near Bend, Oregon.

He had been afraid to leave his prize cargo of auto parts and engines in the back of his truck unguarded.

Anybody with knowledge of engines would have easily identified the two engines in his truck bed as Hemisphere high performance engines.

The next morning Detectives Hannigan, Fitz and Skates were sitting in the Outlaw Cafe having breakfast.

"We need to get over to the apartment before Dustin Silver leaves for the day," Hannigan said.

They had a quick breakfast and after finishing a last cup of coffee, they headed over to locate Dustin Silver at Samantha Fox's apartment.

Dustin was in the apartment parking lot at his pick-up truck, kneeling down and checking tire pressure on his vehicle when Hannigan drove into the parking lot.

"I think that's Dustin over there by the pick-up truck," Skates said from the front passenger seat of the unmarked Police car and pointed towards Dustin.

"Here's a parking space," Hannigan said as he guided the unmarked Police car into the parking slot next to Dustin's pick-up truck.

As they approached Dustin's pick-up truck he raised up from his kneeling position and turned to meet the Detectives.

He had an appraising look on his face and was wiping the grease off his hands before throwing the rag into the back of his pick-up.

"You guys the cops from Wheatland that was here yesterday looking for me?" he asked.

Detectives Skates smiled disarmingly at Dustin and said, "Yes, we came over Satus Pass yesterday to The Dalles hoping to contact you for a few questions."

"How can I help you guys?" he asked.

Hannigan broke in and said, "Dustin, we are here to talk to you about the John Adams murder over in Wheatland, Washington last December 28th. It's pretty cold out here, is there someplace warmer that we could talk?" he asked Dustin.

"Well, I don't want my girlfriend Samantha having to sit there and listen to your line of questions," Dustin said.

They agreed to sit in the unmarked police car and stay parked in the apartment parking lot.

Hannigan sat in the driver's seat and Dustin sat in the right front passenger seat.

"Tell me, Dustin, where were you the night of December 27th and the morning of the 28th?"

"I left The Dalles on the 27th about 9:00 A.M. at the start of my circular route, checking out wrecking yards along the way, checking yards in Pasco and Kennewick. I picked up some 460 Holly double pump carbs at Valley Wrecking in Kennewick and about 35 catalytic converters at the muffler shop down the street. I made it back to Oregon and stayed at the big truck stop at the edge of Pendleton and spent the night in my pick-up. You can check out Valley Wrecking that I was there buying car parts if you don't believe me," he said.

"What time did you leave The Dalles on the 27th?" Hannigan asked.

"Weren't you listening, I just told you I left about 9.00 A.M," Dustin responded, "and got into the Tri-cities and spent the day looking for expensive used auto parts at the salvage yards. I must have cleared out of there and headed back into Oregon about 6:00 P.M. and found my way to Pendleton where I spent the night."

"Is that pick-up parked in the parking lot next to this police car, the one you were driving back then?" Detective Fitz asked.

"Yes, it is my truck and I have had it for over a year," Dustin replied.

"How long have you had those tires on your pick-up?" asked Det. Skates.

"I have had the same mud and snow tires on my truck since last October when I bought them at Orbachs Discount Tire in the Dalles, Oregon," Dustin replied.

"Do you mind if we take photos of the tire treads?" asked Detective Fitz.

"Not a problem, fact is, when we finish our conversation I'll show the dated sales receipt for the tires and you can take your photos," he replied.

"Let's talk about the morning of the 28th," Hannigan said to Dustin.

"Where were you at 6:30 A.M. on the 28th?" Hannigan asked.

"I told you that I was sleeping in my truck near Pendleton, Oregon and I fueled up there before heading over to Baker, Oregon on my route."

"Did you use a credit card to pay for your fuel?" Detective Fitz asked.

"No, I don't have credit cards, I always pay in cash. But I'm sure they have security cameras that will show I was there," Dustin said.

Afterwards I had breakfast at the cafe next to the truck stop where I fueled.

"I guess that would be your job to do the checking since I don't have to prove anything," Dustin directed his comment to Detective Hannigan.

"Wheatland is about 90 miles from Kennewick and you could have driven there overnight or early morning from Kennewick and been back in the Kennewick area in an hour and a half," Detective Fitz said with an accusatory tone to his comment.

"You guys are really reaching, trying to make a case against me," Dustin tersely commented.

"Look at the security video at the Pendleton truck stop before you start accusing me," he continued.

"Well, Dustin, you need to come up with a receipt from the Pendleton truck stop or you don't have an alibi as to your whereabouts," Detective Hannigan said tersely.

"Are you deaf? Didn't you hear what I just said?" Dustin replied to Hannigan.

"I never had anything to do with John Adams murder," Dustin answered.

"You need to look around Wheatland for the killer," he replied.

"Marianne Shutt says she called you about 9:00 A.M., a short time after John's murder, and you told her you were in Pendleton, Oregon headed to Boise to get auto parts," said Detective Fitz.

"Before she told me about John Adams murder I thought she was trying to set up a meeting with me for a tryst when she asked where I was at. No, I was in Pendleton and spent the night of the 27th at the

Pendleton truck stop. I think I'm done talking to you folks so if I'm free to go, this conversation is ending," he said.

"Wait," said Detective Skates, "we need to check your truck for a gas receipt from Pendleton, Oregon and the dated sales receipt for the tires you said you bought the mud and snow tires."

"No problem," said Dustin as he stepped out of the unmarked police car with the three Detectives following close behind.

Dustin opened the passenger door of his pick-up truck and first checked the jockey box for the receipts.

After not finding a gas receipt he sifted through the fast food bags and receipts lying on the passenger floor.

"I found it," he said as he held a piece of paper up and walked around the side of his pick-up truck and handed the document to Detective Hannigan.

The receipt revealed four Hankook mud and snow tires were sold to Dustin Silver on October 16th.

They were Hankook xtreme tires with an aggressive tire pattern.

The tire store logo was imprinted at the top of the receipt.

"I'll take that back," Dustin held his hand out and Detective Hannigan reluctantly handed the receipt back.

"Can't find the gas receipt right now but will let you know when I find it."

"What size are your shoes?" Detective Fitz asked.

Dustin lifted his high top tennis shoes up so they could see the sole and told them he wore a size 9.5 shoe.

"Do you mind if we take a photo of your shoe sole pattern, since we are taking photos of your tire tread on your truck?" asked Hannigan.

"Knock yourselves out," replied Dustin.

"Detective Skates, Samantha told me you wanted my toothbrush and she was told a DNA exam of the toothbrush could clear me as a person of interest. If you want something from me, don't be intimidating my house mate to give you guys my personal property," he said with irritation.

"This apartment has separate bathrooms, one in the Master

bedroom and the other in the hallway, which is where I keep my toiletries, and I have exclusive use of that bathroom, Samantha never uses it," said Dustin.

"In fact, I have a key lock on the bathroom door and no one had permission to enter the locked room and get my toothbrush. Did you have an Oregon Issued search warrant to enter my locked bathroom and locked bedroom?" he asked Hannigan.

"Well, no, we didn't," replied Hannigan.

"So you directed someone to act as an agent for you guys who has no business to get into my locked bathroom and bedroom to obtain a personal item of mine?" he asked pointedly towards Hannigan.

"No, we didn't," Hannigan said lamely.

"Why would she go get my toothbrush from my locked bathroom if you did not direct her? I'm just saying that it looks like you tried to use Samantha as an agent for you guys to gather evidence that was not attainable otherwise. You know, I have nothing to hide, but you should all go back and look at the term "Fruit of the Poisonous Tree" which means anything obtained illegally by the Police cannot be used as evidence against the owner of the property seized. I think I have an expectation of privacy in my locked bathroom and bedroom and you did not have a valid search warrant. I think you all know this is a screw-up on your part," he addressed all three Detectives.

"One last thing. When you talked to Samantha the morning before she left for work, you had asked her to go to Seaside with you, so what made you lie to her?" Queried Det. Skates.

"I did want her to go with me to Seaside because I know how much she likes driving on old highway 101 along the coast," Dustin replied.

"But when she said she couldn't get off work, I changed my mind and thought I would drive my eastern Oregon route," replied Dustin.

"One more thing, Detective Skates, when Marianne called me the morning of the 28th she said John Adams had been shot in the back with a shotgun and I've never owned or even fired a shotgun in my life!" he declared.

"What caliber are the handguns that Samantha owns?" Hannigan asked.

"I think she already told you to screw off when you asked her," Dustin replied.

"It would help you if we knew what caliber and the number of handguns Samantha owned," Hannigan answered back.

"How would that help me?" Dustin quipped as he looked Hannigan directly in the eye.

"The guy was killed with a shotgun, what don't you understand, Det. Hannigan, that shotguns are not handguns?" he continued.

Det. Hannigan averted his gaze and looked embarrassed but did not respond.

"Look, fellas, I'm heading over to Idaho down by Idaho Falls to sell my Catalytic converters tomorrow, but you can reach me by cell phone," he said as he walked up the steps to the second floor apartment he shared with Samantha.

"I think we're through here for now," Hannigan said as they walked back to the unmarked police car.

"I know that bastard and his bitch are guilty, I want the focus on our investigation to bear down on Dustin," Hannigan seethed.

"Did he hurt your feelings?" laughed Det Skates as he winked at Detective Fitz.

When the Detectives were driving back to Wheatland, Detective Hannigan was still seething over the attitude Dustin had directed at him.

"That Bastard is way too cocky and it makes me sure that he is our guy. That bullshit about his toothbrush may come back and haunt him because he thinks we may have overstepped our authority," he said.

"We don't even know if there was good DNA left at the scene or the evidence collected so there may not have been a need to worry about the way we collect Silver's toothbrush," Hannigan said to Detective Fitz and Skates.

They gave each other a sidelong glance knowing that Hannigan had indeed overstepped his law enforcement authority when the toothbrush had been unlawfully obtained.

Detective Fitz thought to himself that a simple screw-up like that could jeopardize the entire investigation.

Satus Pass had been plowed and sanded as they made their way over and were back in Wheatland by 2:00 P.M.

"I am logging the toothbrush into the Evidence Property Room and then will be sending it to the Washington State Patrol Crime Lab in Cheney, Washington," he told Fitz and Skates.

The next morning the packaged tooth brush was on it's way to the Crime Lab for analysis with other evidentiary items from the crime scene.

Smaller law enforcement agencies also used the property room at the Canyon County Sheriff's Office Property room.

It was common for the property room evidence filing clerk to deliver more than one item secured in evidence at Canyon County property storage to the WSP Crime Lab in Cheney, Washington.

Dustin's toothbrush was shipped with 8 other non-case related items that had been requested by other law enforcement agencies to swab the items for DNA.

The following Monday Detectives Fitz, Skates and Hannigan were reviewing the case to glean for more potential witnesses when a phone call came from a man named Eric Savage for Detective Hannigan.

"Detective Hannigan, my name is Eric Savage and I live near The Dalles, Oregon. I'm friends with Marianne Shutt and she was telling me about her boyfriend in Wheatland that was shot in the back with a shotgun and killed last December," Savage explained.

"That's right," Hannigan answered, "what can I help you with?"

"Well, I was having a drink at the Long Prairie Bar last Saturday and there was a guy named Dustin Silver in the bar with his friend Samantha Fox. I overheard them talking about that guy in Wheatland that was shot in the back with a shotgun. I heard Dustin laugh and say that Marianne was saying that he, Dustin, had shot this Adams guy in the back with a shotgun," Eric said.

"I was standing nearby and overheard Dustin say that he would never get arrested, and then I couldn't hear the rest of the conversation," he continued.

"How do you know Dustin?" Hannigan asked.

"Dustin has been a thorn in my side for a long time," Eric said.

"Dustin is a male whore and he was sniffing around my ex-girlfriend Bridgett Farmer when I was going with her. Now he is sniffing around Samantha Fox and I've been asking her out, but now she is living with Dustin," Eric replied.

"As I was saying," Eric continued, "I went to another bar called the Lariat Bar awhile later and I noticed Dustin was standing at the bar and flirting with a bunch of girls sitting at the table behind him. I went up to the bar and stood next to Dustin, kind of hanging back. Dustin and I have never got along but he looked over at me and said hello. I asked him how things were going and he glanced over at the young women behind him and winked. Dustin told me he was doing pretty good and it was going to be a lot better later that night, as he glanced at one of the women and winked at her. Dustin said to me, "I guess Marianne's boyfriend got killed and was shot in the back with a shotgun over in Wheatland," Eric told Hannigan.

"He was kind of joking when he told me and I asked him if he did it. He looked me straight in the eye and told me there was no proof he had shot the guy in the back," Eric said.

Hannigan interrupted and told Eric Savage that John Adams had been shot in the chest, likely by a handgun.

"Maybe Dustin didn't say he used a shotgun when I think about it," said Eric.

"The music was pretty loud in the bar so he may have said he shot the guy with a handgun because handgun or shotgun words could sound alike in a noisy place like the bar that night."

"Do you have a grudge against Dustin?" Hannigan asked.

"Not at all," replied Eric.

Eric paused and told Hannigan he did not like Dustin Silver and the more Eric thought about it, he thought Dustin had told him would not be charged and he had interpreted those words to mean Dustin had confessed and used a handgun to shoot John Adams.

Hannigan paused and considered the sketchy information because from past experience it seemed that Eric Savage had just embellished the story of his conversation with Dustin and Eric's motive seemed to be to get Dustin out of the way so he would have access to Samantha.

"OK, Mr. Savage, we will be traveling to The Dalles in 3-4 weeks and I will obtain a statement from you," he said.

"Fine, I will be here, but give me a day's notice so I can put it on my calendar," Eric told Detective Hannigan.

"By the way, I did telephone Marianne since I have been friends with her when she lived in The Dalles," Eric said.

Chapter 19

Two weeks had gone by as the investigation slowed to a crawl for the CBIT team.

The Washington State Patrol Lab Report for any DNA collected from the spent shell casing came back, and they identified an individual's DNA belonging to Officer Matt Winslow.

"What a fricken idiot, he must have picked the shell casing up with his bare hand," said Det. Fritz.

"I think he was probably carrying the 45 Cal. shell casing around in his coat pocket after he picked it up and placed it in a small plastic bag," he said.

"We don't have the bullet or the gun so we don't have much evidence to present there for comparison with the shell casing. John Adam's girlfriend Nancy Williams told us that Adams had a 45 semi auto handgun with Laser sight, so where is it people?" he said to no one in particular.

"I have the WSP lab report on DNA found on the handcuffs," he said, as he read the results of the DNA identification.

"The handcuffs have a DNA mixture of at least four male subjects and DNA from a single female. Only one person was possibly identified from the DNA and that was Dustin Silver. The DNA from Dustin

Silver was recovered from a toothbrush recovered by detectives in The Dalles, Oregon. The rate of DNA identification on Silver was 1 out of 2400 people. The other three DNA collection from males was roughly about the same as Dustin's but they haven't been identified. The unknown female DNA recovered from the handcuffs was much higher and if DNA samples were collected the donor could be pretty easily identified. The Washington State Patrol Crime Lab Forensic Scientist has said that Dustin can't be positively identified as donor from the small DNA amount recovered from the handcuffs but he also can't be excluded," he said.

"That leaves us nowhere, since 30 other people in Canyon County would have the same small strand DNA markers as Dustin" he said gloomily.

Hannigan walked over to the whiteboard and started making notations and drawing lines.

"Let's take a look and throw in everything we have learned so far."

MOTIVE, he wrote on the board.

"Marianne tells us she was still in a relationship with Dustin and sometimes a love triangle is the motive for murder. Dustin Silver certainly had the motive to kill John Adams because he was losing his girlfriend and son to Adams. Marianne has told us she and John were going to get married."

OPPORTUNITY

"Marianne Shutt was meeting Dustin for their trysts in the area. On the morning of the homicide Dustin could show no proof of his location at the time of the murder and he admitted he had been in Tri-Cities the morning of the 27th. That is 90 miles away from the scene and about 1 1/2 hr. drive, but the homicide occurred at 6:30 A.M. on December 28th and Dustin has no credible proof that he was elsewhere."

MEANS

"A firearm was the weapon used to kill John Adams. I am completing a search warrant to ping Dustin Silver's phone so we can get results of Dustin Silver's location the day of the homicide through phone pings on his phone. The Phone service will download and place the locations on a map once the phone service provider is served a search warrant. We will serve a search warrant for Marianne's cell phone and the additional cell phone she received from her mother," said Hannigan.

"I will also prepare the two search warrants to obtain the downloads off the cell phones. Detective Fitz, please contact Oregon Department of Transportation and have them download their images of all vehicles crossing the Oregon state line from Washington, coming from the Tri-Cities. Tell Oregon DOT we are looking for a specific vehicle possibly tied to the December 28th Homicide. Also, mention that the suspect may have been driving a pick-up with an Oregon License plate."

"Anything new on this Ryan Bates and Juan Garcia pair that two witnesses have said killed John Adams?" he asked Detective Zollars.

"No, and there hasn't been any information from the Crime Check Tip Line related to this case, other than the one phone call," he said.

"Det. Fitz were you able to contact the person that called the Tip Line and provided the information on Ryan Bates?" Detective Hannigan asked.

"No, the number she called from was an encrypted phone number that cannot be downloaded and it is almost impossible to trace" Det. Fitz answered.

Detective Hannigan sat at his desk and prepared a search warrant to obtain Dustin's cell phone for examination and contents.

He added a 4th search warrant to serve on Veracity Communications to obtain Dustin's location through phone tower pings.

After preparing a boiler plate description of his qualifications and experience in law enforcement preparing and obtaining past search warrants, he started on the facts supporting each search warrant and what he was hoping to obtain.

All four search warrants included the same wording:

Dustin had made threats to harm John Adams.

Dustin had been stalking Marianne and John Adams.

Marianne was fearful of Dustin Silver.

Additionally, there was text and e-mail information believed to be located on the three cell phones that would disclose conversations between Marianne Shutt and Dustin Silver that could incriminate Dustin Silver regarding the John Adams murder.

The fourth Search Warrant application sought to prove the whereabouts of Dustin Silver through cell phone pings that would prove the location of Dustin Silver's cell phone during the time of the homicide and the hours before and after the 6:30 A.M. December 28th date of the murder.

The statements of facts also included that Dustin Silver did not have an alibi or could not provide his location at the time and date of the murder.

It took several hours for Detective Hannigan to complete the search warrant applications.

After reviewing the boilerplate and contents of the Search Warrants applications, Detective Hannigan signed each document, under Penalty of Perjury, that the contents of the documents were true and correct.

He then contacted Superior Court Edgar Spartan's legal assistant Mary Winthrop and gave her the completed search warrant for the Judge to review, and sign.

Mary Winthrow assured Detective Hannigan that she would contact him when the Judge was ready to review and sign the search warrant applications.

Chapter 20

Monday, May 13th, the Investigative Team met in the War Room for an update, including Wheatland Police Chief Fife, The Sheriff, and County Prosecutor Walter Colvins.

Dustin Silver's name was at the top of a whiteboard with descending facts that would implicate Dustin in the murder of John Adams.

Detective Fitz started speaking to the group about the circumstances that may prove Probable Cause of Dustin Silver for the murder of John Adams. "We know that there was a love triangle between Marianne Shutt, Dustin Silver and the victim John Adams. Marianne would frequently meet Silver at Motels in the area, often driving John Adam's vehicle and Mr. Silver was very aware the vehicle's owner was Mr. Adams. Marianne has told us during an interview that she observed Dustin Silver looking at the vehicle registration in Adam's pick-up during one of their trysts, so he would know the registered owner was John Adams and his address. Dustin has admitted that he was in the Tri-Cities area the day before the murder which was about 90 miles away or about an hour and a half travel time. He could not provide an adequate alibi for his location the morning of the murder. Search warrants for cell phones and for Silver's cellphone GPS record have been delivered to the Judge for review. His phone was pinged and it showed a location about 30 miles south of Pendleton, Oregon about 9:30 A.M. heading south towards Boise, Idaho. It appears Dustin had intentionally turned off his cell phone from about 10:00 P.M. the night of the 27th and it never came back on until approx. 9:30 A.M. on the 28th near Pendleton, Oregon. We have a witness named Eric Savage from The Dalles, Oregon and he tells us he ran into Dustin Silver at a bar in The Dalles where Dustin was buying the ladies drinks at the bar and probably had a buzz on. Dustin allegedly told Eric that a guy in Wheatland was shot in the chest with a handgun and he would never be charged. Eric thought it was probably the John Adams murder because Marianne had told him about the shooting and she thought Dustin had killed Adams. We submitted the handcuffs found in the front yard of the victim's house to the WSP Crime Lab. They reported there was a mix of DNA from four men and one woman found on the handcuffs. The Forensic scientist said there were partial DNA strands that were consistent with Dustin Silver's DNA. Like 1 in 2400 which means there could be 30 people alone in Canyon County that would have the same small DNA strands as Dustin Silver but that is not enough to say there is a match," Fitz explained.

"That is a little light in DNA standards," Detective Fitz said.

"However, our team has met with Canyon County Prosecutor Walter Colvins, who is here at this meeting, and we feel there is sufficient evidence to charge Dustin Silver with the 1st Degree Murder of John Adams. Judge Edgar Spartan has reviewed the Probable Cause Affidavit and he signed the Arrest Warrant. The actual bond will be decided at Mr. Silver's first appearance in front of Judge Edgar Spartan when Dustin Silver is apprehended and brought back to this jurisdiction for his first appearance. About 8:30 A.M. this morning, Det. Hannigan received a phone call from the Wasco County Sheriff's Office at the jail in The Dalles, Oregon."

The Wasco County Deputy said, "Dustin Silver was arrested last night when he came home about 8:30 P.M. He did not resist and it seemed like he was almost expecting to see us and get arrested."

"The Deputy said that Dustin Silver signed a Waiver of Extradition last night when he was being booked so we won't have to wait for weeks to transport him back to Washington. The Judge will review the signed Waiver of Extradition at 2:30 P.M. today and we will need to be present in case the Judge has any questions regarding the probable cause of the out of state arrest warrant from Washington State," said Detective Hannigan.

"Detectives Skates and Ritz and I will start over to Wasco County Jail and Courthouse right away since it's about a 3 1/2 hours drive," Hannigan said.

"This case is a little thin, so I expect further investigation to fill in the blanks, I want a good case to present to the jury," Prosecutor Walter Colvins told Hannigan.

"There's talk on the streets and several Field Intelligence Cards that Ryan Bates and another guy named Juan Garcia were the shooters, so make your case against Dustin Silver airtight if he is the one," he commented.

"We plan on a lengthy interview with him tomorrow after he has cooled his heels overnight," Hannigan said.

Detectives Hannigan, Fitz and Skates made the uneventful 3 1/2 hour trip to the Wasco County Jail.

They notified the jail they were there to pick up and transport Dustin Silver back to Canyon County Jail after the 2:30 P.M. First Appearance and Waiver of Extradition matter that would be in front of Wasco County Superior Court Judge Abigale Tucker.

They had a quick lunch with Wasco County Major Crimes Sgt. Kim Trenton prior to the 2:30 P.M. court appearance.

"If you fellows need a hand on this side of the state line, let me know and I'll see what we can do," said Sgt. Trenton.

They left the small cafe and bade farewell to the Sgt. when they neared the courthouse.

Once inside the courtroom, they sat behind the wooden rail separating the arena from the spectator section of the court room.

Silver and three other inmates, all dressed in orange jumpsuits, were ushered in by two uniformed Correction Deputies.

A youthful looking attorney from the Public Defenders Office was present and conferred separately with each inmate and would represent the inmates for their first appearance.

The Judge was prompt at 2:30 P.M. and the Bailiff announced for everyone to stand until the Judge was seated.

The Judge called the Court to Order and began reviewing the charging documents that had been placed in front of him.

Dustin was selected to be the last inmate to appear in front of the Judge due to his out of state Fugitive Status and to give time for the Judge to review the signed Waiver of Extradition form.

Judge Abigale Tucker asked Dustin if he had reviewed his Fugitive Status arrest information form and if he had read and signed the Waiver of Extradition.

Dustin respectfully answered the questions the Judge had put forth and affirmed his signature on the Waiver of Extradition Form.

"Gentlemen, if there is no additional information, I am approving the Waiver of Extradition," the Judge explained.

"This court is no longer in session, please stand," said the bailiff as everyone in the courtroom stood as Judge Colleen Biggs left the courtroom through the door located in the alcove on the wall behind the judge's bench.

Detective Skates opened the short wooden gate leading into the arena of the courtroom and stood in front of Dustin before the corrections officers led him away and back to the jail. "Dustin, we'll be right over at the jail to pick you up and take the drive back to Wheatland," he explained.

Dustin looked at Skates and gave a slight nod as he was led away.

Thirty minutes later Dustin, wearing handcuffs attached to a chain around his waist, was led out through the secure backdoor of the jail and placed in the backseat of Hannigan's unmarked police car.

Detective Skates sat in the left rear passenger seat and Det. Fitz was the front passenger.

"We have about a 3 1/2 hour drive back to Wheat, so if you want to talk about this case, we can do it," said Detective Hannigan as he glanced over at Dustin.

Dustin glanced out the passenger window and never replied to

Detective Hannigan as they left The Dalles.

After they crossed Satus Pass, Detective Fitz proposed they stop for a relief break at a small truck stop off Highway 82 at the Prosser, WA. exit.

Detectives Fitz and Skates went inside to use the restroom while Detective Hannigan waited in the car with Dustin.

"Look," said Hannigan to Dustin, "things will go a lot smoother if you just plead guilty in this case and tell the jury you were just planning on going to John Adams's house and talking to him, but when you saw him in his front yard you decided just to shoot him. It might save your neck and you could be found guilty of 2nd Degree Murder with a chance of parole down the road, instead of aggravated murder which could lead to the death penalty,"

Dustin made direct eye contact with Detective Hannigan and replied, "Who the fuck do you think you're talking to, I'm not guilty, for one thing, and whoever killed Adams did it with premeditation which means it was a planned murder and would never be lowered to 2nd degree murder conviction."

Hannigan had an angry look on his face as he turned and looked straight ahead.

"Hannigan, where did you learn how to interrogate someone? Did you get your training from watching cop shows on TV?" Dustin asked, then broke out laughing.

Hannigan turned with blood in his eyes, "Listen, you bastard, I'm going to laugh my ass off when the Judge sentences you to Life without a chance of Parole."

"We'll see about that," Dustin chortled at Hannigan.

Detectives Fitz and Skates returned back to the Police car and Fitz said, "OK, it's your turn."

"Do you need one of us to go with you when you take Dustin to the restroom?" asked Fitz.

"No, if I can't handle one little bastard I need to retire," he said and the others laughed at the comment.

Hannigan opened the back passenger door and grabbed Dustin by the shoulder and pulled him out.

As they walked into the restroom Hannigan said, "Go inside the cubicle and take a whiz, and stay there until I finish my duty over at the urinal. Just try something stupid and I'd love to put a bullet in the middle of your back."

"Not a chance, you asshole, I can't wait to see your face when I walk out of jail a free man," Dustin said with a smirk on his face.

Hannigan's face turned beet red but he never replied.

They got back into the police vehicle with no comments, and although Dustin walked ahead of Hannigan, he never gave him a reason to pull his gun and shoot him in the back.

They arrived at the Canyon County Jail at about 7:00 P.M. and missed the evening meal so Dustin was provided a sandwich, apple and carton of milk for dinner as he was waiting to be booked.

He was listed as "Keep Separate" from other inmates when he was classified at the booking counter.

A plastic identification band was placed on his wrist.

He was taken to an adjoining room where he was strip-searched and issued a bright orange jumpsuit and plastic sandals.

"You can make a phone call before you are placed in a cell," a corrections officer advised Dustin.

Dustin was directed to a telephone mounted on the wall at the booking center.

Who should I telephone that will do me the most good, he thought.

He decided on contacting his brother Gabe who lived in Pendleton, Oregon.

He dialed the phone and as the phone continued to ring, Dustin became concerned he would have to leave a message.

After about the 8th ring, the phone was picked up and answered by a familiar voice.

"Gabe, I've been arrested for murder over here in Wheatland and I am going to need a lawyer, can you help me to get the ball rolling for my defense?" he asked.

"Of course, brother, I will start looking for a good lawyer and come by the jail and put some money on your books so you can buy snacks and other stuff that's allowed in the jail," Gabe told him.

"I have my First Appearance tomorrow morning in front of the Judge and will have an attorney from the Public Defenders Office there to represent me until I can get a regular lawyer," Dustin told him.

"It's just a preliminary thing, but of course I will enter a Not Guilty Plea, and the Judge will decide on the Bond amount, probably in about a week at a Bond hearing to determine how much the bail will be," Dustin continued.

"OK, we'll be in touch and you can make collect phone calls to me when they allow," said Gabe before they hung up.

The next morning Dustin was walked through a back hallway to the Superior Court room for his First Appearance in a Washington Court.

A busy Public Defender Attorney was going down the list of inmates that had been arrested the day before and was hastily scribbling notes.

She explained to the inmates this court hearing was the first of a series of legal maneuvers they would be experiencing.

As each inmate was brought up in front of Judge Robert Benson, the plea would be "not guilty" until their attorneys had time to review the case and receive documents related to the case.

The Judge would appoint a Public Defender for the inmate that could not afford an attorney and a bond would be set.

Finally, it was Dustin's turn to appear and he also put in a plea of not guilty with the Public Defender standing beside him.

The Judge advised the charge was 1st Degree Aggravated Murder and there was no bond at that time.

Dustin turned to the Public Defender, and told her his family would be retaining a Defense Attorney in the next few days and thanked her for her assistance.

The inmates were lined up by two corrections officers and Dustin looked over at the spectator gallery and saw several men pointing their cell phones towards him, taking photos.

He turned his back to the cameras and followed the other inmates down the hallway annex that led to the jail.

Chapter 21

OREGON MAN ARRESTED FOR WHEATLAND MURDER
A half page photo of Dustin Silver dressed in an orange jumpsuit and handcuffed had been positioned under the large headline.

The contents under the headline revealed that a special task force of investigators had broken the case wide open when a witness in The Dalles, Oregon had overheard Dustin Silver bragging about killing John Adams.

A man named Eric Savage had heard about the murder from a woman living in Waterville, Washington and after putting two and two together, had notified authorities at the Canyon County Sheriff's Office.

Dustin Silver, a resident of The Dalles, Oregon was arrested for 1st Degree Aggravated Murder and waived extradition to the state of Washington.

He was transported to Canyon County Jail and made his First Appearance in Superior Court and has entered a plea of Not Guilty.

Canyon County Sheriff Jay Harris and Wheatland Police Chief Will Fife have applauded the investigators for their hard work to identify and arrest the suspect Dustin Silver.

Elected Canyon County Prosecutor Walter Colvins has said he will be the lead Prosecutor for this case.

"Holy crap," Ryan exclaimed after he read the headlines of the crinkled Wheatland Gazette Newspaper while sitting in the recreation room at Canyon County Jail.

He scanned down the contents of the article and the further he read the article, the bigger his smile became.

Ryan still had a half hour left on his 1 hr. time in the recreation section of the jail.

Ryan went to a phone located on the jail recreation wall and directed the jail inmate phone operator to make a collect phone call to Juan Garcia's phone number.

Garcia answered on the first ring and accepted the collect phone call from Juan.

Ryan excitedly told him of the front page news article of the arrest of Dustin Silver for John Adams murder.

Juan reminded Ryan that he was calling on a recorded line.

"When, I get out of jail in a week, we can discuss this matter further," Ryan said.

"I just wanted to let you know before you hear it from someone else," he continued.

Chapter 22

Seattle Attorneys Jackie Skelton and her husband Mark Scalia were sitting in the conference room of their downtown office enjoying a cup of coffee when their Office Assistant Jordan Smith advised them there was a phone call from a gentleman phoning from Pendleton, Oregon and was asking for a Defense Attorney.

Jackie picked up the phone and said, "Hello, this is Jackie Skelton, I am an attorney at this law firm, may I help you?"

"Hello, this is Gabe Silver and I am hoping to find an attorney to represent my brother Dustin Silver who has been arrested and charged for a murder in Wheatland, Washington that happened last December," he blurted out.

"Mr. Silver, this law firm does criminal defense work and some work in Eastern Washington. Attorney Mark Scalia and myself do defense work with another Associate Attorney Colin Thurgood."

Gabe Silver described the history of events that led to his brother's arrest for 1st degree aggravated murder in Canyon County.

"Would you be available to meet with my brother at the Canyon County jail for an interview and see if you will represent him?" he asked.

Mark Scalia had been listening to the exchange that had been placed on speaker phone in the conference room and interjected into the conversation.

"Mr. Silver, we can travel to the Canyon County Jail and if we do take the case, it may be expensive to defend, depending on the circumstances," Mark told Dustin's brother.

"I understand, and I am prepared to take out a loan on my construction business to pay for your services," Gabe explained.

"Our firm will contact Canyon County Jail and arrange for a legal visit with your brother in two days," said Jackie.

"That will be fine and I will be getting a phone call from Dustin tonight and I will advise Dustin you are going to be contacting him in a couple of days," said Gabe.

"Thank you so much, and goodbye," Gabe said as the call ended.

Two days later Jackie, her husband Mark Scalia and Colin Thurgood were well on their way to Wheatland by 6:00 A.M. and had already crossed over Snoqualmie Pass to the Eastside of the state.

About 9:30 A.M. they arrived in Wheatland and arrived at the Canyon County Jail.

The structure had a tall communication tower with microwave and cell phone relay communication towers mounted at the top of the drab flat roofed building.

The three Attorneys walked through the main door of the jail building.

On the far side of the lobby was a heavy metal door with a call button and speaker mounted on the wall.

A window with high impact glass and a metal drawer at the bottom used to pass documents back and forth was installed on the wall beside the metal door.

Jackie pushed the call button and waited for a response.

A female voice came over the speaker and enquired about their business at the jail.

Jackie explained they were there for a legal visit with Dustin Silver.

The Jail attendant asked if any of them had weapons on their person and after receiving an assurance from all three, there was a buzzing sound and click at the door as it swung open.

The jail attendant told them to close the door and make sure the lock clicked after they had entered.

The room they had entered contained another locked metal door.

The locked door buzzed and Colin pulled the door open and they entered the main booking area of the jail.

Mark Scalia notified the Correction Officer at the booking desk of the purpose of their visit.

The corrections officer spoke into the microphone attached to his uniform shoulder strap and requested Dustin Silver be transported to the Attorney Conference Room for a legal visit.

"Sir, the Attorney Conference Room is located directly down the hallway behind you at the far end," the corrections officer told him.

"Oh, and don't forget to sign in and out," as he slid a flat pad attached to a clipboard to Mark Scalia.

Mark signed all of their names and noted the time of arrival.

They proceeded to the Attorney Room and waited for Dustin to be brought down.

The Attorney Room was small, with a concrete bench along the wall.

A metal table attached to the floor jutted out about 4 ft.

On the other side were two plastic lawn chairs of such low quality they could have been purchased at a yard sale.

Dustin Silver walked into the conference room as the defense team stood up and greeted him.

"I've been expecting you guys since I talked to my brother yesterday, I'm Dustin Silver and I need your help," he said matter of factly.

"We're here to help you," said Jackie and she introduced her husband Mark Scalia and associate Colin Thurgood.

"Let's hear from you what circumstances brought these serious charges against you," Jackie stated to Dustin.

Dustin started by saying, "About 3 years ago I broke off a relationship with a woman named Marianne Shutt, when we lived in the Dalles, Oregon. We had been involved in a relationship for about two years and we had a child in common. His name is Zachary and he lives with his Mom Marianne over in Waterville, Wa. where she lives with her mother who works as a traveling nurse. I would phone Marianne at least once every two months to check on my son. This past year Marianne started contacting me, mainly by text messages and she would tell me how much she loved me and missed me. Marianne would frequently text me nude photos she had taken of her body posing in front of a full length mirror. Of course, I enjoyed looking at the photos and reading her messages because it brought back old memories. However, I knew we could never get back together because she was a cheater with every cowboy when I was working out of town. I had to find out from my best friend Cal Jenkins, who owns a taxi service in The Dalles. Cal and I were renting a house together in The Dalles. One night Cal told me that earlier that day he was driving around downtown waiting for a fare pick-up and he got a call for two people to be picked up at a local bar in downtown. He told me he pulled up in front of the bar and some middle-aged guy came out with Marianne draped on his arm and she was pretty drunk. The plastic shield separating the front seat of the cab and the back seat had a slight tint to it and Marianne could not actually get a clear view of Cal as they got into the cab. The guy directed Cal to drive them to the Best West Motel. Cal told me he tilted the rear view mirror down so he had a better view of the couple and Marianne was kissing the guy and rubbing his chest with her hand. When they arrived at the motel Cal parked at the lighted drive up entrance. Marianne and the guy got out of the cab and Cal saw them enter a motel room. I was really upset and I had Cal drive me to the motel and he pointed out the room number he had saw them enter," he continued.

"The guy must have thought it was room service or something because he opened the door and was wearing the white bathrobe furnished by the Motel. I saw Marianne sitting in a dark corner of the room and she was only wearing her bra and panties. Marianne and I looked at each other and I turned and walked away. Cal told me I should have punched the guy out, but he was just an innocent cowboy in the whole scheme of things. I never talked to Marianne or wanted to see her and after awhile the hurt slowly went away. I had laid in bed alone for many nights and suffered from my heartache, but as time went on I knew I had to get out and move on with my life or I might sink into such depression I could never recover. I started going to bars and parties and pretty soon I was my old self, making friends with women of all ages. I met this young woman named Samantha Fox at a college party and we became fast friends and sometimes she would take road trips with me. She especially loved the Oregon coast. She didn't mind when I would make a lot of stops at wrecking yards buying performance auto parts and catalytic converters off wrecked cars or from muffler shops."

"Can you tell us what has been going on the last year," Jackie asked, to get Dustin back on track for the current events.

"Marianne started texting me again and flirting with me. She had attached nude photos with the text messages and kept saying she would like to meet with me sometime and that she had lots of free time. Time had passed and I thought, what the hell, she's a Ho but I guess I should get my share. In between trips I would sometimes meet with her in various small towns with motels for afternoon trysts. Sometimes we would stay together overnight when she could get away from this John Adams fellow. A few weeks before Christmas Marianne came to The Dalles with her mother and our son. She stayed with relatives but contacted me and she would meet me for sex at a motel on the outskirts of town. On the last day Marianne was getting ready to leave back to Waterville with her mother. I was with Samantha having breakfast at a small cafe. Marianne must have drove by and saw my pick-up parked there. Marianne came through the front door looking around and she saw me with Samantha and walked up and started insulting her. I told her to get away from us. Marianne yelled and told me we were through and slammed the door as she was leaving. I thought that was about the end of hearing from Marianne. Sometime after Christmas I got a phone call from Marianne and she was all upset and told me somebody gunned her boyfriend down using a shotgun and the coward shot him in the back. I could tell she was upset and she started threatening me, telling me she was going to kill me if she found out I had shot the guy. I got angry with her and hung up the phone. A few minutes later she phoned me back and was blowing up my phone so I turned it off for awhile," he said.

"She wanted to know where I was that morning and I indicated I was in Oregon headed out to pick up some auto parts and catalytic converters. I had been in Kennewick, Washington on December 27th and bought some car parts from a wrecking yard full of older vehicles. I left there late in the afternoon and spent the night in Pendleton, Oregon at a truck stop and early the next morning fueled up my pick-up truck and had breakfast at the Cafe there on the morning of December 28th," Dustin said.

"How long were you gone?" Colin Thurgood asked.

"I was gone about four to five days and when I got back to The Dalles, Samantha told me the cops from Wheatland were looking for me and she had given them my toothbrush. I wasn't sure what they would want with my toothbrush but I kept it in my private bathroom which was attached to the locked bedroom where I slept. I kept the bedroom door locked at all times because I had a small safe in the closet. Samantha kept all her girlie stuff like makeup and other things a woman uses in other bathroom she claimed as hers. I had the key sitting on a book shelf in the living room, but Marianne had never gone into my bedroom unless I was there and the door was unlocked. Samantha told me the Detective named Hannigan had scared her and told her she could be in big trouble if she did not cooperate, so Samantha unlocked my bedroom door and and retrieved my toothbrush and gave it to this clown Detective Hannigan. Don't I have some expectation of privacy of my belongings in my own room?" asked Dustin, not expecting a reply. "After I got home these three Detectives from some type of Task Force in Canyon County contacted me in the morning after I had arrived the night before. I had been checking out my brake lights on my pick-up in the apartment parking lot when they showed up. We sat in Detective Hannigan's unmarked police car. This Detective Hannigan was an asshole from the get go and started hammering me with questions and where I had been on the night of December 27th and early morning hours of the 28th. I told him that on the 27th I had gone to Kennewick, Washington, to a wrecking yard that sold hard to find car parts for older muscle cars. I told him I stayed there for several hours and when I left I drove to Pendleton, Oregon to a truck stop fueling station where I slept in the cab of the truck. The next morning I fueled my pick-up and had breakfast there. I told them I should have a meal receipt in my wallet or in the pick-up. Of course, when I checked my wallet, there was no receipt and I did a quick cursory search of my pick-up cab but did not locate the receipt. I don't use credit cards so there was no record there. Hannigan yelled at me and told me that I had time to drive to Wheatland early in the morning of the 28th and kill this guy John Adams and drive to Pendleton before 9:30 A.M. I denied it and I thought he was going to grab me and throw a punch at me and the other Detective sitting in the back seat reached over and grabbed Hannigan by the shoulder and told him to cool off. Hannigan told me he was going to get me for the murder and for me not to stray too far. Then this week I got arrested and charged with the guy's murder," Dustin finished.

"We will contact the County Prosecutors Office here this morning and tell them our Law Firm will be representing you on the charges," said Jackie.

"The Prosecutor is required to provide us with all investigation documents or other related material, including photographs they have taken. We understand there may have been Search warrants prepared and we will look into that matter. Until then you will need to sign this document I prepared confirming that you have retained our law firm," said Jackie.

After the paperwork was signed, the documents were dropped off at the Canyon County Prosecutor's Office with a copy filed in the Clerk's Office.

While there, they asked to meet with the Prosecutor involved in the case.

A few minutes later Walter Colvins, the elected Prosecutor, came up to the counter.

"Hello, I am Walter Colvins, how can I help you?" he said in a friendly tone.

"Won't you come back to my office?" he invited.

"Well, thank you for taking the time to meet with us, I know you have a busy calendar and apologize for coming unannounced," Jackie said in a soft tone.

Once seated in the office, Jackie, Mark and Colin introduced themselves and notified the Prosecutor they had been retained by Dustin Silver.

"We came over to your office to ask for the Discovery of this case, including all filing documents, Law Enforcement reports, Autopsy photos, video, search warrants and returns, etc." Jackie said.

"Not a problem, I can have the current Discovery, including the police reports, downloaded and put on a thumb drive today. If you would stay in town for lunch, I should be able to have everything by 1:00 P.M." he said.

Walter Colvins picked up his phone and dialed his Legal Assistant directing her to download the Discovery information on a thumb drive.

"Well, that's done," he said in a friendly tone.

"Thank you for your assistance," Jackie said to the Prosecutor.

"We'll review the Discovery and would like to coordinate with our calendars for the upcoming hearings and motions that we will need to do before a trial date is set," Mark commented to the Prosecutor.

"We will be retaining two Licensed Private Defense Investigators to assist on our case," Mark advised further.

"After we review the Discovery, we would like to get started setting up interviews with the Prosecution witnesses," Colin Thurgood said.

"Not a problem," answered Colvins, "I should have a current list of the State Prosecution Witnesses in our files right now and will give the list to you with the other Discovery this afternoon."

"Thank you, Mr. Colvins, for your assistance and maybe we can talk sometime next week," Jackie said.

"Looking forward to it," he said with a smile, as the defense team left to have lunch and they later returned to pick up the thumb drive from the Prosecutor's Office.

. . .

The following week the attorneys were in their conference room discussing the information they had gleaned from the documents and photographs received from Canyon County Prosecutor's Office.

"We need to retain the Defense Investigators to assist on this case," Colin Thurgood Surmised.

"Let's hire an Oregon P.I. to investigate and contact witnesses in the state of Oregon," Jackie added.

"The other Private Investigator should have an office in Eastern Washington," she continued.

"Let's hire Monty Victor from Portland, Oregon, he was really effective when he worked on that homicide case with us over in Bend, Oregon. He located our star witness and our client was found not guilty, as you guys will recall," she finished.

"OK, I'll give him a call tomorrow to see if he is available," Colin said.

"My former Adjunct Professor Mark Vetos at Gonzaga University is also a Criminal Defense Attorney practicing in Spokane. Do you guys remember the major Hanford Nuclear Facility time card fraud where a substantial number of workers and mid-level Managers were charged by the Feds for Conspiracy to Commit Fraud for falsifying their time cards. Feds thought it was a slam dunk case against defendant Tom Hunter, the mid-level manager, until Mark Vetos, his attorney, tied the Prosecutors Office in knots and they ended up dismissing charges on Tom Hunter who they had claimed was the key figure in the conspiracy. Mark's Investigator was a P.I. named David Anson out of Liberty Lake, Washington. He had located some important witnesses the Feds had failed to contact and interview. The Whistleblower was identified and she admitted to David Anson the Feds had pressured her to write up her statement in their own wording and the document she had signed was grossly exaggerated. The case against Tom Hunt was dismissed and the Federal Judge that had signed the charging document was livid with the two Federal Prosecutors and threatened to charge them with prosecutorial misconduct. Both Prosectors were terminated by the U.S. Attorney's Office and the Judge was satisfied with the outcome and never criminally charged either Prosecutor. The Judge did send a complaint to the Federal Lawyers BAR Association. If you guys are in agreement, I will contact David Anson and see if he can assist in this case," Jackie said.

The next morning Colin phoned Monty Victor in Portland, Oregon and exchanged pleasantries before Colin approached him with an offer.

"What type of criminal case are you defending?" asked Monty.

"It's a murder case that happened last December in Wheatland, Washington and the Prosecutor is charging our client with 1st Degree Aggravated Murder. Our client's name is Dustin Silver and he lives in The Dalles, Oregon," he continued.

"His ex-girlfriend Marianne Shutt is living in Waterville near Wheatland in Canyon County. Her new boyfriend lived in Wheatland and was gunned down last December 28th. CBIT task force fingered Dustin Silver, accusing him of being part of a love triangle that went bad. There is a lot of evidence and witnesses listed in the Discovery documents and photographs. However, we have heard that the true killers are a couple of guys named Ryan Bates and Juan Garcia that are a couple of Wheatland lowlifes that make a living out of car prowling, burglaries and selling meth to other young kids in town. There is quite a bit of follow-up investigation to be done on the Oregon side of the border," Colin continued.

"I would be glad to assist with defense of your client," Monty replied.

"Please, send me the Discovery Documents and photos on a thumb drive and I'll look them over and perhaps in about a week we can meet," Monty continued.

The phone call ended with a promise by Colin to send the information the following day.

"Well, that's one, I just retained Monty Victor to assist in the case," he told Jackie and Mark.

Jackie placed a phone call to David Anson at his Liberty Lake Office.

David Anson answered his phone and Jackie introduced herself.

"Mr. Anson, I have contacted an Attorney in Spokane named Mark Vetos, whom I believe has retained you in the past," she started out.

"Yes, I worked a very successful Federal case with Mark Vetos a couple of years ago," he replied.

"Mark Vetos was very impressed with your work on that particular case," she said.

"Those are kind words from Mark Vetos," Anson said softly.

"If I can call you David, I am contacting you to ask for assistance in resolving a murder case in Wheatland, Washington which is the County seat for Canyon County."

"That's fine, but most folks just call me Anson," he replied.

"OK, Anson," Jackie replied back.

"This is an alleged Love Triangle case the Prosecutor is pushing forward and our client is accused of killing the other man in the triangle. Our client Dustin Silver is accused of the murder since he allegedly had the means and motive. However, we are gathering information that the murder was committed by two meth heads in Wheatland that were prowling cars last December. One of the prowlers obtained a gun from inside the victim's vehicle where the owner was known to keep firearms. The victim had stepped out of his house and had apparently confronted the two thieves. One of the vehicle prowlers named Ryan Bates had armed himself with the owner's gun he obtained from the victim's pick-up and shot and killed the man," she continued.

"His partner's name is Juan Garcia and he has made an admission to others that he was with Ryan when he killed the guy."

"Are you available to assist with this case?" she said.

"How long do you figure it will take for the investigation and the trial to end?" he asked.

"I would guess the investigation and trial should run about 6 months, depending on what you find," she advised.

"It sounds like a challenging case, which is the type I prefer," he answered back.

"I'd be glad to help in this case," he replied.

"Part of this case will involve a lengthy investigation in The Dalles, Oregon area, so we have retained a Portland investigator named Monty Victor," she said.

"I will be e-mailing your retainer documents to sign and will place the case reports and photos on a thumb drive and overnight to you," she replied.

"Give me a week to review everything and then we can meet and create the game plan," he said.

"Thank you for agreeing to assist in the case," she said and hung up the phone.

Chapter 23

Jackie Skelton was true to her word and two days later David received a thick Fed-EX envelope, and when opened the charging documents, prosecution witness list and a series of photos at the crime scene were enclosed with several Thumb Drives containing additional case related information.

He laid all the documents out on his conference table, cleared old case information off the whiteboard on his office wall, opened his laptop and sat down to review the information he had received.

He spent two full days reviewing all of the information, spending long hours until midnight both nights, before leaning back and rubbing his tired eyes.

There is a lot of work to do on this case, he thought as he put his laptop to sleep and rose out of his chair.

Tomorrow I'll contact the Monty Victor and we can decide our next move, he thought.

He was groggy when he came into his office the next day with a hot cup of black coffee he had picked up at the local coffee Drive Thru.

He rummaged through the top drawer of his file cabinet and removed a 5 hr. energy booster drink that was in a small 2 oz. plastic bottle and swallowed the contents down in two gulps.

He woke up his laptop and searched Google for Monty Victor's phone number in Portland, Oregon.

He dialed up the listed phone number and waited patiently while the phone rang before going to voice mail.

After leaving a brief message he hung up.

In a couple of minutes the phone rang and Monty Victor was on the other end and after a brief introduction they discussed the case and the priority of witness contacts.

"I think we should look at the State's witness list and do some follow-up contact and interview them," Monty suggested.

"I agree, and we should do another canvas of the neighborhood because the police never contacted all of the neighbors," Anson replied.

"The attorneys would like to set up a meeting to go over the assignments they would like accomplished," Monty said.

"Jackie just phoned me a few minutes ago and she is setting up a Zoom Conference meeting this Friday at 3:30 P.M.," he continued.

"Check your e-mail, there should be a message from the defense team regarding the online Zoom meeting."

Their phone conversation ended and Anson opened his e-mail and saw the message from Mark Scalia advising of the upcoming meeting.

On Friday at 3:30 P.M. promptly the private on-line Zoom Meeting started.

Jackie asked Anson and Monty if they had reviewed the material that had been sent to them.

"I received the documents, but it appears some of the Discovery documents are incomplete," Monty pointed out.

"Yes, there are other documents you didn't receive," she replied to Monty and Anson.

"We know our client is innocent and your project is to help prove Dustin is innocent and gather evidence proving two other persons committed the murder," she said.

We are naming this case "**The Innocent Project,**" she said.

"What are your plans or goals to start your investigation?" she asked Monty and Anson.

Anson replied, "We are going to canvas the neighborhood again because the police reports reflect that not all of the people in the neighborhood were contacted other than a few that were still home the day of the homicide. Probably most had left for work or school. There is quite a list of witnesses but it looks like Bonnie Crawfoot is a key witness so Monty and I will contact her."

"That sounds like a good start," said Mark, "but remember this woman named Samantha Fox needs to be contacted in the Dalles, Oregon since she has been contacted by the Detectives from Canyon County area."

"When are you guys headed to Wheatland?" asked Colin Thurgood.

"I'm meeting with Monty next Monday in Wheatland and we'll spend about 3 days locating witnesses, and introducing ourselves to Dustin at the jail."

"That sounds like a plan," Jackie said. "In the meantime we are preparing documents for an Evidentiary Hearing and Motion to Dismiss charges. We will hold off filing any documents until we hear back from you guys. Let's schedule an on-line Zoom meeting every Friday at 3:30 P.M. to review your progress," she commented to Anson and Monty.

The following Monday shortly before noon, Monty and Anson both checked into the Best West Motel in Wheatland

"Let's contact some of the witnesses and then after dinner, go over to the jail and visit with Dustin," suggested Anson.

"Good idea," replied Monty, "the jail will be quiet and most attorneys will be gone for the day."

After a quick lunch they drove up to 3rd street and parked in front of Bonnie Crawfoot's house.

They looked across the street towards John Adam's house and the front yard where the murder had occurred.

As they were stepping out of their vehicle, a middle-aged woman walked up and stood at the sidewalk near their vehicle.

"Are you guys more Cops?" she asked.

"No, ma'am, this man is Monty Victor and I am David Anson. We are both Licensed Private Investigators retained by the defense attorneys at Skelton and Scalia Law Firm," he informed her.

"Monty Victor here is licensed out of Portland, Oregon and I am licensed in Washington State with my office located at Liberty Lake," he explained.

"I'm Bonnie Crawfoot," she introduced herself and shook their hands with a firm grip.

Anson noted her strong grip and calloused hands and wondered what her profession was.

From the dark tan on her face and small wrinkles around her mouth and forehead it was obvious Bonnie had spent a lot of time outdoors.

"I live here," as she pointed out her residence which was located across the street from John Adams's house.

"We were going to stop by and visit with you since we are in the neighborhood to contact the neighbors," Monty explained to Bonnie.

"We're checking with the neighbors to determine if they heard or saw anything suspicious in nature the morning of the homicide of John Adams."

"I have wanted to reach out and talk to someone about what else I had observed at the time John was killed," she said.

"I've had time to think and reflect about what I actually saw at the time of the shooting. Let's go inside and I can show you where I was sitting when I heard the shot," she said.

Bonnie directed them to a large kitchen table with 6 wooden chairs that separated the kitchen area from the living room of her modest and well kept home.

"I was sitting right here," and she pointed out a chair facing the table which would give her a view of John's house looking through a large living room window.

"I had been up since about 2:00 A.M. that morning, which is when I do my baking of pastries that I sell to the local coffee stands and restaurants," she continued.

"I had the overhead light on in the kitchen," she continued.

"I was reading the newspaper and having a cup of coffee when I heard the gunshot and I saw a flurry of activity in the front yard. I saw John Adams holding his stomach with both hands and stumble back into his house and close the door," she said.

"I thought it was John and his son Devin shooting off fireworks or something, but I got suspicious and phoned John and there was no answer."

"Did you think that Devin may have followed his dad back into the house?" asked Monty.

"I didn't know for sure, so I put on my coat and went over to John's house and knocked on the front door and there was no answer," she replied.

"I went back to my house and phoned 911 and went back outside and stood on the sidewalk waiting for the police to arrive," she said.

"While I was waiting, John's sister Olive Adams drove up and parked in her driveway. She lives next door to me on the south side and was just coming home from spending the night with her boyfriend. Olive got out of her car and walked over to me and asked me what was wrong. I told her I thought something bad had happened to her brother John and told her what I had observed and that I had phoned 911. About a minute later I saw three Wheatland Police cars driving down the street to the south of us and their headlights were turned off. They parked a couple of houses down from John's house and approached, walking on the sidewalk. Olive and I walked across the street and met the officers. I pointed out John's house and described what I had observed. The one Officer told us to stay back and directed one officer to work along the Southside of the neighbor's yard and position himself at the S/W corner of John's house. The officers I talked to moved across the front lawn and ducked below the window of John's living room window and knocked on the front door reaching over with his flashlight. I saw one officer peer into the living room window and saw him speak into his portable radio microphone that was clipped to his left shoulder," she continued.

"I saw the officers enter the house with their guns drawn. Olive and I waited for a couple of minutes, standing on the sidewalk in front of John's house and then walked up to the front porch and went into the living room because the door was wide open. We were standing behind one officer who was kneeling beside John who was lying in a kneeling position on the kitchen floor. It was obvious to us that John was dead. The officer with John noticed us standing directly behind him and he turned and told us to go outside and wait across the street."

"How far away from John were you when the officer noticed you standing there?" Anson asked.

"We were maybe about 3 feet away from John."

"You mentioned that you had second thoughts about what you observed through the flurry of activity, is that right?" Anson asked.

"Well, yes, I have been thinking about what I saw that morning and was trying to figure why it was so easy to see outside at that time of morning. Then I remembered it had snowed the night before and the snow on the street and ground gave a soft light outside. After I heard the shot and John stumbled inside his house, I saw somebody standing in the yard with his back to me and he ran alongside the truck and disappeared from my line of sight to the north. I could tell it was a man, but he wasn't very tall and I would estimate maybe 5 ft 6 inches in height. I wouldn't say the guy was fat, but he definitely was chubby," she continued.

"Did you get a look at his face?" Monty asked.

"I just got a glimpse but it looked like he was a white man and his cheeks were kind of puffy looking, and he looked about 18-20 years old. Then, just about a second later, I saw a tall guy with short dark hair run across the lawn, right to the left and he was lost from view when he ran behind the bush in John's front yard."

"Did you see his face?" asked Monty.

"No, I just saw his profile, but he reminded me of the kid that lives down the street with his mother, but I can't say for sure it was him," she said.

"He was probably 6'3" and was wearing dark clothing and had something in his right hand," she said.

"It looked like a small power drill or something and at the time I hadn't put two and two together yet because I was so traumatized," she continued.

"After you put two and two together, what did you think?" asked Anson.

"I felt kind of stupid for not immediately thinking about it and now I think it was a gun he was holding," she said.

"I mean, I heard a gunshot and then saw someone run across the yard with a power drill… Naw. I'm really confident that the object I saw was a handgun."

"Have the police ever recontacted you other than the day of the murder, or have you told anyone else besides Detective Anson or me?" asked Detective Victor.

"The day after the funeral I talked to a couple of detectives and I told them I needed time for my recall to return since I was so traumatized. I never talked to any cops about my recall of the events beside you and Detective Anson. I told my daughter and she told me I should contact someone so I'm glad you guys came along today," she said.

"Would you agree to make a written Statement and sign it as a true and correct statement?" Anson asked.

"Of course, I would, I have nothing to hide," she replied.

"I would prefer that you prepare the statement under my direction and I will review it for accuracy and sign it."

Monty opened up his legal type briefcase and removed a small laptop computer and turned it on and started the process.

After several additional additions and deletions Bonnie was satisfied that the prepared statement was accurate.

The statement was downloaded to a thumb drive and Bonnie allowed the use of her printer, to download and print the statement.

The statement was reviewed one last time and she signed the document which was witnessed by Anson and Monty.

They thanked Bonnie and as they were leaving and standing in her driveway, Anson asked one last question.

"Did you see anyone else in the neighborhood or around John's house that morning before the police arrived?"

"Oh my, I plumb forgot about a guy walking down the middle of the street as I was walking back to call 911. The guy's name is Steve and he lives with his girlfriend Lynn Bennett two houses to the north of my house on the same side of the street. Every morning somewhere between 6:30 and 6:45 A.M. I see the guy walking south on 3rd and he goes to the market on Division about a block away. Then about 5 minutes later I always see him walking back with paper coffee cups, holding one in each hand," she said.

"On that day, when he walked by, was he holding a coffee cup in each hand?" asked Anson.

"Oh, yes, he was," Bonnie responded. "So that means he must have been walking to the store right before the shooting and he was coming back from the store with the coffee cups in his hands right after the shooting," she surmised.

"That makes sense," Monty told Bonnie, "and if you don't mind, do we have your permission to stop by and talk some more if we have further questions?"

"Yes, you guys can, but after I bake in the morning I usually go out and work on my farm until about 2:00 P.M. I'm usually in bed by 6:00 P.M.," she continued.

They thanked Bonnie and walked back to their vehicle.

"Let's check this guy named Steve," said Anson.

"I bet he saw something when he was walking back from the store with his cups of coffee," said Monty.

They walked on 3rd Street to Lynn Bennett's residence a few houses north of Bonnie Crawfoot's house.

There was a three foot high white picket fence around the front yard with the gate barely holding on to the post with one hinge.

As the gate was moved to the side, there was a chorus of barks coming from within the residence.

Anson knocked loudly on the door in order for the occupant to hear the knocking over the din of the barking dogs.

The door opened by several inches and a partial view of a woman's face called out and asked, "Can I help you?"

Anson and Monty identified themselves and passed business cards through the narrow opening of the door and asked if Lynn Bennet was there.

"Yes, that's me, just a minute while I do something with these dogs," she said.

She shut the door and they heard her cussing at the dogs and telling them to get back.

The barking became faint and the front door opened again.

"Come on in, I put my three dogs out in the backyard so we can talk," she said and stepped aside and directed them to some kitchen chairs.

"We stopped by this afternoon to contact neighbors that may have seen or heard anything regarding the John Adams homicide last December," Anson told her.

"A neighbor down the street told us she had observed your boyfriend Steve walking down the street holding a cup of coffee in each hand right after there was a gunshot heard in the neighborhood," Anson explained.

"Yes, that's true," she replied.

"On that morning Steve came through our front door and was all excited and said something bad had just happened down the street a couple of houses down on the opposite side. Steve told me the cops were showing up there," she said.

"He noticed the cops when he was just walking through our front gate," she continued.

"Steve told me he had seen two guys run out onto Division Street from the alley behind the house where the guy had been shot. Steve had asked me to call 911 and report what he had observed," she continued.

"Did you call 911 and tell them what Steve had observed?" asked Monty.

Lynn had a sheepish look on her face and answered the question, "No, I never called 911 because the cops were already there. Steve had a Department of Corrections Warrant for his arrest and both Steve and I were afraid he would be arrested if the cops came over and talked to us about what he had observed. About an hour after the cops showed up I saw a cop walking up the sidewalk and he stopped to open the gate, so I went outside and met him. He asked if I had seen anyone suspicious or had heard a gunshot, and I told him no. I did not tell the officer what Steve had told me. I was afraid Steve would be arrested."

"Can I get Steve's full name, please?" Anson asked.

"His name is Steve Paulson, and he is living on the coast near Poulsbo," she said.

"Steve does roofing and new home construction as a carpenter so he moves around quite a bit with this big housing boom going on right now. He lists my address for his mail so we do keep in touch and he stays with me when he is back in Wheatland. I have a hard time reaching him by phone because he works in some pretty isolated areas with poor phone reception," she continued.

"I know he will be calling me from a land line tonight, usually after 9:00 P.M. because of his late work hours," she said.

"Oh, by the way, Steve resolved the issue with the DOC (Department of Corrections) and they dropped the arrest warrant on him. However, he has to come back to District Court later this week to appear on a No Vehicle Operators License on Person charge," she added.

"He actually did not have his driver's license in his possession when he was stopped for a burnt out tail light, so now he has to appear in front of the District Court Judge and display his driver's license to the judge to get the charge dismissed," she replied.

"How long have you lived at this address?" asked Anson.

"We moved here about four years ago when I was still married and I've been divorced for two years now. I have two children, a boy and girl," she revealed.

"Austin is fifteen going on sixteen and my daughter Carolyn is fourteen, and they both live at home," she said.

"A couple of thieves in the neighborhood broke into our house when we were on vacation last summer and stole Austin's X-box. It was Ryan Bates and Juan Garcia that did our burglary from what I learned," she said.

"I heard they might have also been involved in the murder of John Adams," she said.

"Where did you hear that?" Monty asked her.

"Well, actually, Steve described the two guys running out from the alley when John Adams was killed. Steve said he didn't want to accuse them but it looked like Ryan Bates and the shorter kid looked like Juan Garcia. Ryan Bates lives with his mother Kat Bates just four houses down from John Adams and on the same side of the street. Juan Garcia lives with his mother and siblings in the low income apartment buildings at the North end of 3rd street where it crosses Canal Street," she continued.

"His mother is Lawanda Garcia, and she fits the profile of a woman that just keeps popping out a baby every year to get more money from State Public Assistance. I heard she has eight children but the State Welfare came and took away the three youngest because of child neglect. She got caught trading her Welfare food card to some guy in the complex for booze and pills," she said.

"The guy was caught using the food card at Walmart and couldn't match his name to the card so he got busted for EBT card fraud. Lawanda was also criminally charged and put on probation because there would have been no one to take care of her other five children so she got no jail time," she continued.

"But she is right back on Public Assistance and gets a monthly food card and free cell phone paid by the State," she said.

"Did you or Steve ever tell the Wheatland cops who you thought may have killed John Adams?"

"No, because Steve couldn't say for sure who he actually saw running out the alley," she said.

"Ryan and Juan would come over to my house to visit my kids and I would barbecue and buy pizza for the group, and they would all hang out in the backyard," Lynn told them.

"I had an above ground swimming pool set up in the summer and they were always coming over to lounge in the pool. However, Ryan and Juan knew our family was going to be going up to Curlew Lake near Curlew, Washington to our cabin on vacation and would be gone for the week," she said.

"When we were driving back home through Wheatland I saw that Juan Garcia was riding my son Austin's bike down the street. I cut him off with my car and all the dogs and kids were inside," she said.

"I got out and confronted the damn thief," she continued.

"Juan told me that he saw the bike in our backyard and he had just borrowed it to ride around while our family was on vacation. I took the bike back from him and had Austin ride the bike back home. I told Juan he was not allowed at my place for a month," she emphasized.

"When we got home, the window in Austin's bedroom had been broken out and someone had cut themselves because there was quite a bit of blood on the glass and ground below the window. Someone had crawled through the opening because there was smeared blood on the window frame and a dribble of blood drops across the bed cover on Austin's bed. One of Austin's T-shirts was wadded up in the hallway and it had quite a bit of blood on it. We put two and two together because there was a Bandage wrapped around Juan's right wrist when I took Austin's bike from him, and I thought maybe he had sprained his wrist or something. Now I believe Juan had cut his arm on the glass from my son's bedroom window," she continued.

"Our TV was on the living room wall and it was hanging by a piece of the metal wall mount when we got home. The thieves hadn't been able to pull the TV loose," she said.

"The burglars went through my dresser upstairs in the bedroom and stole some old coins and jewelry and a set of my dad's handcuffs. When I called the cops they came up and looked but did not check for fingerprints anyplace or collect blood samples from the bedroom window. My dad was a Cop at Sultan, Washington Police Department, and about 1990 he was killed in a terrible collision with a drunk driver one night while he was on patrol. Our family was in shock and thank God my dad's life insurance paid for his funeral and covered most of our living expenses. My mom bought a house here in Wheatland," she continued.

"We survived on my dad's survivor retirement plan and never went hungry," she explained.

"When I turned twenty-one my mom gave me the pair of Dad's old handcuffs and his service revolver. Thank God I brought the revolver with us when we went on our vacation because the gun had been in the same dresser drawer in my bedroom along with the pair of handcuffs," she revealed.

"Was there anything unusual about the handcuffs that you recall?" Monty asked.

"They had a couple of large loops between the main handcuffs and some of the serial numbers had been ground off," she replied.

"My dad collected old law enforcement memorabilia."

"I want to show you some photos of handcuffs," Monty said as he opened his laptop and located various photos.

He prepared photos of four other handcuffs and the fifth photo was the handcuffs recovered in the front yard of John Adams's house.

He placed the photos on a rotating montage and displayed each photo on full screen on his laptop.

Lynn carefully examined the first three handcuff photos and when the forth photo was displayed, she positively identified the handcuffs that had been her father's, and stolen in her burglary.

She pointed out the unusual characteristics.

Monty downloaded the photos to a thumb drive and received permission to print out the photos on Lynn's color printer.

"Would you please sign and date on the right corner of the photo that you picked from the montage?" Monty asked.

"I'll be glad to sign it," she said and Monty handed her a pen and the photo of the handcuffs she had selected from the photo montage.

"Oh, by the way, do you know John Adams's son Devin?" Anson asked.

"Well, yes, Devin used to come over and play video games with my son Austin," she said.

"Devin would sometimes bring over this little boy named Zachary, but he was only about 3-4 years old," she revealed.

"Zachary's mother was a girlfriend of John Adams," she said.

"Austin used to go over to Devin's and they would all play on the trampoline in the back yard. Zachary was pretty small but the boys would let him play on it with them."

"Did Zachary ever play with your handcuffs that were stolen?" Anson asked.

"Yes, Austin would ask to play with the handcuffs and I would get them out," she said.

"Austin would play cops and robbers with Devin and Zachary and they would put the handcuffs on each other," she replied.

"It was harmless and always when I was in the house with them," she continued

Lynn Bennett was agreeable to sign a Statement based on the information she had provided.

Monty got out his laptop and Lynn Bennet directed him to dictate her statement on the laptop.

After the statement was completed, it was downloaded and copied on Lynn's printer, and she signed the document as true and correct.

They walked down the street towards Anson's vehicle, and once inside, Monty said, "Man, we hit the jackpot with these witnesses and it's just the first two people we have interviewed."

"Let's check online with Canyon County District Courts schedule and see if Steve Paulson's name comes up," Anson said.

The screen opened on the laptop and Steve Paulson's name was displayed with an entry for Failure to Possess a Valid Operator's License on Person from Canyon County that had not been adjudicated yet.

"OK. Let's stop over at the District Court Clerk's Office and see when a court date has been set," Anson said.

The District Court Clerk's Office was located on the second floor of the ancient courthouse.

The court clerk came to the counter and she was asked for a copy of the Traffic Infraction that had been issued to Steve Paulson.

The clerk came back several minutes later with a copy of the document and handed it to Monty.

"This gentleman named Steve Paulson is scheduled to be in Judge Price's court at 9:00 A.M. tomorrow morning," she said.

"The courtroom is located on the third floor," she continued.

"Thank you, Ma'am," Anson replied with a polite smile that she happily returned and nodded.

As they walked back to their vehicle Anson told Monty they should go back to Lynn Bennett's and obtain a photo of Steve Paulson.

"Good idea, let's drop by and get a photo so we can identify him," Monty said.

Lynn's house was only about a 3 minute drive from the courthouse, and as they pulled up and parked, Monty said, "I'll just run up to the porch and obtain a photo of Paulson."

Monty was gone for 2-3 minutes and he walked back to the car holding a photo in his hand.

"This is Paulson," he said as he passed the photo to Anson.

"OK, let's call it a day then and head back to the hotel, clean up and have dinner," Anson said.

"Then we can write up our reports and send to Jackie, Mark and Colin, they will be happy with our news," he continued.

The next morning Monty and Anson were sitting outside Judge Price's courtroom hallway, watching for Steve Paulson to pass by.

At about 8:50 A.M. they spotted Paulson walking down the hallway towards the courtroom.

As he started to pass, Anson called out his name and Paulson turned with a quizzical look on his face.

"Yes, I'm Steve Paulson, can I help you guys?" he said with a hint of suspicion.

"Mr. Paulson, I am Private Investigator David Anson and this is Private Investigator Monty Victor," said Anson.

"We are retained by the Seattle law firm, Skelton and Scalia Law Office."

Monty told Steve Paulson the reason for their contact and Paulson confirmed that it was indeed him that had been walking down 3rd street holding a cup of coffee in each hand the morning of the homicide.

"We would like to talk to you about the incident when you have time," he continued.

"I'm available today right after court. I have to meet with the Judge in the courtroom and as soon as we are done we can discuss what I observed," he said.

"You guys are welcome to sit in court," he continued.

They followed Paulson into the courtroom and sat towards the back while he sat at the front of the courtroom.

When Paulson's name was called from the docket, he stood up.

The Bailiff read the charge which was for Operating a Motor Vehicle Without a Valid Operator's License on Person.

"How do you plea?" the Judge asked Paulson.

"I am pleading guilty of the charge but would like to address the court on the circumstances," Paulson replied.

Paulson made eye contact with the Judge and explained that he had his valid driver's license on him and handed the document to the Bailiff, who passed it up to the Judge.

The Judge handed the document back to the Bailiff and passed it forward to Paulson.

"Mr. Paulson, you have taken responsibility for your traffic infraction and have done the responsible thing by keeping your valid driver's license on your person. I'm going to suspend the fine and you only have to pay the twenty-five dollar court fees."

"Thank you, your Honor," he said to the Judge who nodded as Paulson turned and walked out of the courtroom, followed by Monty and Anson.

They stopped outside in the hallway and decided to walk to a nearby coffee shop.

Paulson said he wasn't a coffee drinker but would like a hot chocolate.

Monty and Anson each ordered coffee and Anson paid and tipped the Barista.

"Your drinks are ready," she said about a minute after the order had been made.

They sat in a secluded corner of the coffee shop and got comfortable with their drinks.

"Steve, can you tell us what happened or what you observed on the morning of December 28th last year?" asked Anson.

"I'll try to describe the details the best that I can," Steve said.

"That's all we can ask," Monty said to Steve.

"Well," he paused, "I was living with my girlfriend Lynn Bennet at her house just down the street from where the guy lived that got shot. Just like clock work every morning, I would walk down the street past the guy's house on 3rd, down to a small market at Division and 3rd. I visited with the lady that was working there as we would often chat because I was such a consistent customer. I got a couple of 16 ounce cups of coffee in those paper coffee cups. I always had to be careful because the cups were hot and I would put a paper sleeve on them, but still had to be careful. So, I was walking carefully and pretty slow so I wouldn't spill the cups or burn myself."

"As I was crossing Division Street heading to 3rd street, headed to my girlfriend's house, I saw a motion to my right and I looked over and saw two guys run out of the alley. They were really running and one guy was tall, about 6'3", and the other guy was short," he continued.

"The shorter guy turned and looked directly at me and I got a pretty good look at his face. They turned and ran east on Division where I lost sight of them. They both were wearing dark clothes and the taller guy had short dark hair," he continued.

"The shorter guy was about 5'6" and pudgy, and had a light complexion like a baby face. I was on high alert and figured they had been up to no good, just by the way they were running like they were in a panic. I walked down the middle of the street and was looking all around while I walked to Lynn's house. Just about the time I got to Lynn's gate I heard a sound of cars coming up the hill on Division and the loud distinctive sound of studded snow tires on the road surface. I stopped at the gate and looked down the street and saw at least three marked Wheatland Police cars coming towards me with their headlights out. The cop cars stopped and parked on the east side of the street, a couple of houses south of John Adam's house. I went into the house because I had an arrest warrant and didn't want the cops to think I was involved. I told Lynn to call 911 and tell the operator that two people had been observed running out of the alley. At that time neither Lynn nor myself were aware John Adams had been murdered. I thought Lynn had called the cops but then found that Lynn never did tell the cops what I had observed," he said.

"About a week later Lynn and I were walking down 3rd street to the market and there was a group of people standing in John Adams yard. We stopped and asked if the person that had shot John had been arrested. A young woman standing there told us a guy named Dustin Silver may have shot John but had not been arrested. Lynn recognized the woman. She told me the woman's name was Marianne and she was Zachary's mother and had been John Adams' girlfriend," he continued.

"Did Lynn Bennet own a pair of handcuffs?" asked Monty.

"Yes, I saw the handcuffs numerous times at Lynn's house," he answered.

"They were older and had big rings between the part that ratchets them closed. The serial numbers had been partially ground off so I kind of thought the handcuffs were stolen," he replied.

"Lynn told me her dad was a cop and he had been killed in a motor vehicle accident in Granite, Washington and her mother had given her the handcuffs and a revolver that had belonged to her dad," he continued.

Lynn told me her dad also collected law enforcement memorabilia

Anson got out five photos of handcuffs in various models and condition and placed the photos facedown across the table.

The 5 photos depicted handcuffs in various models and condition.

"Do any of these handcuffs in the photos look like the pair of handcuffs that were Lynn's?" Monty asked as he handed a photo to him.

Steve carefully examined a photo and, when finished, would lay the photo back facedown before turning to the next photo.

He examined the first three photos, and after viewing the fourth photo, he handed it back to Monty and said, "This is the photo of Lynn's handcuffs."

"Are you sure?" Anson asked.

"Of course, I'm sure, I have handled these cuffs dozens of times and the kids would play with them."

"Would you mind placing your initials and the date on the lower right hand corner of this photo to confirm this is the photo you have identified?" asked Anson.

"Of course," Steve said as he took a pen from Monty and signed his initials on the document.

"Would you be willing to sign a statement with the information you have provided to us this morning, and after reviewing it for accuracy, sign and date it as a true and correct document?" Anson asked.

"I would be glad to, but my work in the construction business has left a lot of arthritis in my fingers and I'm a little clumsy in my writing skills," he said.

"If one of you would write out the statement for me, I could review it for accuracy and sign it," he said.

"That's not a problem," Monty said, "if you have a few more minutes, I will write it out right here and you can look at the statement and sign and date it."

While Monty prepared the statement on his laptop, Anson continued the conversation with Steve.

Steve told him that he and Lynn had cooled their relationship because he had been working out of town and could only get home about every couple of weeks.

He would drive from the westside after work on Fridays and then have to return back to his low rent motel in Tacoma on Sunday afternoons.

Monty finished writing up the statement on his laptop and handed it to Steve.

Steve read the statement out loud to himself and went back and reviewed several segments of the statements.

He looked at Monty and told him that the statement was 100% percent accurate.

Monty printed out the document on his portable printer that was wirelessly attached to his laptop.

Monty handed his pen and the printed Statement to Steve to review for accuracy and he signed and dated the document.

"I hope this helps you out, you have my number so let me know if I will be needed to testify," he said.

Monty and Anson thanked Steve as he walked out the main entrance of the coffee shop.

"The photo of the Lynn Bennett's handcuffs revealed a small amount of rust in one of the locking mechanisms of the handcuffs," said Anson.

"Lynn Bennet said the handcuffs were stolen like in June or July while she was on a family camping trip, so that would have been about six months from the time the handcuffs were found in the front yard of John Adam's house."

Chapter 24

Ryan Bates walked out of the Canyon County Jail five days later after he had posted bond for the assault of Jenna.

He looked around on the street as a white pick-up truck rapidly drove down the street and braked sharply in front of Ryan.

Juan Garcia yelled for Ryan to get into the pick-up truck.

As Ryan walked around the front of the pick-up he noticed there was another man sitting in the front passenger seat.

He easily recognized Bronza, another friend of his.

The three had been on a recent crime wave, causing a sharp increase in car break-ins and burglaries.

The Wheatland cops had a good idea of who was doing it but had been unable to trace the crimes back to them.

"Man, I need some meth, it's been awhile and I'm hurting," Ryan said as he got into the pick-up truck.

"Either of you dudes got any meth that I can get a pinch?" he asked.

"Naw, we're both dry, but I wanted to talk to you about something you and I had talked about doing in the past, before you went to jail," said Juan.

"What do you have in mind?" Ryan asked.

"Remember, we talked about doing an armed robbery at the norteno trap house over at Othello," he continued.

"We can't use this pick-up truck because the norteno gang has members here in Wheatland. The gang members in jail here have wives and kids that have moved here to Wheatland, so they can be closer to visit their jail birds, and sooner or later the norteno's would spot this pick-up and know who ripped them off," he continued.

Bronza said, "My side chick over in Wenatchee has an old beater Honda that her ex-boyfriend left behind when he moved out. It runs and we can use it and then dump it back in her garage out of sight."

"Those are some serious dudes and we might have to pop a cap on some of them," said Ryan.

"Do you still have that handgun?" Juan asked.

"Yeah, I have it hidden out at an old homestead well house up a canyon north of town. Let's see if it is still there," Ryan said and directed Juan to drive up the narrow canyon road from Wheatland and had him stop at the driveway that led to the handgun's hidden location.

He was gone for two to three minutes and returned holding a black colored semi auto pistol, and a box of 45 caliber ammunition.

"Let's check it out," Ryan said, and Juan and Bronza got out of the pick-up.

Ryan aimed the pistol at an old, abandoned refrigerator standing starkly in the field right off the roadway about 25 yards away.

He fired four shots rapidly and had a nice shot pattern in the middle of the refrigerator door.

The shell casing flew back at an angle and one of the hot spent shell casings landed on Bronza's neck, making him yelp and slap at his neck.

"What kind of gun is this?" Juan asked, as Ryan handed the gun to him.

"It's a Smith and Wesson 45 caliber semi auto pistol," said Ryan.

"Do you notice that small object attached to the bottom rail of the gun?" he asked.

"I have no idea, except it looks like a little spotlight or something," Juan answered.

"It's a laser sight that emits a red laser light and wherever it is pointed, if you pull the trigger, the bullet will travel where the laser light is pointing," Ryan explained.

"Cool," Juan said as he pointed the pistol towards the old refrigerator and pulled the trigger three times.

His shot pattern was wider and not as accurate as Ryan's.

Bronza walked over and took the pistol from Juan, dropped the magazine and asked Ryan for more cartridges.

"Nice," Bronza said as he examined the gun and loaded fresh cartridges into the magazine.

He expertly slid the magazine back into the pistol and racked a new round into the chamber.

He stepped ahead and held the gun in a sideways motion commonly referred to as gangster style.

The method was not particularly accurate but gangbangers thought it looked cool when they would shoot their handguns in that fashion.

Bronza held the gun Gangster style as he began walking towards the abandoned refrigerator and fired all of the bullets from the ten round magazine, towards the target.

They all walked up to the refrigerator as Bronza handed the gun back to Ryan.

"Fuck man, you only hit the refrigerator three times out of ten, where the hell did you learn to shoot that bad?" asked Ryan.

Bronza was sheepish and advised the gangster method he used was the only way he had ever shot a handgun before.

"When we do the takeover robbery I will be the guy packing the gun, hell, you might accidentally shoot one of us," Ryan chuckled.

"Bronza, go get that beater Honda and we can meet at the Canyon County Park over by the Remington Irrigation Canal that runs underneath the highway between Quincy and Wheatland," he said.

"Do you know where the Restrooms are located at the Canyon County Park there?" he asked.

"Yes, I can be there about 5:00 P.M. if that works," Bronza said.

"That will work, I can park my pick-up and leave it while we caper," Ryan continued.

Bronza was dropped off at his low rider SUV in the Safeway parking lot in Wheatland and he drove off towards Wenatchee.

"We've got a few hours. Let's smoke a bowl of weed," Juan said, not waiting for an answer as he removed a small baggie from his shirt pocket.

He expertly tamped a small amount of the marijuana into a tobacco style pipe and lit it up, with his lighter,

Juan slowly drew the smoke into his lungs.

He passed the pipe over to Ryan.

He took a long drag off the pipe and coughed violently from the acrid smoke.

After several more exchanges the weed had burned up and Juan tapped out the remaining ashes in the pipe with his shoe heel.

"Man this weed is killer, I can hardly keep awake, Juan you drive," said Ryan.

After trading places, Juan turned the volume up on the radio up and was singing loudly to the music.

Ryan looked around the parking lot and said, "Come on, Juan, let's move away, that barista in the drive-thru coffee stand across the Safeway lot is staring at us."

"Hell with her," Juan said, but started up the engine of the pick-up and slowly drove past the drive-thru coffee stand, flipping the female Barista off and swearing at her through his open window.

"I need to stop by my mom's house and tear up one of my black t-shirts to make masks," Ryan said as Juan drove to his Mother's house.

They parked out front of the house and Ryan went inside.

A few minutes later he came out carrying a brown paper grocery bag.

"I also got a couple of beers for us to drink on our way to meet Bronza," he said.

Juan steered the pick-up away from the curb and guided it towards the Canyon County Park to meet with Bronza.

They arrived at about 4:30 P.M. at the County Park and parked Ryan's pick-up truck near the public restroom, which would be the safest place to leave it unattended until they returned from the Robbery.

After about 15 minutes Bronza drove up in a beat-up Honda Accord.

The car body had rear end damage with a broken tail light and the back left passenger door window had been broken out.

"Geez, Dude, will this piece of shit even make it to Othello and back?" Ryan asked Bronza.

"Oh, hell yeah, the motor is tight," Bronza responded.

"Let's hope some trooper doesn't pull us over," said Juan.

"My side chick was at work when I left and won't even know this car is missing from her garage," he continued.

They got into the car with Bronza driving.

Ryan in the front passenger side and Juan in the back seat.

Othello was about 45 minutes away so they made plans on how the heist was going to go down during their drive.

They arrived in Othello and, after driving through the narrow streets, located the trap house which was located in the industrial side of town.

They sat back several blocks away near several grain silos where the employees parked.

There was a clear view of the front of the norteno trap house and the back yard had a 6 ft. wooden fence with an alley behind the fence that was used for garbage service and garage access to some of the residences.

There was a slow stream of vehicle traffic stopping at the trap house and usually a passenger would get out of the vehicle while the driver remained in the car.

A lookout was observed standing in the backyard by a wooden gate leading to the alley and another man was standing in the front yard looking up and down the street.

A dark blue Dodge Hellcat Challenger was parked on the front yard facing the street and a dark colored Ford Transtar van was parked in the driveway.

"Man, that Hellcat is probably running over 700 horses," Juan mused.

"I don't know, this may not be as easy as I thought," said Ryan.

"I know we can't outrun them if they're chasing us in that Hellcat," he continued.

Let's take a drive down the alley and get our bearings so we can figure out our plan.

"I think we need to wait until it gets dark so we can move up and get close enough to take out the guy in the back," said Bronza.

They drove down the alley slowly and methodically and saw there was a church on the next street over and a large parking lot where they could park their car for a fast getaway.

They noted there were several openings in the back fence from fallen boards and the spaces appeared to be large enough to step through into the back yard.

The lookout merely glanced at them as they passed the backyard driving down the alley.

They continued out the end of the alley and drove around the block behind the trap house, and parked in the church parking lot.

"It will be getting dark in about a half hour and we can make our move then," Ryan said.

"Before I forget, Bronza put the keys on the floor on the driver's side so when we leave, we may be running fast and hard," Ryan told Juan and Bronza.

"We will need a distraction for the lookout in the back yard. So I'm thinking one of us can distract the lookout and one of us can come up behind him and take him out," Ryan continued.

"I will have the gun and will use it only as a last resort because we may have to fight our way out. Gunshots tend to bring the cops real fast," he continued.

"I've got a sharp knife," Bronza said as he reached for a knife sheath on his belt and pulled out a wicked looking knife with a 6 inch blade that glistened in the dusk.

"No," Juan said softly. "We're not here to start a body count, let's get the drugs and cash and get the hell out of town," he said.

"Use this ball bat here for the lookout," he said as he reached into the backseat and handed the bat to Bronza.

The section of the parking lot where they had parked was not lit up by street lights.

They quietly left the Honda and softly spoke in whispers as they walked the short distance to the alley where they crept down the dark alley directly behind the back of the trap house.

There was a soft sound of Spanish music coming from the direction of the house.

The backdoor opened and a figure stepped out and walked down the steps and crossed the lawn where the lookout was standing in the shadows.

The man laughed softly and handed the lookout a bottle of beer.

The man stood at one of the back yard fence openings and relieved himself with the stream flowing into the alley.

He grunted and there was a sound of his trousers being zipped up.

"Enjoy the beer," he said to the lookout, "Jesus is standing out front and Carlos and myself are inside packaging the meth and counting the money."

"We're leaving in a few minutes to bring some more meth from the Potato Warehouse because a customer wants about 120 ounces tomorrow, and if we sell as much as we did today, we'll need to get more," he told the lookout.

Ryan tapped Juan on the shoulder and backed up to where Bronza was standing, "Let's stand back until they come back with a load of meth, then we'll rob them."

About 5 minutes later they heard the low rumble of the Dodge Hellfire as it was started up.

The sound of the vehicle traveling down the street was soon lost.

They stood about a half block back in the dark near the church parking lot.

"Let's try to not get in a shootout with these norteno's, they have a long reach and we don't want them to know who we are," Juan cautioned.

A few minutes later they heard the rumble of the Dodge Hellfire coming down the street until the engine noise ended in the front yard of the norteno trap house.

They waited a few minutes and started creeping down the alley until they reached the edge of the backyard.

Ryan crept down the alley until he passed the location the lookout had previously been standing.

He stood in the dark just outside the opening in the fence.

Juan and Bronza crept up to the opening in the fence on the other side of the lookout.

Ryan stepped through the opening in the fence and called out to the lookout who had not noticed his entry into the yard.

"Hey, man, I'm here to pick up my order," he said to the young hispanic male who had produced a small black revolver and was pointing it at Ryan.

The lookout never had a chance to respond back to Ryan when he was struck from behind with a hard blow to the head and crumpled to the ground.

Bronza had used too much force and the crunch of the lookout's skull was clearly heard by all three.

The norteno lookout would not recover from the lethal blow.

Ryan looked at Bronza and shook his head.

"You stand here in the backyard and watch our back to make sure no one comes up on our six," Ryan instructed and handed Bronza the small revolver the lookout had been carrying.

Ryan and Juan crossed the yard and crept up the steps leading into the kitchen at the rear of the house.

In their excitement and stress they neglected to put on their black face masks.

The door had not been completely closed as they quietly opened the door.

Ryan was the first to enter and was holding his 45 caliber pistol in a two handed shooting stance.

Juan followed close behind and was holding a pillowcase they had brought to grab the anticipated drugs and money.

The norteno gang member named Carlos was standing at the

kitchen table with his back to them and Adolpho was standing at the side of the table.

Adolpho noticed the movement behind Carlos and started to reach for a handgun tucked in the front of his pants.

"Don't do that and no one will get hurt," Ryan said softly.

Carlos turned his head and immediately realized it was either a police raid or a drug rip-off.

"Ok, man. We're cool," he said and held his arms up away from his waist.

Juan came up from behind and swiftly checked Carlos for weapons and located a small semi-auto handgun and removed it from his waist.

"Get down face down on the floor," he directed Carlos.

Juan quickly used flex cuffs to secure Carlos and told him to stay down.

Alphonso had his hands resting on the kitchen table and was ordered to stand in that position while Juan went behind him and removed a small revolver from the front waist.

"Get on the floor beside your friend and turn your head away," he ordered.

Juan knelt down and placed a flex cuff on Alphonso's wrists.

Ryan kept his gun pointed towards the ground in the direction of both men.

Juan picked up the meth that was prepackaged on the table and placed it in the pillowcase he was carrying.

He opened the kitchen drawers nearest the table and found stacks of money that had been bound with rubber bands.

He counted at least 50 bundles of cash as he placed them in the pillowcase.

"If you want to live, tell me where the main cache of meth is located, I know you just brought a new shipment into the house," Ryan threatened as he pushed the barrel of the pistol into the small of Carlo's back.

Carlos raised his head and looked in the direction of the living room.

"It's in the duffle bag in the front room," he said.

Juan darted inside the other room and came back with a large duffle bag.

He opened the duffle bag up and reached in and pulled out wrapped kilo sized meth.

Alphonso said, "You motherfuckers, you have hit the wrong place. This is a norteno trap house and we will hunt you down."

"You two lay here and if you stand up, we will kill you," Ryan told them.

They backed out the door and ran across the yard through the fence opening and down the alley.

They ran to the Honda and Ryan grabbed the car keys while Juan sat in the passenger front, and Bronza dived into the backseat with the money and drugs.

They had only got about 2 blocks, and when they turned onto the main street they saw the lookout looking in their direction and then run across the yard towards the Trap house.

"They must have alerted the lookout in front," Ryan said, "we should have capped them."

They maintained the speed limit to not arouse local police attention and headed back towards Interstate 90 where they would turn off at the Quincy exit.

Carlos had kicked at the front door and yelled loudly, and Jesus, the lookout came running up to the door to investigate the pounding sound and the yelling from inside.

He opened the door and spotted Carlos standing inside the room.

"Cut this flex cuff off me and do the same for Alphonso," he ordered.

Jesus quickly cut the bonds from the men and helped Alphonso to his feet.

Carlos quickly opened the cabinet door beneath the kitchen sink and brought out a sawed off pump shotgun and a 357 Magnum revolver.

He quickly checked to make sure the guns were loaded.

"Come on," he shouted at Alphonso and Jesus.

Alphonso had stepped out into the backyard where he found Michael, crumpled on the ground near the back fence.

He reached down and felt for a pulse.

Not finding one, he felt the skull where a large portion of blood had seeped.

"Carlos, they killed your brother Michael," Alphonso shouted out.

"There were at least two of those bastards," Carlos said with blood in his eye.

"I saw a car pull out from a side street a couple blocks away without lights on," said Jesus.

"I saw their brake light come on and only the right brake light worked," he continued.

"Come on," Carlos said as they jumped into the Dodge Hellcat with Jesus getting into the backseat.

He knew if Ryan continued on the same street, there was only one main road that led to I-90 interchange.

Carlos wasn't concerned with local law enforcement as he roared through town at high speed.

As they left the city limits, Carlos accelerated to over 100 miles per hour, looking anxiously ahead for the suspect vehicle.

They had gone about 5-6 miles when a small car was spotted in the distance.

The small Honda car sped up to approximately 80 miles per hour and the Dodge Hellcat easily caught and kept up with them.

Soon I-90 freeway loomed up and the small Honda braked to maneuver around the curving onramp to I-90 westbound.

The Honda braked when traversing the lane to enter the freeway, and only one tail light lit up.

"That has to be the car," Carlos said as he inched behind the car, almost touching the back bumper.

"They have spotted us," yelled Ryan and handed his semi auto handgun to Juan.

"Put a shot through their windshield, that should slow them down," he directed Juan.

Ryan suddenly changed to the left lane of the freeway, giving Juan a clear shot of the windshield of the Dodge Hellcat.

Juan rapidly fired 3 shots at the pursuing vehicle and saw an immediate result as the Dodge Hellcat slammed on the brakes.

"Godammit," Carlos said as the upper passenger side of the windshield exploded.

"I'm OK," Alphonso said, "let's get those assholes, this is personal now."

Carlos jammed the accelerator to the floor and the car leapt forward, throwing them back in their seats.

They rapidly caught up to the Honda and Alphonso placed his arm outside of the vehicle and fired directly at the vehicle.

They were so close that every bullet struck the vehicle and several bullets passed through the rear window and through the car, shattering the front windshield.

Ryan felt a hot sticky matter on the back of his head and the front windshield was splattered with blood and brain matter.

He glanced over his shoulder and Bronza's face was mostly missing except for his slack mouth and jaw.

Ryan used his right arm to push Bronza's body back against the back car seat.

"You bastards," Juan shouted and emptied a series of rounds of 45 caliber slugs back towards the following vehicle.

Several of the spent 45 caliber semi auto shells landed inside the Honda and the rest had tumbled out onto the roadway.

The Dodge Hellcat suddenly swerved and went off the roadway where it rolled several times before coming to rest.

Carlos had a gaping wound in his right shoulder caused by the slug tumbling after it passed through the windshield before striking him.

Alphonso had been knocked unconscious and Jesus appeared unhurt.

Jesus scrambled out from the wrecked vehicle and removed the shotgun and handgun and threw them over the Freeway property fence so they would not be discovered by responding law enforcement.

Jesus looked both ways and ran up the bank and collected the firearms.

After several minutes Alphonso gained consciousness but had not regained all of his senses when the sound of sirens was heard in the distance.

Carlos was holding the front of his shoulder, and there was steady bleeding from the wound.

The first person to approach the wrecked vehicle was Washington State Trooper Larry Davis who peered inside and assured the two injured occupants that medical help was on the way.

Carlos was barely able to acknowledge the trooper's presence but gasped out that he had been shot.

The trooper shined his light on the blood that was welling out from the wound.

Realizing that the man could die before medical help arrived, the trooper cut the seat belt from Carlos and dragged him out the driver's open door.

He placed Carlos on his left side on the bare ground and began placing direct pressure on the gaping wound, to slow or stop the flow of blood.

There were almost immediate results as the trooper held the pressure on the wound until fire units arrived and an EMT took over treatment.

He later learned that his fast action had saved Carlo's life by staunching the blood flow.

Alphonso was gently removed from the inside of the vehicle after the fire department's Jaws of Life tool had pried the passenger door off it's hinges to gain access.

Alphonso was placed on a backboard and a cursory examination revealed a broken humorous of his right leg and a deep crease along the right side of his skull, in the hair line.

The EMTs recognized the head injury was probably from a bullet passing along between the scalp and skull.

Trooper Davis recognized the incident was more than a simple high speed single vehicle rollover and contacted Communications requesting a total station and the local Sheriff's Office criminal investigators to respond.

The outside lane of I-90 was closed for a 1/2 mile section along westbound I-90.

A Department of Transportation truck responded to slow and direct traffic onto the inside lane of travel.

A tow truck was dispatched and when it arrived on the scene, the DOT truck closed both lanes of travel to allow the tow truck to hook up the totaled Hellcat.

The vehicle was placed on the bed of the tow vehicle to be transported to a local evidence processing facility.

The trooper had looked inside and noticed there were four unfired 357 caliber cartridges lying on the front floorboards and unfired shotgun shells, but no firearms were observed.

The investigators were not aware that Jesus, the third person had left the scene with the firearms.

Trooper Troy Robertson had arrived to assist and was walking along the edge of the outside lane when he saw a shiny metal object lying on the roadway.

He bent down and looked closer and noted it was a spent cartridge casing.

He placed a small evidence cone near the casing and continued walking along I-90 away from the damaged vehicle.

He traveled another 30 ft. and spotted another shell casing located on the shoulder of the road.

After marking the location with another cone he traveled further and located two other shell casings which he marked.

The first shell casing he had located was lying at an angle and he bent down, shining his flashlight on the head stamp, and noted the caliber was 45 caliber semi-auto ammunition.

He walked back to Trooper Davis who was conferring with several deputies.

"I wonder if this was a road rage," Robertson commented.

"I located four 45 caliber shell casings lying along I-90 down there," he said as he pointed towards their location.

"Definitely bullet holes on the windshield and engine hood cover," he continued.

"There were 357 caliber cartridges and 12 gauge shotgun shells found inside the victim's vehicle. This could turn out to be a gang related shoot-out," Trooper Davis said.

The investigation continued until daylight when a Law Enforcement drone with a high resolution camera was used to show the overhead layout of the scene.

The Accident Reconstruction Team completed their investigation and tiredly loaded up their equipment and cleared the scene.

I-90 Interstate Highway westbound, was opened back up to normal traffic flow.

Chapter 25

Ryan had continued traveling at high speed on I-90 and looked through the rear view mirror as he saw the Dodge Hellcat swerve off the roadway and roll after Juan had emptied the magazine of bullets from the semi-auto pistol.

He cut his speed down to the posted speed limit.

They traveled for approximately 20 miles before they took the exit leading to the county park where Ryan's pick-up was located.

They arrived at the Canyon County Park and drove to Ryan's parked pick-up truck.

Ryan reached into the back seat of the Honda and removed the blood covered pillow case bag containing cash and packaged meth and threw it into the back of his pick-up.

Next, he pulled out the large cotton sports type bag containing the large quantity of meth stolen from the norteno's trap house.

He tried to wipe off the congealed blood and brain matter from the sports bag.

"Fuck it," he swore and reached into the opened sports and threw the kilo sized wrapped packages of meth into the back of the pick-up box.

The fresh blood on the wrappings of the packaged meth left blood on the bed of the pick-up box.

Juan walked over and threw the bloody bag into the back seat of the Honda where it landed on the bloody, lifeless body of Bronza.

He remembered to take the handguns they had taken from the norteno gang members and throw them into the bloody gym bag.

Ryan handed the keys to his pick-up to Juan and directed him to follow him as he walked back to the Honda.

He looked at the lifeless body of Bronza, slumped at an angle in the corner of the backseat behind the passenger door.

They drove from the park entrance for a couple of blocks and turned down the road leading to the Coulee Dam Irrigation Company metal gate.

Beyond the blocking gate was a gravel road that paralleled the Remington Canal.

Ryan checked for any oncoming traffic and, seeing none, hit the gate head-on with the Honda at about 20 miles an hour and easily broke the padlocked chain and the gate swung open.

He drove about 1/4 mile down the road where he slowed and pointed the Honda at an angle facing the dark water before coming to a stop.

He stepped outside the open door while keeping his foot pushed on the brake pedal, holding the vehicle in a stopped position.

The Honda transmission was still in drive and he stepped back, releasing the brake pedal.

The vehicle slowly moved forward and traveled over the edge of the concrete lined canal and rolled down the side where it was lost from view as it sank beneath the water surface.

"See you in Hell, brother," he said as the Honda sank.

He walked over to his pick-up truck and got into the passenger seat and they drove back along the canal road.

After they passed the gate, Ryan had Juan stop the pick-up.

Ryan got out and walked back and swung the gate shut and tied the chains together, securing the gate.

They headed back to Wheatland, taking their time so as not to arouse any suspicion.

Chapter 26

Little did they know that an Irrigation District employee named Jeff Winrick was inspecting the canal early the next day.

Jeff found the broken gate and mused it must have been kids gaining access to a hidden location for one of their Kegger parties.

He had checked the security gate padlock yesterday and it had been secure.

The Irrigation District employee had only traveled about a 1/4 mile along the canal road when he noticed tire tracks in the gravel road that led over the edge of the canal and disappeared at the water's edge.

"Oh Gawd, I bet we have a car load of kids that drove into the ditch," he thought to himself.

He ran back to his pick-up truck and notified 911, asking for law enforcement and rescue vehicles to come to the scene.

The second call he made was to his Irrigation District Supervisor.

He stood by nervously peering into the dark waters.

If a vehicle had gone into the canal at that location, the current could have carried the vehicle down the canal to a grate in the canal 1/2 mile away that was used to catch larger floating debris and vegetation.

Canyon County Sgt. Matt Powell was called to the scene and upon arriving he started placing traffic cones and police tape as a perimeter where the tire tracks led into the canal.

He thought the Accident Reconstruction team would appreciate his forethought in protecting the point the vehicle had entered the canal.

Next, he advised radio communications to Dispatch a second Deputy to control the gate that had been forced open.

The second responding deputy's job would be to open the gate for investigators and related personnel and keep the curious folks, and media out from underfoot.

The Incident Commander would arrive shortly with a Mobile Command Vehicle to manage the incident.

The media would be showing up soon, and they would be held near the canal road gate where all Press Releases would occur.

Chapter 27

After dumping the Honda in the canal, Ryan and Juan had drove back to Wheatland and parked in the alley behind his mother's detached garage.

Ryan opened the overhead garage door and looked for boxes and containers to place the drugs and cash in.

After rummaging around the garage he found several cardboard boxes and placed the items inside.

After preparing the boxes he removed a ladder hanging on a side wall and used it to lean against the opening ledge of the attic.

Juan started to hand the boxes up to Ryan but paused and removed four rubber band wrapped stacks of cash and a kilo sized bundle of meth.

"Until we figure how we're going to deal with all this meth and money, we can enjoy some of our spoils," Juan commented.

"Did you grab the hand guns we took from the norteno's?" Ryan asked Juan.

"I left the handguns in the bloody sports bag back inside the Honda," Juan answered.

"Hand me the 45 handgun we got from the Adams guy because it is going to be hotter than hell," said Ryan.

He placed the 45 caliber semi-auto pistol, and box of ammo in the attic, wrapped in a piece of clothing.

Ryan stepped down, then placed the ladder back onto the wall hangers on the inside garage wall.

He lowered the garage door, then walked around to the side door where he turned off the power to the electric operated garage door.

He locked the door and then placed the key above the door trim shelf.

He placed the meth and cash beneath an old woolen blanket on the floor behind the front seat of his pick-up.

"Did all the spent shell casings stay in the Honda when you were shooting at the Hellcat?" Ryan asked.

"I think a couple of the shell casings landed inside the Honda and the rest were ejected onto the roadway," said Juan.

"Let's go into Spokane tomorrow to party, and we can also sell the 45 pistol to one of my brother soreno gang members. We should get four or five hundred for the gun, that's a nice laser sight on it," Ryan said.

Chapter 28

The officers standing along the Canal Road could hear sirens wailing in the distance and several minutes later a van with Canyon County Sheriff Dive Team emblazoned on the side arrived.

Three Sheriff Deputies stepped out of the van.

All were wearing light t-shirts with the Dive Team slogan on the left front portion of the t-shirt and were all wearing shorts.

Sgt. Scott Van Dissel stepped from the group and greeted the on-scene officers.

"We have called for the Chelan County Sheriff Helicopter to respond to locate the submerged vehicle," he said.

"They should be here in about 20 minutes, they were called out before we left," he continued.

"This no longer an emergency so no reason to risk injury for my divers mucking around in the dark water," he continued.

Sgt. Van Dissel announced that it was going to be a recovery mission and no longer an emergency rescue.

Approximately 30 minutes later the Mobile Command Vehicle trundled up and parked behind the Dive Team Vehicle on the road side.

Canyon County Sheriff's Captain Kemph arrived in his unmarked prowl car and parked at the rear of the Mobile Command Vehicle.

Sgt. Matt Powell approached Captain Kemph and advised him of the progress of the investigation and they were waiting for the Chelan County Sheriff's Helicopter to arrive and do a sweep of the irrigation canal, downstream from where the vehicle had entered.

There was about a 5 mile per hour current in the canal.

Their conversation was muted when the loud sound of helicopter rotors approached

The Chelan County Sheriff's Helicopter was spotted approaching at a fast rate.

Sgt. Scott Van Dissel held his microphone close to his mouth and turned his head away from the sound while he communicated with the helicopter pilot.

He walked over to the spot where the vehicle tracks led off the road and into the canal.

The helicopter pilot rotated the helicopter in the downstream direction and raised its elevation to approximately 100 feet.

The forward speed was barely more than a crawl as the co-pilot leaned out of the machine and concentrated on looking into the depths of the water.

They had travelled approximately 300 feet downstream when the machine stopped and the helicopter dropped to approx. 50 feet above the water.

"I can see a red colored vehicle right below our position," he radioed to Deputy Powell and Sgt. Scott Van Dissel.

"Do you see any underwater obstacles around the submerged vehicle that could be a hazard to my divers?" the Sgt. asked.

"No, we can actually see the bottom of the canal and it looks pretty clear from up here," the pilot responded.

"Ok, thanks for the help, you saved our divers a lot of time," Sgt. Van Dissel said and waived to the pilot.

The pilot gave a thumbs up and the engine rpm revved up as it raised to a higher altitude and picked up speed heading back in the westerly direction to the Chelan County Airport.

Captain Kemph asked Sgt. Powell to have the tow truck back down the canal road and stop at the location the submerged vehicle had been spotted by the Helicopter crew.

The tow truck slowly backed down the canal road and the driver was directed to position the tow truck at the proper location, for recovery of the submerged vehicle.

Two divers gripped a strong rope tied to a hook on the back bumper of the tow truck and started to back down the incline of the canal.

They stopped as the tow truck driver unwound a steel cable with a locking hook and handed the attached hook to a diver who continued down into the water and was lost from sight.

Sgt. Van Dissel and Captain Kemph stood on the bank and watched the vehicle recovery process.

The divers were only underwater for a few minutes when they surfaced and used the rope to pull themselves up the wall to the side of the road and stood with the other officers.

"We hooked the front of the vehicle in the water through the CV joints with your cable so it will hold and not come unhooked," one of the divers said.

"We did notice what looks like bullet holes in the rear window glass and the front windshield has at least one shattered section," he said.

"We saw a body inside the red Honda," the diver continued.

The tow truck driver started the process of winding the metal cable back into the housing.

The front and top of the vehicle was the first part of the vehicle to emerge.

There was a baseball sized hole in the front shattered windshield.

The red Honda was pulled completely out of the water and was placed on the middle of the canal road with water draining out the bottom of the door frames.

Sgt. Van Dissel walked up to the vehicle and looked inside and spotted the lifeless body of Bronza wedged on the floor behind the front seats.

Bronza's face was turned up and the exit wound from the 357 caliber to the front of his face was readily observed.

The partially missing face where the bullet had exited was shocking, even to Sgt. Van Dissel.

"This is no vehicle collision, looks like we need the Homicide Investigators called to the scene," he said further.

They walked around the vehicle and several bullet holes were observed in the back window.

"I wonder if this vehicle is connected to the road rage incident on I-90 by Highway 17 that comes from Othello," he mused.

"Looks like a hell of a gun battle," he continued.

Captain Kemph used his cell phone to contact the Major Crimes Unit at the Canyon County Sheriff's Office and requested a team to respond.

He turned to Sgt. Van Dissel and Sgt. Powell and explained that he would be leaving the scene, and Sgt. Powell would be the Incident Commander.

Sheriff Detectives Bob Nickels and Bill Carr arrived on the scene approximately 30 minutes later and reviewed the scene and the body located inside the recovered car.

They walked to the Incident Command Vehicle and sat at a desk inside the well equipped vehicle.

They prepared a search warrant listing the circumstances of the incident and the body located inside the red Honda.

The earlier shooting incident on I-90 was also included in the Statement of Facts portion of the document.

The document was faxed to Canyon County Superior Court Judge Amos Brandon.

After a few minutes Judge Brandon's Legal Assistant faxed the search warrant back with the Judge's signature.

"Let's recover the body and have it sent to the Medical examiner to determine the cause of death, although it is pretty obvious," Nickels commented.

"When we get the body removed, take another series of photos," Nickels directed Detective Bill Carr.

They watched as the ambulance attendants that had arrived on scene struggled to extricate Bronza from the vehicle.

A blue plastic tarp had been laid on the ground so no evidence would be dropped on the ground as the body was moved from the Honda.

A wheeled gurney with an opened plastic covered body bag, was placed on the blue tarp.

Bronza's head lolled backwards as he was lifted and placed on the gurney exposing his destroyed face to the group of onlookers.

One medical responder stepped away to the side of the road and violently vomited after looking at Bronza's destroyed face.

He walked back to the gurney and was thankful that his partner had zipped the body bag closed.

Bill Carr directed the ambulance crew to transport Bronza's remains to the Canyon County Medical Examiner's Office, advising them the Examiner's Office was expecting the delivery.

The Forensic Evidence Technicians had arrived and had folded up the blue tarp to be checked later for potential evidence that may have been dropped.

Next, the two detectives walked to the Honda and peered into the interior from the opened driver's door.

They noted the wet duffle type bag lying on the front seat that was discolored on the top near the handles with what appeared to be congealed blood that had been partially washed away from submersion in the canal water.

The detective observed three handguns inside the duffle bag.

Lying on the floor behind the front passenger seat were two spent cartridge shell casings.

They were photographed and collected by a Forensic Technician and placed in glassine evidence containers.

Detectives Carr and Nickels looked closely at the recovered shell casings.

"These are 45 caliber ACP shell casings," Carr murmured.

"If there is a 45 caliber handgun found inside this car, I would think this incident is connected to the shooting and vehicle rollover along I-90."

A wooden baseball bat with the handle taped with black grip tape was found wedged between the two front seats.

The bat was removed and wrapped in brown butcher type paper and secured with evidence tape.

Detective Carr walked over to Sgt. Powell and told him they were leaving and the scene could be opened up.

They followed the ambulance and the tow vehicle from the scene.

As they passed through the gate near the highway there was a group of vehicles parked along the highway with news crews filming their departure.

Chapter 29

Othello Police Department received a 911 call of a dead body located behind a fence in the back yard of a residence.

The officers immediately recognized the dispatched location as a norteno gang trap house from past Othello citizen complaints of drug activity.

The 911 caller had identified himself as Jose Fillipe with his home address and phone number.

Othello officers Jay Simmons and Rob Ethridge coordinated their approach and each parked their patrol vehicles in the alleyway, effectively blocking all vehicle traffic into the alley at both ends.

A lone figure was standing in the alley, and as they got closer, an older Hispanic man was nervously standing near a fence with boards missing in several locations.

"Did you call 911?" officer Simmons asked the older man.

"Yes, I was taking a shortcut down this alley, going to visit my daughter who lives over on Grant Street," he replied.

"I was looking in the backyard through the fence openings when I saw what looked like a pair of tennis shoes, but then I saw they were attached to a pair of jeans," he continued.

"That dead guy is laying facedown and there is blood on the back of his head," he continued.

"I noticed the back door of the house is standing open but I did not walk up there because someone might be hiding inside," he said nervously as he looked at the house.

"Ok, it might not be safe here," Simmons said and directed Mr. Fillipe to walk down the alley away from the house and stand by Officer Simmon's marked police cruiser.

Officer Simmons notified communications that the backdoor to the norteno trap house was open and had not been cleared for additional victims or suspects.

He requested backup and assistance from other law enforcement officers to respond to the scene.

In a matter of minutes three Washington State Patrol Troopers had responded to the scene and two of the troopers had stationed themselves behind their patrol cars with law enforcement grade AR-15s' pointed towards the front of the residence.

WSP Trooper Reed had parked near Officer Simmons's patrol car and approached down the alley with his pistol held at his side for instant use if needed.

He stood behind a garbage dumpster in the alley.

Officers Simmons and Ethridge crept over to the trooper who was warily watching the open back door.

"We are going to the back door and announce ourselves and check the rooms starting at the open door. We don't know if there are other victims or if there are suspects holed up in there," Officer Simmons said.

"This is a hardcore norteno gang trap house and the Drug Enforcement Administration Agency has been receiving information of an uptick in activity coming out of that house," he continued.

"Once Officer Ethridge and I make entry, we will start sweeping each room," he continued.

"As we clear a room, would you cover our backs as we continue our search in case we missed someone in the rooms or they come up behind from someplace?" Officer Simmons said.

"I understand," the trooper replied.

Officer Simmons walked along the left fence line of the property while Officer Ethridge and Trooper Reed walked along the right side of the fence line, cautiously approaching the back door.

The officers inched their way on both sides of the open door and Officer Ethridge loudly shouted, "Police, show yourselves!"

They waited a full 60 seconds and officer Ethridge again shouted out the warning.

There was no response except for hispanic music playing inside the residence.

Officers Simmons and Ethridge both entered and spread out on either side of the door, making sweeps with their handguns.

The kitchen area was the first to be searched and then the living room was cleared.

Trooper Reed had entered and was sweeping the kitchen and living room and double checked behind the sofa and curtains in the living room.

He proceeded to a narrow hallway that led to a bathroom and two bedrooms.

He heard the word "clear" as each room was searched by the Othello Police Officers.

The house sat on a concrete slab and was a single story structure.

"Wait!" Trooper Reed said and pointed to an overturned chair in the kitchen.

Directly above the turned over chair was a trapdoor in the ceiling that opened to the attic.

Officer Ethridge grabbed a broom from the kitchen and lifted the corner of the trapdoor about a foot high with the broom stick.

Officer Ethridge called out for anyone that might be inside the attic.

"I'm coming out," shouted a voice from the attic.

There was a sliding sound in the ceiling and a pair of legs came out of the opening.

A figure slid further out of the opening and grabbed the edge of the opening and swung down landing on the kitchen floor.

He was directed to lay on his stomach with his arms spread out from his side.

Officer Ethridge approached the figure lying on the floor while Officer Simmons held his gun in a downward position while the man was handcuffed and searched.

Trooper Reed had been pointing his pistol at the opening of the attic in case anyone else was hiding inside, preparing to ambush the officers.

"What is your name?" Officer Ethridge asked.

"My name is Jesus Chaco," he replied.

"Is there anyone else up there?" Officer Ethridge asked.

"No, there is no one else up there, I thought you might be the guys that ripped us off coming back so I went into the attic," he explained.

"Are there any firearms in the house?" the officer asked.

Jesus hesitated, then nodded.

"I have a revolver and a sawed-off shotgun in the attic," he said.

"We got robbed by some Gringo's and we chased them down the road and they shot up our car and we wrecked. I grabbed the guns out of our car and ran because I thought they might turn around and come back and kill me."

"What kind of car were you guys driving?" the officer asked.

"We were driving a Dodge Hellcat," he replied.

"How did you get back here with the guns?" Officer Simmons asked.

"I made a phone call and a friend gave me a ride back here. I have only been back here about a 1/2 hour until you guys showed up," he answered.

"Do you live here at the house?" Officer Simmons asked and Jesus nodded yes.

"Why would the guys come back?" Officer Simmons asked Jesus.

"Because they never got all the cash and meth," he said and instantly regretted his outburst.

"Look, Jesus, you know we can get a search warrant to do a thorough search of this house using a drug dog," Officer Ethridge stated to Jesus.

"I'm requesting that you cooperate and sign a search consent form so we can save time and it will prove that you are cooperating in this investigation," Officer Ethridge said to Jesus.

Jesus hung his head for about 30 seconds, then said, "Give me the Search Consent Card and I will sign it."

"Where are the drugs and money hidden?" Officer Ethridge asked.

Jesus directed them to open drawers where Ryan and Juan had stolen the money and meth.

"Those drawers have false bottoms and you will find meth and packets of money beneath the false bottoms," he said.

"If you pull the bottom drawers completely out along the kitchen cabinets you will find more stuff on the bottom half of the drawers, attached underneath," he said.

"We need to call our Crime Scene Techs to process the crime scene for the body in the backyard and also take photos of the drugs and other evidence that are found," Officer Simmons said.

"Stand by, keep an eye on the attic opening and I will be right back with my under vehicle inspection mirror so we can make sure the attic is clear," Trooper Reed said.

He was gone for several minutes and returned carrying what looked like a round 10 inch mirror on the end of a metal round aluminum broom type stick.

Trooper Reed sat the fallen kitchen chair up beneath the attic and inserted the mirror up into the opening so he could sweep the mirror around the attic for other suspects.

Finally, he said the attic was clear, except there was a handgun and sawed-off shotgun located right beside the opening of the attic.

Trooper Reed picked up the overturned chair beneath the attic opening and placed it upright, and stood on the chair, reaching up and recovered the firearms.

Othello Police Sgt. John Price had arrived on the scene and was given an update on the incident starting with the initial call of a dead body.

"We have a search waiver signed by Jesus Chaco who is a resident," Officer Simmons told Sgt. Price.

Sgt. Price held his portable radio near his mouth and called for detectives from the Major Crimes Unit, the Medical Examiner's Office, and the ambulance to transport the deceased male after it had been examined and cleared by the Major Crimes Detectives and the Medical Examiner.

"I'm also calling in the Forensic Evidence Recovery Unit to process the inside of the residence and recover found evidence, including the firearms inside."

He quickly radioed his orders to the Communication Center.

He also requested four Reserve Police Officers to respond and manage the security points and within 45 minutes the reserve officers were on the scene, blocking alley entrances and two were stationed at the front and rear of the residence.

The three Washington State Troopers were cleared from the scene after many thanks for their assistance.

Shortly afterwards the Forensic Evidence Recovery team arrived as well as three Major Crimes Detectives and Sgt. Randy Evans.

Sgt. Price and officer Ethridge provided the information to the two groups when they arrived.

Sgt. Randy Evans, the supervisor of Major Crimes detectives, was provided the Search Consent Card obtained from Jesus Chaco.

"Ok, thanks," he said, "I'd like one of the Major Crimes Detectives and myself to place Jesus Chaco in the back area of our van where we can interview him. I will call for a patrol car to transport him to the Othello City Jail when we are finished with him."

"Great!" said Sgt. Price and he notified Officer Simmons that he could clear the scene and resume normal patrol activity, and prepare reports of his involvement in the case.

He directed Officer Ethridge to wait and transport Jesus Chaco to the Othello jail after the Detectives had conducted an onsite interview with him.

The Medical Examiner approached the body and carefully inserted a sharp tipped instrument into the back kidney area of the body to check for the internal temperature to determine the time of death.

"The internal temperature of the body indicates time of death was ten hours to fifteen hours ago and rigor mortis is almost fully involved," he explained.

Sgt. Price stepped away and made a cell phone call to Fred Pruitt, the Othello Police Chief, and explained what had transpired that day.

"You know, these past 24 hours have been crazy in our region," the Chief commented.

"One car in an irrigation canal with the driver found dead inside from a gunshot to the head, connected to a possible road rage on I-90 near the Quincy Washington exit that left the driver with a gunshot wound and his passenger injured," he continued.

"All of the incidents are likely gang related," he finished.

Chapter 30

Ryan and Juan were sitting in Ryan's mother's living room watching the news to see if the robbery and murder had been reported by the local media.

The T-BYU Cable News reported police activity at a residence located in Othello and a body had been discovered in the back yard.

A Police Spokesman was tight lipped and promised a press release in the coming hours.

There was a report of a one vehicle collision on I-90 near Quincy, Wa. exit.

The driver was injured with a gunshot wound and transported to the Hospital in Wheatland.

The only passenger received leg injuries and was treated and released to police custody.

"What the hell," Ryan shouted, "there was a third guy in that car so what the hell happened to him?"

"I know there were three of them and why didn't the cops mention the guns in the car? They sure as hell weren't throwing rocks at us," he continued.

"Maybe the guy that took off probably took the guns with him," he said thoughtfully.

The News barely mentioned that a vehicle had been driven into the Remington Canal near Quincy and the lone driver had perished.

"No one seems to have connected the dots yet," Ryan said.

"Let's head to Spokane and get rid of the 45 caliber pistol," he said.

"I know a couple of soreno dealers that we can sell some kilos at a discount price," he continued.

"Ok, let's drive the pick-up around the back in the alley and get some more money and 3-4 kilos of meth to sell," Juan said to Ryan.

They parked in front of the rollup garage door and retrieved more cash and 3 kilos of meth.

They left Wheatland and headed to Spokane, driving East on Highway 17, passing through small villages of Wilson Creek, Odessa and Davenport where they connected to Highway Two and drove through the small towns of Wilbur and Reardan.

By driving the speed limit they were not stopped in any of the speed traps often set up by the local police in the small towns.

"Hey, let's stop at the Tribal Casino in Airway Heights just west of Spokane and do some high rolling gambling and stay at a high priced master suite and party," suggested Juan.

"Good idea," Ryan said and turned onto the road leading to the Casino.

"Pull over for a minute," said Juan, "we need to stow those kilos in a bag or something when we go inside and check out a room."

"We're OK, just put the meth and gun in the center console and I can lock it with my console key," said Ryan.

They drove to the entrance and had the parking valet take the vehicle and drive it off to park it.

"I hope your ignition key doesn't open up the console," Juan said.

"No, I have the only console key in my pocket," Ryan replied.

They checked into a deluxe suite on the upper floor and the female desk clerk looked closely at them as Ryan peeled out $3,000 in $100 bills to pay for the room in advance.

He handed the clerk a hundred dollar bill as a tip, which won him a smile.

Chapter 31

The following Monday morning Othello Police Chief Fred Pruitt, Task Force criminal investigators from Chelan County Sheriff's office, detectives from Othello Police Department and Sgt. Matt Price were present for a meeting in the Othello Police Chief's conference room.

Detectives Hannigan, Fitz and Skates sat at the back of the room as spectators.

When everyone was seated at tables with their coffee and pastry, Chief Pruitt moved to the front of the room with whiteboards located on the wall behind him.

"Gentlemen, it seems like the event on I-90, the trap house homicide in Othello and the Honda in the Remington Canal are all connected," he began.

"The two male subjects involved in the rollover on I-90 are both identified norteno gangsters and they reside at a known norteno trap house in Othello where the murder victim was found in the back yard. The driver of the vehicle in the rollover was shot in the right shoulder and his vehicle swerved and rolled over several times. The driver did survive the incident but will lose the use of his right arm due to nerve damage," he continued.

"The doctors removed a 45 caliber slug from his shoulder. The passenger in the vehicle suffered a broken leg but he is not talking to us. The only thing the passenger told us was that "they would handle it", so it seems we may have some more revenge shooting deaths involving gang members. There were four 45 caliber shell casings located along I-90 and spaced about a quarter mile or so from the rollover," he said.

"The victim found in the backyard of the Othello trap house is Michael Guzman, 27 years of age. Michael died from a fractured skull and the shape of the skull fracture would indicate a baseball bat or some other rounded weapon was used. He is the brother of Carlos Guzman, the driver that was shot and lost control of the Dodge Hellcat that wrecked on I-90. We conducted a safety search of the Othello residence and located a male subject named Jesus Chaco hiding in the attic section of the house. We located a 12 gauge sawed off shot gun and a 357 caliber revolver where Jesus had hidden the weapons. Jesus was really scared and traumatized. He told us that he had been a lookout in front of the residence and checking out customers before they could go into the house to buy their drugs. He said he noticed a red Honda four door drive out from a side street headed towards the highway. He noticed the Honda because the lights were off on the car. When the car slowed, one of the brake lights came on, but only on the left side. About that time he heard Carlos yelling loudly so he ran into the house and found Carlos and Alphonso secured with flex cuffs. He quickly cut off the flex cuffs and told Carlos about the red Honda he had seen leaving town with the lights out and a brake light out. Jesus said Carlos grabbed a sawed off shotgun and a 357 Magnum revolver. They all piled into Carlo's Dodge Hellfire and left at a high rate of speed to catch up to the red Honda. Jesus said they had traveled on the highway at high speed for about five or six miles when they caught up to the red Honda and got so close they may have bumped the back bumper of the Honda. He said that Alphonso took the 357 revolver and started shooting into the back of the red Honda. The passenger of the red Honda started shooting back at them from the passenger window and probably fired five or six times. That was when Carlos got shot and lost control of the car and crashed. Jesus said he crawled out of the wrecked Dodge Hellcat with the shotgun and revolver and ran from the scene. He said he called a friend that picked him up and took him back to the norteno trap house in Othello. He was afraid to go into the backyard to cover Michael's body because he thought the robbers would come back and kill him. He was actually relieved that it was the cops that came into the trap house. Jesus admitted that the 357 revolver we recovered in the attic at the house was the gun that Alphonso was using to shoot at the fleeing Honda. He also disclosed the location of packets of meth valued at $300,000.00 and $900,000.00 in cash that was hidden under the drawers in the kitchen that the robbers missed. There were 3 fired cartridges and three unfired cartridges in the 357 caliber revolver cylinder. The revolver was test fired at the WSP Forensic Crime lab and the bullet matched the slug found on the floor of the red Honda. The slug was somewhat deformed and it appears the damage was done when it passed through the skull of Bronza. The search warrant that had been executed on the Dodge Hellfire turned up some twelve gauge shotgun shells and four 357 magnum cartridges. They were probably placed in the car by Carlos Guzman when he jumped in the Dodge Hellfire prior to the chase. Now, turning to the murder victim found in the backyard at the Othello Trap house," he paused. "Like I said, the victim with the smashed skull is Michael Guzman. I would guess that the victim may have been facing one of the takedown crew and someone must have sneaked up behind him and hit him in the back of the head with such force that the back of the skull was driven into the brain pan. The Medical Examiner doubts if the victim even knew he had been struck since death was probably instantaneous. We have reviewed the reports related to the red Honda that was pulled out of the Remington Canal the next day after the incident at 1-90 near the Quincy exit. A male subject, later identified as Bronza Miller, was found inside the vehicle and he had a severe head injury possibly caused by a 357 caliber bullet that had hit him in the back of the head and exited and struck the dashboard and fell onto the floor. We also located several 45 caliber ACP shell casings inside the interior of the red Honda. We would suspect that the shooter was firing a 45 caliber semi auto pistol from the right passenger side of the Honda. The 45 caliber shell casings from the submerged red Honda were sent to the WSP Firearms Crime lab to check for specific markings on the head stamp of the shell casings. The four 45 Caliber shell casings found at the accident scene on I-90 near the Quincy Exit were also collected and sent to the Washington State Patrol Crime Lab. The shell casing head stamps were photographed for comparison. Then they were sent to the WSP Crime Lab in Olympia for a DNA swab. I can tell you that the firing pin markings on the two 45 caliber shells recovered at the vehicle in the Remington Canal and the four shell casings recovered at the I-90 and Quincy off ramp all matched. The extractor marks were the same on all of the shell casings. The four shell casings from the I-90 scene were then sent to the WSP lab for DNA swabbing. For now, we are waiting to see if there is identifiable DNA on the shell casings. There is a rush at the DNA lab so we can move forward with this case and identify suspects. A baseball bat was found between the front bucket seats of the red Honda and that is the likely weapon used to kill Michael Guzman. The Baseball bat has been forwarded to the Medical Examiners Forensic Office to determine if the baseball bat matches the crushed skull of the victim Michael Guzman. And one last thing," he continued, "the registration on the red Honda came back to Georgio Rasmussen with a Wenatchee address. We located him in Chelan where he is working at an Apple warehouse. He seemed surprised that his Honda had been found in the Remington Canal. He told us, as far as he knew, the car had been stored in the garage at his ex-girlfriend's house. He was adamant that he had given no one permission to drive his car. His ex-girlfriend is Marigold Summer and she was located at 2307 N Orchard Lane in East Wenatchee. We contacted her and checked inside the garage with her and the red Honda was missing. She said she did not give permission for anyone to be driving Georgio Rasmussen's red Honda and the car must have been taken from the garage while she was at work. Marigold advised her on again and off again boyfriend was Bronza Miller and he knew about the Honda that was located in her garage. She revealed that Bronza's vehicle was currently parked in her back yard, but she had not seen or heard from him for about a week. Marigold gave permission to allow investigators to enter her property, and they had Bronza's vehicle towed to the WSP evidence processing garage in Wenatchee.

She told the investigators that Bronza lived in Wheatland on 3rd street about a block north of the Division street market," Chief Pruitt finished.

Chapter 32

After the meeting Hannigan, Skates and Fitz sat back in their chairs to see which direction they would be taking on the investigation.

"Remember, we did put out an APB asking for any information law enforcement agencies had regarding 45 caliber handguns and ammunition they might recover from their department activities," Hannigan said.

"Fitz, would you take the recovered 45 caliber shell casing in the John Adams case and hand carry it to the WSP Firearms Crime Lab? We need to see if it matches the six 45 caliber semi auto shell casings found at the scene of the shooting at I-90 and Quincy exit and the shell casings found in the red Honda," Hannigan said.

"Sure thing, it's only a 2 hour drive so I'll leave right away," Fitz replied.

"I will phone ahead for you," said Detective Skates.

"Maybe they will be able to give us the answer this afternoon," he continued.

"I will check with the WSP Lab in Cheney, Washington and see if they can do the comparison today," said Detective Fitz.

About 4:30 P.M. Detective Hannigan received a phone call from Detective Fitz, calling from the WSP Forensic Firearms Crime Lab.

Detective Hannigan put the phone on speaker mode as Detective Skates was the only person in the War Room beside himself.

"Well, the 45 caliber shell casing found in John Adams's front yard is a match to the other six shell casings recovered from the Remington Canal and along I-90," he exclaimed.

"The firing pin markings and ejector marks all matched."

"What the hell," blurted Detective Skates.

"We have Dustin Silver sitting in jail so we know he wasn't involved in any of the shootings from those incidents," he continued.

"Bronza Miller lived right across the street from Ryan Bates's mom," he said.

"Bronza must have taken the red Honda from his girlfriend's house in Wenatchee. Bronza takes a bullet and is DOA but who was with him at the norteno trap house in Othello? I would bet the other Mutts are Ryan Bates and Juan Garcia since they all hung around together. Maybe one of them found the pistol that was used to kill John Adams and is using it on their crime spree," Hannigan said thoughtfully.

"Let's go by Ryan's house and Juan's apartment and run them down."

"This still doesn't mean they killed John Adams, I think Dustin Silver is still responsible," Detective Hannigan said.

"Let's wait until tomorrow and we will start a search for them," Detective Hannigan said.

"This case is spreading out all ways," Detective Skates said thoughtfully.

Chapter 33

Anson and Monty sat in the hotel lobby having a cup of coffee and discussed their strategy to locate other witnesses to the event.

"I think our next step is to contact known associates of Ryan Bates and Juan Garcia here in Wheatland," said Monty.

They had sent a Public Records Request to Wheatland Police records for all police reports on Ryan Bates and Juan Garcia.

Several names appeared in the police reports that listed addresses of associates in the same neighborhood as Bates and Garcia.

"The name Martin Nelson is mentioned in several police reports connected to Bates, so let's pay him a visit today. His address is on First Street, about 6 blocks from John Adam's house," said Anson.

About 15 minutes later they arrived at the front of the residence and parked across the street.

The house was a rancher style design with a one car garage.

A 4 ft. chain link fence surrounded the back yard and a Beware of Dog sign had been attached near the front fence gate.

Anson leaned over the fence and knocked loudly on the side of the residence.

The front door opened and a large man, at least 6 ft 7 inches tall, weighing at least 300 lbs. stepped out onto the small front porch landing.

His voice was tight and suspicious as he asked what the Private Investigators wanted.

Anson explained they were canvassing the neighborhood for clues to the recent homicide of John Adams.

"Are you Martin Nelson?" Monty asked Martin in a neutral tone of voice.

"Yes, I am Martin," he replied.

"Look, I think I can help you but I have to be careful," he said as he looked up and down the street to see if anyone was watching.

"My wife Karen and kids are in the house so do you guys mind talking to me in the back yard?" he asked.

They walked around the corner of the house and sat in chairs on the small concrete patio.

"I do have information on the murder but I haven't come forward to the local cops because I don't trust them. The guy that killed John Adams has come by my house and told me someone has snitched on him and he will find the snitch and pop a cap on him," Martin said.

"Why don't we start from the top," Anson said to Martin.

"OK," he began, "on the day of the murder, at about 10:00 A.M., I was over at my friend Trampus Byrne's house right down the block from here. We were in his bedroom playing video games when this guy Juan Garcia shows up and his mom, let him in the house. Juan came into the bedroom where we were playing video games. Juan was in a cold sweat and was fidgeting like he was coming off meth. But this time it was different because he seemed actually frightened. Juan told us that he and Ryan Bates had been out all night breaking into cars and stealing whatever they could find. He said there was a pick-up truck parked on the street about 1/2 block from Ryan's house. Juan said he was the lookout and Ryan was in this guy's truck looking for guns. Ryan thought the guy had kept his guns there periodically because he had observed the guy carrying guns back and forth to his house in the past. Ryan found a gun under the storage compartment between the front seats of the truck. Juan told us that the guy started to leave his house through the front door and he saw Ryan getting out of the guy's truck. He told us the guy yelled and started to walk down the sidewalk and Ryan shot the guy with his own gun. Juan told us that he ran from there and went home and climbed back into bed with his girlfriend. Juan said he couldn't sleep so he finally got up and walked over to Trampus Byrne's house because he was stressed out and thought he was going to get sick. He stayed there in the bedroom with us and played some video games and he seemed to calm down. A little later Trampus' mom came to the bedroom door and said Ryan was at the front door. Juan seemed to freak out and begged us not to tell Ryan that he was there. I went out the backdoor and walked around the corner and called Ryan's name, and he turned and looked at me. I said, "Hi Ryan, Trampus is amped up on meth in his bedroom, let's go over to my house and share some weed," Martin explained.

"Ryan and I walked down the alley and made our way to my house," said Martin.

"We sat on the front porch and shared a joint. Ryan seemed freaked out and I thought taking on some weed would calm him down. After about twenty minutes Ryan had become pretty mellow. He told me that he and Juan had been out breaking into cars and had got into a guy's pick-up truck that had been parked on the street. Ryan told me the guy came out of the house and spotted him, and he just panicked and started to run away. He told me he had found a 45 semi-auto handgun in the truck with a box of ammo and when the guy stepped out, he pointed the gun at him and pulled the trigger. Ryan told me that if he got arrested he was just going to tell the cops that he accidentally shot the guy. We sat on the front porch for about an hour and my mom came home so Ryan left," he continued.

"Do you mind making a written statement and signing it?" Monty asked Martin.

"Let me think about that, I don't want to endanger my family because Ryan can be batshit crazy."

"OK, that's fair enough, I'm sure we will be in touch and check with you in about a week," said Anson.

Anson and Monty left their car parked on the street and walked about 1/2 block to Sharon and Trampus Byrne's house.

When they approached, a middle aged woman was seen sitting in a cheap plastic chair on the side patio of the house and was smoking a cigar.

She seemed lost in thought and was startled when she was alerted by Anson and Monty approaching.

"Excuse us, ma'am, my name is David Anson and the gentleman beside me is Monty Victor. We are both Washington State Licensed Private Investigators and we are hoping to speak with Sharon Byrne."

"That is me," she replied and looked suspiciously at them.

"We understand that you may have some information on the murder of John Adams," he continued.

"Oh yes, I have a lot of stuff to tell you," she said.

"I heard the cops had been going door to door but no one ever knocked on my door, beside you guys," she said.

"Well, I need to clarify with you that we are not the cops, we are Licensed Private Investigators just trying to find out what happened," Anson told her.

"I understand," Sharon replied. "I've been waiting for someone to show up. I knew that Ryan and Juan had killed John Adams because I heard Juan make a confession to my son and to the neighbor kid, Martin Nelson," she continued.

"I heard there had been an arrest in the case and found that a guy named Dustin Silver had been arrested for the murder of John Adams. The news said the guy was an ex-boyfriend of the woman named Marianne Shutt and this guy named Dustin Silver was jealous and killed John Adams," she said.

"The newspaper article said the guy had the motive and opportunity to kill John," she continued.

"I went to a lawyer named Robert Lee in Wheatland and told him what I had overheard," she continued.

"The Lawyer wasn't sure if I was telling him the truth so he had me submit to a Polygraph Examination. The Polygraph took several hours to complete and when we finished, the Polygrapher notified me that I had successfully passed the polygraph and was truthful. He told me he was writing up his report and was forwarding it to the Attorney Walter Colvins."

"What did you see or hear?" Monty asked.

"It was about 10:00 A.M. on the morning of the murder when I heard some knocking on the side of my house. I stepped outside onto my front porch and saw this kid named Juan Garcia knocking on my son's bedroom window. I asked him what he wanted and Juan told me that he was there to see my son Trampus," she continued.

"I told him to stop knocking and he could come into the house and see Trampus," she said.

"When he entered he had a strong, sweaty smell and looked really nervous and jumpy. I took him down the hallway and knocked on the door before opening the door. I opened the door and Trampus and the neighbor kid named Martin Nelson were sitting on the bed playing video games. Juan went into the room and I stepped out and closed the door," she continued.

"I stood out in the hallway and listened so I could figure out why Juan was in a panic," she said.

"I heard him say he thought he was in big trouble. Martin asked him what he was talking about. Juan said he was prowling cars with Ryan that morning and Ryan had stolen a handgun out of a guy's pick-up truck and shot and killed the owner," she said.

"Juan also said that it was an accident, that Ryan had just panicked," she continued.

"I heard the floor creak and thought someone was coming out of the bedroom so I went back into the living room," she said.

"Just before noon there was another knock on the front door and Ryan Bates was standing there. Ryan wanted to know if Trampus was there and I told him I would check and see if he was awake."

"That gave me the opportunity to walk back and let the guys know he was outside. Juan said he didn't want Ryan to know he was there," she continued.

"Martin said he would go around the side of the house to the front and have Ryan go over to his house. As far as I know, that's what he did," she finished.

"You have been very helpful," Monty told Sharon.

"Would you mind signing a statement containing the information you just told us?" Anson asked.

"Not at all, and I'm also available if you want to do a recorded interview," she answered.

"Is Trampus available this morning so we can talk to him for a few minutes?" Anson asked.

"He was awake in his bedroom playing video games about an hour ago. He plays those dumb ass video games 24 hours a day," Sharon said with a look of disdain.

"Hang on, I'll have him come outside and talk to you, it might help him get some fresh air," she said.

About 5 minutes later Trampus walked out to the side patio of the house.

"Hey Trampus, I'm Monty Victor and this is my partner David Anson. We are both State Licensed Private Investigators," he explained.

Trampus held his closed fist out in front of him and did a knuckle bump greetings with both investigators.

He looked up and down the street to see if anyone might be walking nearby.

"Have you guys talked to Martin Nelson about this?" he asked.

"Yes, we talked to him earlier this morning," Anson answered.

"Did he tell you what Juan Garcia said to us the day that dude got capped by Ryan Bates?" he asked.

"Yes, he pretty much told us what happened, but it's always better to talk to other witnesses that heard what Juan Garcia said in your bedroom," answered Anson.

"Witnesses will often forget key information, so when several witnesses are questioned, the fine details can be found and fleshed out," Monty said.

"OK, let me start out by saying that on the night before the guy was killed, Martin had come over to play video games and had ended up spending the night. We had played until the early morning hours, about 2:00 A.M. We woke up at about 8:00 A.M. on the morning of the murder," he said.

"Martin and I had been playing a progressive video game online with other gamers and were playing for bitcoin," he continued.

"We were up by 75 bitcoin when Juan came into my bedroom. When I looked at Juan, he looked pretty bad," Trampus said.

"What do you mean?" Monty asked Trampus.

"I mean, Juan looked scared and his hand was shaking so bad he could hardly hold his bottle of Gatorade I gave him. He actually puked in a trash can in my bedroom," he continued.

"I was pissed off with him, but wanted to hear what the hell happened that would upset him so badly," he continued.

"Juan started out by saying, "I'm screwed, that damn Ryan." Juan told us that he was out with Ryan prowling cars the night before and they had a good haul of cash and jewelry. He told me that Ryan had a great idea to try and steal guns out of a guy's truck that was parked over by his mom's house. Ryan had said that he knew where there was a major norteno trap house in Othello, Washington that was selling a lot of meth. He thought it would be an easy robbery and a quick way to make a lot of money and steal a bunch of drugs if he had a gun," he said.

"Getting back to the John Adams murder, what else did Juan tell you?" asked Monty.

"Juan told Martin and me that they walked on the sidewalk beside the guy's truck just before daylight. They saw the guy inside his house through the front window and he was sitting at his desk in the living room, and he was playing on his computer. Juan told me he stood at the corner of the guy's house where he could see if the guy was getting ready to leave, and was supposed to warn Ryan," Trampus continued.

"Juan told me he got distracted and was watching Ryan as he was in the truck. When he turned his attention back to the guy in the house, the guy already had put his coat on and was walking to the front door with a set of keys in his hand. Juan said he whistled at Ryan but it was too late. Juan said the guy yelled at Ryan, and Ryan started to turn to run from the guy, but instead turned and shot at the guy one time. He said the shot was really loud and he saw the man clutch his stomach and struggle to get back inside his house. Juan told us he ran across the front yard and ran through an opening between the guy's house and his neighbor's house to the north. He didn't know how Ryan got away, but they met each other when they were running down the alley to escape," he continued.

"Juan told me that when they ran out of the alley on Division Street there was a guy walking from the convenience store and coffee shop and was crossing the road and headed on 3rd street towards where Ryan shot the guy. He said the man was holding a couple of paper cups of coffee and the guy looked directly at him. Juan didn't know if the guy got a good look at his face but he was really worried. Juan told us that he split up with Ryan and went back home. He said when he went into his house through a slider, he had forgotten that his brother's girlfriend was sleeping on the couch, and she rolled over and looked at him as he came through the door. He said he went to the bathroom and took his jeans and shoes off, then crept into his bedroom and slid back into bed without waking his girlfriend, Tiffanie Weeks."

"Are you willing to sign a Declaration regarding the information you just provided?" Monty asked him.

"Sure, I will do that, but you better get Ryan off the street before he kills somebody else," he replied.

Chapter 34

Ryan lay on one of the queen beds in the deluxe suite at the Casino where they had checked in.

Juan and Ryan had gambled heavily at the high stake poker tables and spent a lot of time and money doing the slots.

They had lost thousands of dollars gambling and had used room service numerous times.

Several of the high price prostitutes that prowled the Casino in search of high rolling Johns had noticed the large amount of money Ryan and Juan were throwing down.

It wasn't long before they were focused on the two young men and were having conversations with them.

As the night went on, Ryan and Juan continued to drink, and by midnight they both had a serious buzz on.

"You boys want to go up to your suite and party some more with us?" Star and Shontell asked.

"What do you have in mind?" asked Ryan with a sloppy grin on his face.

"Whatever you would like," the woman named Star said and slid her hand down on the front of his pants and rubbed on the front of his zipper.

Ryan said, "Come on, Juan, let's go back to our suite and bring these ladies."

They all walked out of the casino together to the main lobby where they took the elevator to the 9th floor two bedroom suite.

Once inside, Ryan took one of the high priced hookers' hand and took her into the bedroom.

Before he closed the door he told Juan he would see him in a couple of hours and winked at Juan.

Star wrapped her arms around him and thrust her hips forward.

"Look, honey, no pay, no play," Star said to Ryan.

"How much?" Ryan asked as he started to rub the woman's shapely hips.

"Five hundred dollars an hour or One-thousand dollars for the rest of the night." she said.

"If you're a real cowboy, I'll show you a real rodeo," she said as she laughed.

Meanwhile, Juan had sat on the sofa in the suite with the other attractive hooker and poured her a glass of wine.

"By the way, what's your name?" he asked.

"They call me Shontell," she answered.

"Care to share a joint?" he asked.

"No," she said, "I have some high grade coke if you want to do a line."

"How much for one line?" he asked.

Juan had little experience using cocaine because of the high cost.

"Three hundred dollars a line, but of course, you'll pay for mine, won't you?" she said as she turned towards him and rubbed the inside of his leg.

"Sure, baby, lay out a couple of lines," and peeled out six One hundred bills from his pants pocket and laid them on the coffee table.

Shontell laid out two lines of cocaine on the coffee table.

Juan placed a straw into a nose nostril and sucked in the white powdery substance.

His nose turned numb and his senses were unbelievably sensitive.

Shontell deftly inserted a cocktail straw in her nose and sucked the other line of cocaine into her sinuses.

She turned towards Juan and started kissing him deeply and rubbing her hand on his chest.

"Honey, if you want some of this, it's not free. If you want to play," she said as she kissed the tender part of his neck.

"How much?" Juan asked as he stood up from the sofa and took her hand and led her into the bedroom.

By then, Juan was so excited he would have agreed to any price but she quoted the same price as Star.

Several hours later the women had emerged dressed from the bedrooms and tucked the cash into their small purses.

"Geez, this dude Ryan tipped me another $200 dollars," she bragged.

"I left Juan my phone number because he wants more, maybe later tonight. That kid does not have a clue how to treat an experienced woman like me," Shontell said as they left.

Both women left the hotel room while both Ryan and Juan slept their intoxication off.

"Oh Gawd, that was the most talented woman I have ever been with," said Ryan as he sat at the kitchen table of the suite drinking mimosa with a breakfast of ham and eggs followed by black coffee ordered from room service.

Juan was also sitting at the table, holding his head between his hands.

He was trying to get over a case of vertigo from his use of the cocaine the night before.

He had a plate of dry roast, a glass of ice water and a small glass of apple juice.

Juan looked at Ryan's plate of food and had to fight down nausea.

"Let's call them for another date tonight," Ryan said.

"That's a great idea," he said to Ryan, let's give them a call later this afternoon.

"That woman taught me stuff I had only heard of," he said with a grin.

"That Shontell is the most experienced woman I have ever been with," he continued

"All this gambling, drinking, expensive food and the cost of this suite has pretty much depleted the money. I think I have four or five thousand left but let's go downstairs and pay for another five or six nights here," Ryan said.

"We'll take the meth we have locked in the pick-up and go into Spokane and sell the gun and the three kilos of meth. We still have some 8 balls of meth we can keep for ourselves. The meth is good grade and we can dump the meth for a good price per kilo in town. It's normal to pay $15K for a kilo of the same grade. I know a couple guys down in the Zone located west of the Spokane County Courthouse. The Cops and Lawyers call the area "Felony Flats" because it's wide open," he continued.

"I used to stay there with a guy named Tim Bolt when I was hiding from the cops, we'll look him up," Ryan said.

They got into the pick-up truck and drove into Spokane downtown, then turned west and drove past the County Courthouse and Jail on Broadway Avenue.

"Man, don't ever spend a night in that rat hole jail unless you are crazy," Ryan said and shuddered.

"You share a small cell with another inmate and they let you out of the cell only one hour a day."

Ryan slowed down as they continued westbound on Broadway and pointed out a small park.

"When you want to score any kind of dope, this is the place to go," he continued.

"They call this place "Peace Park" but it's so bad the cops hardly ever walk into the park unless there are three or four cops together as back-up," he continued.

"We'll go around on the far side of the park on Bridger Street," he advised.

As they slowed down they saw five dangerous looking men standing around a picnic table.

They appeared to be the muscle and security for the drug trade going on.

Another man was stationed about a hundred feet to the side of the group on Broadway Avenue and it was obvious he was the lookout if cops were spotted.

They parked the pick-up on Bridge Street.

"Just be cool and sit in the truck, we're going to get checked out by some of this gang," Ryan warned Juan.

A couple of the men stepped away from the group.

The larger of the two wore all dark clothing and was wearing a black stocking cap and sunglasses.

The second gang member was shorter and was wearing tan pants and a wife beater shirt.

The gang banger with the wife beater shirt had a handgun tucked down in the front of his jeans with the butt of the gun clearly visible.

They never said a word as they approached Ryan's pick-up, then slowly walked around, doing an inspection.

Finally, the taller of the two gangsters tapped on the driver's side window and Ryan rolled the window down.

"What you boys doing in my hood?" he asked in a menacing tone.

"Hey, Cisco, it's me, you know, the farm boy from Wheatland," he said in a soft tone.

"Tell your boss I can score him some good meth if he is interested and there's no fentanyl in the mix. It's pure grade straight from the Mexican source," he continued.

"Wait here," Cisco said and walked back to the group.

Cisco talked to a man sitting at the table who was obviously the gang leader.

The large Hispanic man stood up and they both started walking back to the pick-up.

"That's the guy I deal with, his nickname is Paco, but nobody knows his real name," said Ryan.

Paco walked up to the driver's window and recognized Ryan immediately.

"Hey, Farm Boy," he exclaimed. "I thought you got capped or something, it's been so long," he said with a loud laugh.

"Naw, man, I been in jail for the past 6 months off and on, and had to do the pee tests," he lied.

"You haven't been in the lockup here or I would have known about it," Paco said as he looked directly at Ryan.

"No, I was on DOC Violation in Oregon," he replied.

"Who's this Dude?" he asked and looked over at Juan who had been watching several other gang members standing in the park.

"Hey, man, he's cool, we are like brothers," he said and introduced Paco to Juan.

"Look, man, we got a large load of meth down in Oregon and we need to dump extra so we can pick up a load of Blow (cocaine) next week."

Paco looked suspiciously at Ryan and said, "If you give me a deal, I'll buy some, but the meth better be the grade of pure quality."

"I say it is," replied Ryan.

"Let's see it," Paco said.

"Get in the truck here in the front seat and we can deal. Juan, get out of the front seat and stand outside," Ryan ordered.

Ryan knew Juan would have his hand close to the 45 Semi Auto pistol tucked in his jeans with his shirt concealing the gun.

Once Paco was seated in the front seat, he looked around and the group of men were standing about 20 feet in front of the pick-up.

"OK, let's see what you got," Paco said to Ryan.

Ryan raised the cushioned center console of the front seat and pushed it back until it was standing straight up.

He then reached and grasped a strap, and pulled up the bottom compartment cover of the console.

Three kilo sized bundles of meth were clearly visible.

Ryan removed one kilo and lowered the console back to it's original position.

He handed the bundle of meth to Paco who looked at the outside covering, turning it over to check for markings and feeling the weight.

"Hey, Farm Boy, there's dried blood on the outer wrapper," he exclaimed with surprise.

"Like I said, I got it down in Oregon," he explained.

Paco knew Ryan was lying but he knew he would be paying a low price for the meth, with a potential to make a handy profit.

"I need to check on the quality first," Paco said.

He reached into his pants pocket and pulled out a small bladed folding knife.

He plunged the blade into the top of the packet and twisted the blade, making a small opening in the covering of the meth kilo wrapping.

He slid the blade sideways into the bundle and removed a small amount of a tan substance.

Paco motioned for Cisco to step forward.

"Take this and use a drug test kit to make sure it's not crap."

Cisco gingerly picked up the knife, holding the blade sideways and walked across the street where a standard looking Chevy Impala with darkened windows was parked.

Cisco got into the Impala on the passenger side and closed the door.

Ryan nervously tapped the steering with his fingers while they waited.

"I can supply you with more of this stuff when you need it," he said to Paco.

A few minutes later, Cisco got out of the Chevy Impala and walked over to the pick-up passenger side.

He handed the knife back to Paco and told him the contents of the meth packet was high quality.

Paco knew he could cut the meth down at least 5 times and sell at a good price.

"How much a kilo?" asked Paco.

"$15K per kilo and that's a good deal," Ryan told him.

That's a great price, Paco thought to himself, *I've been paying $20K a kilo.*

There is blood on the bundles, so they are probably from a rip-off somewhere, he thought.

I'll watch the news and I bet there will be a report of a gang style shooting and that's where this meth will be from, he mused.

"That's $45K for all three," Ryan told him.

"I've got a pretty steady supply but I'll do you a favor and take it off your hands for $35K," Paco said.

"Fuck, man, you don't know how involved it was for Juan and me to buy this stuff," he said to Paco.

"As nervous as you are, I don't think you want to be going around trying to get rid of this stuff to other trap houses," Paco said to Ryan.

"Look at the blood on the wrappings, I wouldn't want to be you if the Sinaloa Drug Cartel finds out who you are and track you down. Those markings on the wrappings are symbols of the Mexican Sinaloa Drug Cartel and they will kill you and your family if they find out you ripped one of their dealers off," he said.

"I know they supply the nortenos in this area," Paco continued.

"Tell you what, I'll raise to $40K and that's as far as I can go. I will destroy all the meth wrappers with the blood on them," he finished.

"If you obtain more kilos of meth, be sure and tear the wrappers with the cartel markings off before you try to sell them. I'll buy as much as you want to sell but you have to sell to me at a discount," he said.

"OK, you have a deal, I need the $40K in large bills," Ryan said.

"Hold on," Paco said and motioned for Cisco to come to the pick-up.

"$40K," he said to Cisco and passed the single kilo packet to Cisco.

He walked across the street and opened the trunk of the Impala and placed the kilo into the trunk, and reached down and appeared to be placing something in a brown shopping bag.

The other gangsters were standing in a semi circle near the pick-up watching for cops or worse, from an attack from other ruthless drug gangs in Felony Flats.

Finally, Cisco walked back over to the pick-up and passed the bag through the open side window and handed the bag to Ryan.

Ryan removed one bundled money packet out of the bag and noted there was a stamped sign of $5,000 dollars on the paper wrapping around each bundle.

"There are eight of these packets and it looks like $5,000 in each pack," he said to Juan who had been standing outside Ryan's window.

Ryan lifted up the center console and handed the other two kilo packets to Paco.

Ryan dumped the money packets inside the console and handed the bag back to Paco.

"Bring me some more," Paco said and laughed as he slapped Ryan on the shoulder and stepped out of the pick-up and closed the door.

They drove away from the park and they headed east on Broadway Avenue before turning south on Monroe Street and entered the on-ramp for westbound interstate 90.

They turned off at the Airway Heights exit.

They stopped at a western themed restaurant that specialized in "Barbecued beef with all the fixings, that was advertised on a large sign alongside the road.

"Let me text Tim Bolt and we can get rid of this gun, we definitely do not want to get caught with it," Ryan said.

"We could never explain how we ended up with this gun," he said wryly.

Ryan sent a text message to Tim Bolt and asked if he was interested in a Piece.

"What kind?" the responding text came back almost immediately on Ryan's phone.

"A 45 caliber pistol and where are you at?" Ryan texted back.

"I'm down at my new apartment down in the Zone," he replied.

"Let's meet somewhere, have you got a set of wheels?" Ryan replied.

"Where do you want to meet?" Tim answered.

"We're up at that barbecue restaurant and bar at the top of Sunset

Hill, do you know where it's at? I'll buy you a beer and some great barbecue," he continued.

"We are on our way, see you in fifteen minutes," Tim replied.

Ryan put his iPhone in his pocket as they got out of the truck and walked into the restaurant.

They picked a corner booth and Ryan sat in a position where he could see the front entrance of the restaurant.

The restaurant was filled with mostly blue collar workers and men in Air Force uniforms that were assigned at nearby Fairchild Air Force base.

A pretty young woman with dyed red hair wearing a cowboy hat, tight blue jeans and low heeled cowboy boots walked up to the two and handed them each a menu.

The waiter returned a few minutes later and asked if they had made a selection.

"We're waiting for a couple of friends but we'll have a couple of tall Lager beers while we wait," Juan told the waitress who walked away and returned several minutes later and placed the tall bottles on the wooden table top.

Juan leaned back in the chair and took several swallows of the ice cold beer.

"Damn, I don't know if we want to go back and deal with that dude Paco again, his muscle, Cisco, gave me the fucking creeps," said Juan.

Ryan answered, "Yeah, I think we have to be real careful if we sell them more."

Ryan was watching the door when he saw Tim Bolt and an older thin male walk into the area in front of the cashier counter.

He waived and Bolt saw them and the two of them walked over and slid into the two remaining chairs.

"Hey, man," Bolt said as he did a fist bump to Ryan, and introduced his companion as Rufus.

They did small talk and waited until after the waitress had came and took their orders and walked away.

"What are trying to sell?" Bolt asked Ryan.

"We got a real hot Smith and Wesson 45 caliber semi-auto pistol with a laser sight that we need to sell," Ryan told Bolt.

"How hot?" asked Bolt.

"A guy in the Wheatland area got capped with the gun. The gun hasn't been used around here," he continued.

"That gun may be too hot for me," said Bolt.

"My man Rufus might be interested," Bolt continued.

Rufus asked what kind of money they wanted for the gun.

Juan said, "I just want to get rid of it so you can have it for $300 and that includes a half box of cartridges."

"I'll take it if the gun is in decent shape," said Rufus.

The waitress arrived with platters of food and they spent the next 45 minutes concentrating on the generous portions of barbecue beef with all the fixings.

The waitress dropped off the check and Ryan placed a hundred dollar bill on the invoice tray left by the waitress and they walked out of the business.

"Come out to the back parking lot where we are parked," Ryan said and pointed to the pick-up that was parked on the very last row with a barb wire fence directly behind.

Bolt and Rufus drove up in a mid 80's Ford Bronco and parked next to Ryan and Juan.

They got out of the Bronco and walked over to the open passenger door of the pick-up truck.

Juan removed the semi auto 45 cal pistol from the console and handed it to Rufus.

"Careful, the gun is loaded," said Juan.

Rufus reached down on the ramp below the gun barrel and found the "On" button for the laser sight.

The light came on and there was also a switch to change the color of the laser sight from red to green.

"The green laser is used best in the daytime," Juan advised.

Rufus said that he would buy the gun and pulled out three hundred dollars in twenties and handed them to Juan.

"Well, guys, we got a couple of dates with some wild ladies," Ryan said as they prepared to leave the parking lot.

They drove to the Casino and arrived there within ten minutes and pulled up in the courtyard of the hotel.

"Let's take the money with us, I don't want to leave it in the console," said Juan, and they placed the $40K in a paper bag.

When the parking attendant walked up Ryan asked for valet parking.

Ryan passed a one hundred bill to the valet who had a happy smile on his face and thanked Ryan several times.

"Would you text Star and see if she is available and if her friend would like to be with me?" Juan asked.

Once they got to their suite Ryan texted Star and found that she was available and her friend Shontell would be with her.

They agreed to meet in the Casino at about 10:00 P.M. near the card games.

Ryan had removed two five thousand dollar packets from sales and placed the remaining thirty thousand dollars in the freezer section of their refrigerator.

He handed a five thousand dollar packet to Juan and said, "Let's go tear up this casino and I can't wait to party with Star."

They went down to the card section of the casino and played the Stud poker table and 21 game.

When 10:00 P.M. came Ryan had lost about two thousand at the poker table and Juan was up by about six thousand dollars when he cashed in his chips.

Star and Shontell met with them after Juan had cashed in his chips.

Shontell was a gorgeous creature with long legs and they looked great in her black spandex tights.

"Let's get this party started," Ryan urged and they walked to the main elevators in the lobby.

They were soon inside the suite on the 9th floor and the curtains were pulled open which revealed a spectacular view of commercial airlines taking off and landing at the nearby Spokane International Airport.

Juan called room service and ordered up drinks and expensive finger foods.

A short time later an attendant arrived with a cart with bottles of wine, rum, scotch and other brands of alcohol they had requested, along with various mixers.

Some of the food they had ordered was hot so they sat around the large counter in the open kitchen and noshed while Ryan made them drinks.

After the snacks they moved back into the living room and had more drinks.

Ryan and Juan were buzzed and a few minutes later, took the two hookers into their separate bedroom suites.

Shontell told Juan a brief history of her life and then asked Juan questions about his life in order to relax him.

They had been sitting on the edge of the king size bed with the lights low, watching the airport activity.

Chanel began rubbing the inside of Juan's leg as she kissed him deeply and made small sounds of pleasure.

She gently pushed Juan back onto the bed and she knelt down in front of him and removed his shoes and socks, then reached up and unzipped his jeans and pulled the pants and underwear off, throwing them on a nearby chair.

Juan pulled off his long-sleeved shirt and was now naked and lying on his back.

Shontell stood in front of him and disrobed slowly, allowing Juan a clear view of her naked body, which he would soon be enjoying.

She lay beside him and, with a soft whisper, told Juan he could do anything he wanted with her.

Star and Ryan had changed out of their street clothes and into the luxurious robes, furnished by the upscale suite.

The lights were dim and Star was running her hand along the back of Ryan's neck, giving him a small massage on his tight muscles.

"Do you want to play the same games like we did last night?" she whispered in Ryan's ear.

"Oh yes," he whispered back.

"Do you want to do a line of coke before we start?" she enquired.

"I will guarantee all your sexual nerves will be real sensitive and the sex will be dynamite like you have never had before," she finished.

Can it get any better? he thought to himself, remembering the previous night.

"Okay, let's try it out," he said softly to Star.

Star removed a small glass bottle from her purse and produced a small round mirror and laid the mirror down on the counter.

She laid out two lines of cocaine, approx. 5 inches long.

She took a short plastic straw approximately 6 inches long and placed one end in her nostril, pinched off the other nostril opening, and breathed in a line of the white powder through the single nostril.

"Wow," she said as she blinked her eyes.

"Your turn," she said as she had him lean down and suck in the cocaine through the straw.

Ryan felt his nose go numb but almost immediately nerve sensations in his body became sensitive and he was ready to enjoy the skills of Star.

Both of the women came out of the bedrooms at about 3:00 A.M., and each had fifteen hundred dollars they had received from Ryan and Juan.

"Jeez, those guys don't know much about coitus and getting a woman aroused, do they?" Star said and they both laughed as they walked out the door.

As they walked to the elevator they talked about the appointment with Juan and Ryan that was set for the upcoming 10:00 P.M. session that evening.

Juan was up at 11:00 A.M., sitting at the small kitchen table, having a light breakfast and sipping on orange juice with a carafe of coffee.

Ryan had just stepped out of his bedroom and was holding his head like he had a severe hangover.

"I think it was the cocaine I used last night that has given me this killer headache," he commented.

"I'm getting in the shower and hope the steam will do me good," he said as he walked back into his bedroom.

He never came back into the kitchen until it was almost noon.

Ryan picked up the phone and ordered home fried potatoes and bacon with a glass of apple juice and a carafe of coffee.

He walked over to the sofa where he fell back and was sitting halfway up.

Juan handed Ryan a cup of black coffee he had poured from his carafe.

"Thanks, man, I'll be all right when I get some food, I'm weaker than a kitten," he said as he rubbed his forehead.

The food service arrived on a cart and after tipping the attendee a twenty dollar bill, Juan rolled the cart over to the sofa where Ryan proceeded to hungrily eat the food he had ordered.

After he finished his breakfast he poured a fresh cup of coffee.

"Let's schedule a full body massage at the salon this afternoon," Juan suggested.

"Gawd, that would be great, my body is really sore from wrestling around with Star," Ryan said.

"They are coming back at 10:00 P.M. for another night of hardcore sex and I better be up for it," Ryan said to Juan.

Juan nodded in agreement and said, "Man, you get what you pay for and those hookers are well worth it."

Ryan phoned the Beauty Salon located on the first floor of the luxury casino hotel and made two hour massage appointments for both of them for 3:30 P.M.

"Guess we'll see what a $350 massage feels like," he said to Juan.

They showed up for their appointment and were placed in a bubbling hot tub to relax their sore muscles.

One attractive massage attendant directed Ryan to a massage table and placed him face down.

He had ordered a complete deep massage that would leave his muscles relaxed and stretched.

Juan had been led down the hallway and the young woman placed him face down on the massage table.

He had ordered a hot rock massage and at first flinched when the warm rock was placed on his bare skin.

The attractive masseuse would continuously slide a hot rock pressed into his back muscles.

The full pleasure of this type of massage became apparent and Juan fell into a drowsy stupor from the pleasure.

Shortly after 6:00 P.M. Juan and Ryan were finished with their massages and were sitting on a sofa in the main lobby of the deluxe hotel.

"Man, I am so relaxed, let's go have dinner and get some strength up for the hookers that are showing up tonight."

They walked down to the expensive casino restaurant and ordered 12 ounce prime rib dinners.

"Hopefully, this will get our strength up," Ryan said with a grin.

"Did you ever think you would be so tired from tangling with those tigresses," he said and laughed.

"Hey Juan, let's do a switch tonight, I've been with Star two nights in a row," Ryan said.

"It don't matter to me, Star will be a new woman to me tonight," replied Juan.

They left the restaurant and walked over to the main casino where they both stood at the card table and gambled, playing 21.

After an hour of the game, Juan was up a couple of hundred dollars.

Ryan was playing recklessly and making heavier bets, so at the end of the hour he was down a couple of thousand dollars.

"Come on," he said to Juan, "Let's go play some slots."

Juan was a little irritated at Ryan for pulling him away from the card game.

They went to the more expensive slot machines with a higher maximum bet.

"Let's try these two," Ryan said as he sat down in front of one of the game consoles.

Juan picked the machine to the left of Ryan's machine and inserted $500 into the machine.

"I'll play a ten dollar bet each push of the slot button and get at least 50 turns," he said to Ryan.

Juan had pushed the slot button about a dozen times when he got a good roll of the tumblers and won $300.

He continued playing the game and when his amount left in the slot machine was down to $200, he cashed out.

Juan continued to watch Ryan making bets on his slot machine until he ran out of the money he had placed in the machine.

He placed another $500 in $100 dollar bills in the slot machine.

Ryan was pissed off because he had lost about $1,500 so far on that gambling machine.

"Hell with it," he said and started making $100 bets on the slot machine.

He won $30 one time and another $130 on another slot entry.

Ryan was down to $200 and after a couple more rolls he was out of money.

As he got up he told Juan that he had blown $3000.

They went over to the cashier and Juan cashed in his receipt and was given $700 back.

"I only lost about $300 on the slots," he said to Ryan.

"I'm done," Ryan said dejectedly. "Let's go up to the room and get ready for our dates," he said with a wink.

They walked out of the casino and took the elevator to the 9th floor where they entered their room.

"They should be here in about half hour," Juan said, "I'm going to jump in the shower."

"Go ahead," Ryan responded, "I'm going to order up some bottles of wine and rum with some mixer."

"Order up some good snacks," Juan told Ryan just before he stepped into the shower.

Shortly after ten o'clock there was a knock at the door and the two ladies stepped into the suite.

Juan was still in the bedroom when Ryan told Star and Shontell that he and Juan would like to trade the women for the night.

They both shrugged and smiled.

"Honey, we don't care if you want to switch out," Star said.

"As long as you pay to play, we're up for anything," Shontell said with a wink.

"You ladies will get a bonus," Ryan said and winked back at Shontell, anticipating what the evening would bring.

Juan walked out of his bedroom and was only wearing the white cushy bathrobe furnished in the deluxe bedroom suite.

Star walked over to Juan and gave him a soft hug, leaving no doubt that she was his for the taking.

They sat on the comfortable sofas facing out towards the open window with the beautiful night time view.

An expensive bottle of wine was opened and shared with Ryan and Shontell.

Juan and Star opted for hard liquor.

Star went over to the open kitchen and grabbed two 6 oz. glasses from the cupboard.

She opened the freezer compartment and filled the glasses with ice.

"What is that," she said to herself and saw a paper bag partially covered with ice at the back of the shelf.

She partially opened the paper bag and saw bundles of currency that appeared to contain $100 bills.

She turned and no one had noticed that she was doing anything other than placing ice in the glasses.

Next, she poured 3 ounces of rum and filled the remainder with coke.

Walking back to the sofa she handed Juan one of the drinks and kept one for herself.

As the night went on Ryan opened a second bottle of wine and drank freely.

Juan would go to the kitchen and prepare more rum and cokes for Star and himself.

Juan didn't notice that Star was drinking far less than him.

"I have to use the powder room," she said.

"That's a good idea," Shontell said and they both got up and walked into Juan's bedroom.

Star was excited and spoke in a low voice, "When I went into the refrigerator to get ice I saw a paper bag that had about six packets of money and they looked like all $100 bills."

"Hell, there could be thousands of cash in that freezer," Shontell said excitedly.

"I don't know where those rubes got that kind of money but I bet they would not report the theft if we stole it," Star said.

"I have a couple of Rohypnol pills (street name roofies), let's give them some. They are in my purse," she said as she opened the clasp on her small purse and withdrew two white tablets.

"Then, we'll empty their pockets and grab the bundles of cash in the freezer," she continued.

Star handed Shontell one of the white pills and said, "Let's slip them in their drinks when we go into the bedrooms with them."

"Let's head to your bedroom for some real nasty fun," Star said to Juan as she picked up both of their glasses and carried them into the bedroom.

Juan didn't notice when Star dropped the small white roofie pill into his drink.

It dissolved almost instantly.

The door was closed as they walked into the bedroom where Star sat down on the bed next to Juan and leaned over. "Are you ready for a rodeo?" she whispered as she reached through the gap in his robe and teased him.

Juan stood up in front of Star as he took a drink from his drug laced glass of rum and coke.

Shontell and Ryan were still in the living room when she went to the kitchen bar and refilled their wine glasses and discreetly dropped the roofie into Ryan's wine glass.

Ryan was craving a carnal romp with Shontell and quickly gulped down the glass of wine.

Shontell filled his wine glass again and led him into his bedroom and closed the door.

She did a slow strip tease in front of him as he stared wolfishly at her primary body parts.

She drew her black silk teddy across his face and eyes.

She kneeled behind Ryan and massaged the tight muscles on his back and after a few minutes he rolled over on his back and stretched out on the bed.

Ryan started slurring his speech and was clumsy as he reached for Shontell who was standing in front of him.

Next, she straddled him cowboy style.

After a couple minutes of his gyrations his body slowed and finally refused to move and he fell asleep.

She got out of bed, dressed quickly and looked down, and gave Ryan a kiss on the forehead.

She rummaged through his trouser pockets and discovered there was over $3,000 in $100 bills.

I wonder how things are going with Star, she thought as she walked across the hall and quietly pushed the unlocked bedroom door open.

Juan was naked and lying on his back with his legs hanging over the bed.

"We never got past that position when the roofie took effect," Star said with a laugh.

"Let me get dressed and I'll check his pockets for any money he had on him," she said.

Star rummaged through the trouser pockets lying on a chair beside the bed.

"Jackpot," she said as she removed a thick bundle of cash and placed it in her purse.

They went into the kitchen and opened the freezer and removed the paper bag containing the bundles of cash.

There were 6 bundles of cash and Star handed Shontell 3 of the bundles.

They left the suite and took the elevator to the main lobby where they were soon lost in the pedestrian traffic.

Their fashionable wide brimmed hats and sunglasses concealed their features from the casino security cameras.

The concierge was standing at his station and quickly summoned a taxi for the women.

"Take us to the Blue Ruby Hotel on 3rd," Chanel said.

They were soon dropped off in front of the hotel and they walked into the bar for a drink in celebration of their good luck.

"I think we got over $30K out of the freezer in addition to the money in their pockets," Shontell said.

Star took her burner phone out of her purse and removed the sim card.

She placed it on the hard table and crushed it by tapping it with the drink glass.

She went into the women's restroom where she stomped on the burner phone and placed it under running water, then threw the broken instrument into the trash.

"Did you use your burner phone to talk with these fools?" she asked Shontell.

"Yes, the guy named Ryan texted me earlier yesterday afternoon, but I am going to ditch it and get a new one," she replied.

"Then give it to me," Star said and held out her hand.

Shontell handed the phone over and Star expertly accessed the sim card and crushed it with the bottom of her thick bottom drink glass and wrapped the sim card in a bar napkin.

"Those guys could be pretty dangerous so let's leave tomorrow morning and travel to Missoula, Montana where we can work some of the high class Casinos there. I'll pick you up in my car at about 8:00 A.M. in the morning. The roofie shouldn't wear off until 9:00 or 10:00 A.M. so we will have time to get out of town."

They both walked out of the upscale bar together and separately summoned taxi rides.

Chapter 35

Ryan was the first to stir from the drug induced sleep and had no memory of the events that occurred after he had walked into the bedroom with Chanel the prior evening.

He picked up his phone and ordered breakfast from room service for both Juan and himself, including apple juice and a carafe of coffee.

Walking around the living room in his underwear, he looked at the view outside the large deluxe suite window and stared out at the sunny day for about 10 minutes when there was a knock on the door.

"Room service," came a voice from outside the door.

"Just a minute," Ryan said as he went back into his bedroom and put on the white bathrobe.

He opened the door and the attendant pushed in a cart containing the food, carafe and glasses of apple juice.

Ryan signed the invoice card and added a $20 tip to the bill.

"Hey man, rise and shine, we got stuff to do," he said as he opened Juan's bedroom door.

"Oh, Gawd," Juan said as he turned over and looked into Ryan's face.

Let me splash some water on my face as he walked naked across the room and stepped into the bathroom.

The cold water revived him somewhat and he put on his underwear and a T-shirt.

He walked into the small kitchen area and started eating the substantial breakfast with Ryan.

After downing the glass of apple juice Ryan commented that he needed a glass of ice water.

He picked up a glass and opened the freezer section of the refrigerator to place ice in his glass.

"What the hell? He said, the money is gone. Those hookers must have slipped us roofies and stolen our money. Do you remember actually having sex with Star?" he asked Juan.

Juan paused and said, "Hell, I thought I had but I may have passed out from the alcohol, I don't remember."

"I've still got Shontell's number," Ryan said and rapidly checked recent phone numbers on his iPhone.

He dialed the number and the message came back that the number was not a working number.

"I bet they had burner phones, so we are screwed," he said.

"Let's get dressed and get the hell out of here," said Juan.

Juan went into the bedroom and was putting on his trousers when he reached his hands in the front pockets and found they were empty.

He searched around for his wallet and found it in the dresser drawer by his bed.

"At least that bitch didn't find my wallet," he said as he looked in the contents and was relieved there was over $500 in mixed bills tucked inside.

He walked next door to Ryan's bedroom suite and saw Ryan sitting on the bed, holding his pants pocket and noted the front pockets of the trouser were turned inside out.

Ryan had a look of shock on his face.

"That bitch took a couple thousand dollars out of my pockets," he said angrily.

"I found my wallet in the trash can in the bathroom and she left me a one hundred dollar bill," he said.

"If we find those whores they are dead meat," he said and was so angry spittle sprayed out of his mouth.

"There's not much chance of that," Juan said glumly.

They quickly left the casino hotel without paying their alcohol and food bill.

"We're still paid up for 4 more nights and there's no chance for a refund," said Juan.

"They can take the unused nights and use the funds to pay that breakfast bill," Juan continued.

They drove out of the casino parking lot and headed west towards Wheatland.

Ryan pushed the pick-up and exceeded the posted speed limit, slowing down only to drive through Moses Lake and Ephrata, then he would again exceed the posted speed limit.

After about 20 miles they continued on State Highway 2 and crossed over into Canyon County.

"Better chill out, man, we don't need the locals to pull us over," Juan warned.

Ryan ignored the warning and after traveling another 3 or 4 miles they met a Washington State Patrol Trooper driving in the opposite direction.

The brake lights immediately came on the Trooper's Patrol Unit 737 and Ryan saw the cruiser make a U turn and head back towards them at a high rate of speed.

"Dammit, my driver's license is suspended," Ryan said as he looked for a wide spot on the road shoulder to pull over and park.

Trooper, Tarina Dobson, walked up to the passenger window and motioned for Juan to roll the window down.

She directed her attention towards Ryan who sat with his hands clasping the steering wheel.

"Do you know what the posted speed limit is?" she asked Ryan.

"60 miles per hour," Ryan answered.

"Radar shows your speed at 72 miles per hour," she said.

"Hand me your vehicle operator license, registration and proof of insurance," the trooper ordered.

"And shut your vehicle ignition off," she ordered.

"I don't have my license or proof of insurance with me," Ryan explained to Trooper Dobson.

"What is your name and date of birth?" she asked.

Ryan was honest when he provided his correct name and DOB.

"I'll be back," the trooper said as she turned and walked back and entered her patrol vehicle.

Ryan nervously tapped his hands on the steering wheel and watched the trooper in his rearview mirror, talking on her radio.

"Come on, bitch," he said as he continued to watch the trooper sitting in her patrol unit.

"Look ahead," Juan said to Ryan as he saw a Canyon County Sheriff car approaching from the opposite direction.

The Sheriff's patrol car slowed as it passed by and then made a U-turn and parked behind the trooper's patrol unit.

His emergency flashers were turned on and he had parked his patrol unit partially out into the lane of travel to protect the trooper when she walked up to the driver's door of the pick-up.

Deputy Brett Farr conferred with Trooper Dobson and learned that Ryan Bates was a suspended driver.

Trooper Dobson walked towards the stopped pick-up and ordered Ryan, to step out of the pick-up, and walk backwards to the rear of the pick-up truck.

"You have a suspended driver's license and you have an outstanding arrest warrant for failure to remain in contact with the Department of Corrections. Place your hands behind your back," she ordered as she placed the handcuffs on his wrists and locked the ratchets.

"Your vehicle will be towed unless you want to release the vehicle to your friend in the truck and if he has a valid driver's license," she said.

"That will be fine, my friend can drive my pick-up," Ryan answered.

The trooper placed Ryan in the secure caged area of her patrol car.

As she turned she heard Deputy Farr shout a warning to her as he had unholstered his firearm and was pointing towards the back of the pick-up.

"Passenger, put your hands on the dashboard," he ordered and Juan placed his hands upon the dashboard.

"Passenger, open the door with your hand by reaching out to the outer door handle," Juan was directed.

"Back towards me with your hands clasped behind your head," Deputy Farr ordered.

When Juan had backed up to the end of the pick-up truck he was ordered to get on his knees and lay flat on the ground with his arms outstretched and have his face turned away.

Deputy Farr safely approached Juan at an angle while covered by Trooper Dobson and quickly searched and placed handcuffs on Juan.

He had had felt a small bulge inside the sock on the right leg.

Deputy Farr removed a small plastic bag of a light brown substance, then walked Juan back to the Canyon County Sheriff patrol car, placing him inside.

He walked back to Trooper Dobson and showed her the bag containing the light brown substance.

"I saw the passenger lift up the center console and it looked like he was rummaging around until he saw me and closed the lid," he stated.

Trooper Dobson opened the trunk of her vehicle and got out a drug identification field test.

She placed a small amount of the light brown substance in the small clear plastic pouch that contained several small glass vials.

She closed off the open end, then squeezed both vials inside the pouch until they broke open and the liquid inside mixed with the unknown substance.

She rapidly shook the container back and forth and the color of the light brown substance immediately turned bright blue, which was an indication the content was methamphetamine.

Trooper Tarina Dobson held the clear container up to show Deputy Farr and remarked how quickly the substance had changed to color blue.

"Let's search the pick-up truck and justify the search as an incident to and arrest since they could have secreted a firearm or other contraband in the console," she said.

Trooper Dobson opened the pick-up door and looked under the front seat and opened up the center console.

"Nothing else but a partial box of ammo, looks like 45 caliber," she said to Deputy Farr.

"Wait," Trooper Dobson said after she received a message on the secure channel of her handheld portable police radio. "Ryan Bates is currently on parole with the Department of Corrections and is a convicted felon. That makes it a DOC violation if Bates is found in possession of a firearm or ammunition," she said with a smile.

"We also have Juan Garcia in possession of a controlled substance, methamphetamine, so he also gets a ride downtown," she continued.

A request for a local tow company was made and they walked back to Ryan's pick-up to obtain the vehicle registration number on the left side of the upper dashboard to determine if the serial number matched the number on the registration document.

"What is this?" Deputy Farr said as he pointed out some dark stains on the inside bottom of the pick-up bed.

Trooper Dobson stood on her toes and looked over the edge of the pick-up box.

"It looks like dried blood on those spots," she said as she pointed out the locations in the pick-up box.

"There was a recent shooting over on I-90 by Quincy and there were 45 caliber shell casings found along the freeway that investigators thought were involved. I will call the Canyon County investigators real quick and find out the brand and caliber of the shell casings that were collected," Deputy Farr said.

Deputy Farr used his cellphone to make the call and while he was on the phone with the Canyon County Sheriff's Office, Trooper Dobson walked back to the pick-up truck and noted the brand on the 45 caliber box of ammo was Winchester.

"They are Winchester 45 caliber semi-auto cartridges," Trooper Dobson informed Deputy Farr.

Deputy Farr told the detective on the phone line that a partially full box of Winchester 45 caliber semi auto cartridges had been found in the pick-up console.

The Canyon County detective told Deputy Farr the shell casings found at the shooting scene were the same brand and caliber that were found in Ryan Bate's pick-up.

"We're towing the vehicle and will have it processed," he informed the Detective.

Once the tow truck arrived and was hooked up, Trooper Dobson told the tow truck driver the location of the Washington State Patrol Vehicle Processing location.

Deputy Farr had requested that communications dispatch a second Canyon County Sheriff patrol car to respond and transport Ryan Bates to jail. Upon arrival Ryan was transferred from Trooper Dobson's patrol unit to the Canyon County Sheriff patrol unit without incident.

When both deputies arrived at the Canyon County jail, the Correction Sgt. was told to keep Bates and Garcia separate.

Trooper Dobson followed the tow truck driver to the evidence process garage where it was unloaded and the tow driver cleared the garage and the roll-up garage door was lowered back down and locked.

Deputy Farr was on the phone with Canyon County Sheriff Detectives Carr and Nickels and provided them with the information that had resulted in the arrest of Ryan Bates and Juan Garcia.

A few hours later Detective Nickels contacted Deputy Farr and advised the magistrate had signed a search warrant for the vehicle.

Detective Hannigan was notified by Detective Carr and agreed to attend the interviews of Bates and Garcia.

Arrangements were made with the WSP Evidence Recovery Unit to process Ryan's pick-up the following day.

Detective Hannigan and Detective Carr met at the jail where they had Ryan Bates brought into the interview room.

Bates had not been in front of the presiding Judge for his first DOC criminal complaint and had not yet been appointed legal counsel.

Ryan sat across the table from both detectives and rattled the handcuff chains that were attached to an eyebolt mounted on the table in front of him.

Detective Hannigan looked at Ryan and made eye contact.

Ryan was advised of his Constitutional Rights, which he stated he understood and waived the requirement to have an attorney present.

"Look, Ryan, we have some questions for you about those 45 caliber cartridges in the cardboard ammo box found in your truck," Detective Carr said as he placed the cardboard box containing ammunition on the table.

Ryan got a sick look on his face when he recognized it was the same box of ammunition, that he had stolen from John Adams' pick-up truck.

"I don't know where that box of ammo came from, it must have been Juan Garcia that put it in my pick-up," he said.

That dumb bastard, Juan never gave that box of ammo to Rufus when we sold the gun to him, so now the ammo box is in Police custody, he thought.

"Do you have information about the shooting that occurred on I-90 about a week ago?" Hannigan asked.

"I have no idea, I never heard about it," he answered.

Ryan thought to himself that as long as he wasn't connected to the red Honda found in the Remington Canal, he would be fine.

"We found dried blood on the bed of your pick-up box," Detective Carr said as he looked closely at Ryan, who averted his eyes away from the Detective.

"How did it end up on the bed of your truck?" he asked.

"I hit a pheasant a couple of weeks ago and stopped and threw it in the back," he replied.

"Bull shit," Detective Carr said loudly and leaned over the table and made direct eye contact with Ryan.

"The WSP Crime Lab has tested the substance and it is human blood," he continued.

Ryan's eyes widened and he remembered that after Bronza had been shot there had been copious amounts of blood and brain matter on the gym bag located on the back seat where he had died during the chase.

He realized he had not completely closed the partial open travel bag of meth packages when he ran out of the trap house and threw the bag in the back seat of the red Honda.

Blood and brain matter from Bronza apparently had spilled into the gym bag and got onto the meth packages.

The blood on the floor of his pick-up bed must have transferred when he tossed the blood covered containers of meth onto the pick-up bed.

He remembered the dried blood left on the paper wrappers on the kilos of meth that he has sold to Paco in Spokane.

As long as the cops don't find the red Honda with Bronza's body I will be OK for awhile, he thought to himself.

This possession of ammunition will only get me 30 days in jail from DOC (Department of Corrections), he thought to himself.

"I want to stop the questioning," he said to the detectives.

"Let me mull this over and maybe we'll talk more," he finished.

Ryan was taken back to his solitary cell.

Next, the detectives had Juan Garcia brought to the interview room and he sat quietly, looking at the chain attached to his handcuffs.

"Juan, we're here to talk to you about that 8 ball of meth you had hidden in your sock," said Detective Carr.

Juan gave a disinterested looked and stared at the mirror on the interview wall, knowing other people could be on the other side of the one sided mirror watching him.

"Look, you have substantial points accrued in your criminal convictions record and you could end up with a long prison sentence. I think we might be able to help each other if you are willing to cooperate with us. I'm going to advise you of your Constitutional Rights and I'm aware you have not made a first appearance with the judge."

Juan nodded and verbally told the detectives that he understood his Constitutional Rights and would be willing to talk to them.

"Where have you been the past week and a half?" Detective Hannigan asked.

"Ryan and I were hanging out in Wenatchee, just hanging out with friends," he replied.

"Do you know anyone that drives a red Honda in Wenatchee?" Hannigan continued the questioning.

Juan's eyes looked upwards and he quickly turned his head down.

"No, I don't think we saw a red Honda when we were hanging out," he said as he cleared his throat with an obvious sign of stress.

"What about that box of 45 caliber ammo in Ryan's pick-up console, do you know where that came from?" he was asked.

"Hey, I never even touched that box of shells and have no idea where Ryan got them," Juan answered, but his facial expression changed and he blinked rapidly, averting his eyes away from Hannigan.

Juan remembered the box of ammo had been stolen by Ryan from John Adams' pick-up truck along with the handgun.

"I want you to think about what you know," Detective Hannigan said to Juan.

"We will be checking back," he finished.

"Give me some time," Juan said, "and maybe we can make a deal."

"Don't wait to long because if Ryan talks first you won't get a deal," Hannigan said to Juan.

The detectives left the jail cell and travelled to the War Room where Detectives Fitz and Skates were seated.

Hannigan walked over to the whiteboard at the front of the room.

"Let's look at the similarities of the shootings in Chelan County and Canyon County over the past two weeks. Number one - the murder and robbery at the norteno trap house in Othello. The victim, identified as Michael Guzman, was killed from blunt force head trauma. He was the lookout in the back yard of the trap house. The kitchen cupboards inside had been ransacked, likely searching for methamphetamine and cash," he said.

"A witness named Jesus Chaco was the lookout in the front yard of the norteno trap house and tells us the rip-off men were driving a red Honda. Number two- the shooting and road rage incident at I-90 and Quincy cut-off rd. Involved Carlos Guzman, Alphonso Ruiz and Jesus Chaco. Jesus Chaco was a passenger in the Dodge Hellcat when Carlos Guzman was shot and the vehicle lost control and rolled. Jesus Chaco has said Alphonso had earlier shot into the rear of a red Honda with a

357 caliber revolver. Alphonso and Carlos have refused to cooperate with law enforcement. Four 45 caliber semi auto shell casings were found along the roadway and a 45 caliber slug was removed from Carlos Guzman shoulder, which was consistent with the spent 45 caliber shell casings. Number three - the red Honda located in the Remington Canal is suspected of being the vehicle used in the robbery. When the vehicle was pulled out of the canal there was a body inside which was likely one of the robbers. The victim suffered a severe head wound and a misshapen 357 caliber bullet apparently passed through the back of the victim's head and struck the dashboard and dropped to the floor. A gym type bag was found on the floor behind the front seats and even after being submerged there were small amounts of blood and traces of methamphetamine in the material at the bottom of the bag. In the bottom of the bag were three handguns. One was a Smith and Wesson 380 semi auto and the other two were 38 caliber Smith and Wesson five shot Detective Special revolvers with 2 inch barrels," he continued.

"All the handguns were fully loaded and apparently had not been discharged. Two 45 caliber Remington semi auto shell casings were found on the back seat of the Honda. They are the same brand and type as the four shell casings found along I-90 at the shooting and vehicle rollover. The Honda was registered to a man in Wenatchee and, when contacted by Chelan County Deputies, he told them the Honda was parked in his ex-girlfriend's garage in Wenatchee. The Wenatchee Police Department checked by and the woman living there did not know the Honda was missing from her detached garage. Parked in her back yard was a low rider vehicle that she said belonged to her friend Bronza Miller and he lived in Wheatland. When the man's body was removed from the red Honda it was taken to the Medical Examiner's Office for autopsy. Dental records and fingerprints collected have identified Bronza Miller as the gunshot victim found in the red Honda. His last address was listed on 3rd street in Ephrata and is a short distance from John Adams' residence. We suspect that Bronza parked his vehicle in the backyard of his girlfriend's house in Wenatchee and took the red Honda from the enclosed garage. We think Bronza and two other mutts drove to Othello in the stolen Honda and did the robbery at the norteno trug house. Their plan was likely to drive back to Wenatchee and put the red Honda back into the garage. We're not sure how the norteno gang members knew the robbers were in the red Honda but it appears they caught up to the Honda and put some shots into the back of it. Bronza was apparently shot in the back of the head with a 357 magnum bullet and the suspected bullet was found on the floorboards. The recovered slug from the Honda is at the WSP Firearms Forensic and Ballistic Lab. The recovered 357 mag. revolver found in the attic of the norteno trap house is being test fired with a similar type of cartridge and the recovered slug that went through Bronza's head will be compared to the test fired bullet to determine if it is a match to the slug found on the floorboards of the red Honda. A baseball bat was found in the red Honda but it's unknown if there is any evidence on the bat because it was submerged in water. The baseball bat could have been used to bash in the head of Michael Guzman who was a lookout in the back yard of the norteno trap house. Yesterday a man named Ryan Bates, 24 years of age, was stopped for speeding by Washington State Trooper Tarina Dobson a few miles out of Wheatland. The passenger was Juan Garcia, 23 years old. They both gave Wheatland, Washington addresses and Ryan Bates's residence was only three houses south of John Adams. Ryan Bates was driving on a suspended driver's license. A Canyon County Sheriff Deputy had rolled up and assisted taking Bates into custody without resistance and placed him in the trooper's cruiser. The Deputy had been watching the passenger and he seemed to be leaning down like he was trying to secrete a weapon. They did a felony stop and walked Garcia back to the Deputy's cruiser where he was hooked. A small packet of meth, probably an 8 ball, was found tucked up in Garcia's sock. The two officers checked the vehicle for weapons or other drugs and did not find anything in the interior of the pick-up truck, other than a partial box of Winchester 45 semi-auto cartridges was found in the center console. The deputy used his cellphone to send us photos of the base portion of the 45 caliber cartridges found in the ammo box. They appear to be the same as the shell casings found along the roadway near the I-90 /

Quincy exit near the shooting of Carlos Guzman. The cartridge box and contents have been forwarded to the WSP lab. The items will be examined and swabbed for DNA. The four shell casings found along I-90 have also been sent to the lab for DNA collection and analysis. The deputy and trooper noticed what looked like dried blood in several spots on the bottom of the pick-up bed. Ryan Bates told the investigators he had struck a pheasant with his truck and stopped and picked it up and threw it in the back of his pick-up. There were actually three or four areas of the dried blood. The WSP Crime Lab Techs took samples of the dried substance and confirmed it was human blood. We're standing by, waiting for the results from the lab," he continued.

Detectives Skates and Fitz stared thoughtfully at the notes on the white board.

"Is the 45 caliber shell casing found in John Adams' yard the same type as the other four 45 caliber shell casings found along I-90 and the two 45 caliber shell casings found in the red Honda?" Detective Fitz asked.

"Yes, they all look like they are the same, but there were no fingerprints and the only DNA found on the shell casing in John Adams' yard was the officer's DNA that collected the shell casing," Hannigan said with disgust.

"I still think Dustin Silver is guilty but we will see how the ballistic and DNA evidence comes out," he continued.

"Let's give the cases a few days to percolate," he finished.

Chapter 36

Detective Hannigan and the Investigative Team were back in the office the following Monday and they reviewed the lab reports with surprise.

DNA findings on the four spent 45 caliber shell casings recovered along I-90 were identified as belonging to Juan Garcia and another unknown male.

The DNA analysis from the swab of the Winchester Ammunition box found in the console of Ryan Bate's pickup also came back to Juan Garcia and two other unknown male contributors.

There was no DNA found on the remaining cartridges located inside the Winchester Ammo box.

"How did Juan Garcia obtain the ammunition box?"

"I think after Dustin shot John Adams he threw the 45 semi auto pistol and the box of cartridges out of his vehicle somewhere and Juan Garcia must have found the discarded gun and ammo," Detective Hannigan said.

Detectives Fitz and Skates looked skeptically at each other.

Hannigan saw their mutual glances which irritated him.

"Have you got a better theory?" he said as he stared Fitz and Skates down.

"Have you even considered that it was actually Juan Garcia and someone else, perhaps Ryan Bates, that shot John Adams?" asked Detective Skates.

"No way, and I told Dustin Silver that I was going to see him going away for the murder of John Adams," Hannigan said defensively.

"Let's see how things come to light and not get all excited until we know more," Detective Skates said in order to cool Hannigan down.

Hannigan read the next report from the WSP Crime Lab.

The WSP Crime Lab had received blood samples from the body of the man found in the red Honda.

They had also obtained the sample of dried blood found on the Ryan Bates pick-up box bed.

The blood samples found in the Honda and back of Ryan Bate's pick-up were identified as belonging to Bronza Miller.

The man had also been identified from dental records.

"I know this evidence is going to cause a stir with Dustin Silver's defense team, but we need to send all the lab results to Canyon County Prosecutor Walter Colvins. The prosecutor can provide the information to Dustin Silver's defense team and their investigators," said Hannigan.

Chapter 37

The defense team was provided with the Washington State Patrol Lab findings the following Friday afternoon.

"Why does the Prosecutor's Office always provide additional reports and documents on Friday afternoon?" said Jackie to Mark and Colin.

"They know the court is closed on weekends and we have to scramble and respond to the allegations by the next Monday," she continued.

They read the lab reports with excitement.

"WSP Lab says the firing pin marks and ejection marks on the shell casings found in a red Honda matched the markings on the shell casing that was recovered in John Adams' front yard last December 28th. The four 45 caliber shell casings found along I-90 a week ago also have the same markings. There was a partially full box of 45 caliber brand ammunition found in the center console of Ryan Bates's pick-up truck. The ammo box was swabbed for DNA and five different contributors were found including one from a female. DNA of Juan Garcia was found on the ammo box recovered from Ryan Bates's console in his pick-up. DNA was located on the four 45 caliber semi-auto shell casings found along I-90 of 2 male subjects. Juan Garcia was also identified as the contributor," Jackie laid it out.

"Did they figure out the identity of the other contributors?" asked Colin.

"Could one of them be John Adams' DNA?" he continued.

"Let's prepare a motion before Judge Charles Parker to compel the prosecution to submit John Adams' DNA for comparison to the cartridges and also on the ammo box," Mark Scalia said.

"We can present the motion next Monday at our next court hearing," Colin Thurgood volunteered.

"How is the investigation with witnesses developing?" asked Mark.

"We have obtained video, audio and written declarations from Martin Nelson, Trampus Byrne, Leslie Byrne, Lynn Bennet and Steve Paulson this past week," Monty disclosed to the attorneys.

"I gave the documents and video recordings to Colin," he continued.

"That's right," Colin said, "they are included in the packet I prepared for this morning's meeting."

"Thanks, Colin," Jackie told Colin.

"I have some other news that will affect the evidentiary value of the handcuffs found at the scene," Colin Thurgood said calmly.

"We were sent crime scene photos that included the pair of handcuffs found in the front yard," he started.

"However, as part of the mix, there was a series of photos taken by Wheatland Police Officer Matt Winslow that were taken with his personal cell phone," he continued.

"I reviewed the first of the photos from Officer Winslow's cell phone and there were three fallen leaves covering about half of the handcuffs on five of the images. I looked at the rest of the handcuffs photos and the handcuffs must have been picked up and examined and then placed back onto the ground. I compared the handcuffs photos the other investigator took and it was obvious the handcuffs were not in their original position. Look here," he said and spread out 8 by 10 photos of the leaves on the handcuffs and the following photos with the leaves removed.

"If you compare Officer Winslow's photos, you will see that the grass beneath the handcuffs is flattened in the opposite direction and one of the leaves that was first photographed on top of the handcuffs is now lying beneath the handcuffs," Colin finished.

"Great job Colin," said Mark.

"Let's go over the signed search warrant Detective Ralston Hannigan submitted for Dustin's cell phone records and photos," said Jackie.

"Then let's review the particular search warrant they prepared to obtain cell tower pings on Dustin's phone number to find his location," Jackie said.

"We'll meet in a week for updates on those search warrants," Mark said as the meeting ended.

Several days had passed when Anson's cell phone rang.

He didn't recognize the number.

He picked up the phone and a woman's voice asked for Investigator David Anson.

"This is me," he responded.

"Hello, Mr. Anson, this is Lynn Bennet, Steve Paulson's girlfriend. Steve is at the Wheatland County Jail and he phoned and told me to get in touch with you and he gave me your number. He said he had something important to tell you on your case, but he couldn't say any more on the phone."

"What is he in jail for?" Anson asked.

"Remember when you guys met with him at the Canyon County Courthouse?" she asked.

"Yes, I remember, it was for a driver's license violation and the judge dismissed the case because Steve had obtained his driver's license," he said.

"Well, the court clerk did not make a notation that Steve's case was dismissed by the judge and the charge went to warrant status since the record showed Steve never paid his fine or something," she continued.

"With the long holiday weekend Steve goes to court on Tuesday and everything should get straightened out but in the meantime I am getting some cash gathered up to pay for his bond," she continued.

"Thanks for the information, we will go over and visit Steve this morning," he said to Lynn before ending the phone call.

Anson walked over to Monty Victor's room at the hotel where they had set up a table for their laptops and documents related to the case.

A metal file cabinet with padlocks securing the file drawers was next to the table.

Anson told him about the phone call he had received.

"I thought Paulson had taken care of his traffic warrant," Monty said.

"Just a screwup by the judge's court clerk," Anson answered.

"Let's stop by the jail before visiting hours closes for lunch and see what is so important that Paulson asked his girlfriend to pass us a message," he continued.

They arrived at the Wheatland County Jail and pushed the button beside the jail security door.

A camera was mounted above the door.

A detached sounding voice on a small speaker enquired who they were.

They identified themselves as part of the Dustin Silver Legal Team.

The small room they entered had a heavy metal secondary door leading into the jail lobby.

An attendant sat behind a thick glass window with a medal sliding tray beneath.

They presented their credentials and asked to visit with Steve Paulson for a professional visit in the attorney room.

The electric lock switch on the metal door buzzed and they pushed through the door into the booking lobby of the jail, where they were directed to a room designated for legal visits for attorneys and investigators with their clients.

The attorney client visiting rooms were small rooms with a bench along one wall, a metal table was secured with bolts to the concrete floor.

Two plastic lawn type chairs sat on the other side of the table.

They entered the room and sat in the plastic chairs, waiting for Steve Paulson to be brought into the room.

A few minutes later there was a rattle of chains and Paulson was brought into the room wearing waist chains with attached handcuffs placed on his wrists.

He shuffled over to the bench on the wall and sat down, placing his hands on the table top.

"Can you believe this bullshit?" Paulson said.

"What are you in here for?" Monty asked.

"I got arrested for that traffic charge that the court had already dismissed," he said.

"Do you remember when I met you guys in court?" he started.

"The judge dismissed charges because I had obtained my vehicle operators license. Then I got stopped on an equipment violation yesterday and the cop told me there was an arrest warrant out on me for not having a valid vehicle operator's license," he said.

"I see the same judge that dismissed my case next Tuesday and my girlfriend Lynn Bennett is going to post my bond today," he said.

"She will be here probably right after lunch time."

"I asked her to contact you because I have some important information that will really help your case," he said.

"Let's hear it," Monty said with renewed interest.

Paulson told them that when he was booked into the Canyon County Jail he was placed in C tank, which is where the newly arrested men are kept until they are classified and moved to different jail dorms, or they are waiting to bond out.

"When I was in C tank I was sitting on my cot when another man came up and sat down on my cot. We just started with small talk and he asked what I was in jail for, so I embellished the reason for my arrest. He told me he was in jail for being a felon in possession of ammunition," he continued.

"He bragged about some robberies he had committed and had not been caught, and I figured it was just braggadocio on his part. I don't know if he was on meth or something but he told me he lived in Wheatland, and around last December he had killed some fool that caught him breaking into the guy's pick-up truck," Paulson said.

"He told me that some other dude had been charged for the murder, and then he laughed about it. Then he laughed again and said he shot the guy with his own gun that he had taken from the truck," Paulson said.

"I was instantly on alert because I knew he was talking about the John Adams murder," he continued.

"This guy told me he lived down the street with his mother," he finished.

"Right after that the corrections officer called out his name so he got up from my cot and went to the booking counter and was classified and moved into another cell block."

"The corrections officer called out the name Ryan Bates," he exclaimed.

"I'm almost positive he was the taller of the two guys that ran out of the alley behind John Adams' house the morning of the murder."

"Are you willing to sign a declaration regarding your conversation with Ryan Bates?" they asked.

"Sure I am, that worthless punk needs to pay up and your client needs to get out of jail for a crime he never committed," Paulson said.

Paulson was supplied with a pen and paper and he reduced his story to written form.

When he finished he laid the pen down and gave one final review of his declaration.

He signed the document under the Penalty of Perjury and handed it to Anson.

"Where can we reach you when you get out of jail?" Anson asked.

"I'll be staying with my girlfriend Lynn," he answered.

As they left the interview room a corrections officer called out Steve Paulson's name and directed him over to the counter.

"Your bond has been paid and you are free to leave the jail after we do the paperwork to release you," the corrections officer said to Paulson.

"Here is my business card," said Monty and Paulson accepted it as he walked over to the Jail counter.

Monty and Anson walked the short distance to Monty's hotel room where they reviewed the startling information Paulson had provided.

Chapter 38

"I was just thinking about something," Monty said as he stood up to make his point.

"According to Lynn Bennett, Marianne Shutt's son Zachary used to come over to her house with Devin Adams and play with her son Austin," he started.

"What does that have to do with anything?" Anson asked.

"Remember the handcuffs that belonged to Lynn Bennet were the same handcuffs that were found in John Adams' yard? The lab said there were possible traces of Dustin Silver's DNA on the handcuffs. It didn't make sense, but now it is starting to," Monty said.

"Let's go have a visit with Lynn Bennett and ask her some more questions," Anson said.

They left the hotel and drove to Lynn Bennet's house on 3rd street.

Lynn answered the door almost immediately and startled the two investigators.

"I was standing in the kitchen and saw you guys drive up, what can I do for you?" she asked.

"Ms. Bennet, we stopped by to ask you a few more questions about your stolen handcuffs," Anson started.

She invited Anson and Monty into her residence and had them sit in kitchen chairs clustered around an antique round oak table.

"Do you remember John Adams's girlfriend Marianne Shutt and her little boy Zachary?" Monty asked.

"Yes, her little boy was probably over here at my house three or four times a week when he would come over with Devin Adams," she said.

"He was over here a lot last spring and summer," she continued.

"Did you ever let the kids play with your handcuffs?" Monty asked.

"I did let the kids play cops and robbers with their plastic toy guns and my handcuffs, but only when I was supervising them," she replied.

"Did little Zachary ever bring over toys when he would visit?" he continued.

"He did bring over a small electric game and the kids would play on it," she said.

"I think it was an Atari game that they would hook up with Austin's TV in his bedroom, but Zachary always took it back with him," Lynn said.

"Anything else?" Monty asked.

"Let me think," she paused, "Zachary had a bright red sports whistle that he wore around his neck and he would about drive me crazy with his incessant noise. I warned him that I was going to take it from him and he was pretty good about not blowing it for a week or two," she continued.

"Zachary came back a couple of days later and started blowing the whistle so I took it away from him and put it on top of the refrigerator," she said.

"Zachary left my house later in the day and I forgot to give the whistle back to him. After that, maybe a week or two later, Zachary came back with John Adams' son and they played games with Austin. I plumb forgot about the whistle, let me check and see if it is still there," she said.

She tipped on her toes and exclaimed, "It's still there but in the far corner of the top of the refrigerator, I can't reach it."

Anson stood at 6 ft. 1 inch and he could see over the top and spied where the red whistle was located.

"Do you have any unused paper school lunch bags handy?" he asked.

"Yes, I have some in the pantry because I buy them in bulk for the kid's lunches that I pack," as she directed Anson to the pantry where the container of paper lunch bags was stored.

A box of clear plastic sandwich bags was sitting on the same shelf.

Anson removed a sandwich baggy and carefully avoided touching any part of the outside of the sandwich baggy and placed his hand inside.

He picked up a paper lunch bag and snapped it open.

Holding the opened bag with his other hand he reached up onto the refrigerator top and grasped the red whistle with his covered hand and dropped the whistle into the open paper lunch sack.

He deftly rolled the top closed.

"That whistle has been up there since the day I put it up there last year," she said.

"Has anyone touched it?" asked Monty.

"None of the kids saw where I placed it," she said.

They thanked Lynn and drove back to the hotel where they placed the red whistle in the locked metal filing cabinet.

Monday morning came and Monty and Anson met with Mark, Jackie and Colin for the scheduled weekly Zoom meeting.

Jackie started off with her weekly updates on the case preparation.

"We have compared the interview reports Detective Hannigan did with Marianne Shutt," she said.

"I compared those interviews with the probable cause information Hannigan wrote in the search warrant for Dustin's cell phone numbers and text messages. I also compared the same information to the statement of facts Hannigan had placed in the probable cause section of that second search warrant applied to locate Silver's phone by pinging the phones location history," she continued.

"Marianne told Hannigan that Dustin Silver had never made threats to harm him or come to Wheatland and confront him. I reviewed Marianne Shutt's audio recordings and Hannigan purposely lied in both search warrants in the probable cause section of both search warrants and said that Dustin Silver had made threats towards John Adams. He swore under penalty of perjury that the information he had placed in the search warrant application was the truth," she said.

"Hannigan is a Brady cop for lying!" Monty exclaimed.

(Brady cop is a term used for police officers that have been deemed dishonest and the prosecutor is required to notify the Jury the officer has a history of being untruthful.)

"Yes, he is," Jackie said and we are going before Judge Charles Parker to make a motion to exclude both search warrants.

"Anson and Monty, have you anything new to discuss?" Jackie asked.

Anson started out by telling the defense team about the phone call he had received from Lynn Bennett who notified him that Steve Paulson had been jailed on a mistaken arrest warrant.

"Paulson had requested contact with us," he said.

"The warrant was issued for the same charge Paulson had on him when we contacted him at Wheatland District Court. Paulson had a citation for no valid driver's license and the judge dismissed the charge because Paulson had obtained a driver's license. The judge's clerk neglected to make a notation on Paulson's court file showing the charge had been dismissed by the judge. It will be all straightened out on Tuesday and Lynn Bennet has posted the bond so he didn't have to spend the weekend in jail," he continued.

"Monty and I went to the jail and visited with Paulson before lunch this past Saturday. Paulson tells us that when he first got booked into the jail he was placed in C Tank which is where all newly booked men are placed prior to being classified and sent to the various jail pods. He tells us he was sitting on his cot and this guy named Ryan Bates came over and sat at the end of his bed and started making small talk, asking why Paulson was in jail. They talked further and Ryan told him he had been stealing a gun from a guy's pick-up parked on the street and he had smoked the fool with his own gun. Ryan told him it was last December. Paulson knew exactly what Ryan was talking about. Paulson said he was almost positive it was Ryan, that he had observed run out of the alley with a shorter guy on the morning of the murder of John Adams," Anson explained.

Monty showed Paulson a photo of Ryan Bates and he positively identified him as the person he had talked with at the jail.

"Steve Paulson signed a declaration with the information."

"That is great, you guys," Mark said.

"Just another brick on the wall," he continued.

"Anything else?" Jackie asked.

Anson started out by talking about the strands of DNA found on the handcuffs from John Adams's yard that could not be excluded as belonging to Dustin Silver but could also not be identified as belonging to Dustin Silver.

"Monty and I talked about it and Monty reminded me that Dustin's son Zachary would play over at Lynn Bennet's place with her son Austin and John's son Devin. We knew the handcuffs were owned and possessed by Lynn prior to being found in the front yard at John Adams. Lynn Bennet told us she did allow all of the boys, including Zachary, to play cops and robbers and they would play with the handcuffs. I asked Lynn if there were any objects Zachary would have touched that were still at her house. She told us that Zachary had a red whistle that he would bring over. That Zachary would blow that whistle incessantly and loud so she finally took it away from Zachary and placed it on top of her refrigerator," Anson continued.

"Lynn checked the top of the refrigerator and the red whistle was still up there. She told us that no one else had touched that whistle after she put it on top of the refrigerator," he said.

"We collected the red whistle to check for DNA for comparison of DNA found on the set of handcuffs. The whistle is locked in our file cabinet back at Monty's room," he finished.

"Great work, you guys," said Mark.

"We have the DNA markers and sequence of the DNA threads found on the handcuffs that the Prosecutor thinks are Dustin's," Mark said.

"Monty, are you available to transport the red whistle to the private DNA Research lab we have worked with?" asked Jackie.

"If Zachary's DNA is connected to his father's DNA, it will explain how those DNA strands ended up on the handcuffs," he continued.

We know that Dustin Silver had no connection to Lynn Bennet," he continued.

"That will destroy the prosecutor's theory that the handcuffs belonged to Dustin and he accidentally dropped them when he shot John Adams. I can drive to Portland tomorrow morning and deliver the securely packaged whistle," Monty finished.

"Great! I will phone the lab tomorrow and let them know to expect the whistle," Jackie said.

"We already know Dustin never had possession or contact with those handcuffs," Jackie said.

"Let's meet next Monday afternoon, Mark and I will make a motion to exclude the two search warrants Hannigan falsely prepared and presented to the judge next Monday morning, she continued."

"Oh, one more thing, I mailed the signed declaration from Steve Paulson to Colin," said Anson.

Chapter 39

Jesus Chaco had been sitting in the Othello Jail since the day of the murder and robbery of the norteno trap house in Othello.

He had been formally charged with conspiracy to transport and distribute controlled substances, including methamphetamine, cocaine and fentanyl.

He was sitting in the jail open recreation area watching the small television set to get over his boredom.

A corrections officer called out his name and had Jesus step out in the hallway outside the recreation room where he was handcuffed in waist chains.

Two correction officers escorted Jesus to a large interview room with a mirror located on one wall.

When the door opened Jesus was surprised to see four plainclothes men standing along the interview table and his court appointed attorney was standing on the other side.

The corrections officers left the room.

"Come in and sit down," Sgt. Price said to Jesus and directed him to sit next to his court appointed defense attorney Jana Gerber.

The Sgt. introduced Randy Evans of the ATF task force, DEA

Agent Jeremy Brown and Hank Shover from the U.S. Marshals Office Eastern Washington District.

Agent Jeremy Brown started the conversation and told Jesus that he would be receiving lesser charges and a reduction in jail time if he cooperated.

"Let me advise you that your charges are going to be transferred over to the U. S. Attorney's Office for prosecution. We know the drugs were shipped across state lines and that makes it a felony under Federal jurisdiction. You were with Carlos Guzman and Alphonso Ruiz when they were involved in the chase that ended up in an accident. You know Bronza Miller was shot and killed by Alphonso Ruiz when he shot into the back of the red Honda," Agent Brown said.

"You admit you grabbed the guns from inside the Dodge Hellcat Carlos was driving, and it is evidence in the homicide. You ran from the scene and ended up back at Carlos Guzman's house," he continued.

"The officers in Othello and the State Troopers found you hiding in the house and recovered the guns, including the 357 Magnum Revolver that Alphonso used to kill Bronza Miller. When the officers interviewed you, the locations of drugs and large amounts of cash in Carlo's house were pointed out by you. Perhaps we can come to an agreement but it will require you to provide testimony. The trial will probably be in the fall."

Jesus paid rapt attention to Agent Brown's comments.

"You will be charged as an accomplice to 2nd Degree Murder of Bronza Miller who was the passenger in the red Honda and was shot and killed by Alphonso Ruiz during that crazy car chase. Police reports show that you provided the location of a large cache of the drugs and money that belong to Carlos Guzman and the Sinaloa Cartel. What will happen to you when Carlos finds out you gave the cops the information?"

Jesus face blanched, but he just sat there, looking down.

"How would you like to save your life?" Deputy Marshal Hank Shover said to Jesus and Jesus looked up sharply.

"You will be a dead man walking if we throw you in a federal prison cell," he explained further.

"If you are willing to disclose the pipeline of the drugs coming into the area we are open to a deal."

"However, the names and contact points of the Sinaloa Cartel will be required. As you know, the Sinaloa Drug Cartel and norteno gang will put a reward out on your head," he continued.

"You won't last long," Deputy Marshal Shower said.

"Do you have family in the United States?" he asked Jesus.

"No, I am originally from El Salvador and my family was killed off in the drug wars there," Jesus answered.

"I have no relatives that I know of," he continued.

"I can get you into the U.S. Marshal Witness Protection Program and issue you a new identification and move you to another region in the U.S. and find you meaningful employment," Shower said.

"You will never be allowed to contact anyone from your past because you could be found by the Cartel and the norteno's if you do. You will have a U.S. Marshal Agent to contact that will be your handler if there is a problem, or you think you have been compromised," he finished.

"It's a hard choice," said Sgt. Price, "but it will save your life."

"We know that you are just a small cog in the drug distribution chain so we are willing to drop all charges, including the accessory to murder charge, if you cooperate and testify in the upcoming federal trial on Carlos and Alphonso. Carlos will be charged with 2nd Degree murder along with Alphonso because he played an important part in the murder by chasing the red Honda, although it was actually Alphonso that pulled the trigger. The Sinaloa Cartel is involved so Carlos and Alphonso will probably get a maximum sentence in a federal high risk prison for conspiracy. What do you think?" Agent Brown asked, and all eyes were on Jesus' face.

Jesus turned and looked at his court appointed attorney and asked her what she thought of the deal.

"I've told you of the pending charges on you and the lengthy prison sentence in a Federal Prison you will get if you are convicted," Jana Gerber told him.

"I can't tell you to take the deal or not, that's up to you, but you need to look at what will happen if you don't," she continued.

"OK, I'm ready to talk and will cooperate and give you the information you want," he answered.

"Great," said Agent Hank Shower.

"We are going to move you to the Sea-Tac Federal Prison near Seattle where we can keep you in protective custody until we get everything ironed out. You will be under heavy protection," he continued.

"I have an agreement for you to review with your attorney Jana Gerber."

Jesus reviewed the document and scribbled his signature and the date on the bottom line.

Chapter 40

Almost two weeks had passed when Detectives Hannigan, Fitz and Skates walked into the Canyon County Jail and requested that Juan Garcia be brought into the Sheriff's interview room.

Juan's Public Defender Ozzie Kryer was waiting in the jail hallway with Canyon County Prosecutor Walter Colvins.

The door was opened and the Detectives, Public Defender Attorney Ozzie Kryer and Prosecutor Walter Colvins filed in.

Juan Garcia was brought into the room through a heavy metal door and he sat down beside his attorney.

He slid the handcuffs he was wearing up and down as if his skin was starting to chafe.

Prosecutor Walter Colvins started out by asking Garcia if he knew why he was there meeting with the Detectives and himself.

"Yes, my attorney told me that I could give a free talk and nothing I say about myself can be used against me. If I tell the truth, consideration will be given on my criminal charges for sentencing if I am convicted," Garcia replied.

At that point Detective Skates started the conversation with Juan.

"Do we have your permission to audio video this interview?" he asked Juan.

"Yes, you have my permission," he replied.

Detective Skates pointed out each person attending the free talk and only started the interview after everyone had given permission for the recorded interview.

"We know that the empty shell casing found in John Adams' yard matches the four shell casings found along I-90 last week at the scene of a collision where the driver had been shot and wounded. We also found two more shell casings in the red Honda that was pulled out of the Remington Canal and they also match. All of the firing pin markings match and all were fired from the same 45 caliber semi auto handgun," Det. Skates continued.

"Of course, you already know there was a body found inside the Honda with a gunshot wound to the back of the head which resulted in the guy's face being blown off. Juan, you know the dead man's name was Bronza Miller because you were with him when he died," he finished.

Detective Fitz took over the interview task and coached Juan to describe the incident in detail.

"There's not much to tell," Juan started.

"We had information the norteno trap house in Othello was really busy so we decided to drive over there and do an armed robbery for drugs and money," he said.

"What kind of gun were you going to use?" Fitz asked.

"A 45 caliber handgun," Juan answered.

"Where did you guys get the gun?"

"I don't know where Ryan got the gun."

"Come on, Juan, you know the first one to talk always gets a better deal and we are going to contact Ryan tomorrow," Detective Fitz coaxed.

"We know a 45 cal. semi auto pistol and a box of Winchester ammunition was stolen out of John Adams' truck in the early morning hours of this past December 28th. It was you and Ryan that did the deed and shot and killed John Adams, wasn't it?" he said with a raised voice.

"Why do you think that?" Juan said weakly.

"Let me tell you," Det. Hannigan interrupted.

"The partial box of 45 caliber semi auto cartridges was found in Ryan's pick-up when you guys were stopped by the WSP Trooper. The Washington State Patrol Crime Lab has found your DNA on the ammo box. The firing pin markings on the head stamp of the found shell casings are the same on the two 45 caliber shell casings found in the red Honda, the shell casings along I-90 at the scene of the collision all matched, and last but not least, they are a match to the shell casing found in the front yard of John Adams house on December 28th morning. This means the gun that fired the fatal shot into John Adams is the same and ties you into that murder."

Juan looked down and didn't say anything.

"We know Ryan Bates was driving the red Honda when Carlos Ruiz and gang were chasing you on I-90 after the robbery," he continued.

"Bronza Miller wasn't the shooter because he was shot and killed by someone in the other car. The only other person in the red Honda was you. It was you that fired into the windshield of that Dodge Hellcat and shot the driver Carlos Ruiz, causing him to lose control and roll a couple of times."

"They were shooting at us and they killed Bronza," Juan blurted out. "They shot Bronza in the head and blew his brains out," he said, barely holding back tears.

"Look, we didn't plan for anyone to get wasted," he explained.

"What the hell happened to the guy in the backyard?" Hannigan pointed out to Juan.

"Oh Gawd, I know," he said, "Bronza had a baseball bat and was supposed to sneak up behind the guy while we distracted him and hit him on the back of the head and knock him out. Bronza was excited and hit the guy in the head with the bat as hard as he could, and I heard the guy's skull crush."

"Did anyone in the norteno trap house hear the noise outside?" Detective Fitz asked.

"No, because Ryan and I immediately went into the house through the back door which was partially open," he admitted.

"What happened inside the trap house?"

"The two guys inside didn't see us until we had the drop on them," Juan continued.

"We took their guns away from them and tied their wrists with flex ties."

"What did you take from inside the house?" Fitz asked.

"We picked up all the bindles of meth that were packaged sitting on the kitchen table and we found more meth in kitchen drawers. There were also bundles of cash we found in a separate kitchen drawer," Juan continued.

"There were probably 30 bundles of cash and all contained $100 bills. I placed all the stuff in a pillowcase we had brought with us. There was a gym bag sitting on the floor in the living room that we checked and it was loaded with probably twenty more kilo sized packages of methamphetamine. They were packaged in light paper with the Sinaloa Cartel markings on each package."

"What did you guys do then?" Detective Fitz asked.

"I placed the handguns in the gym bag and we grabbed the gym bag and pillowcase and went out the back door," he continued.

"Let me interrupt and tell you that the names of the three guys in the house were Carlos Guzman, Adolpho Ruiz and Jesus Chaco," said Detective Skates.

"The dead guy in the backyard was Michael Guzman and he was the brother of Carlos."

Juan told the detectives that Ryan had threatened to kill Carlos and Alphonso if they shouted out before Juan and Ryan left.

"Bronza had been standing outside as our lookout so we all ran down the alley and got into that red Honda," Juan said.

"We never heard any shouting and when we got to the Honda we drove out of the church parking lot and headed back towards I-90," he continued.

"Ryan was driving, Bronza was in the backseat and I was in the passenger seat," Juan said.

"Bronza was going to drive the red Honda from the Canyon County Park, where Ryan had parked his pick-up truck back to Wenatchee and park it back into his girlfriend's garage and he would pick up his own vehicle," Juan continued.

"Ryan was driving with no headlights until we got out of sight from the norteno trap house so we didn't think anyone would know where to look," he continued.

"Someone must have seen us leaving the area, We were driving down the road about 80 miles per hour and we noticed this big high performance car rapidly approaching us from the back and we thought the driver was going rear end us," Juan told Detective Fitz.

"Then the car backed off about 20 feet and the front passenger started shooting at us. I heard bullets hitting the back of our car, so I leaned out the passenger window of our car and started shooting at the following car," he continued.

"I couldn't tell if I hit anyone but the car swerved off the road and rolled a couple of times. My neck felt wet and when I reached up and touched my neck, I looked down and there was blood on my hand. I couldn't tell if I had been shot, but then I looked over in the backseat and saw Bronza. The lower part of his face was missing, it was horrible, and he was dead," he said shakily.

"We drove the Honda back to the Canyon County Park where Ryan had parked his pick-up. We took out the pillow case of drugs and money and threw them in the pick-up bed of Ryan's truck. When I had grabbed the sports bag in the norteno trap house I had not closed it after I had looked inside. There was congealed blood and brain matter from Bronza inside the gym bag and some of it had covered the upper kilo sized bundles of methamphetamine. We emptied the bloody gym bag and tossed all of the bloody bundles of methamphetamine in the back of Ryan's truck. We threw the gym bag containing the norteno guns into the back seat of the Honda. We didn't know what to do with the car and Bronza's dead body inside, so we drove the car to the gate of the roadway that ran along the Remington Canal. Ryan broke through the gate by ramming it with the red Honda and drove on the road along the canal for about a quarter mile where we stopped. The engine was still running and the automatic transmission was left in drive position. Ryan stepped out of the car and took his foot off the brake. The Honda idled down the side of the canal and sank in the canal," he continued.

"We drove Ryan's pick-up back to the gate and closed the gate after we went through. We never thought the cops would find it so soon," he finished.

The room was silent as everyone digested the information Juan had just provided.

"Juan, do you need a break, or would you like a soda or water?" Detective Fitz asked.

"Sure, I need a bottle of water and could use the restroom," he said and stood up and rattled his handcuffs.

Several serious looking corrections officers were summoned and they left the interview room with Juan who was flanked on both sides.

"Alright, let's get started," Detective Hannigan stated after Juan had returned and sat in the chair holding the bottled water.

"Where did you go after that?" Hannigan asked.

"We drove back to Ryan's mother's place and hid the money and packaged drugs in the attic inside her garage," he answered.

"We had talked about taking some of the cash and bundles of methamphetamine into Spokane to a guy Ryan knew that would buy the meth from us. The next day we went to the attic and grabbed some bundles of cash and three wrapped kilos of methamphetamine. We sold the three meth kilos to the drug buyer that Ryan had done business with this last year," Juan continued.

"We got $40,000. dollars cash for the 3 kilos. Next, we arranged to meet a friend of Ryan's that worked at the mineral shop in the Spokane Valley. His name is Tim Bolton. We agreed to meet later in the day at a barbeque restaurant just west of Spokane. We met him and another guy in the parking lot," he said.

"The other guy bought the 45 caliber handgun from Ryan that evening. His name was Rufus. After that we went out to the Tribal Casino and checked in and got a deluxe suite on the top floor. It cost us $3k for 5 nights and we spent most of the time gambling and having hookers up in our room. We had brought thousands of dollars from the norteno robbery with us and had the majority of the $35K left. We were doing some gambling but not doing very well. I contacted a couple of hookers and we set up their service at the casino hotel. I think their street names were Star and Shontell," he continued.

"They showed up at our hotel suite. We were having a few more drinks up in our room and we had decided to switch the women that night. Ryan had been with Star the other times and he wanted to try out Shontell," he explained.

"Ryan took Shontell into his bedroom and I went into my room with Star. I remember having another drink and lying on the bed beside Star, but that's the last thing I remember until I woke up the next morning. Star was gone and my pants pockets had been emptied of cash. I took a shower and then went out to the kitchen and discovered Ryan was already up and had ordered breakfast. He told me that he didn't really remember having sex with Shontell the night before. We decided we were going to head back to Wheatland later in the day," he said.

"Did you head back?" Detective Fitz asked.

"Yes, we did but, I forgot to tell you guys that we had the packets of money and also part of the $40 K from the meth sales, hidden in the freezer section of the refrigerator. All of the money was stolen out of the freezer by Star and Shontell," he said angrily.

"We tried phoning Shontell but it was apparent it was a burner phone and there was no answer. We had no idea where they were so we just headed home and were stopped by the cops on our way home."

"How much money and drugs would you guess are still up in the attic in the garage at Ryan's mother's house?" Det. Skates asked.

"There were about 50 bundles of cash we took out of the drawer at the norteno trap house. We took about nine or ten packets when we went to the Spokane Casino, so there was probably around $200K left in the attic," Juan answered.

"How many kilo sized packages of meth were in the sports bag?" Detective Fitz asked.

"When we placed the packages up in the attic I counted 30 packets and we only took 3 kilos with us to Spokane."

"Does anyone else between Ryan and yourself know the location of the drugs and money?" Detective Fitz asked.

"No, I don't think Ryan would have told anyone."

Detective Hannigan changed the direction of the interview and Juan looked at him questionably.

"Juan, we need to talk about the John Adams murder from last December," Detective Hannigan started.

"Your DNA was found on the ammo box found in the jockey box from Ryan's pick-up when you were arrested."

Juan looked at Detective Hannigan but did not respond.

"Your DNA was also found on the shell casings found at the I-90 shooting incident. The firing pin strike mark on the primers of all the recovered spent shell casings match the shell casing in John Adams' front yard. You have admitted you were the shooter when you were shooting at the Dodge Hellcat that was chasing you on I-90. We can put you in possession of that 45 caliber handgun that was stolen from John Adams pick-up truck."

"I wasn't there and I didn't shoot John Adams," he said.

"I think Bronza Miller was with Ryan Bates and Ryan killed Adams. I was in bed all night with my girlfriend, you can ask her," he said.

"I want you to think again about your answers," Hannigan told Juan.

"So far you haven't actually killed anyone yourself so we may be able to help you out as long as you continue to be truthful," Detective Hannigan told him.

Prosecutor Colvins interjected into the interview, "Mr. Garcia, you need to answer the detective's questions truthfully, and perhaps we can be helpful to you."

Juan looked over at his attorney for direction.

His attorney told him that he had already disclosed information to the detectives so he should continue to be truthful.

Juan held his head down without speaking for several minutes and then he raised his head and started speaking.

"Alright, I will tell you what happened when John Adams was killed," he said.

"Ryan Bates telephoned the night before John Adams was killed and wanted me to go with him to do some vehicle prowls and he knew where a guy had a gun in his pick-up truck. I got out of bed and dressed and met Ryan over at the church about Division Street and 3rd Street," he continued.

"We went over to the Southwest side of town and got into a couple of vehicles and stole a wallet, jewelry and some coins. Then we went over to a dealer's house and bought some meth. After that we went over to this guy's place about half a block from Ryan's house. The guys' pick-up truck was parked in front and Ryan got into the pick-up truck and I was the lookout. The guy came out of his house and yelled at Ryan and he started coming down the sidewalk towards Ryan. I saw Ryan point the handgun at John Adams and shoot him in the chest, and the guy ran back inside his house," he said.

"Several weeks later we went to Spokane and sold the gun to a guy named Rufus. Ryan knew a guy named Tim Bolt and he arranged the gun to be sold to a guy named Rufus in Spokane," Juan said.

"Are you willing to sign a statement of the facts regarding the John Adams Murder?" Prosecutor Colvins asked.

"Are you willing to testify, and tell the Jury of Ryan Bate's involvement in John Adams murder?"

"Yes, I will do that," Juan said in a shaky voice.

"If everything you tell us is true I will recommend a lesser sentence from Superior Judge Charles Parker. Do you understand that you can be charged with 1st Degree Murder regarding the death of Michael Ruiz because the crime occurred during the commission of a robbery? The same goes for the death of Bronza Miller, even though he was actively involved in the robbery, so you could also be charged with the 1st Degree Murder of Bronza. Now, getting back to the John Adams murder, you could also be charged with 1st Degree Murder since you were the lookout person when Ryan Bates killed John Adams," Prosecutor Colvins said.

"If you testify truthfully and not back out of an agreement, the State will charge you with 2nd Degree Murder for each of the described murders. I will make a recommendation to Judge Charles

Parker that you be sentenced to 15 to 20 years in a state penitentiary and you can receive "good time" credit," he finished.

Juan looked at his attorney and they had a brief conversation before Juan answered that he would agree to the terms.

"You will be placed in protective custody and moved over to the Benton County Jail where you will be safe. We will be back with you today with a prepared Statement based on the information you have provided," said Detective Skates.

He finished as everyone stood up and Juan was led away by corrections officers.

"I think we have pretty much solved the murders at the norteno trap house and the death of Bronza Miller and John Adams," Detective Skates said.

"After we obtain Juan Garcia's signed confession, I will send a copy and the Juan Garcia recorded interview to Dustin Silver's defense team," Prosecutor Colvins stated.

That defense attorney Jackie Skelton is the worst of all of them," Detective Hannigan thought to himself

Chapter 41

The following Monday the defense team met to discuss updates. Jackie had received the Juan Garcia recorded interview and signed confession, and she had also e-mailed them to defense investigators David Anson and Monty Victor.

Anson commented that law enforcement apparently had not followed up tracking the location of the 45 caliber handgun in Spokane, to find where it was currently located.

"Can you guys do a follow-up on the gun history just to tie up loose ends regarding Juan Garcia's Statement," Mark Scalia said.

"I know Tim Bolt, I know where to locate this guy, he lives in the zone west of the County Courthouse which is commonly called Felony Flats," Anson continued.

"Are you and Monty available to go to Spokane and run down this guy?" Mark Scalia asked.

Monty looked at Anson who nodded back at him.

"We can leave tomorrow," Monty answered.

"When reviewing the transcript of Juan's interview, it pretty much ties Ryan into Adams' murder," Monty surmised.

Jackie Skelton told the team that the DNA lab had contacted her and they were starting to compare the DNA markers on the red whistle to the DNA on the handcuffs.

"I expect a telephone call from them probably tomorrow and then a written report and decision with the results in a few more days," she said.

"Good luck with your interview of Tim Bolt," Jackie said to Anson and Monty.

Chapter 42

"I was contacted by Prosecutor Walter Colvins yesterday and he forwarded more police reports to us regarding the 45 caliber shell casing issue," said Jackie Skelton.

Prosecutor Colvins advised he had received a report from Detective Massee who had been at the crime scene the day of the murder.

Detective Massee had assisted in the collection of evidence inside the residence and he performed a cursory search of the clothing John Adams was wearing.

He located three 45 caliber cartridges and six spent 45 caliber shell casings in the pocket of the light jacket John Adams was wearing.

He collected the items and placed them in a protective plastic holder.

The Detective placed the items in the pocket of the coat he was wearing.

Detective Massee writes in his report that he had forgot to put the evidence in the evidence property room until almost three weeks later when he discovered the cartridges and shell casings inside his coat pocket that had been hanging up in his office.

The found spent shell casings were sent to the Washington State Patrol Crime Lab.

"This past week we got a response back from WSP and they determined the firing pin markings on the head stamp of the shell casings recovered from Detective Massee are the same as the two 45 caliber shell casings found in the red Honda," Jackie said.

"The shell casings found along I-90 at the scene of the collision are also match," Jackie continued.

"And last but not least, those shell casings also match the shell casing found in John Adams' yard on the morning of the murder," she finished.

Jackie could barely contain her excitement from the good news disclosed by the Prosecutor.

"Just a minute, I am getting Prosecutor Walter Colvins on the phone," Jackie said.

The phone was answered by Prosecutor Colvins and Jackie Skelton confirmed with him of the accuracy of the WSP lab report.

"This pretty much clears my client of this murder, doesn't it?" she asked Prosecutor Colvins.

"Let me go through the information I have and we can talk about a settlement to this case," he said.

"It looks like the defense investigators have stirred the pot so the truth has floated to the top," he continued.

"Tomorrow we have a motion to dismiss the two search warrants of Dustin's phone text messages and phone call records," said Prosecutor Colvins.

"The other motion is to dismiss the second search warrant for phone pings and locations of Dustin's phone. OK, see you in court tomorrow," Prosecutor Colvins finished and the call ended.

Chapter 43

Jackie Skelton, Mark Scalia and Colin Thurgood sat in Judge Charles Parker's courtroom awaiting the Judge's appearance.

Dustin had been brought over from the jail with his hands cuffed and attached to belly chains around his waist as he sat between Mark and attorney Colin Thurgood.

Prosecutor Walter Colvins, and Detective Ralson Hannigan were sitting at the adjacent table with the podium used to address the judge between the tables.

The court reporter and bailiff entered the room ahead of Judge Parker.

Judge Parker was a large intimidating man and the rumor was the Judge kept a 44 magnum revolver in a holster under his Judicial robe.

The bailiff announced the Judge's presence and everyone stood, in respect to Judge Parker.

"Your Honor, we are here today to respond to the defense, the motion to suppress several signed search warrants that were prepared by Detective Ralston Hannigan," said Prosecutor Colvins.

"Your Honor, I have read the motion to suppress document, and I will have a response to the defense accusations of Detective Hannigan's dishonest behavior. He allegedly used improper information in the preparation of both search warrants prepared on January 3rd and 4th," he continued.

"Please respond for the defense Ms. Skelton," said Judge Parker.

"Your Honor, if I may please make reference to page #2 line 23, where Detective Hannigan's affidavit states that Marianne Shutt told him Dustin Silver had been making harassing type phone calls to her and he had threatened to come to John Adams in Wheatland and take care of him. If you will read page twenty-three, lines 13-21 of the Marianne Shutt recorded interview transcript, Marianne is positive that Dustin never made any threats towards John Adams or threatened to confront John Adams," Jackie said to Judge Parker.

"Your Honor, we have reviewed all text messages from July this year back through December 28th of last year. Marianne was texting Dustin almost daily and was encouraging him to meet her at hotels on Moses Lake and Wenatchee," she continued.

"Dustin was resistant to meet with Marianne in most instances, as you can see by his responses to Marianne. We have served subpoenas to the various hotels Dustin and Marianne were using to confirm they were staying there," she noted.

"Your Honor, I request permission to approach the bench and hand you hotel receipts from those hotels which disclose that Marianne Shutt was actually paying for the hotel rooms. The additional text messages show that Marianne Shutt was sending text messages, telling Dustin that she couldn't wait to see him. As you can see from the attached photos, Marianne Shutt was constantly sending Dustin Silver nude provocative photos of herself. Your Honor, as you can see, Detective Hannigan purposely placed false information in the probable cause section of the search Warrant request for the purpose of obtaining an invalid misleading search warrant," she continued.

"What the defense team finds astounding is Detective Hannigan prepared a 2nd search warrant for the location of Dustin Silver's phone by utilizing the GPS cell tower pings the day before the homicide and two days after the event. He provided the same inaccurate information that he used in the first search warrant probable cause affidavit. Again, we feel the information was incorrect in the probable cause section of the search warrant. We stop short of accusing Detective Hannigan of deliberate criminal activity, but feel the information may have been manipulated," she finished.

"Mr. Colvins, care to comment on the motion to dismiss?" Judge Parker asked.

"Yes, your honor, I am calling Canyon County Sheriff's Investigator Ralston Hannigan to respond to these serious allegations," he replied.

Detective Ralston walked across the room to the witness box and stood while Judge Parker swore him in.

"Your Honor, I can explain the discrepancies in the two search warrants," he began.

"I must have read my notes incorrectly from the interview I did with Marianne Shutt. I apologize because I didn't actually listen to the recorded interview I did with Ms. Shutt, otherwise I would have noticed that the probable cause affidavit I prepared was incorrect," he said with his eyes refusing to meet Judge Parker's gaze.

Judge Parker began with, "I have read the motion to dismiss prepared by Dustin Silver's defense team and the attached photos of text messages back and forth between Marianne Shutt and Dustin Silver. I see that Detective Hannigan's statement of facts does not match up with the documents contained in the motion to dismiss." He finished and looked down at his hands which were visibly shaking.

"Do you have any comments or argument to this motion to dismiss the search warrants?" Judge Parker asked Prosecutor Colvins.

"No, your honor," Prosecutor Colvins turned and glared at Detective Hannigan.

Judge Parker took off his glasses and stared down at the persons sitting in his courtroom.

"I have never been made aware of such an outrageous blurring of the accuracy of a search warrant," he said to Prosecutor Colvins.

"This Detective claims that it was just a basic mistake and confusion of the circumstances. Detective Hannigan is an experienced investigator and had the ability to review evidence and documents that he possessed. Yet, he claims it was an honest mistake, that he failed to check for accuracy before he submitted the search warrant to my court," he continued.

"I'm torn to decide if Detective Hannigan committed a criminal act or it was just plain incompetence. I am denying the use of both search warrants argued before my court this morning and nothing contained in the results will be deemed admissible," he ordered.

"One last thing, Prosecutor Colvins, in the future I believe you better review any search warrants related to this case that was prepared by Detective Hannigan."

"Your Honor, we still need to address the tampering incident at the crime scene of the handcuffs that were reportedly found in John Adams's front yard," Jackie Skelton requested to Judge Parker.

"Let's hear your motion on that matter," Judge Parker said as Defense attorney Colin Thurgood stood up to address the Judge.

"Your Honor, you will see a police report prepared by Wheatland Police Officer Matt Winslow," he started.

"Officer Winslow took a series of photographs when he first found the handcuffs lying on the grass in John Adams's front yard," Colin Thurgood continued.

"Your Honor, if you would look at the first five photos taken by Officer Winslow on his cellphone camera, you will see several leaves covering the handcuffs with snow on top of the leaves. In the next 3 photos you will see the leaves are no longer on the top of the handcuffs. If you look closer and compare the direction the grass has flattened between the handcuffs and the ground, between photo 5 and photo 6, you will notice the grass has been pressed down in an opposite direction which indicates some unknown person actually picked up the handcuffs and manipulated and contaminated them. Your Honor, it is suspect the evidence was manipulated and contaminated," Colin Thurgood finished.

Judge Parker turned his head towards Prosecutor Walter Colvins.

"Your Honor, I would like to have Officer Winslow explain the situation so the air can be cleared on that matter," Prosecutor Colvins stated to the Judge.

"Very Well, Mr. Winslow, please step forward and sit in the witness chair if you will, please," Judge Parker ordered.

Matt Winslow was nervous as he walked across the arena and stood in front of the witness chair until the court bailiff had the officer swear that his testimony would be truthful.

Prosecutor Colvins walked over to the front of the witness chair and looked directly at Officer Winslow. "Officer Winslow, is it true that you placed the handcuffs on police evidence property as evidence?"

"No, sir, I placed the handcuffs in a paper bag and sealed the bag, placing my initials and the date on the bag," he answered.

"I carried the bag over to the Incident Command Post and left it on a table there with other evidence," he said.

"Your written report does not mention that there were leaves covering the handcuffs and your report does not disclose that you had actually picked up the handcuffs to examine them, is that true?" Prosecutor Colvins asked.

Officer Winslow replied, "Well, I didn't see any evidentiary value to the handcuffs and they looked like they had been on the ground for several days, so I picked them up to check for a serial number. There was not a complete set of serial numbers, they looked like they had been ground off so I placed the handcuffs down where they had been laying on the grass."

"Why didn't you include in your report that the leaves had been covering the handcuffs and that the serial numbers had partially been ground off?" Prosecutor Colvins asked.

"I don't know, I guess I should have," he said and looked down.

"Any other questions for Officer Winslow from the defense?" asked Judge Parker.

"No, Your Honor," Colin Thurgood started, "but I move to have the handcuffs suppressed as evidence in light of this information we learned today from Officer Winslow."

"I will take this matter under advisement and make a finding next week," the Judge said.

"Prosecutor Colvins, I believe this is another officer that you should request a follow-up internal investigation to the Wheatland Police Chief, regarding this handcuff matter," the Judge continued.

"I suspect Officer Winslow may not be trained for the preservation of evidence, or he purposely did not include the information in his report," the Judge said.

"He could be another Brady Officer," the Judge said and glared down at Officer Winslow, who was still sitting in the witness chair.

"That will be all, you can step down Officer Winslow," Judge Parker said as he stood to leave the room and all spectators hastily stood until the judge left the courtroom.

Prosecutor Colvins walked out of the courtroom with Detective Hannigan and Officer Winslow and stood at the end of the hall, away from the defense team.

He had an angry look on his face when he stood in front of Detective Hannigan and Officer Winslow.

"I haven't decided if I am going to have your boss start an internal investigation on both of you," he said.

"If you can't get the information you want, the answer isn't to falsify a search warrant just to get a conviction on someone that might actually be innocent," he spoke loudly and turned to Officer Winslow. "Your fucking report doesn't even match the photographs that you took or the position of the handcuffs in later photos. You don't even know the chain of evidence on the handcuffs after you dropped them off at the table in the command vehicle or who may have handled them. Thanks for embarrassing me in front of the judge and everyone else in the courtroom," Prosecutor Colvins said as he walked away from Detective Hannigan who had a worried look on his face, and Officer Winslow stood in the hallway with his head looking down.

Jackie, Mark and Colin had stepped out of the courtroom into the hallway and had witnessed and overheard the confrontation between Detective Hannigan, Officer Winslow, and Prosecutor Colvins.

"Wow," Colin Thurgood said as they walked down the hallway. "I wonder what he thinks of the case now."

"There's more to come," Mark Scalia replied with a smile.

"The prosecution can't even identify Dustin's location during the time and date of the murder and they cannot provide any information about the text messages or anything related. Just another brick on our defense wall," Jackie said and they gave each other a high five as they walked out of the courthouse.

Detective Hannigan sat on a park bench across from the courthouse and watched the defense team walk to the car parked in front of the courthouse.

He was trying to think of his future as an investigator and realized his career was in the hands of Prosecutor Colvins who could deem him a "Brady Cop".

The anger of Judge Parker towards him could come back and haunt him more than one time during the investigation.

I know that bastard Dustin Silver did the murder and I'm not giving up, Hannigan thought to himself.

A common mistake often made by inexperienced law enforcement investigators.

Detective Skates and Fritz spoke in low tones after they had separated from Detective Hannigan.

"Look, I think the case is going to be a shit show because Hannigan has done a pretty good job of screwing it up," Detective Fitz said.

"Yes, I think Ryan Bates did kill John Adams, but Hannigan has tunnel vision and is going to make questionable claims and still try to push the murder charge on Dustin Silver," he continued.

"So far the judge hasn't shown any interest in sanctioning us, but the prosecutor can request that you and I also be the target of an investigation along with Hannigan," Detective Skates said.

"Hannigan seems focused on the Attorney Jackie Skelton, which has nothing to do with this case," he continued.

"I think Hannigan is about to have a mental break down and he definitely needs to take some time off for his mental health."

Chapter 44

Anson and Monty had been reviewing the reports received from Prosecutor Colvins' office which contained the law enforcement interviews of Juan Garcia and Ryan Bates.

"It looks like there was some type of free talk conducted with Jesus Chaco which will probably be very valuable for us," Monty said as he phoned Jackie Skelton and she put the phone on speaker so Mark Scalia and Colin Thurgood could hear the conversation.

Colin Thurgood responded, "I will ask for the document. I wonder why they haven't sent the rest of those documents."

Mark Scalia thought about the situation and said, "I wonder if Jesus Chaco is going to the Witness Protection Program? That might explain it and perhaps the county prosecutor's office may not have been told. It takes time for the U.S. Attorney's Office and the U. S. Marshalls Office to set up the Witness Protection Program and other federal law enforcement will be working cases from the information Jesus Chaco reveals."

Anson said, "Monty and I are going to Spokane and try to track down John Adams' 45 caliber pistol."

"Good luck, let's meet next Monday morning for a team meeting," Jackie Skelton replied.

Chapter 45

Monty and Anson were on the two hour trip to Spokane to find Tim Bolt, who had worked on cases as an informant with Anson in the past and provided excellent and accurate information.

"Tim Bolt has the pulse of the zone west of the Spokane County Courthouse and can pretty much tell you who is doing what. His house is a shelter for some of the criminals in town but he also lets street kids crash when they are hiding out from one thing or another. His house is a neutral zone and any beefs between people staying there are left outside at the door, or they are kicked out," Anson said.

Monty was directed to take the Monroe Street exit off I-90 Freeway and they headed north on Monroe Street.

Anson directed Monty to turn west on Broadway Ave. that went right past the Southside of the County Courthouse.

After they had travelled six or seven blocks they slowed and Anson pointed out a small community park on the Southside off the road.

"You can see a lookout standing at the corner and then another about 50 feet back in the park," Anson told Monty.

"If you want to deal with these guys on drug deals, this is the place to come, but you have to be at least a mid-quantity dealer," he said.

"A person just trying to buy personal quantity would get their ass beat down or capped if they tried. That's a paranoid crew, as you can see," he continued.

"Drive about 6 blocks down to Edgerton Street and take a left. About two blocks down is River View Street and Tim Bolt resides at that blue corner house. Pull over and park here on Edgerton and we won't get out for awhile. It will give Tim Bolt or one of his runners a chance to scope us out so they don't get trigger happy," Anson said.

"Tim and his flunkies knows me so we will be fine," Anson said with confidence.

They stayed parked at that location and the curtain of a side window in the house opened slightly, and they knew they were under surveillance and getting checked out.

A few minutes later two young men in their late teens walked around the corner from River View and walked on the sidewalk towards their car.

"Just sit tight, they are scoping us out, looking for any signs we are the cops," Anson told Monty.

The taller of the two men pretended like he was talking on his cell phone, but Monty noted he was taking photos.

Anson's cell phone buzzed and he picked up the phone without looking.

"Hey, Dude, why didn't you just walk up on my front porch and knock," said a laughing voice on the other end.

"My Hood Rats sent me cell phone photos of you two sitting in plain view in your vehicle," Tim Bolt said.

Anson laughed back and said, "Hey, we're just about to walk up and knock."

They got out of the pick-up truck and locked it before walking up to the front porch of the two story modest home.

Tim opened the front door before they had reached the front porch.

He stepped onto the front porch and stood there until they had arrived.

"How you been, man?" he asked Anson and gave him a fist bump and a wide smile.

He glanced at Monty as Anson introduced him.

Bolt gave Monty a friendly fist bump as a greeting.

"Come on in," he said and directed them into the living room that had decent furniture and the house was reasonably clean.

"I didn't know you got into the drug trade," said Anson.

"Oh, hell no, man, I'm into something a lot better that doesn't get the Narcs and Feds on my ass," he said in mock horror.

"Come with me," he continued and had them follow to the basement stairs where they went downstairs into the basement.

Tim turned on the basement light and Anson and Monty just stood there and stared.

"I'm helping to clean up Felony Flats," Tim said almost proudly.

There were hundreds of catalytic converters stacked on one section of the basement.

"My crew has been stripping the catalytic convertors from the abandoned cars that are parked all over in vacant lots, parked on the street and maybe a few more non abandoned vehicles," he said with a wink.

Next, Tim pointed out rolls of copper household wire that had the insulation burned off and the rolls were bare wire.

The copper wire was stacked to the ceiling.

"As you know, there are many condemned and vacant houses in this part of town and they are slated for razing. My crew goes into the houses and strips out all the copper wiring," he revealed.

"I'm just cleaning up the neighborhood," he said with a wink.

"There's a lot of money value here. How do you get rid of that much stuff? Doesn't anyone get suspicious?" Anson asked.

"We are careful and sell the stuff in Idaho around Idaho Falls at a big recycle company. I actually have a business license to buy and sell scrap metal that I present at the recycle business and there are never any questions asked," Tim replied.

Anson changed the subject and asked if he knew Ryan Bates.

"I'm not sure, the name sounds familiar, I think he had a girlfriend around here if it's who I am thinking."

Monty showed Tim a photo of Ryan Bates and also Juan Garcia.

"Yes, I know this guy as Ryan Bates," Tim confirmed.

"The other guy in that photo was with Bates a couple of weeks ago," he said.

They walked back up the stairs and sat down in the living room.

Tim sent the two young men sitting in the kitchen area to go outside for a few minutes.

"Have you heard of Ryan Bates trying to sell a 45 caliber semi auto pistol?" Monty asked.

"I know that Bates was trying to sell a gun like that down here in the zone, including to me," Tim answered.

"Ryan sold the gun to a guy named Rufus. He sold the gun out in the parking lot at that barbecue joint on the westside by the airport. Fact is, I was there but never had any part of the transaction," he said.

"That gun was probably worth a good $700 and Rufus bought it for $300. Ryan told us he had ripped the gun off and it was hot in Wheatland, but you won't be able to recover the gun from Rufus," Tim continued.

"Why not?" Monty asked.

"Because Rufus made a "Ghost gun" with that gun's components, that he can sell for up to $2k."

"What do you mean?" asked Anson.

"Rufus buys pistol components online and assembles handguns with no serial numbers. He will strip out the components and parts from the handgun he bought from Ryan and put them in a new gun frame without a serial number. He puts a new barrel in the ghost gun and it cannot be traced. The rest of the gun is probably on its way to a landfill," Tim explained.

"Look," he paused, "I know Rufus will never meet with you guys but I can give him a call and see if he hasn't stripped the gun down yet."

"I would appreciate it if you would," Anson said.

Tim picked up his cell phone and dialed a number.

"Hey, Rufus," Tim said as he spoke into the phone.

"Do you still have that 45 you bought from Ryan?" Tim Bolt asked Rufus.

"I have a buyer," he continued.

"You don't?" Tim said on the phone to Rufus, while Monty and Anson listened to one side of the conversation.

"What happened to the gun?" he asked Rufus.

"Oh, OK," Tim Bolt said, "I'll check back later with you."

Tim turned to Anson and Monty and told them the gun had already been stripped down for parts that had been used for the components of a ghost gun.

"He told me that if you wanted the gun frame, barrel and firing pin, you would need to take a swim in the Spokane River," he continued.

"I'd like to have you sign a written Declaration if you would," Anson said.

"There's an innocent guy that is sitting in the Canyon County Jail for a murder he didn't commit and Ryan Bates is the actual shooter," Anson continued.

"I'll do it man, only because it's you but I won't name Rufus in the Declaration," Rufus told them.

Monty quickly prepared a declaration on his laptop and attached it to his portable printer.

"Look this over," he said to Tim and handed the printed document to him.

"It is accurate so I will sign it," Tim replied and handed it back after signing it.

"If Ryan Bates tries to intimidate you let us know and we can take care of it by going to the court and getting an intimidation of a witness arrest warrant on him," Monty said to Tim.

"He won't have the backbone to come into my neighborhood without my permission, or he might never leave upright," Tim said with a laugh at the humorous comment he had made.

"Thanks, man, you have been real helpful," Anson said before they stepped out of Tim's house and walked back to their pick-up.

One of Tim's street guards had been standing by Anson's unoccupied pick-up truck, protecting it from being stripped.

They nodded at the young man who was barely out of his teens, and he stepped back when they got into the pick-up.

"Let's find a place for a cold beer and sandwich," Monty said to Anson.

As they drove East on Broadway Avenue they stopped at a well known Bar and Grill on the corner of Monroe Street.

"Give us a couple of prime rib sandwiches and cold bottles of beer," Anson said to the friendly waitress.

Chapter 46

They had barely finished their lunch and second beer when Monty's phone rang.

"This is Jackie, did you find Tim Bolt?" she asked.

"We not only found him, but we also got a confirmation from him that Ryan Bates had sold a 45 caliber semi auto handgun with a laser sight. Bates also told the buyer the gun was hot in Wheatland," Monty replied.

"Bolt was present when the gun was sold to an illicit gun dealer named Rufus that does business in Felony Flats. The 45 caliber handgun was parted out and placed in a gun frame without serial numbers. Rufus threw the recognizable parts like the gun frame, barrel and firing pin mechanism into the Spokane river, probably downstream from the Felony Flats location. In other words, Rufus used the components of Adams' gun to build a ghost gun. Rufus would not meet with us and he is a serious arms dealer," he said.

"The local police and ATF would love to bust up his operation. He is a very careful and a very dangerous man," Monty cautioned.

"According to Tim Bolt, Rufus buys many handgun frames, pistol barrels and mechanisms online without serial numbers or other distinctive markings, and he builds ghost guns which are new untraceable firearms. All isn't lost, though, since we now have Tim Bolt as another great witness," Monty told Jackie.

"When are you guys coming back to Wheatland?" Jackie asked.

"We thought about spending the night here and returning tomorrow if that works, but what's going on?" Anson asked.

"I got a call from an attorney named Robert Sylvester in Wilson Creek and he had just came from the jail in Wheatland. A corrections officer at the jail is a friend of Attorney Sylvester and he pulled him aside after the Jail Commander had left for the day. The corrections officer told him that an inmate named Alex Johnson told him his cellmate had admitted to him he had killed John Adams when he was breaking into the guys truck," Jackie said.

"They were cellmates for only a couple of days until Alex Johnson told the corrections officers that he wanted to be in a cell by himself, so Ryan Bates was moved to another cell," Jackie continued.

"What is Alex Johnson in jail for?" Monty asked.

"Alex Johnson is a norteno gang member and is waiting for his sentencing for a double murder of some soreno gang members over in Mattawa, Washington," she replied.

"Alex Johnson has no dog in this fight and he will not gain anything towards his prison sentence by coming forward as he has done. Johnson is waiting for sentencing and is expected to get life without parole so he has no incentive to lie."

"Man, he sounds like an ideal witness," Monty said.

"Exactly, and that's why I would like you guys to come back to Wheatland and do an interview with Johnson and see if he will make a Declaration," Jackie said.

"Legal professional visits can be made at the jail until 9:00 P.M.," she added.

"We're on our way in a couple of minutes and will let you know what we find out after interviewing Alex Johnson."

"Ready to head back to Wheatland to do another interview?" Monty asked Anson.

"What's up?" Anson asked back.

"I'll fill you in after we get in the pick-up," Monty said.

Anson finished his bottle of beer.

The two hour travel to Wheatland gave them opportunity to talk about the upcoming interview they would be doing that evening.

When they arrived back in Wheatland and traveled to the County Jail, it was noted that most of the lights in the jail administration windows were dark at 6:00 P.M.

They went to the Jail exterior entrance door and Anson pushed the button next to the metal door.

A security camera and speaker were mounted on the wall above the door.

Almost immediately a voice came from the speaker and a woman's voice enquired about their business.

Monty explained they were there for a legal visit with Alex Johnson.

Monty and Anson displayed their private investigator credentials directly in front of the camera.

The corrections woman asked if either of them was armed.

After receiving an answer, the door clicked and Anson pulled the door open and they entered a small bare room except for a metal bench attached to the concrete floor.

The second inner door made a buzzing sound and an audible click was heard, signaling the door was unlocked.

When they opened the door a corrections officer met them and escorted them down the hallway and stopped at the designated visiting room door, unlocked it and pushed it open.

The room was separated by a waist high concrete table with a concrete counter top and the remainder was a heavy metal screen except for an opening approximately 1 inch by 14 inches that could be used to transfer documents back and forth between an attorney and client.

Two cheap straight back metal chairs sat on either side of the room.

Anson and Monty sat in their chairs and after a few minutes the sound of keys clanging on the door on the other side was heard, then the door opened.

Alex Johnson shuffled into the room wearing a belly waist chain attached to a set of handcuffs that rattled as he moved his arms around.

He never said a word until the corrections officer had stepped out and locked the door.

Anson started the conversation by introducing Monty and himself, telling Alex Johnson they were part of Dustin Silver's defense team.

"I thought you guys might show up after I talked to the corrections officer," he started.

"That C.O. is a good man and I trusted him to get the word to you guys," he continued.

"Tell us what happened and we won't interrupt," Monty told Alex Johnson.

"OK, well, to start out, several weeks ago this guy named Ryan Bates was put in my cell. He talked and talked and just wouldn't shut up and kept telling me the shit he had done, I guess to impress me so I would think he was tough and dangerous. He told me he and another couple of dudes had ripped off a norteno trap house over in Othello and a couple of the norteno's got killed. He bragged about all the money and drugs he had stolen from them and he laughed about it. Ryan told me about another fool he had smoked over in Wheatland. He said he was in the guy's truck and, when the guy came out of his house, he shot the guy with a gun that had been in the truck."

"Did he tell you the name of the guy he shot?" Anson asked.

"No, but Ryan said there was snow on the ground and the guy lived near Ryan's house," he continued.

"Why are you telling us about this? You have already been found guilty of a couple of murders and you probably wouldn't get any time off for telling us?" asked Anson.

"I know that," Alex answered. "But my reason is more basic than that. Ryan didn't know that I am a West End L.A. norteno Gang member. He thought I was a heavy duty soreno gang member and I never showed him my norteno gang tattoos on my back," he smiled.

"I know that when Ryan goes to prison he will be someone's bitch for awhile, and then he will be totally humiliated. Word travels fast in prison if someone has wasted a fellow norteno brother," he said.

"Are you willing to sign a statement that contains the information you just provided us?" Monty asked.

"Hell yeah, man, I want the dude's ass in person at the prison as soon as we can get him there. I know he will go to Shelton Corrections center for screening to determine which prison he will be sent. He will likely end up over in Walla Walla Prison in the Maximum Security Section. Wouldn't that be funny if we became cellmates there?" he said with a laugh.

"I might be the one to sink the sharpened end of a toothbrush handle right into his neck in his carotid artery a dozen times. Then I can look at his face and he will see who killed him as he bleeds out," Alex said with a laugh.

"How come you didn't kill him here in the jail when he was your cellmate?" Anson asked.

"Because I wasn't sure if the guy was telling me the truth about ripping off the norteno trap house. I read about the norteno murders in the Columbia Review newspaper after I had kicked Ryan out of my cell, otherwise I would have already killed the dude," Alex replied.

"What are they going to do to me, give me another life sentence? There's no Death Penalty in this state," he finished.

Monty hand wrote a declaration at Alex Johnson's direction and after reviewing the contents, Alex signed the declaration as a true and correct document, witnessed by both Monty and Anson.

"I'll be leaving on the prison transport bus in about two weeks for my lifetime home, but I have no regrets," Alex said, and there was a hint of somberness in his voice.

They both thanked Alex and stood, and prepared to leave.

As they closed the door, Anson looked back and made eye contact with Alex before turning away and walking out of the room through the heavy door.

Chapter 47

The following Monday morning the defense team were seated in Judge Parker's courtroom and Prosecutor Walter Colvins sat on the other side of the lectern podium.

The court clerk was seated.

The only other person in the room was Wheatland Daily Herald reporter Danielle Lily who was sitting in the front spectator seating area behind Prosecutor Walter Colvins.

He glanced over his shoulder at Danielle and had a worried look on his face.

Jackie had observed the worried look on Walter Colvins' face and she gave a smile to Danielle.

Whatever happens here is going to hit the newspaper no matter what the outcome, she thought.

Judge Parker's Bailiff Garfield West entered the courtroom through the judge's chamber door.

He announced Judge Parker and everyone stood as the judge walked over to his bench and sat down.

He looked down at the Defense Attorneys and Prosecutor Walter Colvins.

"Ladies and gentlemen, I have carefully reviewed the legal arguments provided to me regarding the Motion to Suppress for the first two search warrants prepared by Detective Ralston Hannigan. First, I am going to make a finding on the first search warrant requesting the phone and text messages between the defendant Dustin Silver and Marianne Shutt. Detective Hannigan prepared the search warrant, and he interviewed Marianne Shutt including, the audio/video interview of Ms. Shutt. She told Detective Hannigan that Dustin Silver had not made text, telephone or e-mail messages to her threatening to do harm to John Adams. Mr. Colvins and the defense team have filed briefs with me so no need to argue the merits, I have made my decision. I am approving the defense motion to suppress the search warrant and contents, and none of the information gathered from the search warrant can be used for the trial. Prosecutor Colvins, I am also adding that if Detective Hannigan would have been called to testify as to the probable cause contents of the search warrant, I would have found that he committed perjury. I'm not telling you how to do your job, but you need to think about the impact it will have on the prosecution case if Detective Hannigan testifies at any part of this upcoming trial," he said.

Prosecutor Colvins stood and answered, "Your Honor, he is the lead investigator on this case, I'm not sure of the integrity of this case."

"Now, on my ruling of the second search warrant requesting to do telephone pings of Dustin Silver's cellphone locations, Detective Ralston used the exact wording for the probable cause that he had used in the body of the first search warrant application," he continued.

"Therefore, I am ruling in favor of the defense team and the second search warrant will be suppressed. I have the same misgivings of Detective Hannigan's signed Affidavit of Probable Cause," the Judge stated.

"Now, the next subject I wish to discuss with both prosecution and defense attorneys because I plan to make an evidentiary decision on the handcuffs that were found in the front yard on the day of the murder by Wheatland officer Matt Winslow. Officer Winslow has stated under oath that he removed leaves covering the top of the handcuffs, and picked the handcuffs up and examined them, then placed them back on the ground and not in the position he had found them. Officer Winslow never disclosed the improper handling of the handcuffs and never made a notation in his prepared police reports. I'm also inclined to believe the chain of evidence was not followed. Therefore, I am not going to allow the introduction of those handcuffs to be used as evidence in this upcoming trial," he stated.

"Mr. Colvins, I am admonishing you for even making an argument to maintain the evidence of the handcuffs. If you had called Officer Winslow as a witness to testify on the stand during the trial, you could have put him in peril of a perjury charge. Again, Mr. Colvins, you have the ability to call for an internal affairs investigation on Detective Hannigan, and also for Detective's Skates and Fitz to determine if they had knowledge and were complicit in the false information Detective Hannigan placed in the two search warrants," Judge Parker said.

Defense attorney Mark Scalia looked over his shoulder and watched reporter Danielle Lily feverishly writing down notes.

"Your Honor, may we set up a trial readiness hearing two weeks from today?" Mark Scalia asked Judge Parker.

Prosecutor Colvins stood up and told the judge his schedule would also make him available for the trial readiness hearing.

The Judge addressed Prosecutor Colvin and the Defense Attorneys, "This should give you enough time to see if some type of resolution can be made before the trial."

He turned and got up from the bench as the courtroom occupants stood up to show respect for the judge's position.

The defense team walked out of the courtroom, followed by Prosecutor Walter Colvins. He walked up to Mark Scalia, Jackie Skelton and Colin Thurgood that were, standing at the end of the hallway.

"Look," he said, "can we have a meeting at the end of the week and see if we can make a resolution and perhaps a lesser charge on your client Dustin Silver?"

"Yes, I think we could agree to a dismissal of all charges on our client," Jackie Skelton said, looking coyly at Prosecutor Colvins.

"Well, I don't know if we can go that far, but let's meet next Thursday if that works," he said.

"That will be fine," Mark told the Prosecutor, "but let's meet at our office, we have some additional evidence to show you and perhaps we can make a deal right there."

They parted and the prosecutor walked down the hallway and left the Courthouse ahead of the defense team.

As they were leaving the Courthouse and walking down the steps, the reporter Danielle Lily was standing at the bottom, awaiting the team to step down.

"Excuse me," she said, "are you satisfied with Judge Parker's decision to find both search warrants invalid and the introduction of the handcuffs also not allowed in the trial?"

"You heard what the Judge said in court," Jackie Skelton replied.

"I heard what the Judge said about Detective Hannigan and Officer Matt Winslow," she said.

"Does that mean they can be arrested for lying in their reports?" she asked.

"You are asking the wrong person," Jackie responded, "you need to ask Prosecutor Walter Colvins his intentions."

"What about all the other cases the officers have been and will be involved in, I mean, if they have been untruthful, will they throw out those other cases?" the reporter continued.

"Again, you will need to talk to the Prosecutor," Jackie said.

"Well, thanks for the time," Danielle Lily said, "This is front page news."

"Man, I would not want to be the Prosecutor because the prosecution case is going to go into the tank and that young reporter will make sure the whole county reads about it," Jackie commented.

"Colin, would you get in touch with Anson and Monty and we will start making a list of all evidence that clears Dustin and all the evidence that discloses Ryan and Juan as the true killers of John Adams. We will prepare the information in bullet form and give a presentation with copies of documents to the Prosecutor when we meet next Tuesday. I expect this week will be stressful for Prosecutor Colvins. he will probably meet with John Adams' family and explain the situation. The Prosecutor cannot place Dustin in the area of Wheatland or present any text messages they had recovered from the search warrants. They can't even put Dustin any closer than Pendleton Oregon."

Jackie's cell phone buzzed and as she responded she heard Anson's excited voice on the other end.

"Wait a minute," Jackie answered, "we're walking back to the car and I will put my phone on speaker phone. OK, what has got you so excited?"

"I've got Monty here with me on my speaker phone," Anson started.

"We were looking at anything related to firearms that were placed on property as evidence. We looked at evidence placed on property on the date of the homicide and didn't see anything unusual about items placed there as evidence. Then, we looked at an additional unrelated investigation report and property number prepared by Detective Massee who had been one of the investigators there on December 28th. Detective Massee's report states that when John Adams was still lying in the kitchen, he searched the light jacket Adams was wearing. He found three semi auto 45 caliber cartridges and six spent 45 caliber shell casings," Anson continued.

"Massee put the items in a small plastic bag and put them in his own coat pocket. He forgot they were in his coat because they weren't actually placed in the property room as evidence until a couple of weeks later and under a different evidence property number from the rest of the evidence. Monty and I noticed the spent shell casings were never sent to the WSP Crime Lab for a comparison with the 45 caliber shell casing found in John Adams' front yard. If the spent shell casings found in John's jacket pocket do match the shell casing and firing pin marks of the shell casing found in the front yard, then that should absolutely prove that the 45 caliber gun used in the homicide came from John's pick-up truck. It will help prove that Ryan Bates and Juan Garcia were truthful, when they told witnesses they stole the gun from John Adams' pick-up truck the morning Adams was killed," Anson finished.

"I don't know how you guys keep finding such helpful evidence but I love it," Jackie said, and Mark and Colin voiced their agreement in the background.

"We will be contacting Prosecutor Colvins and will voice our concerns about the lackluster investigation Detective Hannigan and his team have accomplished. Mark is going going to make a call right now so we can alert Prosecutor Colvins. I will phone you guys tomorrow and let you know what the Prosecutor says," she said and ended the call.

Mark Scalia made the phone call to the Prosecutors Office and the receptionist transferred the call into Walter Colvins' Office.

"What can I do for you?" Walter Colvins said when he picked up his phone.

"I wanted to give you a heads up on another situation where evidence collected was not placed in the evidence property facility for over two weeks after it was collected and removed from John Adams' coat pocket."

Mark Scalia had Prosecutor Colvins full attention as he waited to hear the details of another fuck-up that had occurred in the investigation.

"Detective Massee had been on the scene of the homicide and had assisted in the interior crime scene investigation of the residence, and he had located 45 caliber cartridges and spent shell casings in John Adams' jacket pocket that he was wearing when he was killed. Detective Massee did not submit an investigative report or place the cartridges and spent shell casings in the evidence property room until two weeks after the event. He used a different property evidence tracking number other than the evidence property tracking number assigned to the case. None of the criminal investigators noticed or prepared a request for the Washington State Patrol Firearm Forensic Unit to compare those shell casings to the spent 45 caliber shell casing found in John's front yard, to see if they are a match. If the shell casings are a match, it will pretty much prove the 45 caliber firearm came from John's pick-up truck," Mark finished.

Prosecutor Colvins agreed to send the shell casings immediately to the WSP Forensic Crime Lab in Cheney, Washington and would send an officer first thing the next morning.

"You know that if there is a match, your case is going to fall apart, don't you?" Mark Scalia asked Prosecutor Colvins.

"I just want to get to the truth in this case so there can be some closure for the victim's family," Prosecutor Colvins replied and ended the conversation.

Next, Prosecutor Colvins picked up the phone and dialed Wheatland Police Chief Will Fife.

Chief Fife answered his phone and agreed to meet next door in Walter Colvins' office.

"What's going on?" Chief Fife asked as he walked into Walter Colvins' office.

"My case is going to hell in a hand basket," Prosecutor Colvins answered dejectedly.

"The case is getting stronger for the defense and weaker for the prosecution. Detective Massee was one of the investigators at the crime scene and he located some 45 caliber cartridges and spent 45 caliber shell casings in John Adams' jacket pocket that he was wearing when he was shot. He never wrote a report until a couple of weeks later and had not placed the ammo and shell casings in the evidence property room until he wrote the report. Now it looks like our criminal investigators totally overlooked the items Massee placed on property and the defense team found the report. The defense team is raising hell because of our fuck up, and it really is our fuck up," he said to Chief Fife.

"We need to fix this as soon as possible, so will you have one of your officers obtain the shell casings from property evidence and prepare a WSP lab request for a comparison to the spent shell casing found in John Adams' front yard?" he asked Chief Fife.

"I don't want Detective Massee or Detective Hannigan doing this assignment. If we can get a rush on the project with the WSP lab it will be appreciated, and I want the results sent directly to me," he directed Chief Fife.

"I have determined the four shell casings found at the shooting along I-90 and Quincy turnoff match the shell casing found in John Adams' yard. There were two 45 shell casings found in a red Honda that was pulled out of Remington Canal and the dead body inside was, killed by gunshot. We know both of those shell casings from the red Honda also match the shell casing found in John Adams' yard," he continued.

"If the shell casings found in John Adams' coat pocket by Detective Massee match the spent shell casing found in Adams' front yard, I would say we have the wrong man in jail," he finished.

"OK, I will have a Wheatland Officer transport the evidence early tomorrow morning so the officer will be at the WSP lab front door when they open at 8:00 A.M.," Chief Fife answered.

Chapter 48

Two days later at 10:00 A.M. Prosecutor Walter Colvins received a phone call from a forensic scientist named Jeffery S. Stevens at the Washington State Patrol Firearms Forensic Unit located in Cheney, Wa.

"I'm contacting you because there had been a rush order placed on the spent 45 caliber shell casings delivered by the Wheatland Police Officer, regarding the connection to the John Adams case," he said.

"Yes, I have been waiting to hear the results," Prosecutor Walter Colvins responded.

"I can tell you that the extractor markings and the firing pin impressions on the base of the shell casings found in the victim's jacket pocket all originate from one firearm. That includes all of the 45 semi auto shell casings recovered along I-90 in that shooting, the shell casings found in the red Honda, and the shell casing found in John Adams' front yard," Jeffery Stevens confirmed.

"Thank you, and please send the written results as soon as possible," Walter Colvins requested.

"I'll send you a forensic lab report of the results in the mail and also e-mail the results this morning," he finished.

Walter Colvins wondered how he would weather the front page

news articles that were going to break in this case, as he reached for a bottle of antacid tablets.

The Prosecutor closed the door to his office and dialed up defense attorney Jackie Skelton on his phone.

"Hello, this is Jackie Skelton," she said as she picked up the phone.

"Hello, Ms. Skelton, I would like to talk to you about the shell casings that Officer Massee had placed in evidence property using a different evidence property tracking number," Prosecutor Colvins said.

"Hold on, please, I am putting you on speaker phone so my team can listen and join in on our conversation," Jackie Skelton said to Prosecutor Colvins.

Prosecutor Colvins revealed that the spent shell casings recovered by Officer Massee had been sent to the WSP Crime Lab for comparison to the other 45 cal. shell casings.

"I just got a preliminary response from the WSP forensic lab and they have confirmed all of the spent shell casings have the same forensic markings as each other," he said.

"I am waiting for written confirmation from the crime lab," he finished.

Mark said, "I guess we should talk about dismissing all charges on our client, wouldn't you agree?"

"They are all connected, so that means the gun came from John Adams' pick-up truck, is that right?" Colin Thurgood asked.

"I suppose so," Walter Colvins replied.

"I know your client couldn't have possibly been involved in the murder in Othello at the trap house or the gunfight along Interstate 90," he admitted.

"Let me review the case and I will check with you next Monday," he said and then hung up the phone.

Jackie broke the good news to Anson and Monty and they talked on speaker phone mode.

"Wow, that is really great news," Anson said.

"Should we just back off continuing the investigation?" Monty asked.

Jackie answered, "Oh hell no, any extra evidence that will clear

Dustin we will still need as backup. We haven't worked with Prosecutor Walter Colvins in the past so we can't trust him 100%."

"We plan on traveling to The Dalles and searching the interior of Dustin's pick-up for any receipts or other documents that will add to Dustin's alibi just in case," Monty said.

"We know that Dustin spent the night at that truck stop on Pendleton, Oregon where he fueled up and had breakfast before heading further south in Oregon picking up classic era auto parts," Anson added.

"Dustin had a regular route he would follow so there is a good chance that people would know or remember Dustin," he continued.

"OK, good luck on your trip and keep us informed," Jackie said and ended the phone call.

Chapter 49

"Let's pack up and head over to The Dalles," Monty said. "It's about a 3 hour drive and we might be able to look at Dustin's pick-up late this afternoon."

The three hour drive to The Dalles was without incident and Monty Victor placed a phone call to Samantha Fox.

She was at home and advised Dustin's pick-up truck was still parked in the apartment parking lot.

Samantha met them at Dustin's pick-up and handed them the key to the pick-up.

The truck was opened and Monty and Adams literally looked in every nook and cranny in the pick-up truck without finding anything useful.

"We didn't find any potential defense evidence, or anything useful inside the pick-up cab," Anson said.

"Oh, that's because I removed Dustin's travel bag inside the pick-up so vehicle prowlers would not see it and break into the truck," Samantha explained.

"I grabbed the bag and some paperwork lying on the front seat," she finished.

"Can we see it?" Anson asked Samantha.

"Sure, let's go up to my apartment and we'll look things over," she replied.

They followed Samantha into the apartment and sat at her kitchen table.

A small travel bag was placed on the table where Monty and Anson sifted through the contents without finding anything of value.

"You mentioned some paperwork that was in the truck and you had brought it here?" asked Anson.

"Oh, yes," she said and reached over to a brown manila envelope lying on the kitchen countertop.

"This is the paperwork I found on the floor of Dustin's pick-up," she said and handed the envelope to Monty.

"We need to find a gas slip or meal receipt for Pendleton, Oregon," Anson said to Samantha.

The documents were examined and no helpful information was found.

"Thank you, Samantha, we will be in touch," Monty said, as they left her apartment.

"I think we better travel to the truck stop in Pendleton, Oregon and spend the night, and see if anyone remembers seeing Dustin on the morning of December 28th," Monty said.

"I agree," said Anson, "we will check with the employees at the truck stop and the cafe in the morning because they were likely working when Dustin was there to fuel up and have breakfast."

Early the next morning they left the Red Top Motel in Pendleton where they had spent the night and drove to the truck stop where Dustin said he had fueled up on the morning of December 28th.

"Let's park in the Sunrise Cafe parking lot and we can walk over to the gas station before having breakfast," Monty said.

The gas station cashier was sitting behind a counter with various cigarette lighter displays, small flashlights displays and other memorabilia on display so last minute purchases could be made by customers getting ready to pay.

They both approached the cashier and identified themselves and explained the purpose of the contact.

Anson showed the cashier a photo of Dustin and asked the cashier if he recalled Dustin as a customer.

"Yeah, I remember this guy, he comes through here about every couple of months and fuels up. I think he told me he is in the market for classic car parts and he makes a drive through Eastern Oregon and southern Idaho and buys used auto parts, mainly from Mopar powered vehicles," the cashier said.

"Do you recall if Dustin came through here on December 28th in the morning?" asked Monty.

"I remember Dustin coming through about that date but can't recall the exact date," the cashier told them.

"Do you have security cameras here?" asked Monty.

"Why the hell didn't I think of that?" replied the cashier.

"We do keep the video on file for at least a year," the cashier disclosed.

"My employee gets here in a few minutes and if you care to wait we can check the video for the past December 28th," she said.

"That's great!" said Anson. "We will go next door for breakfast and come back after a while."

"I know this Dustin fellow would eat over at the Sunrise Cafe after he would fuel up," the cashier said.

"Thanks, we'll ask at the Sunrise Cafe," Anson said as they walked out.

Chapter 50

They entered through the front door of the Sunrise Cafe and stood by the counter until a busy waitress saw them.

The attractive waitress was in her middle forties and very friendly.

Her name tag with the name "Rita" was pinned to her clean, crisp uniform left shirt pocket.

She sat them down at a booth and handed them menus, then told them she would be right back with water and coffee.

Rita came back with two glasses of water and two steaming cups of strong dark coffee.

"What can I get you, gentlemen?" she said as she got out her order pad.

They placed their order and after a few minutes Rita returned with their breakfasts served on large platters.

Rita stood and chatted with them, which gave them the opportunity to identify themselves.

"Do you remember if a customer named Dustin Silver was here last December 28th in the morning and had breakfast?" Monty asked.

"Oh, sure, I know Dustin, he is a handsome man and quite the flirt," she said with a smile.

Anson pulled out the photo of Dustin and handed it to Rita.

She looked at the photo and immediately identified Dustin.

"I think he was here on that date," she said, "but wait a minute."

"The last time he was here he wrote his phone number on the back of his customer receipt, because he wanted to take me out," she said with a grin.

"I have another customer that just walked in, but I will check for the receipt in a couple of minutes," she told them.

They had another refill of coffee and patiently waited for Rita to return.

A couple of minutes later Rita returned with a narrow slip of receipt paper.

"Here it is, Dustin wrote his phone number on the Sunrise Cafe customer receipt and gave it to me."

Rita handed the piece of paper to Anson and he checked the date and time of the receipt.

Monty was watching Anson's face as he saw it suddenly light up.

Anson smiled and handed the receipt to Monty.

"Jackpot," said Monty, "this receipt is for December 28th at 6:45 A.M. at the Sunrise Cafe."

"We have Dustin's alibi," he said happily.

"Rita, this document is very important, can we have it?"

"Of course you can, if it will help Dustin, he is a nice guy," she said with a wink.

They paid their bill for the food and left a generous tip for Rita.

After leaving the restaurant they checked back with the gas station cashier.

"I have it right here," the cashier said and handed Monty a thumb drive.

"Dustin Silver was on our video where he was standing fueling up his pick-up truck at the number # 6 pump," said the cashier.

"Does it show a date and time stamp?" asked Anson.

"It shows a 6:00 A.M. time stamp on December 28th," the cashier stated.

"The defense team is going to be so happy with this news," said Anson.

"Damn straight," said Monty, "this means Dustin never had the opportunity to kill John Adams because he wasn't even in the state."

Anson dialed up Mark Scalia's phone number which was answered almost immediately.

Anson had placed his phone on speaker mode so Monty could hear the conversation.

"Mark, please put the speaker phone on so the others can hear us," Anson said.

In a few seconds Jackie and Colin said hello in the background of Mark's phone.

"The cashier at the truck stop recalled that Dustin was a pretty regular customer but couldn't recall what day it was in December that Dustin had stopped other than it was early morning," Monty said.

"We went next door to the Sunrise Cafe for breakfast and talked with a waitress named Rita," he continued.

"Dustin apparently was quite the flirt with her and she recalled he would stop by for breakfast at the Sunrise Cafe every couple of months. Rita recalled that sometime in December Dustin had breakfast there. She said Dustin wrote his phone number on the customer copy of his receipt and he gave it to her, hoping for a date with her. Rita still had the receipt and she gave it to us," said Anson.

"The receipt was dated December 28th at 6:45 A.M.," shouted Monty.

"We also have the video of Dustin fueling up his pick-up at the gas station at Pendleton, Oregon," said Anson.

"What time did Dustin fuel his pick truck up?" asked Jackie.

"Dustin fueled up at 6:00 A.M. on December 28th," Monty answered.

"Wahoo!" shouted Jackie Skelton over the phone. "Dustin would not have had the opportunity to kill John Adams since the murder occurred at 6:30 A.M. clear over in Wheatland, which is 250 miles away."

"This case would have been over if that lackwit, Detective Hannigan and his crew had bothered to do a follow-up and check Dustin's alibi here in Pendleton," Monty said.

"We're on our way back to Wheatland," Anson told the defense attorneys.

Mark said, "Let's meet tomorrow and go over our evidence and Jackie, Colin Thurgood and myself will start preparing a motion to dismiss all charges on Dustin."

Chapter 51

The next morning, Mark started the meeting at Jackie and Mark's suite where there had been a long table placed as a location for files, printers and laptop computers.

"Let's assemble a list of all the information we have received that proves Dustin's innocence and provide the police investigators with the evidence to prosecute Ryan Bates and Juan Garcia," said Jackie.

Colin got up from behind his laptop and stood at the front of the room with a large whiteboard on a tripod. "Let's just go down the list and I will write the points on the whiteboard," he said.

1. Dustin can prove he was in Pendleton, Oregon at the gas station at 6:00 A.M. on December 28th because was identified on the gas station video, and the meal receipt for 6:45 A.M. from the Sunrise Café.

2. Prosecutor Walter Colvins had confirmed Wheatland Police Officer Massee found empty 45 caliber shell casings in John Adams' jacket that he was wearing when he was killed. The spent shell casings match the 45 caliber shell casing found in John Adams' yard, the shell casings found along I-90 at the scene of a homicide and 45 shell casings found inside the submerged red Honda with Bronza Miller's body located inside.

Dustin was in jail when the freeway shooting, at the norteno trap house robbery and murder occurred and when the submerged red Honda with the body inside was found.

3. Our witness Tim Bolt would testify that he observed Ryan Bates sell a 45 caliber semi-auto handgun with a laser sight to a man named Rufus in Spokane Felony Flats area for $300.

Bolt overheard Ryan tell Rufus the gun came from Ephrata.

4. Detective Hannigan misrepresented the truth in two search warrant affidavits seeking phone records and ping locations of Dustin's phone.

Judge Parker threw both warrants out.

5. The WSP Crime Lab scientist has said under oath that based on the DNA found on a pair of handcuffs, they could not identify Dustin Silvers' DNA from the sample collected.

6. Lynn Bennet would testify the handcuffs found at the crime scene were her property that had been stolen in a burglary of her residence the summer prior to the John Adams' homicide.

Lynn Bennet had also listed Ryan Bates as the suspect in that burglary.

7. Steve Paulson would testify that on the morning of the John Adams murder he saw two male subjects run out of the alley behind John Adams' house.

He would describe them as one tall and the other shorter than average height.

Steve Paulson would testify further that when he was an inmate in the Canyon County Jail he talked to Ryan Bates and Bates admitted he had been in a guy's pick-up truck and smoked the dude when he came outside.

That Ryan Bates admitted to Steve Paulson that he killed the guy with the gun, that he had stolen from the man's pick-up truck.

8. Trampus Byrne will testify that on the day of the John Adams murder Juan Garcia visited with him and Martin Nelson and Juan admitted that he had been with Ryan Bates when he got into Adams' truck and stole a 45 caliber semi auto pistol with a laser sight and used it to shoot John Adams when he stepped out of his house.

9. Sharon Byrne is the mother of Trampus Byrne and she will testify that at approximately 10:00 A.M. the day of the homicide Juan Garcia showed up at her house and went into her son Trampus' bedroom. She would testify that she heard Juan Garcia say that he was out prowling cars earlier that morning with Ryan Bates and Ryan had shot and killed a guy with a gun he had stolen from the guy's truck.

10. Martin Nelson would testify that he was in Trampus Byrnes' bedroom playing video games on the morning of the John Adams homicide when Juan Garcia showed up. That Juan was shaky and nervous and said he was with Ryan Bates when Ryan Bates shot and killed John Adams.

11. Martin Nelson will testify further that on the day of the homicide that Ryan Bates was at his house sitting on the front porch and Ryan admitted he had entered John Adams' pick-up truck and stole a 45 caliber semi-auto handgun with a laser sight.

Ryan told him that he pointed the gun and shot and killed John Adams when he stepped out of his house and surprised Ryan Bates.

12. Jenna Edward is Ryan Bates's ex-girlfriend and she will testify that Ryan had assaulted her and choked her and told her he would kill her just like he killed John Adams.

That she drove Ryan up the Canyon Road to hide something at an old well house on the day of the murder.

13. Alex Johnson was a cellmate of Ryan Bates in the Canyon County Jail and he will testify that Ryan Bates told him that he had been in some guy's truck and had smoked the fool. He had told Alex the guy lived on the same street as his mother and it was in December of that year.

14. Susan Mattern is the girlfriend of Juan Garcia's brother and frequently sleeps at his mother's apartment on the couch.

She will testify that she saw Juan sneak out of the house about 11:00 P.M. the evening before the homicide and she saw him sneak back into his mother's house about 7:30 A.M. the next morning.

15. Tiffanie Weeks would testify on the evening of December 27th Ryan was staying with her at her house and left the residence at about 10:30 P.M. and did not return until 6:45 A.M. on the date of the John

Adams homicide. She will testify further that Ryan was frantically scrubbing his hands, and took off his clothes and showered. That Ryan changed his clothes and then left her residence.

16. Bonnie Crawfoot will testify that on the morning of the homicide she looked across the street after hearing a gunshot coming from the front yard of her neighbor John Adams front yard.

She will testify that she saw a tall male and a medium height male run away from the front yard as John Adams stumbled into his house.

Colin Thurgood stood back and looked at the list.

"This all looks good," Jackie said.

"Colin, would you mind preparing the motion to dismiss document with all of the items on the list on the whiteboard?" she asked.

"When the motion to dismiss is finished we will meet with Prosecutor Walter Colvins and lay everything out for him. Then we will file the document in the Canyon County Clerk's Office and send a copy to the judge. Monty and Anson, if you would continue doing follow-up investigations for additional information, that would be great. OK, team, let's get the ball rolling!" she finished.

Two days later the motion to dismiss document was finished and delivered to Prosecutor Walter Colvins' office with a copy to Judge Parker and the third copy was filed in the Canyon County Clerk's Office.

The next day was a Friday and Walter Colvins contacted Jackie, asking for a meeting in regard to the motion to dismiss.

He wished to have the conversation outside of the courtroom.

"Let's meet Monday morning in my conference room, if that will work for you," he addressed Jackie.

"That's fine, our defense team will see you there," she replied.

"If you don't mind, I would like Wheatland Police Chief Will Fife and the Sheriff at the meeting," he said.

"That's fine," Jackie answered.

"Remember, that when we eventually have a hearing in front of Judge Parker, the news media will be very interested," Jackie told him.

"I'm hoping we can come to a resolution and not have to go that route," Walter Colvins said.

Hmm, thought Jackie, *I wonder what offer Prosecutor Walter Colvins is going to present for a resolution.*

Chapter 52

Carlos Guzman was released from Kadlec Hospital in Quincy, Washington after surgery on his shoulder after spending four days recovering.

Two Deputy U.S. Marshals had arrived at the hospital with a transport van.

He was immediately arrested on a federal charge of trafficking in controlled substance and transported and booked into Canyon County Jail.

"Why am I facing a federal charge?" he had asked the arresting Deputy U.S. Marshal.

"A search warrant was served at your house in Othello and meth packages wrapped with Sinaloa Cartel stamp markings were found. It's obvious the meth was transported across state lines in order for you to be in possession. You're also under investigation for the murder of a man named Bronza Miller. You will receive all the documents from your legal counsel when we get you booked into the Canyon County Jail. In a few days, you will go in front of a Judge to arraign you on the murder charge. Your co-conspirator Alphonso Ruiz is also in the Canyon County Jail on the same charges and will also face a Judge and make a plea. He will also be charged with the murder of Bronza Miller," said the Deputy Marshall.

The drive to Canyon County Jail was made without incident.

Carlos was a confirmed norteno gang member and was housed in Unit B at the jail.

Alphonso had been housed in the jail infirmary section but had recently also been moved to Unit B in the jail.

This was an oversight made by the jail staff that assigned the newly arrived inmates into the facility because co-defendants are normally not housed in the same cell block.

Carlos was placed in a separate cell than Alphonso but they still were allowed out of their cells at the same time for recreation, to make phone calls, or use the weight training room at Unit B.

After several days Alphonso stood with Carlos in the weight room.

Carlos was doing weight training for his legs and Alphonso was doing an upper body workout.

Alphonso came over by Carlos and quietly said, "Do you know who is in this jail with us?"

"No, I haven't really talked to any of our norteno brothers that are here," Carlos replied.

"The soreno dudes that ripped us off and killed your brother Michael at our house in Othello are both sitting here in jail," said Alphonso.

"The one dude is Juan Garcia and he is locked in the Protective Custody Section here. This means he is a confidential informant or he has ratted on his partner. There's little chance that we can get close enough to kill him as long as he is in that protective section of the jail," he continued.

"The other dude is Ryan Bates and he is housed in Unit D which is the location where inmates with more serious or violent crimes are housed. Inmates already convicted and awaiting transport to prison are also housed in the same Unit," Alphonso said.

"Do we have any norteno brothers that are in Unit D?" Carlos asked.

"I've been checking and a brother norteno is Alex Johnson in Unit D," Alphonso said.

"He was convicted of two violent murders at a small bank in Wilson Creek, Washington. He has two consecutive life sentences so he will die in prison," he continued.

"We have to get word to Alex before he leaves on the Chain (The Washington State Prison Inmate Transport System). Let's get a message to him and see if he will kill Ryan Bates since Alex cannot receive a longer sentence than he already has been sentenced," Carlos told Alphonso.

"We need to send a warning to the soreno gang members that we will strike back when we kill soreno gang member Ryan Bates," said Carlos.

"We can use one of the norteno gang inmates that work as trustees and do maintenance in the jail. They move through the different units, mopping the floors, emptying garbage and scrubbing the cells to disinfect therm," Alphonso said.

"Alex Johnson can be contacted by a norteno jail trusty," Alphonso said.

"I'll see what I can do," Alphonso told Carlos.

That afternoon Alphonso was in the main exercise room at unit B when the trusty inmate crew came through to do their job.

Trusty Greg Smith had leaned against the wall of the room, waiting to scrub the floor of a vacant cell in unit B.

Greg was a confirmed norteno gang member.

Alphonso leaned down as if adjusting the plaster cast on his right leg.

"I need a hit on a soreno named Ryan Bates, he is in unit D, and he killed a brother norteno."

Alphonso passed a small piece of paper to Greg Smith.

"Give this to Alex Johnson up in unit B," he said.

"No problem, I will get the note to him," Greg answered and looked around to see if he had been spotted by the corrections guard.

Alex Johnson was lying on his thin mattress in his cell when he heard a light tap on his door and a slip of paper was slid under the door.

He picked it up from the floor and unrolled the piece of paper and slowly read the contents.

Hey, brother norteno, there is a soreno gang member named Ryan Bates in the same unit as you. He was responsible for killing my brother in Othello and he ripped off the Sinaloa Cartel and myself. Bates' life needs to end as a lesson to other soreno gang members. When Jail Trusty Greg Smith comes by, just tell him yes or no. If you say yes, a shiv will be passed under your door to use on Ryan Bates. Stab Bates in the neck because I want him to slowly bleed out knowing no one can save him.

What do I have to lose? Alex thought. *It will make me a celebrity and well respected with the norteno inmates at Walla Walla prison since I will be killing a soreno.*

The next day Alex was in the exercise area of unit D when Greg Smith came by to perform his mopping duties.

"Yes, I will do it," he said to Greg Smith.

"Watch for something under your door tomorrow," Greg Smith told him in a low voice.

Chapter 53

The next morning Alex was doing a sit-up next to his cot when he heard a light tap on his metal cell door.

Then he saw an elongated object pass under his door.

Alex reached over and picked up a makeshift knife commonly called a shiv.

He closely examined the instrument which was made from a toothbrush.

The toothbrush had been shaped to a very sharp point, and the bristle end had rags tightly wrapped around for a makeshift handle.

Not much of a cutting knife but a hell of a stabbing tool, Alex thought to himself. *This will do what I want it to do.*

This afternoon Ryan will be out in the main recreation room with me and the other inmates, he thought as he planned his attack.

At 2:00 P.M., the individual cell doors in unit D were electronically unlocked.

Alex sat up in his bunk and then stepped out and looked around to check on the location of the other inmates.

He spotted Ryan Bates standing near some of the exercise equipment with other inmates waiting to use the weight bench.

Directly behind the weight bench, about 8 feet away, was a wooden bench that was used by inmates to sit and do isolated arm curls.

Alex stood back and watched until Ryan Bates was taking his turn doing arm curls while sitting on the bench.

Alex had moved the shiv from his waistband and was holding it concealed along his arm.

Ryan was concentrating on his arm curls looking down when Alex stepped in front of him and grabbed him by the hair and pulled his head upward facing him. At the same time he plunged the shiv clear to the hilt into Ryan's throat. He rapidly stabbed Ryan another five or six times before leaving the shiv imbedded deeply in Ryan's neck.

Alex stepped back and watched as Ryan grasped the shiv and pulled it from his neck.

Ryan looked into Alex's eyes with a look of confusion as his life blood spurted out.

His strong heart was pumping out blood in spurts as the corrections officers rushed through the inmates, but their frantic attempts were not able to save him.

Alex felt wildly excited as he watched Ryan's eyes become frozen in a wide eyed terror expression when he died.

He walked back to his cell and began washing the blood from his right hand until his hand was sterile of any blood remaining from the attack.

Alex stepped out of his cell and stood by other inmates watching the corrections officers.

He noticed bloody inmate sandal prints scattered throughout the floor of the recreation room.

The corrections officers directed the inmates to return to their cells for lockdown since they would need a clear area to conduct the investigation.

Chapter 54

Prosecutor Walter Colvins was sitting in his office, lost in thought on how he was going to resolve the John Adams case.

If he took the case to trial he had about a 100% chance of losing the case because the defense attorneys would prove Dustin Silver's innocence.

I still have to deal with the John Adams' family who want their pound of flesh from Dustin Silver, he thought.

The ringing of his phone startled him and as he answered the voice of Jail Captain Gary Brady came on the phone.

"Sorry to disturb you this late in the afternoon but the Sheriff has asked me to contact you and have you meet him at the County Jail," Captain Brady said.

"What is it about?" Walter Colvins asked.

"You know that guy named Ryan Bates who was charged with the homicide of the norteno gang member over in Othello?" he asked.

"He was murdered this afternoon," Captain Brady continued.

"The Sheriff thought you should know since this guy named Ryan Bates was also a person of interest in the John Adams murder."

"I'll be right over at the jail," Walter Colvins said and hung up.

He put on a light jacket and arrived at the jail a couple of minutes later.

He was met by Jail Captain Gary Brady and Sheriff Harris.

"Tell me what happened," he asked Captain Brady.

"We have our investigators on scene and Detective Hannigan thinks it is a gang related homicide," said Captain Brady.

"Jesus Christ!" Walter Colvins exploded.

"Get that Detective Hannigan off the case, I am considering making him a Brady Cop from his actions in the John Adams case," he continued.

"Why haven't I heard of this?" The Sheriff asked as he looked directly at Walter Colvins.

"It is part of the John Adams case and I just didn't have time yet to request an internal investigation done on Detective Hannigan. Let's meet after we leave here, but please get Hannigan off that investigation and replace him," Walter Colvins said to the Sheriff.

"Was the victim a gang member?" asked Walter Colvins.

"Yes, I believe he was a soreno gang member," the Captain said.

"When Ryan Bates was classified booked at the jail, did they ask if he was a gang member?" Walter Colvins asked.

"I don't know," Captain Brady answered.

"Are there norteno gang members in the unit D?"

"Yes, there are a significant amount of norteno gang members since they are the majority of gang members in Canyon County," said Captain Brady.

"What a cluster, if Ryan Bates was a soreno gang member, which we believe he was, and he was placed in a nest of norteno gang members, we are going to pay millions to Ryan Bates' family for failing to protect him," Walter Colvins said.

"We haven't located the killer because other inmates stepped in the blood or touched Bates, so his blood is literally transferred all over the unit."

"Nobody is talking," he finished.

"Let's go over to my office and talk," Walter Colvins said to the Sheriff and Captain Brady.

When they arrived Colvins closed the office door and laid out the reasons Detective Hannigan was on the path to be labeled a Brady Cop and Hannigan could very well lose his certification as a law enforcement officer.

"Jesus," said the Sheriff, "do you want me to start an internal affairs investigation and put him on paid leave until this gets ironed out?"

"I think that would be the prudent thing to do, but hold off because I am trying to get a resolution on the John Adams murder case that Hannigan helped investigate," Walter Colvins said.

Colvins' desk phone rang and he answered.

"This is Lieutenant Steve Johan, Mr. Colvins, is the Jail Captain there?"

Walter Colvins handed the phone to Captain Brady.

Lt. Johan told the Captain that the local news media and TV station had reporters waiting at his office to speak with him.

"I won't even ask who it was that leaked the information to the media," he said in disgust.

"Alright, I will be right over and have the Sheriff's Public Information Officer meet me in my office before the media is allowed in. It was probably an inmate calling his family outside the jail that tipped off the press."

"Well, gentlemen, let me know what you find out and who I will need to prosecute," Walter Colvins said.

He held his head in his hands and thought how badly this day would go. *What is the defense team going to do when they find out the real killer of John Adams was murdered while in the custody of the Canyon County Sheriff's Office? I'll give them a call before they read it in the newspaper tomorrow or see the event on the television news.*

He dialed Jackie Skelton's number and let it ring 4 or 5 times before Jackie picked up the line.

"Hi, this is Walter Colvins calling, I need to give you some information," he said in a serious tone.

"It must be pretty good if you are calling me after office hours," Jackie said.

"Your alternate murder suspect, Ryan Bates, was murdered in the Canyon County Jail this afternoon," he said and waited for the response from Jackie Skelton.

"Wait a minute, I am going to turn on my speaker phone so Mark Scalia and Colin Thurgood can participate in this conversation," she said.

"Are you telling me Ryan Bates was murdered this afternoon while under the protective custody at the County Jail?" she asked.

"I guess that's one way of saying it," Colvins bleakly answered.

"What happened?" Colin Thurgood asked.

"All I know is Bates was stabbed in the neck with a shiv numerous times and he bled to death," Walter Colvins told them.

"It's still an active investigation. You will see the news in tomorrow's newspaper and on the local late news TV channel tonight," he continued.

"OK, we will need to meet next Monday and discuss a motion to drop all criminal charges on Dustin Silver before we meet with Judge Charles Parker next Friday," Jackie Skelton told the Prosecutor and the call ended.

"Wow," said Jackie, "I've never worked a case with so many ups and downs before, and our defense case just keeps getting better and better. Colin, would you give Anson and Monty a call and we can meet tomorrow?"

"Let's go by the jail and give Dustin an update on this case," Mark Scalia said to Jackie Skelton and and Colin Thurgood.

"I can't wait to see the look on Dustin's face when we give him an update with the great news," Mark said.

They arrived at the jail just as the meal time for the inmates was winding down.

"We are here for a legal visit with our client," Jackie said into the intercom located on the wall beside the exterior door of the jail.

They held up their photo identification in front of the security camera next to the intercom.

There was a distinctive click and Mark pushed the door open, and they walked down the narrow hallway to the attorney visiting rooms.

Within minutes Dustin was brought into the small room wearing handcuffs attached to his belly chain and he sat down across the metal table from Mark, Jackie and Colin.

After the corrections officer had left the room, Dustin looked over at the team with an excited look on his face.

"Hey, we had a guy get killed today in the cell pod next to mine," he said.

"You'll never guess who it was," Dustin continued.

"Was it Ryan Bates?" Jackie asked, knowing full well that it was Ryan Bates.

Dustin had a look of consternation on his face.

"We were notified by the Prosecutor Walter Colvins of the incident earlier this afternoon," Colin Thurgood disclosed.

"I think it was a gang related situation since Ryan Bates was a soreno gang member and there are a lot of norteno gangsters incarcerated in here," Dustin said.

"I heard it was a retaliation murder on a soreno gang member for the norteno murder at the trap house in Othello. The guy's brother is here in jail so I bet he put a hit out on Ryan Bates."

"What will that do for our case?" Dustin asked.

"We're still examining that case to see how important it is for your defense," Colin Thurgood answered.

"But we have other great news we just received from our investigators Anson and Monty," he continued.

"They travelled to Pendleton, Oregon at that truck gas station and the Sunrise Cafe next door. After Mark reviewed the police investigation reports we could find no police reports that Detective Hannigan or other investigators ever went to Pendleton to determine if you had even been there," Jackie said.

"Do you remember the waitress named Rita at the Sunrise Cafe next to the gas station in Pendleton?" asked Jackie.

"Oh, yes, lovely Rita," Dustin said, "I always stopped there and had a meal when I was driving through there."

"Did you ever give your phone number to Rita?" Jackie asked.

"Yes, I did the last time I was there," he replied.

"Do you remember what type of paper you used to write down your phone number and gave to Rita?"

Dustin had a blank look on his face.

"It was your customer receipt for the morning of December 28th at the Pendleton Sunrise Cafe," Jackie replied.

"That is your alibi for the John Adams murder in Wheatland since you would have been probably 3-4 hours away. I think the time stamp on that receipt was about 6:45 A.M. and Rita can vouch that you were there at the restaurant while she was at work at the time of the time stamp on the receipt," Jackie said.

"Monty and Anson also recovered security video from the truck stop next door to the restaurant. The video clearly shows you pumping gas in your pick-up at 6:00 A.M. on the morning of the 28th."

"You have an airtight alibi!" shouted Mark Scalia.

"We are meeting with the Prosecutor tomorrow morning and propose all charges on you to be dismissed," Jackie said.

"We will get this mess cleared up and get you out of jail as soon as possible," Jackie said to Dustin.

Chapter 55

At 9:00 A.M. sharp the defense team filed into Prosecutor Walter Colvins' conference room and were seated across the table from Prosecutor Colvins, Wheatland Police Chief William Fife and Sheriff Jay Harris.

Detectives Hannigan, Fitz and Skates sat in chairs along the wall behind them.

"I wanted to start out with the latest information our defense investigators Monty Victor and David Anson have uncovered, which we believe will put an end to this case," Jackie said.

Colin Thurgood handed out photocopies of the receipts from the gas station and Sunrise Cafe in Pendleton, Oregon.

"Our client Dustin Silver told Detectives Hannigan, Fitz and Skates that he had been in Pendleton, Oregon at the truck fueling station on the morning of the murder of John Adams," Jackie said.

"Your investigators assigned to this case failed to travel or enquire at the Pendleton, Oregon locations to determine if Dustin Silvers' alibi was true or not," she stated.

Hannigan glared defiantly at Jackie as she continued her accusatory tone.

"The photos I am handing you display that Dustin fueled up at the gas station in Pendleton at 6:00 A.M. that morning and then a short time later at 6:45 A.M. had breakfast at the Sunrise Cafe next door. I have also included a video our investigators recovered from the security camera at the gas station showing Dustin Silver fueling up his pick-up truck at 6:00 A.M. on the morning of December 28th. I believe any prosecution conducted is moot at this point," Jackie said.

"Detective Hannigan should be assigned to school crosswalk duty for the incompetent way he handled this case," she continued.

Detectives Fitz and Skates glanced at each other and Detective Hannigan stood up as his face turned beet red and he leaned towards Jackie.

"Look, you Bitch," he shouted, "you haven't proved a thing to me."

"Sit down and shut up!" the Sheriff said to Hannigan.

"Another outburst like that and not only will you be kicked out of this meeting, you will face disciplinary action," he said loudly to Detective Hannigan.

"Let's talk about Ryan Bates and Juan Garcia," Mark started out.

"Mr. Colvins, in this next packet we are providing information of witnesses we have located that prove to Ryan Bates and Juan Garcia are the actual killers of John Adams, and several eyewitnesses saw two suspects run from the area of John Adams Murder immediately after John Adams was killed. John's neighbor Bonnie Crawfoot has disclosed that she saw two other people in the front yard of John Adams' house when she heard the gunshot and looked up. She described one male as about 6'3" inches and the other as shorter and stocky. Steve Paulson, another neighbor, was walking back from the store down at Division street when he was crossing to walk back to his home. He saw two male subjects run out of the alley behind John Adams' house. He described one male subject, about 6'3" and the other was shorter. Mr. Paulson was later in the Canyon County Jail with Ryan Bates and Bates admitted his involvement in killing John Adams. Alex Johnson was also a jail cellmate with Ryan Bates and Bates admitted his involvement in the killing of John Adams. Jenna Edwards was on a date with Ryan Bates and after he became furious with her, he became violent and assaulted her and told her he would kill her like he did John Adams. Trampus Byrne and his mother Leslie and neighbor Martin Nelson all stated that on the morning of the murder Juan Garcia came to the Byrne residence and he admitted he was with Ryan Bates when Bates killed John Adams," he continued.

"Martin Nelson will state that about noon on the day of the murder, Ryan Bates came to his residence and Ryan Bates admitted to his involvement in the murder of John Adams. Susan Mattern is the girlfriend of Juan's brother and she stated that Juan had sneaked out of the apartment she was staying at around 10:30 P.M. the night before the murder and at about 7:30 A.M. in the morning of the murder she saw Juan Garcia enter the apartment through the living room slider door and cross the room and enter his bedroom. Detective Ralston Hannigan was not truthful in the probable cause affidavits he to prepared detailing our client's movements and location around the time of the murder. As you are all aware, Judge Charles Parker dismissed both of the tainted search warrants," added Jackie.

"Mr. Colvins, as you are aware, our client cannot be tracked from December 26th to December 29th thanks to the manipulated probable cause affidavit for the search warrant Detective Hannigan presented to the Judge which was dismissed as tainted," she continued.

Colin Thurgood added, "We are aware Ryan Bates was murdered in the jail apparently for revenge for the killing of Carlos Guzman's brother Michael during the robbery committed by Juan Garcia, Bronza Miller and Ryan Bates in Othello. The only suspect you have left is Juan Garcia and he has been talking about the various crimes he and Ryan Bates committed. Your big concern now is how to keep Juan Garcia alive and away from norteno gang members before he is taken to trial."

I guess our agreement we made with Juan Garcia is moot since Ryan Bates is dead and we don't need Juan to testify against him, thought Walter Colvins.

"You have information that Officer Winslow lied in segments of his investigation and manipulated the handcuffs found in the front yard. Another officer did not place 45 Caliber cartridges and spent shell casings which were key evidence into the Evidence Property Room until several weeks after the event and did not send the evidence to the Washington State Patrol crime lab for examination."

"I didn't lie in my affidavits for those search warrants," shouted Hannigan as he stood up and glared at Colin Thurgood.

"Detective Hannigan, sit back down," shouted the Sheriff.

"You idiot, the audio video interview of Marianne Shutt distinctly reveals that Dustin Silver did not threaten to injure John Adams," the Sheriff said back to Hannigan.

"It's time for you to leave this meeting," the Sheriff said to Hannigan and pointed towards the meeting room door.

"I am placing you on administrative leave, pending a full investigation of your conduct in this investigation," he finished.

Hannigan looked across the room at Anson and Monty and had a slight smile on his face but his eyes were as cold as ice.

He quietly got up and left the room.

The room was quiet until Walter Colvins cleared his throat and began talking, "I'm convinced your client Dustin Silver has been wrongfully accused and I will go in front of the judge this coming Friday and dismiss all charges against Dustin Silver. I have always been interested in the truth. I apologize and tip my hat to your investigators David Anson and Monty Victor, and they have uncovered the correct evidence that has revealed the real killers of John Adams. The Sheriff is going to create a new task force to gather additional evidence on Ryan Bates and Juan Garcia to show they were the killers of John Adams. Of course, since Ryan Bates is dead, Juan has already made admissions so it should be pretty easy to convict him. I can switch your defense witnesses over to prosecution witnesses against Juan Garcia. I believe he will agree to a plea bargain and this mess will be cleaned up."

He finished the meeting by saying, "I think we are done here."

They all filed out of the office.

Chapter 56

Walter Colvins sat in his office for several minutes and then made a call to Judge Charles Parker.

The phone was answered by the judge's bailiff and she advised the judge would be off the bench in about five minutes, and he had no proceedings until earlier in the afternoon.

The Prosecutor asked the judge's assistant to leave the Judge a message that he would be stopping by in about 15 minutes.

Walter Colvins put on his light jacket and walked over to the courthouse and climbed the stairs to the second floor where the Judge's chamber was located.

"Sit down, Walter," said Judge Parker as he was taking off his robe.

After he hung up the robe he turned and sat down behind his desk, after placing his 44 magnum revolver that he carried under his robe, in his top desk drawer.

"Your Honor, I will cut through the chase and let you know this Friday at your courtroom I am going to use my scheduled time to announce I am dismissing all charges on the defendant Dustin Silver," he revealed.

"The investigators David Anson and Monty Victor have found compelling information and witnesses that clearly prove Dustin Silver was not involved in the John Adams murder and Dustin Silver was actually in Pendleton, Oregon," Walter Colvins stated.

"Mr. Silver will be released from custody right after I announce that all charges will be dismissed in my court." Judge Parker said.

"It sounds like maybe the Sheriff and other agencies need to do some housecleaning," the judge commented.

"When local defense attorneys find out Detective Hannigan has been dishonest and lied in the Adams case and is a Brady cop, there will be a flurry of appeals for new trials from their cases," the Judge said with a sigh.

"I may push for criminal charges on Hannigan and will definitely put him on the Brady list," Walter Colvins continued.

"The Sheriff has mentioned contacting the Washington State Criminal Justice Training Center to have them decertify Hannigan's certification to remain a law enforcement officer," he stated.

"I'm actually looking forward to Friday because I honestly believe Dustin Silver is innocent. Thank you, your Honor, for meeting with me," the Prosecutor finished and left the Judge's Chamber.

Chapter 57

"Let's all meet at the little restaurant called "The Cookery" down on main street, near the courthouse and we can talk about shutting down the case," suggested Jackie.

"Monty, after the case is dismissed, you and Anson can start contacting all of the defense witnesses that they will no longer be needed to testify in the trial because charges are going to be dismissed on Dustin Silver," she continued.

"They will probably be contacted by other law enforcement detectives trying to build the case on Juan Garcia for the murder of John Adams. We are going to the jail to contact Dustin with the good news after we finish with lunch,"

"Colin, would you notify Dustin's brother and Samantha Fox and give them an update that the charges will be dismissed?" Mark Scalia asked.

"Perhaps they can be present in the courtroom on Friday," he finished.

Conclusion

The Friday court hearing was scheduled to begin at 10:00 A.M.

John Adams family members, including his son Devin, were seated in the second row of the courtroom.

Dustin's brother and Samantha were sitting in the courtroom with Monty and Anson in the aisle behind Dustin, and the defense attorneys.

The media filled up the remainder of the first and second rows of the courtroom and the rest of the courtroom seating was filled with law enforcement and curious citizens.

Seated in the back bench of the courtroom was Detective Hannigan who had been placed on administrative leave following the meeting at Prosecutor Walter Colvins' office.

There was a deep scowl on his face.

The defense team was seated when Dustin was brought into the courtroom wearing the orange jail jumpsuit and belly chains with handcuffs attached.

Dustin stood behind his chair while the corrections officer removed the handcuffs from Dustin's wrist, and Dustin sat down beside his defense team.

It was obvious that he had been briefed by his defense team from the smile on his face when he turned and winked at Samantha.

The judge entered the courtroom and everyone stood out of respect for the judge at the direction of the Court Bailiff.

"Please, be seated," the Bailiff said and announced the Honorable Superior Court Judge Charles Parker.

"Please proceed," the judge directed the order to Prosecutor Walter Colvins.

"Your Honor, we are here to discuss Superior Court Case number #13246 State vs. Dustin Silver," he began.

"The Prosecutors Office has received information from third parties that supports the defense attorneys' stand that the defendant Dustin Silver clearly had no responsibility for the death of John Adams. The Canyon County Prosecutors Office is no longer seeking criminal charges on Dustin Silver and is moving to dismiss all charges on the Defendant. My office is requesting the court, to order the immediate release of Mr. Dustin Silver from custody at the Canyon County Jail."

"Very well, Mr. Colvins," the judge began, "I am ordering that the defendant Dustin Silver be immediately released from custody and all related criminal charges be dismissed. Is there any other business related to this case?"

"No, Your Honor," said Prosecutor Walter Colvins.

"Would the defense team like to make a comment?"

"Yes, Your Honor, the defense team would like to thank you for the professional way you have handled this case," Mark said.

"My client would like to say thank you," he continued as Dustin Silver stood.

"Your Honor, thank you for your decision and I pray that John Adams family will receive some closure when the real perpetrator is identified and will be prosecuted," Dustin Silver said to the judge and looked back into the courtroom at the Adams family.

"Thank you for the comment, Mr Silver," the judge responded.

"This case is closed and court is adjourned," the judge said as he pounded his gavel down.

The courtroom started to empty and as the crowd spilled into the hallway there were cell phone camera flashes and the media had video audio set up in the hallway.

"Any statement you care to make?" asked an eager reporter that held a microphone near Dustin's face.

"I'm just glad to get this nightmare over," he said as he was escorted out of the courthouse by his defense team, his brother and friend Samantha Fox.

When they reached the sidewalk, John Adams' mother walked up and stood in front of Dustin.

With tears in her eyes she said, "I'm so sorry you had to go through the nightmare of being accused of causing my son's death. I hope the Prosecutor does something about that detective lying about you in his investigation that caused you to be arrested."

Dustin looked into the woman's eyes and gave her a hug to show he had no ill feelings for John Adams' mother and family.

Little did he realize a local news reporter had been taking photos of the exchange.

The photo would grab the front page of the local paper the next morning.

As Dustin and the entourage walked away from the courthouse, Detective Hannigan stepped out from a business doorway and stood in front of Jackie and said, "You bitch, it's all your fault that I'm under investigation and could lose my job."

He gave her a shove backwards.

"Get away from me," Jackie Skelton said and tried to walk around Hannigan.

Hannigan felt a tug on his shoulder as he was spun around and his face was smashed by a hard punch from Mark Scalia.

There was a loud crack associated with a broken jaw as Hannigan was knocked to the sidewalk.

"You are under arrest for assaulting a law enforcement officer," Det. Hannigan said while holding his jaw.

"I think not," said Prosecutor Walter Colvins who had walked up on the scene as he was coming from the courthouse.

"Mr. Hannigan, the way I saw it, you were assaulting Attorney Jackie Skelton and Mark Scalia merely defended her," he said.

"Now you need to move on before Jackie Skelton decides to file criminal assault charges on you," he told Detective Hannigan.

Hannigan walked away holding his jaw.

"Nice working with you folks," Prosecutor Colvins said to the defense team and bade them a good trip home.

"Anson and Monty, we are having a victory celebration so we have made overnight reservations for two nights for everyone at a winery and lodge on the Icicle River in Leavenworth, Washington," said Colin Thurgood.

"It has a great view of the Icicle River and the food and wine are excellent."

"See you all there," Jackie said as the group broke up and prepared for the celebration.

THE END

Made in the USA
Middletown, DE
16 April 2023